THE BARRACKS OF THE HOLOCAUST

THE COMPLETE SERIES

ELYSE HOFFMAN

ISBN: 978-1-952742-07-1 (paperback)

Project 613 Publishing
Project613Publishing.com

Dedicated to my mother and father for their enduring support
To my grandfather whose stories I never heard
To all of the victims of the Holocaust
And to God, Who makes all stories

BARRACK FIVE

Vilém Rehor had been dealing with graffiti since the day he was born. For one reason or another, some people felt the need to write their name or initials everywhere they went. Perhaps they were insecure. Perhaps they thought if they didn't make a point of leaving their name etched onto every wall, they would one day fade into obscurity.

Vilém had grown reluctantly accustomed to seeing signatures almost everywhere. On bathroom stalls, on desks in school, spray-painted on buildings, and once, while visiting the local courthouse on a civics field trip, he had even seen signatures scribbled on the walls of a holding cell.

But really, he thought with a frustrated shake of his head, *at a concentration camp?*

He couldn't say he enjoyed working at the Camp. Few people would, barring the overly enthusiastic historian or the odd sociopath, but Vilém, whose grandfather had once been imprisoned behind the barbed wire fence, felt particularly uneasy being stuck in such a place.

It wasn't a large concentration camp, certainly not the largest in the Czech Republic, but it had been the target of neo-Nazi attacks in the past. The Camp's director had thus decided a vigilant night guard was a necessity to prevent the fascists from destroying the terrible, precious history held within the barracks.

And that was his job. He patrolled the Camp all alone until 5 AM, when he could finally go home.

The Camp was a museum and memorial site now, but it wasn't like the polished-if-dreary Holocaust museums Vilém had visited in the past. It had a melancholic air to it, an ominous aura that made his skin crawl whenever he came to work. The curators might have fitted it with commemorative plaques and educational placards to give visitors information on the Camp's dark history, but all the denim-clad guests and golden plaques in the world couldn't banish the dreary ghosts that seemed to plague every corner of the complex.

Vilém hadn't thought being a night guard at a concentration camp would be like guarding an amusement park. His grandfather had never said much about his time in the Camp, but his silence had been forlorn enough for Vilém to know that the horrors he had witnessed in the barracks were beyond description.

He had only taken the job because he needed the money. Desperately. So desperately that he was more than willing to return to the Camp every night, even though the place made his stomach churn and his spine shiver.

But although the paycheck was his primary incentive, Vilém had also hoped that working at a concentration camp would give him a reprieve from graffiti. The guests were normally quiet and respectful while touring the grounds. He had hoped they would respect the memory of the murdered Jews and refrain from leaving graffiti in their wake as they walked through the somber site.

So much for that.

He looked at the two words somebody had scratched onto one wall of Barrack Five.

RAYA POMNENKA

It was an unfortunate fact that teenagers were often insensitive and prone to vandalism, but Vilém had never encountered one as pompous and egocentric as Raya Pomnenka must have been. To be so thoughtless and self-absorbed, to deface a Holocaust memorial...

It was sickening, and although he hesitated to touch the barrack walls most of the time (they seemed particularly tainted by the sorrow that pervaded the rest of the Camp), he would have washed the graffiti off himself if he could. Unfortunately, the tactless teen that had defaced the barrack wall hadn't used a pen or marker. She had actually scratched her name into the wood.

The jagged letters stuck out on the otherwise blank wall of the barrack, and yet when Vilém examined the carving closely, he noticed that it didn't look like the average graffiti signature. The names he had seen written on past walls were almost always flamboyant and pretentious, with bright flashy colors and ornate bubbly letters to make them stand out.

This etching wasn't ostentatious at all. It seemed almost frantic, the way she had carved it onto the barrack wall. It looked like the last words of a dying person, one who was so desperate to leave a final message before their life was stolen away that they clawed it into the nearest structure.

If he hadn't known better, and if he hadn't been in Barrack Five just yesterday, he would have thought an inmate had scratched her name onto the wall during the war.

But just last night there had been no writing on the wall. It was far too fresh to have come from the hand of a Holocaust victim.

Regardless, Raya Pomnenka's name was now a permanent part of the exhibit. There was no way to remove it. It would be there until the day that the old wooden floors and walls of Barrack Five crumbled into dust.

THE NEXT DAY, AFTER THE last tour group left the Camp, Vilém made his rounds through the barracks to make sure that everything was in order and there were no straggling visitors wandering the grounds. He wouldn't want to lock some poor kid in the Camp overnight. Even he, an armed security guard, felt his blood congeal once the sun sunk under the horizon and the bitter night-time breeze began to blow through the grounds. A teenager trapped in the Camp would be terrified.

But then again, there was one particular teenager that he wouldn't mind locking in the Camp overnight: Raya Pomnenka.

The brat would definitely deserve it, he thought as he made his way to Barrack Five. *Maybe it would scare some decency into her.*

He entered Barrack Five and his anger at Raya Pomnenka tripled when he saw two more names carved beside the one he had discovered last night.

RAYA POMNENKA RAYA POMNENKA RAYA POMNENKA

Seriously? Vilém thought, grinding his teeth together in indignation. Once was bad enough, but the delinquent had actually returned to the Camp just to deface it even more? He would have to report this to his boss. They needed to watch out for a girl by the name of Raya Pomnenka and make sure she didn't enter the Camp again.

He examined the girl's graffiti and realized how fresh it was. He could see wooden shavings hanging off the final frantically-etched *Pomnenka*. He almost wanted to touch the letters, if only to sweep the shavings off the wall, but he hesitated.

There was something about the flimsy wooden walls that frightened him. The walls had been another prison for the inmates. They had been shoved into the tiny barrack and forced to sleep suffocatingly close to one another. They had wept for their lost families in the barrack. They had gotten sick in the barrack. They had died in the barrack.

Vilém didn't relish the idea of touching the walls that had once surrounded so much misery and death, but the letters Raya Pomnenka had carved...he almost felt as though they were calling to him. He knew they were mere markings, but still he felt his fingers twitch as the urge to touch the letters consumed his arm.

He raised his hand and swept the wooden shavings away. A frigid chill skittered through his body as his fingers brushed against the barrack wall. He pressed his hand against the graffiti and paused, waiting for some sort of epiphany.

Nothing happened. He sighed in disappointment. He wasn't sure what he had been expecting, but the desire to touch the letters had been so sudden and overwhelming that he had expected *something* to happen.

But as his fingers lingered on the letters, he suddenly felt drowsy. He blinked wearily and allowed his heavy eyelids to slide down.

Your name is Vilém, right?

Vilém's eyes sprung open. He pulled his hand away from the wall. It felt cold, numb, as though he had dipped it into a tub of icy water. He flexed his fingers in an attempt to get the frozen blood flowing again and glanced around Barrack Five. He could have sworn he heard someone speak to him. He could have sworn he heard a timid female voice inquire about his name.

Vilém shook his head. It was late, dark, and the Camp's foreboding atmosphere was getting to him. He needed some coffee and a nap.

Vilém's pupils flitted to the defaced wall and he felt his hand tingle when he looked at the trio of *Raya Pomnenkas*. Narrowing his eyes at the girl's name one last time, he exited the barrack.

As soon as he was away from the etchings, his hand became warm again.

Six.

When he went into Barrack Five the next day, there were six *Raya Pomnenkas* decorating the wall. How the girl had once again evaded security and carved her name onto the wall without a soul noticing was anyone's guess. Vilém had told his boss about the graffiti and was promised that the guides and guards would keep an eye out during the day.

But somehow or another, the little lawbreaker had made it into her preferred barrack and left behind three more markings for Vilém to moan about.

Had the girl been vandalizing something other than a Holocaust memorial, Vilém might have been rather impressed. She had determination, but that didn't change the fact that she was insulting the memory of everyone who had died in Barrack Five.

Not to mention she was getting Vilém into a hell of a lot of trouble. His job was to stop vandals from ruining the Camp's structures, after all, and even though he wasn't there all day, his boss still expected him to keep the Camp clean and safe from dark 'till dawn. Since the new markings didn't seem to show up until his shift, it was highly likely that Raya Pomnenka struck on his watch.

Because of this apparent fact, he stayed in Barrack Five throughout the majority of his shift. He figured that if the girl somehow managed to linger after hours and sneak into the barrack, he would catch her and all of this irritation would finally end.

Nobody crept into Barrack Five, however, and Vilém started to get bored and tired. He had been smart enough to bring a small coffee thermos since he didn't want to fall asleep on the job like he nearly had last night. The caffeine, unfortunately, was barely having any effect. Normally, he was rather jumpy during the late hours of his night shift, but now he had to struggle just to keep his eyes half open.

Once he finished the last drop of his coffee, his weary eyes started to roam about the tiny barrack until they finally landed on the offending carvings. Each seemed more desperate than the last. The *a*'s had been so hurriedly scrawled that they almost looked like *o*'s. He could tell the words hadn't been carved with a stick or tool of any sort. They had been clawed into the wood with Raya Pomnenka's fingernails. He had to wonder how her nails hadn't worn down or broken after scratching out her name so many times.

Vilém walked towards the letters. Without truly thinking, as if he were sleepwalking, he lifted his hand and touched the sixth *Raya*. His eyes instantly closed.

It is Vilém. I can see it right there, on your uniform. You're a guard here, yes?

He gasped and opened his eyes. That voice...it was the same from last night. The same soft, worried female tone.

Vilém almost pulled out his gun, but instead he kept his hand on the markings. He scowled at the serrated script.

RAYA POMNENKA RAYA POMNENKA RAYA POMNENKA

RAYA POMNENKA RAYA POMNENKA RAYA POMNENKA

He pursed his lips curiously. *Well, no, it can't be.*

Vilém didn't exactly believe in ghosts, at least not the sort that they showed in movies. He didn't believe in translucent ghouls that could phase through solid matter and possess some poor character's body.

But he believed in spirits. He believed in them because he could feel them whenever he was in a place of death and sorrow.

When he stood by the grave of his grandmother, he could practically feel all of her regrets, the sadness she felt at leaving the world before she could do everything she wanted. When he visited Prague and stood where Reinhard Heydrich—the Nazi General who had ruled Czechoslovakia with an iron heart—had been assassinated by Czech agents, he could sense the German's furious spirit lingering at the spot where the heroes had struck him down.

And he sensed the mournful spirits of the Jews every night when he walked through the barracks where they had lived and died. That was why the Camp made him squirm. Not only because of what *had* happened, but because the unfortunate victims *still* seemed to be there, languishing over their lost lives.

Yet while he often sensed such grief-stricken spirits, he had never thought one would wholly remain in the place of its pain, that it would try to communicate with the living.

Maybe he was overtired. Maybe he had dozed off and was stuck in a strange dream.

But if that were the case, if this was just a dream, it wouldn't hurt to reply.

He inhaled and closed his eyes once more.

"Yes," he muttered under his breath. "My name is Vilém. I'm the night guard."

You're better than the last guard who was here.

He felt his skin become icy, as if the spirit carried the coldness of death with her, a coldness that clung to him as he communicated with her. He almost wanted to run out of the barrack and never return, but his curiosity kept him in place.

"Last guard? The one they fired or...are you talking about a Nazi?"

Vilém could swear he heard the spirit sigh.

Both, I suppose. The last guard here, the last Czech one, he always used to bring beer with him. Sat in the corner and just drank himself stupid.

"In a concentration camp?"

He wasn't a very good man. Not respectful at all. You don't seem so bad, though.

Vilém faintly recognized how odd this was. He was either having a conversation with a figment of his drowsy imagination or he was actually talking to a ghost, and neither option made him feel very good about his sanity. Perhaps he had been spending too much time in the Camp. It was driving him bonkers.

"Am I asleep?"

Your eyes are closed.

"I'm asleep, then. Good."

Good? Why?

"Because otherwise I'd be insane."

If you're asleep right now, you're a very talkative sleeper.

"I'm definitely asleep. You're in my head. You're not real."

There was silence for a moment. Vilém frowned.

"Hello?"

More silence. He thought he might have finally woken up. Yet as he stood there, with his eyes still closed and his fingers still touching the cold barrack wall, he could feel the gloomy presence close by.

"Hello?" he said again, softer this time, his tone almost apologetic.

I exist. I do. I exist.

The return of the voice made Vilém flinch, but his stomach sunk when he heard the spirit speak in a quiet and solemn manner. He had said something wrong, made her sadder than she already was. Even though he was still slightly dazed, he felt guilty right away.

He decided to end this conversation before something else went wrong. It was probably best not to tempt madness and mystic forces by responding to ethereal voices.

But just as he was about to open his eyes and take his hand off the barrack wall, the voice spoke up.

Please come back tomorrow and talk to me again. Please? I promise I'm real. I promise you aren't crazy. Please, I'm not going to hurt anybody, but I want to talk. Just try to talk to me tomorrow. Please?

The poor phantom sounded so frantic and frightened that he couldn't refuse. He gave a single nod and scurried out of Barrack Five. He figured that if she was merely a fantasy created by his fatigued mind, she wouldn't speak again.

And if she talks tomorrow...I guess I'm crazy, Vilém thought with a sardonic smirk. He considered himself to be of sound mind and didn't truly think he was going insane. His head felt fine, and he only heard strange things when he stood in Barrack Five. If his brain was on the fritz, surely he would be seeing and hearing things outside of the barrack. He wasn't, though, and thus he was almost certain that this was nothing but a drowsy delusion.

But there was a possibility that a troubled spirit was stubbornly clinging to Barrack Five, refusing to move on to the next world. If that was the case, he didn't think the spirit was a threat. She didn't feel like a malevolent force.

Still, his curiosity was aroused. He would get plenty of sleep once he got home so he would be wide awake for his shift tomorrow. Either the spirit truly didn't exist, or she would still be there, waiting to tell him why she refused to leave.

RAYA POMNENKA RAYA POMNENKA RAYA POMNENKA
RAYA POMNENKA RAYA POMNENKA RAYA POMNENKA
RAYA POMNENKA RAYA POMNENKA RAYA POMNENKA
RAYA POMNENKA RAYA POMNENKA RAYA POMNENKA
RAYA POMNENKA RAYA POMNENKARAYA POMNENKA

Twenty-four. Before the gates of the Camp had even opened the next day, Raya Pomnenka quadrupled the number of times her name was scrawled on the wall of Barrack Five. Even the visitors had noticed the carvings, and several had asked their tour guides if some unfortunate inmate had made the markings during the Holocaust.

Vilém's boss was convinced that the Graffiti-Girl (as she had dubbed her) struck sometime during Vilém's shift. Suffice to say, she wasn't happy. Vilém was, as far as his boss was concerned, failing at his job. She assured him that he would face severe consequences if another *Raya Pomnenka* appeared on the wall.

Vilém, fortunately, was prepared. He had slept for as long as he could and arrived at the Camp just as dusk started to conquer daytime. He brought along a full thermos of extra-caffeinated espresso, as well as an emergency bottle of ice-cold water that he could splash himself with if all else failed and fatigue started to wear him down.

As soon as the last tour groups started to trickle out of the barbed-wire gate, Vilém scurried into Barrack Five and counted the *Raya Pomnenkas* on the wall. Once he was sure no new markings had been added to the barrack since his boss had scolded him, he sat beneath the graffiti and waited for the sun to slumber.

Soon, the sun vanished, the crickets started to chatter in the distance, and the wintry night-time wind made its way into the barrack. Vilém pulled his coat tightly around himself. He was waiting for a different kind of coldness to come into the barrack. The coldness that would accompany the anguished spirit once she arrived.

At last, he felt it. The eerie, icy feeling that only a woeful wraith could provide. He stood and looked around for some sign of the specter, but although he felt her presence, he didn't see her.

"Hello?" he called out. He waited a moment, but there was no response. His eyes traveled around the barren barrack for a moment as he searched for the spirit. Eventually, he looked at the twenty-four *Raya Pomnenkas* written up on the wall and remembered how he had communicated with the ghost yesterday.

He placed his hand on the markings and closed his eyes.

"Hello?" he said again.

You came back.

She sounded so relieved, as though her very soul had been at stake. Hearing the spirit while he was wide awake confirmed that she hadn't been a hallucination crafted by his erstwhile-exhausted brain. He cringed and chewed on his tongue, wondering how to respond to such an anomaly.

"So..." he muttered. "You were right. You do exist...that or I'm losing my marbles."

You're not crazy, I promise.

She sounded almost amused.

"Thank you for your assurance...ghost. I guess you were telling the truth before, so I'll take your word for it now."

The spirit didn't reply for a moment, and when she did, her tone was noticeably dejected.

Telling the truth about what? Existing? I've existed for a long time, but nobody...

Her voice drifted off. He winced when he felt her arctic aura distance itself, as though she was taking a step away from him.

"I didn't mean to upset you," he said. "I'm sorry."

He felt her cold presence creep close once more.

It's all right. You didn't say anything bad, not really. It's just me...

"I'm a...bit curious, though. How long have you existed *here*, at the Camp?"

Forever.

He might have raised an eyebrow if his eyes weren't firmly shut. "Forever? That's not possible."

It feels like it's been forever.

"Are you trapped here?" asked Vilém. "Do you need help?"

Trapped?

"Are you stuck here, at the Camp? Is there something preventing you from...well...you know..."

Moving on?

"Yes. To...whatever's next."

I don't think I'm trapped here. I think I could leave...but I can't.

"You can but you can't? Or is it more like you can, but you won't?"

The spirit was silent.

"I see," said Vilém. "Well then...I assume your name is Raya Pomnenka."

It is.

"That's what I thought. And you're the one that's been scratching your name onto this wall."

I'm sorry.

"You don't need to apologize. I thought you were some stupid kid, but I guess I was wrong."

Half wrong. I am a kid, but I'm not stupid.

He almost chuckled. The spirit's tone had become slightly brighter, and he definitely preferred to hear her soft voice when it was filled with mirth rather than melancholy.

"Well, young lady," he said, "I'll forgive you for vandalizing the memorial site if you'll please explain why you did so."

There was silence for a moment, yet he didn't feel her presence recede like it did when he said something wrong. He could tell that the spirit was pondering his request, deciding whether or not he was worthy of being answered.

Finally, Raya spoke in an almost hopeful manner.

Instead of telling you, how about I show you?

Vilém's brow furrowed. "Show me? How on earth will you show me?"

I'll show you what happened to me. I think you'll understand better if I show you. Just keep your hand on the wall and your eyes closed.

"Hold on a minute, Raya," he started to say, and he could feel a small surge of warm happiness radiate from the nearby spirit when he uttered her name.

"You want to get inside my head?"

In a way.

"I'm not sure I can do that, Raya. It's weird enough that I'm hearing ghosts. I don't think having one mess with my mind would be good for my health."

You won't get hurt, I promise. It's just my memories. I just… want to show them to somebody. Please, please, Vilém? Please let me show you! It's been so long since I've talked to somebody. I'm not sure I'll ever get another chance! Please…

She sounded almost frantic, as though the world would end if he didn't concede.

Poor girl, he thought. He wouldn't be able to sleep with a clear conscience if he refused her poignant plea. The girl's spirit was, somehow or another, stuck in the barrack, and it was his job to make sure that no children were trapped in the Camp. Perhaps if he watched her memories, he could figure out a way to free her troubled spirit, help her find peace.

"All right, Raya," he said, heaving a small sigh and bracing himself for the mighty headache he would most likely receive once he was thrown into the girl's recollections. "Go ahead. Show me what happened to you."

The transition from the dark, ominous interior of Barrack Five to Raya Pomnenka's memory was so fast and painless that it was almost startling in and of itself. One second he could feel the cold draft nipping at his nose, and the next he was in a warm bedroom with lavender walls, standing in front of a mirror.

But the reflection that looked back wasn't his own. Rather, it was a young girl, no more than nine years old. She had curly auburn hair that had been clumsily tied into two pigtails. An extended family of freckles was splashed across her beaming face.

Her chestnut-brown eyes sparkled with excitement as she straightened out her bright blue dress.

Vilém was astonished. It was as though someone had tossed him back in time, right into the body of little Raya Pomnenka. Although he couldn't control what the girl did, he could see everything that she saw and feel everything she felt. He could feel the excitement that was bubbling in the girl's chest as she spun around and admired her new dress.

"Raya?" he called out.

Yes, Vilém?

"Oh, good, you're still there," he said as he watched little Raya giggle with delight and blow her reflection a kiss.

I wouldn't leave you.

"Thanks. So...how old are you here?"

Nine. This is the earliest memory I have.

"The earliest? At nine?" He could tell from the spirit's voice that she must have been a teenager, no older than seventeen, when she perished. She hadn't lived long enough to gain senility and lose most of her early memories. Vilém himself could easily remember many incidents from when he was a toddler.

Watch for a minute.

He obeyed and observed silently. Raya brushed a small lock of hair behind her ear and, apparently satisfied with her appearance, dashed out of her room. She ran down a hallway that was lined with portraits and family photos before skittering down the stairs and into the dining room.

"Raya! There you are!" laughed a stout woman with the same chestnut-colored eyes as the little girl. Vilém assumed she was Raya's mother. Mrs. Pomnenka kissed her daughter on the forehead and stepped back, smiling widely.

"You finally wore your new dress!" she cried happily. Raya nodded, pinching a corner of her dress and curtsying gracefully.

"Uh huh!" chirped the little girl. "I wanted to save it for the last day!"

"And speaking of the last day!" cried a man with a lampshade moustache and beady black eyes, no doubt Raya's father.

"Raya, sweetie, come here," said Mr. Pomnenka, stepping aside to reveal an eight-pronged candelabra.

"A menorah?" Vilém observed. His grandfather had never been pushy about his Jewishness, but he had possessed an impressive menorah collection. His menorahs had always been coated in wax, however, while the Pomnenkas' shimmered like new.

Yes, it is. This was the eighth night of my ninth Hanukkah, and Papa had promised to let me light the candles. I was finally old enough.

Vilém could feel Raya's heart race ecstatically as she scuttled over to her father. Mr. Pomnenka dragged a small stool in front of the table so Raya could safely reach the menorah. Raya hopped onto the stool and her eyes shifted to her father, her fingers tapping the table with impatient fervor.

Mr. Pomnenka lit one candle and handed it to his daughter. He almost grabbed her wrist so he could guide her shaky little hand, but she pouted and pulled away.

"Papa!" she whined, "You promised! By myself! I'm older now, I can do it all by myself!"

Mr. Pomnenka let his hand fall to his side. Vilém felt a pang of guilt shoot through Raya's stomach as she saw her father's eyes sparkle sadly. Slowly, however, an accepting but still somewhat despondent smile came to his face.

"Yes, Raya, I suppose you can," Mr. Pomnenka sighed. It seemed like he had just realized that his baby girl was no longer a baby that needed him to hold her hand at every moment.

"Be careful, dear," said Raya's mother, shuffling conspicuously close to the sink. "Fire is pretty, but it's also dangerous. If you don't respect it and treat it with care, you'll get burned."

Raya nodded, looking down at the candle and feeling a surge of pride, no doubt delighted that she was now old enough to handle such a powerful element. Carefully, under the watchful and somewhat frightened gaze of her mother and father, she used the candle to light the others on the menorah, spreading the light while her mother and father prayed in a lovely, familiar tongue.

"Baruch atah Adonai..."

"What are they saying?" asked Vilém. He could remember attending his grandfather's ceremonies for Hanukkah and Passover, but he had never learned more than three words of Hebrew.

Blessed are thou, O Lord...

"Eloheinu melech ha'olam..."

Our God, the King of the Universe...

"Asher kidishanu b'mitz'votav..."

Who sanctified us with his commandments...

"V'tzivani 'lad'lik neir shel Chanukah."

And commanded us to light the lights of Hanukkah.

As he listened to the spirit's solemn translation of the prayer she clearly knew by heart, Vilém was almost tempted to ask her if she still believed in God. He could only assume that a specter stuck in a concentration camp had witnessed many horrors, perhaps enough to make her question the Creator's existence. Even though his grandfather had clung to his Jewishness, Vilém had always sensed that Grandpa Fabian's devotion was more to his people than to the God that had seemingly abandoned him back then.

He decided that asking about Raya's faith right at that moment would be insensitive, however, and stayed silent.

"Amen!" cried Raya, gazing proudly at the candles she had lit.

The flames swayed to and fro, dancing gracefully in place, celebrating their temporary vivacity.

Raya turned around and curtsied once more as her parents applauded her achievement.

"Very good, Raya!" said Mr. Pomnenka, putting his hand on her shoulder and squeezing tenderly. "I should stop underestimating you."

"That's right!" chirped Raya, eliciting a chortle from her father.

"Well," cried Raya's mother, reaching into the living room and picking up a brightly-wrapped box that had been hidden behind the door.

"Since you're old enough to be responsible now, your father and I think you're ready for this," said Mrs. Pomnenka, setting the present at her daughter's feet.

"What is it? What is it?" squealed Raya, dropping to her knees and tearing the red bows and yellow paper to shreds. Raya opened the box and her eyes bulged in bewildered astonishment as she pulled out her Hanukkah present.

It was a large, bulky machine that Vilém barely recognized as a camera. The old contraption was nothing like the sleek devices that he was used to. It looked like a gray metal box with a giant lens stuck to the front. Raya's little hands could hardly hold the heavy object, yet the little girl gawked at the gadget with wonder, as though it was the most precious treasure in the world.

"A camera?" Vilém said as nine-year-old Raya jumped to her feet and hugged her parents, thanking them over and over for the gift.

I've always had a terrible memory, you see. That's why I have such trouble remembering anything earlier than this. After I got the camera, though, I could capture moments, memories. Then I didn't forget.

"Here! Let me try it out!" cried little Raya, lifting the camera and waving for her mother and father to stand beside the menorah. Her parents dutifully obliged and posed beside the golden candelabra. Raya fumbled with the camera a bit, trying to get it to focus and making sure that her parents were properly in the frame. Once the shot was perfect, she gave a small, satisfied nod.

"Smile!"

CLICK!

A blinding flash absorbed the memory. As it dissipated, Vilém was surprised to find that the scene had changed. Raya was grasping her father's sweaty hand, and Vilém could feel small beads of moisture clinging to her brow. It was hot as a desert. The sun's brutal rays battered the father and daughter as they marched down a small pathway. Raya could feel her exposed flesh sizzling in the heat, yet she was too happy to truly care. She looked to her left and grinned when she saw a sign.

"Lions: This Way."

"Come on, Papa!" she cried, pulling on her father's arm, yanking him towards the lion exhibit.

"We're at a zoo now," Vilém observed.

I grew up in a very small town. There weren't any big theaters or amusement parks, but there was a little zoo. Papa and I...we used to go to the zoo all the time.

Vilém realized that the girl's Hanukkah present, her precious camera, was lovingly tucked under her arm. Once she and her father arrived at the lion's cage, her father picked her up and sat her on his shoulders, giving her a good view of the lone lion that was lying on a small patch of hay.

"Nudný!" the girl cried to the creature, holding up her camera. "Come on, Nudný! Stand up! Pose for a picture!"

"Nudný?" repeated Vilém with a snort, recognizing the Czech word for 'boring' right away.

I named him that because he never moved. He was always lying down whenever I came to visit.

And the lackadaisical lion clearly wasn't about to change its stationary schedule for the sake of the little photographer. Raya released a disappointed sigh.

"Wow," she grumbled, glowering at the lethargic feline. "Nudný's real lazy. Papa, are all lions as lazy as Nudný?"

"Not at all," Mr. Pomnenka chuckled. "Nudný's just spoiled. Most lions are fierce and strong. They don't just lie down all day. The coat of arms for Czechoslovakia is a lion, you know."

"'Cause we're fierce and powerful?" asked the girl.

"That's right."

"Not 'cause we're lazy like Nudný."

Mr. Pomnenka laughed. "No, not because we're lazy like Nudný. Why don't you take a picture of him, Raya?"

"He's not doing anything."

"Well, just for posterity's sake. So in the future you can remember how lazy Nudný was."

The girl pursed her lips for a moment, no doubt pondering whether or not the sluggish feline was worth the film. She eventually conceded, however, and raised her camera.

CLICK!

With a flash, the memory dissolved and was quickly replaced with another. Raya stood in a dark little room, putting on gloves. There was a sink in front of her, and in the sink, there was a large tub filled with chemicals.

"Where are we now?" Vilém asked.

My developing room. I used to carry my camera with me wher-

ever I went. I loved taking pictures. I loved being able to capture moments and keep them forever. Mama and Papa set up this room for me, a place I could develop my pictures. They helped me at first, but pretty soon I could do it all by myself.

Vilém watched as Raya carefully soaked a sheet of paper in the chemical tub. After the sheet had bathed long enough, she took it out and hung it on a clothesline where it could safely dry.

The memory dissolved into darkness.

"Uhm..." muttered Vilém when a new memory failed to fill the void. "So...what happened next?"

Everything you just saw happened in 1937. The year after that...

"The Munich Betrayal!" Vilém blurted. He hadn't been the best student in school, but he had paid enough attention in history class to know what that dreadful year meant for his homeland.

The Western Powers were as lazy as Nudný in 1938. Hitler asked for part of Czechoslovakia, the Sudetenland, and Chamberlain handed it to him on a silver platter. Mama and Papa were worried, but they didn't even consider moving. Papa said that Czechoslovakia was our home, and we couldn't let a maniac like Hitler drive us away. So we stayed, and we hoped that Hitler would be satisfied with the Sudetenland.

"He wasn't."

No.

Color came to the darkness and Vilém was thrust into another memory. Shouts and cheers assaulted Raya Pomnenka's ears as she stood on the side of the street, stuck in a small sea of adoring onlookers that hollered happily and waved little red flags as a troop of soldiers marched by.

Vilém felt his (or perhaps it was Raya's) heart go cold when he looked closely at the marching men. As they walked, they lifted their legs high into the air. Under normal circumstances, their odd and stiff strut would have seemed comical, but there was nothing funny about the black-clad men who marched through Raya's little hometown. Vilém knew who they were: minions of a madman, harbingers of the Holocaust.

"Those are **SS** soldiers!" Vilém cried, almost fearing that Raya's spirit wouldn't be able to hear him over the din that the spectators were making. "Why are they cheering? This is a Czech town!"

It was. But there were also many Germans living alongside us. To them, the Nazis brought freedom.

"Freedom..." Vilém growled, glancing at the swastika-emblazoned flags that the German civilians waved with pride.

Raya Pomnenka bit her lip, gripping her beloved camera with both hands and watching the Nazis. Slowly, as though she was afraid that documenting this disaster would only make it worse, she raised her camera.

CLICK!

The memory melted away.

Raya could feel her father grasping her little hand. He was squeezing a bit too hard in an attempt to comfort her, and her hand was beginning to feel sore. But she didn't ask him to loosen his grip. She was too focused on the metal gate in front of her.

There were two signs hanging on the gate. One bragged in bright blue letters that this was the entrance to the zoo. The other showcased a proclamation in harsh gothic script:

JUDEN VERBOTEN
JEWS FORBIDDEN

Vilém felt Raya's stomach sink like a ship in savage seas. She stared at the sign for a few more seconds before her eyes traveled to a rigid Nazi officer that stood by the gate, inspecting the visitors' identification cards as they entered. His cold gray eyes flitted sideways, falling upon Raya. He scowled at her, as though the little girl that cradled a camera to her chest was an enemy soldier that he needed to keep at bay, and she shivered.

"Raya, sweetie," Mr. Pomnenka whispered warily. "Raya, we should go. Nudný probably wasn't going to move anyway."

"But he might have," she muttered somberly, wrenching her hand from her father's grasp, raising her camera, and snapping a picture of the "Jews Forbidden" sign. Vilém was startled when the memory didn't fade right away. Instead, Raya lowered her camera and grabbed her father's hand again, allowing him to lead her away from the zoo and the glaring guard.

"Will I be able to see Nudný again?" she asked her father.

"I don't know, sweetie."

"But I want to see him!"

Raya's father released a rather forced laugh. "You always complain about him! You always say he's boring and lazy!"

"He is, but I still like to see him." Raya looked down at her mud-encrusted shoes, loneliness settling in the pit of her stomach, weighing it down like an anvil.

I really did love that lion. Actually...I can't remember the names of any of my old friends or classmates. I remember Nudný, though. Poor Nudný.

"What happened to him?" asked Vilém as Raya and her father walked in uncomfortable silence for some time.

This whole town was bombed to smithereens near the end of the war. Navigation mistake by some Allied pilots, apparently. All the buildings were destroyed, all the documents burned, and the zoo was obliterated. I think Nudný was killed during that bombings. Or maybe he starved to death before then. I don't know.

"Raya, look!"

Mr. Pomnenka's cry startled both Raya and Vilém. Raya's father seemed both astounded and elated as he looked at a graffiti-clad wall.

"What is it, Papa?" asked Raya. Her father placed his finger on the symbol that had grabbed his attention: a freshly painted "V."

"Do you know what this is, Raya?" he asked. The girl squinted and leaned closer, examining the "V" as carefully as possible, but she couldn't figure out what made it noteworthy. She shook her head.

"'V' for 'Victory,'" he said, the English word tumbling clumsily off of his tongue. "Or maybe it stands for '*ven.*'"

"Get out?" said Raya, standing on her tiptoes and trying to brush her hand against the smooth edge of the defiant letter.

"As in, '*Ven*, Nazis! Victory for the Czechs!'"

"*Ven*, Nazis!" chirped Raya a bit too loudly. Her father pressed his hand over her mouth and glanced nervously over his shoulder.

"Hush," he said once he was sure that no nearby Nazis had heard her outburst. "I don't want you to say something like that out loud, understand?"

Raya nodded timidly.

"Good girl. Not that I disagree, though. And this letter here, it shows that our people aren't going to put up with this. We won't let the Germans beat us down. We'll have victory."

He knelt before his daughter and gently tapped the covered lens of her camera. "Take a picture, sweetie. So you can remember the 'V.'"

An optimistic smile bloomed on Raya's face and she lifted up her camera.

CLICK!

With a snap and a blinding flash, the memory faded.

An abrupt stab of pain caused Vilém to wince.

"Ouch!" cried Raya, who was sitting on the edge of her bed. Vilém almost felt embarrassed when he realized that a mere prick from a needle had caused the sudden sting. Mrs. Pomnenka's hand had slipped while she was trying to sew something onto her daughter's dress.

"I'm sorry, darling," said Raya's mother, pursing her lips and carefully completing her work.

Raya hopped off her bed and made her way to the mirror. Vilém noticed that the lavender walls of the girl's bedroom had been almost completely covered with hundreds of black-and-white pictures. He could hardly imagine how much film the little photographer went through in a year.

He wasn't allowed to focus on the photos for too long, however, as Raya stepped in front of the mirror.

No longer was she the bright-eyed little girl that had twirled in front of the mirror on her ninth Hanukkah. Now her chestnut eyes were dimmed with dejection, most of her childish freckles had abandoned her cheeks, and a tattered, pale-blue dress was draped over her lanky thirteen-year-old frame. Her auburn hair was no longer tied into girlish pigtails but hung freely, without a ribbon or braid to restrain it. She had grown into a glum, pretty girl.

And the current cause of her gloominess was obvious. On the breast of her dress, right above her heart, was a yellow patch. It was a six-pointed star, and in the center of the star was a single word, written in black ink.

JEW

Mrs. Pomnenka moved to stand behind her rigid daughter, putting a hand on her head.

"There," she said, gently stroking her daughter's hair. "Not so bad. A bright, golden star. Just like you, Raya."

"It's yellow," said Raya, her bottom lip trembling. Vilém could feel dread ballooning in Raya's chest.

"Raya…"

"It's yellow and it's ugly and I hate it!" the girl squeaked, biting down on her tongue, forcing a sob to stay in her throat. "N-nobody's gonna want to talk to me…"

Mrs. Pomnenka's smile fell away and her lips tightened. She moved her hands to Raya's shoulders and squeezed tightly, as if she was trying to transfer some of her strength into the scrawny body of her daughter.

"Listen here, Raya," she whispered. "If someone won't talk to you because of that star, well, they aren't worth talking to. The Nazis are making us wear these stars so they know who we are. We mustn't be ashamed to show who we are. Wear the star with your head held high, Raya."

The girl stared at her reflection, at the star that had become the focal point of her being. Although dismay had not abandoned her heart, a small spark of pride joined it and the two sentiments began to banter over the girl's emotional state.

Finally, pride gained the upper hand long enough to convince Raya to wriggle out of her mother's grasp and run to her night-stand. Her camera was patiently resting there, waiting to capture another memory that Raya could add to her bedroom walls.

She grabbed the machine and darted back to the mirror. Keeping her elbows out so that the star would show in the picture, she lifted up the camera.

CLICK!

Once more, the memory dissolved into darkness.

"And then what happened?" asked Vilém when a few moments passed and no new memory cleared the gloom away.

Reinhard Heydrich happened.

"Heydrich!" Vilém exclaimed. "The Hangman of Prague!"

I figured you'd know about him.

"Ha! I failed history class, but they made sure even a piss-poor student like me left school knowing that Heydrich was a monster. I went to Prague once. I stood where he was killed. It felt...odd... angry almost. Like he was still there."

I wouldn't be surprised. Heydrich was an evil man, an arrogant man. He must still be mad about getting killed by a bunch of "inferior" Czechs. He became the Reichsprotektor of Czechoslovakia in 1941, about a month after they forced us to wear the stars. He was brutal.

"And in 1942...the Czechs finally got sick of him."

He prodded the lion. It bit off his hand.

"But what does Heydrich have to do with your story?"

The Nazis weren't happy that a gang of Czechs assassinated their top man, and they made sure we all paid for it.

"Right, I remember that. They completely destroyed a Czech village somewhere...Lidice, I think it was called."

You're right again. They destroyed Lidice as part of their revenge, but only part. They also deported hundreds of Jews, including me.

"Get up!"

A shout caused the darkness to stir. Vilém felt Raya's heart lurch as her eyelids fluttered open and she saw her mother standing above her.

Raya's vision was hazy from fatigue. Her mother's face was foggy, so foggy that Vilém could hardly tell what expression she was wearing. Judging purely by her frantic tone, however, he could deduce that something was horribly wrong. The exhausted

Raya could apparently tell as well. Her pulse started to race with worry.

"M-Mama...?"

Before Raya could ask any questions, Mrs. Pomnenka grabbed the groggy girl by the arm and yanked her out of bed. Raya nearly tripped as her mother dragged her out of the room.

"Mama!"

"We have to go now!"

"Mama, my camera!" cried Raya, her bleary vision beginning to clear as her mother yanked her down the stairs.

"We don't have time, Raya! We have to go *now!*"

Mrs. Pomnenka threw the front door open and Raya shivered. It was almost dawn, and the air was still crisp and cold. Wearing nothing but a nightgown, Raya felt the breeze bite at her flesh. Confusion, discomfort, and fear whirled about in her mind like items swept up in a tornado.

"Where's Papa?"

"He went out! We'll have to find him later!"

"But...!"

Raya stopped speaking as her mother pulled her out of the house and they ran down the street. She could hear glass shattering, children crying, horrible screams. The smell of smoke drifted through the air. She saw people lying on the streets in fetal positions as black-garbed men with truncheons beat them. She saw soldiers dragging writhing people away. She saw houses on fire, houses that Vilém could only assume belonged to Jews.

The sun was peeking out over the horizon, as though curious about the hubbub down below. A lovely assortment of orange and red hues were splashed across the sky. It was a beautiful sunrise, a beautiful morning, and Vilém could tell that Raya would like nothing more than to walk back home, sit on her porch, and watch the sun wake up. Maybe even take some pictures.

But when she dared to look over her shoulder, dared to glance back at her precious house, she saw fire spreading across the roof. Sadness stabbed at her heart. She no doubt realized that her beloved home would soon be nothing more than a singed shell.

Raya wasn't given much time to dwell upon her house's demise. As soon as she turned towards her mother, something smacked her on the back of the head.

She fell to the concrete, her head throbbing, stars dancing in front of her eyes. From above, she heard a scream.

"Mama..." Raya mumbled as Mrs. Pomnenka's fingers were wrenched from her wrist. The girl tried to sit up, but her efforts were rewarded with another strike to her skull.

She lay on the street, barely able to look up. Her vision cleared just enough for her to see a man in black kick her mother's head.

"Mama..." Raya moaned pitifully, her head pounding with pain, her limbs heavy as iron weights. She heard two unfamiliar voices above her talking in an alien tongue. Vilém immediately realized they were speaking German, and while he was by no means fluent in the foreign language, he could pick out a few words.

"Girl...Jew...small, but healthy...camp..."

After they came to an agreement of some sort, they yanked the girl to her feet. Raya, terribly dizzy and terribly confused, shook her head to banish the bleariness from her eyes.

She saw her mother on the ground, trying to crawl towards her daughter despite her hands being covered in blood and punctured with broken glass. She saw the SS officer shove her mama against a wall.

"M..."

But before the word could even escape her lips, before Mrs. Pomnenka could even hope to run, the Nazi took out his gun.

BANG!

And when he fired, the memory didn't melt. It shattered.

All of Raya's shock, pain, anguish, and anger hit Vilém like a massive wave, melding with his own emotions until he felt like they *were* his own. Until he felt like he had just witnessed *his* mother's death.

"*N-no!*"

The void was gone, the shattered memory was gone, and he was standing in the middle of Barrack Five once more. His whole body was shaking, coated in sticky sweat, and his heart was beating so fast that he had to put his hand over his breast and breathe slowly to steady it.

Calm, he commanded his frenzied pulse. *Calm...calm...*

The frantic beat died down and he wiped the sweat from his brow. He was still quivering, and his hand felt like he had shoved it into a bucket of snow.

My hand...

He looked back up at the wall, at the twenty-four *Raya Pomnenkas*. He had been so overwhelmed by Raya's agony that he had taken his hand off the wall, yanked himself out of her memory.

And part of him wanted to stay out. That last memory had been too brutal, too much for him to handle. He didn't want to go back and feel the pain of the tormented spirit. He didn't want to see anymore.

But he could still sense her. He could sense Raya's spirit lingering by the letters, anxiously awaiting his return. He couldn't let her down now. He couldn't leave her to suffer alone. As much as he wanted to walk away, he needed to stay.

His legs sluggishly protested, but eventually his determined mind convinced his limbs to haul him back to the wall. He lifted his cold, heavy arm and placed his hand against the jagged letters.

Vilém took a deep breath, bracing himself for the impending sorrow, and shut his eyes.

Darkness greeted him. Then, a voice.

You came back.

"I...I'm sorry. About your mother...and about leaving. I was..."

You came back. That's what matters. Thank you.

"What happened after...that?"

I was put on a train...

"Your father...?"

I never saw him again.

"I...I'm very sorry..."

You didn't do it.

"So you were all by yourself...and the train..."

It took me right to the Camp, the one you're guarding now. Of course, the guards back then...they weren't as good as you.

"Well," said Vilém, finding an almost morbid urge to chuckle, "I would think not."

We got to the Camp, me and the other Jews, and the Selection started.

Vilém didn't need to ask what the Selection was. He had spent enough hours at the Camp reading the educational placards to know what happened to the new arrivals once they reached their destination. The Selection meant either slave labor or death.

And in Raya's case, the Selection meant fogginess. At least it seemed that way when the memory finally materialized. It took a moment for Vilém to realize that the weather wasn't the cause of the hazy cloud that had descended upon Raya's recollection. Without her camera, Raya's memory was fuzzy. Faces were blurry, sounds distorted, and a strange mist was covering the whole campground.

"It's hard to see..." Vilém commented, focusing as hard as he could on the few spots of complete clarity.

I'm sorry. Like I said, my memory's always been bad. It's been so long, and without my camera...

"Don't apologize, Raya. I understand."

Raya was roughly shoved to the front of the winding line that had formed. She gazed up at the SS guard in charge of the Selection, who had been rendered faceless by the fog.

"Age?" he asked, his voice echoing about the memory.

"Sixteen." She was stifling a sob. He could feel her heart sitting at the bottom of her stomach, too heavy to lift itself back up to its rightful place.

"Scrawny," the Nazi observed, a hint of malice coming to his strange voice. "Do you have any special skills? Useful skills?"

Raya swallowed and stayed silent for a moment.

"Right. Well..."

"I can develop..."

The Nazi, clearly angered about being interrupted, barked, "What?"

"I can develop photos. I'm a photographer."

The fog cleared away from the lower half of the SS guard's face, revealing a wide smirk.

"Well!" he exclaimed. He looked over at another featureless SS man and shouted something in German. Vilém caught the word "Kommandant."

"Kommandant?" Vilém repeated as the guard yanked Raya out of line. The frightened girl didn't struggle as the Nazis took her from her fellow Jews and pulled her towards Barrack One, the Kommandant's barrack.

A fellow photographer.

The memory shifted suddenly. Raya was standing in a well-furnished office. The mist of forgetfulness had noticeably cleared, though the Nazi that stood beside her remained faceless.

However, another Nazi, one with more medals and patches

decorating his dark uniform, stood before her. His face and voice were clear as day: blonde hair, blue eyes, the ideal Aryan. He smiled down at the girl, his sapphire irises twinkling.

"Be that the case, Little Jewess..." the Kommandant said.

"Raya..." the girl whispered. "Raya. My name is Raya Pomnenka."

The Kommandant's dark blue eyes flashed with amusement.

"Is that your price?" he asked. Raya felt a twinge of confusion, but she didn't respond.

"Fine then," said the Kommandant. "You won't get a number like the others, *Raya*. I have to say, you're very lucky I found you. I've been waiting forever to find somebody who loves photography as much as I do. If you can develop and develop well, you'll be perfectly fine."

He had sensitive skin, sensitive eyes, a sensitive nose...at least when it came to developing chemicals, so he never learned to develop the photos he took.

"What sort of...photos?" asked Vilém while the memory trickled into oblivion.

He couldn't stand the smell of chemicals. Corpses, on the other hand...well, he couldn't get enough of those. At least as long as they were Jews...

The abyss that followed the last memory twisted itself into a new recollection. Raya was standing in a dark, stuffy room, her hands stinging from the chemicals she was using to develop the photos. The Kommandant had given her thin, tattered gloves that hardly protected her flesh from the burning liquid.

Raya, though, scarcely seemed to notice the pain. She hung a newly developed photo up on a wire where it could properly dry. Her eyes darted from picture to picture and Vilém felt her stomach coil in disgust as she saw what moments in time the Kommandant had been so keen to capture.

The crowded Selection platform. Men, women, and little children crying as the SS guards shoved them into line.

The train that had transported the Jews to the Camp.

The boxcars filled with the bodies of those who hadn't survived the long journey.

Prisoners lined up outside for roll call, shivering as snow fell upon them. Their thin black-and-white uniforms couldn't hope to keep them warm in such weather.

A prisoner dangling limply from a piano wire. He must have broken one of the Camp's many rules. His executioner, a young SS guard, seemed proud of his handiwork. The youthful killer posed by the body and smiled at the camera.

Emaciated prisoners lifting heavy bags of sand. It was a wonder that their skeletal frames could support their own scant weight, much less that of a burdensome bag.

A man tangled in the electrified barbed wire that surrounded the Camp. Perhaps he had been trying to escape, or perhaps he had merely wanted to end it quickly. Either way, his scorched corpse hung lifelessly on the wire, like a ragdoll that had been carelessly tossed onto the fence.

Raya's gut roiled violently, but she refused to vomit. She didn't want to end up like the people featured in the Kommandant's photographs. She had to keep going.

She tugged on her frayed gloves and got started on the next picture.

The memory faded.

"Why...?" Vilém started to ask, woozy with nausea. "Why would the Kommandant take pictures like that?"

Same reason I did, I suppose. Memories. He wanted to remember all of his...achievements. Funny thing is, I remember he had a son, a sweet little boy, but he never took pictures of him growing up. I think I only ever developed three pictures of his child.

I guess the Kommandant didn't want to waste film on his own son when there were so many miserable Jews to photograph.

"Those pictures...the pictures of the Camp...I think some of them are in the exhibit."

Exhibit?

"For the museum, for the Camp. I didn't know you developed them."

Raya was silent for a moment.

"Raya?"

I developed all the Kommandant's pictures. I worked for him for two years, until 1944.

"What happened then?"

The war. The war started to get bad for the Germans. They started getting worried. Worried they would lose, and worried that once they lost and everyone found out what they did...well, you understand. The Kommandant stopped photographing his work.

A new memory appeared. Raya's heart was pounding so loudly that it almost gave Vilém a headache. The girl was crouching by the door of the Kommandant's office, peeking inside.

The Kommandant had placed his camera on the floor. He looked down at the machine, his eyes shimmering with fearful regret. He took a deep breath and raised his foot over the device.

The Nazi's steel-lined boot crushed the camera, smashing its lens and causing bits of metal to scatter across the floor. Raya whimpered and began to tremble in terror, no doubt realizing that, with the camera's destruction, the Kommandant no longer needed a developer.

The memory dissolved.

The Kommandant stopped taking pictures, and he also stopped giving me special treatment. A few weeks later, he transferred me to Barrack Five. I never saw him again, but I know he bit down on a cyanide pill just as the Russians made it to the Camp. Never got interrogated. Never got punished.

"What happened to you, though?" asked Vilém.

After the Nazis moved me to Barrack Five, they gave me a new assignment. I was to clean the latrines.

As soon as he heard the word "latrines", Vilém braced himself for sludge. He was tossed into another memory and an atrocious stench promptly assaulted his sinuses.

Raya was kneeling down before a toilet, her fingers covered in filth. She was forced to reach in and scoop out the muck with her bare hands. Vilém squirmed with disgust as he felt the grime stick to the girl's skin. He felt anger and humiliation burn in Raya's chest as she listened to her supervising SS officer laugh at her.

Vilém was more than grateful when the memory dissipated.

"Revolting," he commented.

And unsanitary. You can imagine doing that every day without ever really washing or wearing gloves...

"You'd get sick...." Vilém muttered, his stomach sinking with dread when he realized what was about to happen.

I did.

Slowly, the shadows that surrounded him morphed into a new memory.

Heavy. Her body felt heavy. Her arms and legs felt like they were made of bricks rather than flesh and blood. Her bones felt like they had been encased in steel, rendered far too cumbersome for her to lift.

She was lying on the rough wooden plank of her bunk, watching as the last prisoner left Barrack Five to report for roll call. Raya Pomnenka whimpered. Her fingers twitched and she tried to reach for her fellow prisoners, tried to beg for their help, but her throat was too dry. Water. She wanted just a sip of cold water to soothe her arid throat.

But more than that, she wanted a hand to hold, an ear to whisper a few last words into. She didn't want to die here. She didn't want to die like this. Sick, silent, alone.

She could feel her spirit slipping out of her body, as if she had been shot and her blood was slowly draining away, leaving only her lifeless corpse behind. She frantically tried to keep the Grim Reaper at bay, to get his cold, clammy hands off of her.

Yet Death refused to yield. She looked up at the wall beside her and tried to lift her arm, tried to touch the wall. It was her last desperate deed. Vilém could tell right away what she wanted to do.

But she didn't have the strength to write her name on the wall of Barrack Five. Her arm fell to her side and she wanted to cry, but she wasn't even strong enough to shed a tear.

The barrack became blurry, the dull colors fused together to form an appalling blob of brown and gray, and the very last thing that Raya Pomnenka felt was a horrible mixture of loneliness and regret.

Darkness.

Vilém opened his eyes.

He felt cold, numb, as though he too had been embraced by the Grim Reaper's icy arms. Yet he felt his heart beating, he felt his blood slowly warm and rush through his veins, and he had never been more grateful to feel his soul resting securely within his functioning body.

He looked at the words on the wall, the twenty-four *Raya Pomnenkas* that the spirit had carved so anxiously, and he understood.

Raya Pomnenka's hometown had been destroyed, her parents had been killed, everything she had ever known had been wiped out. And on top of all that, everything that had ever known *her* had been obliterated.

The Kommandant had died before he could tell anyone about the girl who had developed his morbid pictures. Her parents had died before they could tell the world about their beloved daughter. Her classmates and neighbors had died before they could utter a word about her. All of the pictures she had taken, all of her memories, had been destroyed the same day she had been shipped to the Camp.

There was no diary of Raya Pomnenka that hundreds of people could read. There was no memoir about her sitting on a library shelf. She didn't even get her name inscribed on a commemorative plaque.

It was as though she had never even lived. The Nazis had taken her home, her family, her pictures, her very name, and they had all but taken away her existence.

The carvings on the wall were a desperate effort to exist, to make sure somebody, anybody, at least knew her name. To make sure she didn't completely fade into oblivion.

Vilém clenched his jaw. As far as he was concerned, the girl deserved better than this. She deserved more than graffiti on a barrack wall. She deserved a plaque at least. He would have to work something out, talk to his boss, see what he could manage. Of course, he could hardly say that the ghost of the girl who had developed the pictures displayed in the museum's exhibit had come to him and told him her tale. But no matter what, he would find a way to share the spirit's name and tell her story.

For now, though, he was exhausted and rather depressed. He needed to go home and start planning.

But before he did that, he looked back up at the twenty-four *Raya Pomnenkas*. He could still sense the spirit's cold presence close by. She had something else to say.

He placed his hand on the markings and closed his eyes.

Vilém...

"Yes, Raya?"

Can...I ask you something?

"Of course, Raya."

Will you remember me?

Without a moment of hesitation, he replied, "Of course, Raya. I'll always remember you."

Raya Pomnenka's icy aura became warm as a ray of sun. Slowly, he felt her fade away.

No more markings appeared on the wall of Barrack Five.

BARRACK FOUR

"So then my dad shot it!"

"No way!"

"It's true! Right in the head! Knocked it out!"

"Was it a big snake?"

"Mm hm..."

"How the hell'd he hit it on the head?"

"Dad was a great shot!"

"I don't believe you!"

"Vilém, Vilém, back me up here!"

Vilém Rehor, who was midway through his third beer of the night, barely heard his friend over the hubbub of the bar. He, his best friend Erik, and a pretty girl that his friend had been trying to put the moves on for the last half-hour were clustered around the counter. Erik was standing close to the girl, leaning on the table, while she sat beside the slightly slumped-over Vilém.

Vilém was far too exhausted to try and score himself. He had been hoping for a nice night out with his buddy, a few beers and some jokes, but Erik had never been one to pass up a conversation with a lovely lady.

He finished his drink, exhaled, and glanced over at his two companions. The bar was so dark that he could hardly see either the girl or his friend, but he could make out Erik's features enough to see him mouth three words: *help me out*.

Normally, he wouldn't. Their tradition was that Erik would make up some story off the top of his head and Vilém would teasingly decry it as either false or exaggerated. The girls never cared: it was a story, and as long as the story was good, they normally didn't mind if it was one hundred percent true or not.

But this time he was just so damn *tired* that he didn't feel like doing his usual routine. Besides, for once Erik had told a story that was above seventy-five percent true—his father *had* shot a snake with a BB gun once, Erik had just exaggerated his own bravery. From what Vilém remembered, Erik had been cowering in his tree house for hours on end, sobbing even after he was told the snake was gone.

"All true," Vilém assured the girl, gesturing to himself. "Witness."

"Wooow!" she cooed, finally giving him her full attention. "So you two have been friends for a real long time?"

"Since we were kids," said Erik, looking worriedly over at Vilém and quirking his head to the side, obviously finding the fact that Vilém wasn't taking part in their usual repartee disturbing.

"Hey, buddy, you okay?" he asked. "You're looking a little, eh..."

"Dead?" Vilém supplied, rolling his aching shoulders and smirking. Erik and the girl both snickered.

"Yeah," agreed Erik.

"Too much to drink?" the girl queried, snatching Vilém's

empty glass and putting it upside-down on the counter. He shook his head.

"Nah ah, I was just up all day," he explained.

"Ya' mean all night?" asked the girl.

"Nope, night-shifter," replied Vilém, smiling at her playful theft of his cup. He tried to steal it back, but she moved it before he could. He chuckled and decided to wait until she let her guard down.

"Ooh," she said with an understanding nod. "What are you, security?"

"Yep, good guess!"

"Yay, I'm smart!" the girl giggled. "Where?"

Vilém and Erik exchanged awkward glances. They had made a list long ago of "Topics To Avoid While Trying To Score." While they had never officially added "The Holocaust" to that list, ever since Vilém had gotten a job at the local concentration camp it had become that list's unspoken #1. There was no better way to spoil the mood than to bring up the most infamous genocide in world history, after all.

But since Vilém was fairly sure that Erik had already charmed this girl, he decided there would be no harm in being honest tonight.

"You know that concentration camp right outside town?" he asked. The girl's eyes—which Vilém had just noticed were a lovely shade of chestnut brown—widened.

"*There?*" she gasped. Erik cringed at her horrified tone, shaking his head at Vilém, silently chastising him for bringing up the #1.

"He guards that shitty place during the night, I fix up clogged sinks during the day," Erik joked, trying to add a hint of humor to the dark subject. "I'm boring, he's depressing."

"Oh, yes," concurred Vilém. "I'm depressing."

"You don't seem *that* depressing," the girl noted with a brightness in her tone that made Vilém raise a surprised eyebrow.

"Man, I'd never be able to work there," she sighed, fiddling with Vilém's empty cup and gazing at her distorted reflection in the glass. "Too…"

"Depressing?" queried Vilém.

"Yeah, yeah. And it's kind of worse for me cause I'm Jewish, so it'd be like…wow, that could have been me! You know? I've never even been able to visit that place. My family's been avoiding it for basically three generations."

"Totally understand," he said.

"You're Jewish?" queried Erik with a smile. "Hey, cool! Half Jewish right here!"

"Mazel tov!" she declared. She looked over at Vilém, nodding her head as though to question his Jewishness (or lack thereof.)

"Grandpa on my mom's side," Vilém said. "You should have heard the argument he and my pa had when my folks decided not to get me circumcised."

She laughed and Erik, sensing the chemistry brewing between the two (a chemistry based on a bleak history, but any chemistry that didn't blow up in Vilém's face was good chemistry), decided to search elsewhere. He spotted a pretty brunette sitting by herself and pretended she was an old classmate of his.

"Have fun, Vilém! Don't be a moron!" he cried as he sauntered over to the other girl.

"Look who's talking!" Vilém retorted. The chestnut-eyed girl giggled and scooted closer, finally allowing Vilém to get a good look at her as the light illuminated her face and body. She was most certainly pretty. Maybe a little chubbier than the cultural ideal, but she had a nice body, a beautiful face, and the cutest dimples he'd ever seen.

"Oh, I'm Vilém, by the way," he said, offering his hand. She gave it a firm, genial shake.

"Jana, in case you missed it," she said. "Sorry. I guess I was giving Erik all my attention. You barely got a glance at my ugly face!"

"Nooo!" he said, shaking his head. "I'm the only ugly one here! I know I look like crap. I got *no* sleep."

"Why not?"

"Well, I was *gonna* sleep during the day like I usually do and hang with Erik tonight, but I had stuff I wanted to get done and by the time Erik came to pick me up I was just..."

He pretended to fall over dead. Jana snickered and he took advantage of her distraction to reclaim his cup.

"Heeey, cheater!" she cried as he hugged his glass protectively.

"We weren't *officially* having a competition. Besides, I'm not drunk *yet*," he said.

"So, what were you doing that robbed you of your beauty sleep?" Jana inquired.

"Writing!" he declared with a hint of pride. Her eyes brightened.

"Oh, you're an author?"

"Well, not yet. I'm practicing. It takes a million words of crap before you write something decent."

"What're you writing about?" Jana asked. Vilém glanced idly at the ceiling.

Since he didn't want her to think he was *completely* insane, he decided not to tell her about Raya Pomnenka, the ghost of the Holocaust victim he had promised to always remember. He was writing her story as insurance for that vow. Even if someday he wasn't around to remember her, a book or short story could memorialize her for eternity. He had failed to get a plaque dedicated to her installed in the Camp. To get permission to erect such a memorial, he would have to prove her existence, and there was nothing material left of her. A book, even if people thought it was fiction, would have to do. It was better than nothing.

But telling Jana all that likely wouldn't be the best way to get her number.

"Something I thought of at work. Maybe I'll show you when I'm done," he said.

"Cool!"

"I'll warn you: it'll be depressing. Holocaust and all that."

"I don't mind. I grew up reading about it, I just wouldn't be able to be *there* constantly. Why'd you take that job?"

"Well, to be honest I mostly took it 'cause of the paycheck. Times are tough."

"Right, right."

"And I *hated* it at first, it completely creeped me out. But y'know, I'm actually really glad I took it. It's been...an experience. It's depressing, but I feel like it's important."

"Oh, yeah. And hey, it gave you inspiration!"

"Right!"

"Do you have to do a lot at night? Like, do people stick around after dark?"

"Not...willingly," Vilém said, remembering the shy, gentle presence of Raya Pomnenka. "But when they do, I help them out. That's my job."

Jana nodded, smiling softly.

"You seem like a really nice guy," she observed.

"And you," he declared, waving towards the bartender, "are a really nice and really pretty girl. So...let me buy you a drink and let's talk about you. Are you as depressing as I am?"

"Not really," Jana said, smiling at the bartender as he filled Vilém's cup and plopped a beer in front of her.

"Then let's talk about happy things," Vilém suggested.

"Rainbows and butterflies for the rest of the night?" Jana joked.

"Rainbows and butterflies," he agreed, raising his glass. She clinked her cup against his.

"Cheers!" she declared, and the rest of their stay at the bar consisted of drinking, laughing, joking, and sharing stories that were anything but depressing before they ended up stumbling out of the building together.

VILÉM WOULD NEVER DESCRIBE HIMSELF as a player. He'd had his fair share of one-night stands, but he'd never been the sort to skedaddle the second he awoke, leaving the poor girl potentially confused and hurt. Even if it was a girl he found significantly less lovely come morning when the beer goggles dissipated, he always stayed until she showed him a smile.

He didn't need to force himself to stick around for Jana's sake: she was just as pretty in the morning as she had been when his brain had been addled with alcohol. His tradition of staying ended up serving him well. They had gone back to her apartment, and not only was her kitchen fully stocked, but she knew how to make chocolate-chip pancakes.

"Haven't had these since I was...ten? Probably ten," Vilém declared with a boyish smile after getting dressed and sitting down at the table. Jana chuckled.

"What? Shame! I'll just have to spoil you."

"You're already spoiling me!" he cried as she served him a sumptuous mountain of pancakes.

"Aw, you deserve it. You're a sweetheart," she said, pulling her hair out of a ponytail and letting it fall over her shoulders. "Thanks for not jumping outta my window when I wasn't looking. I can sometimes get pretty dumb at the bar. I've taken some real bastards home...nothing too bad, but y'know, sometimes sweethearts turn sour in the morning. You're great, though...in more ways than one."

She smiled coyly and he felt his face heat up.

"Er...thanks..." he mumbled, practically hiding behind his tower of pancakes so she wouldn't see how red he was.

"Eat up!" giggled Jana. He grinned.

"Happily!" he declared, taking a bite.

"Well?" she asked.

"Great! Really sweet!" he proclaimed, and Jana's face lit up with joy.

"I'm glad," she said. "I'd have to quit my job otherwise!"

"What's your job?"

"You know that candy store on Klammer Street?"

"Sladký Sweets? Mm hm! Love that place! Too bad I didn't spend my whole childhood here, I would'a spent my whole allowance there!"

"Haha! You would'a given *me* your allowance if you had! It's my shop!"

"You *own* the place?"

"Family business. Since my dad ran off with some Hungarian girl and my big brother's off in Berlin studying, I'm in charge. My grandma lives right above the shop. She still helps run it, but she signed the shop over to me. Said I have the most passion for the place."

"Is she all right on her own?"

Jana snorted.

"What?"

"Nothing," said Jana, sipping her coffee, a smirk peeking out over the rim of the mug. "It's just that if you knew my grandma, you wouldn't say that. She could kick your butt."

"Really?"

"Yep!"

"I *am* a security guard."

"She could do it."

"All right, I'll take your word for it. So what's it like, running a candy shop?"

"Both wonderful and awful."

"Awful? I work at a concentration camp—you're gonna have to try *hard* to convince me that working at a candy shop is awful!"

"Oh, I love it, and I imagine it's a more...*cheerful* environment than what you have to deal with. It's just I love it too much—I'm *so* freaking fat because of that place."

"Oh, come on, you're beautiful!"

"And you're a liar...but a real sweet one."

"I'm not a liar. Actually, the only one that's gonna end up fat around here is me. I'm gonna be coming over to your house for breakfast every day now!"

"Haha! Won't even bother with the pleasantries, you're just gonna climb through my window every morning," she giggled.

"That's the plan, I'm part of your morning routine now," Vilém said.

"Sounds good to me!" Jana said, quickly tidying her countertop. "I've got to run to work. You gonna steal everything I own?"

"Nope!"

"Then stay as long as you want and finish up."

"You're an angel!"

"You deserve it. Did you give me your number last night?"

"Let me check...nope!"

They exchanged numbers, an embrace, and a promise to meet up again before Jana ran upstairs, did her makeup, and hurried to work. Vilém looked down at the new contact on his phone with glee before noticing a missed call from Erik. He inhaled deeply and called his friend.

"Before you even ask, yes, yes we did," he said as soon as his friend picked up. Erik chuckled.

"Good one, Vil! She was hot! Where are ya' now?"

"Her house. She made breakfast and let me stay for a little while. Real sweet girl."

"Oooh, do I sense domestic bliss already settling in?"

"Shut up. Speaking of sweet, did you know she owns that little candy shop?"

"Sladký's?"

"Yup!"

"Oh, yeah, awesome place! They have great fudge."

"I think she might be a keeper."

"Because of the candy?"

"Erik..."

"I'm kidding. Hey, Vil, if she's a nice girl, go for it. Just because your job's depressing doesn't mean your life has to be depressing too."

"Guess you're right. Hey, listen, bud, I'm gonna finish up here and clean up, maybe hang out at home before I run to work. I'll meet up with ya' when I can."

"Sounds cool! Gotta head to work myself. Not all of us are night owls like you!"

"See ya, bud!"

"Good luck at work, Vil. Don't let that place get to you!"

"I'll try."

Although he had grown morbidly accustomed to the Camp, it was hard to obey Erik's command and not let the place get to him. Even when he was in the best mood he'd had in a while, the second the bus screeched to a halt and he saw the tall, warped barbed-wire fence, his smile wilted like a neglected rosebush.

"Another night," he sighed, adjusting his uniform and skittering off the bus, carefully pushing his way through a small cluster of college students. He grunted when he saw two girls pose as one lifted up a selfie stick and snapped a picture of her and her friend in front of the Camp. At least they weren't smiling. Nevertheless, he felt the need to speak up.

"Girls, *please*," he sighed. "Show some respect."

One girl blushed in embarrassment. The other huffed.

"We're just getting a picture. Everyone's doing it," she said, pointing towards another student, who was taking a picture of one of the wooden watchtowers.

"They're taking pictures of the Camp for school. You're treating it like a vacation," Vilém pointed out. "People died here. A lot of them. Try to keep the focus on them instead of you."

The huffy girl's scowl melted away and she gave a small, resigned nod.

"'Kay, sorry," she said, gesturing for her girlfriend to follow her back to the bus.

"Thanks for that, Rehor," a familiar female voice grunted. Vilém inhaled deeply and turned to face his boss, Ms. Doubek. Alica Doubek was a senior with curly silver hair and a perpetual scowl; it seemed as though she was constantly annoyed with all Creation. She always dressed in a suit (he had never seen her wear a dress and the day she wore one was likely the day Hell froze over) with a blood-red tie. A pair of reading glasses hung from her collar, reading glasses she never seemed inclined to put on: she always insisted on leaning horribly close to anything she felt like reading rather than don her spectacles.

Erik had once described Ms. Doubek as having a six-foot pole permanently stuck up her ass, and Vilém couldn't disagree. Compliments were a rare gift from the woman, and a smile...well, he didn't even know what it would look like if she were to smile. Some of the other employees at the Camp even referred to her as "The Kommandant" behind her back. Vilém never went that far.

"Ma'am?" he queried, and she pointed stiffly towards the retreating girls.

"Those girls," she said with a tut. "If one more idiot teen takes out one of those phone sticks, I'm going to grab it out of their greasy little mitts and beat them with it."

Vilém could easily visualize that, and the fact that he could do so without difficulty scared him.

"Disrespectful. My..." Her voice trailed off. "Well, never mind. Good work there, Rehor."

"No problem, ma'am. I agree; it is disrespectful," said Vilém, smiling slightly. Ever since the Raya Pomnenka graffiti incident, his relationship with his boss had been rather sour. He knew he was constantly walking on a tightrope with her. She hadn't forgiven him for failing to capture the vandal. Even though the girl had stopped carving her name onto the wall, the damage had been done to both Barrack Five and Vilém's reputation. Any amount of praise from his boss was a step towards forgiveness and was, to Vilém, almost as precious as his paycheck.

"Camp's closing up. You have your flashlight, Rehor?" asked Doubek. Vilém nodded, holding up the hefty tool.

"Good. I want you to stay near the Heydrich Exhibit for the next three weeks."

That made Vilém raise an eyebrow. "Heydrich Exhibit?" he repeated. Doubek beckoned for him to follow her. He obeyed, trailing behind his boss like a lost puppy as she strutted past Barrack Five and into Barrack Four.

A few straggling visitors were snapping pictures of the red and black placards and glass cases that were strategically spread out across the barrack. A new mini exhibit had been set up, probably last night while Vilém had been off. The placards prominently featured pictures of the Nazi official that had been in charge of Czechoslovakia during the war, the "Butcher of Prague", Reinhard Heydrich.

"It's actually supposed to be an exhibit about perpetrators," explained Doubek. "But we couldn't find much about the Kommandant except basic biographical information, and that's not enough to interest most people. So Heydrich gets to take center-stage this time."

"Yay for him," grumbled Vilém, leaning over one of the glass cases and gazing at a small, slightly rusted pen that had evidently belonged to the Butcher.

"Don't touch!" snapped Doubek as Vilém's hand brushed against the glass. "That's the sort of behavior I need you to keep under control. Half of this stuff is on loan from other museums and the other half was from the bastard's family. I do *not* want to be getting a call from his son at six-in-the-morning asking why we destroyed his daddy's favorite pen. Until the folks in charge give us permission to take down the exhibit and send all this shit back, this room is your number one priority. Got it?"

"Yes, ma'am," said Vilém with an obedient nod.

"Good. Then stay here until closing. And if we have another Graffiti Girl incident, Rehor, you're fired."

"Y-yes, ma'am," said Vilém, bowing his head. She peered at him for a few seconds before giving a curt nod and marching out of the barrack. Vilém sighed and leaned against a placard without looking.

Once he'd recovered from his boss' threat, he glanced idly to the side and cringed when he discovered he was leaning right beside a picture of Heydrich. The Nazi's narrow eyes seemed to glare straight at him, as if Heydrich's ghost was possessing the photograph and trying its hardest to exude hatred even in his petrified state.

"Fuckin' hell," hissed Vilém, leaping back and wringing his arm, fearing that merely touching an image of the Nazi would infect him with whatever filthy disease had consumed the Butcher's soul.

"Bastard," he growled, glaring into the still eyes of Heydrich. Although he had (obviously) never been fond of the long-dead Nazi, his recent encounter with Raya had changed the dull, obligatory hatred he had once felt towards Heydrich into a personal fire. It was Heydrich's fault that poor, sweet girl had been forced to suffer so much.

Vilém stepped away from Heydrich's visage and glanced at the accompanying paragraph:

Reinhard Heydrich: The Butcher of Prague (1904-1942)
Dubbed "The Man with the Iron Heart" by Hitler himself, Reinhard Tristan Eugen Heydrich was the head of the SD (Sicherheitsdienst), a Nazi intelligence division tasked with organizing the arrest and murder of the Third Reich's enemies, political and racial. Heydrich was one of the primary architects of the "Final Solution to the Jewish Question."
He was the chairman of the infamous Wannsee Conference, a secretive meeting of German officials where plans for the Holocaust were discussed and finalized. Heydrich's brutality earned him the position of Reichsprotektor of Nazi-occupied Czechoslovakia in September of 1941.
Heydrich was responsible for mass-scale executions and terror throughout Czechoslovakia, earning him the epithet "The Butcher of

Prague." He was assassinated by two Czechoslovak agents, Jan Kubis and Jozef Gabčík, in 1942 during Operation Anthropoid. After Heydrich's demise, Hitler ordered several reprisals that resulted in the deaths and incarcerations of thousands of Czechs and Jews. Although historians continue to debate whether or not his assassination was worth the high cost, almost all agree that he was one of the most evil men in the Third Reich.

"...and that's saying something," sighed Vilém, turning away from the Butcher of Prague's arrogant features and letting his eyes wander to another display.

A familiar face caught his eye: a man, barely younger than Heydrich, dressed in black SS garb with a severe look on his face. He, unlike Heydrich, did not look at the camera as he was photographed. Instead, his eyes (which were light-colored, though Vilém couldn't tell their exact shade from the black-and-white photograph) wandered to the left, as if someone standing beside the cameraman had caught his eye.

Vilém didn't need to read the blurb under the picture to know that the man was the Camp's Kommandant. He remembered him from Raya's memories. He scowled at the man for a moment before curiously reading the snippet.

The Kommandant
Hans Gerber (1909-1945)
Born to an upper-class couple, Hans Gerber joined the SS in late 1932. His enthusiasm and loyalty to the ideals of Adolf Hitler caused him to rise through the ranks swiftly, and in October 1941, Reichsprotektor Reinhard Heydrich made him the Kommandant of this small camp.
Gerber, a sociopath with a morbid fascination for photography, took many pictures of his grisly work. Survivors and witnesses would often

describe how he would climb to the top of the watchtower and take pictures during executions. Though many of these pictures were destroyed during the war, many more remain and are currently on display throughout this memorial site. Hans Gerber committed suicide shortly before Soviet forces arrived at the campground in 1945.

Vilém almost sighed in disappointment. Baseline information, and little of it was new to him. He hadn't known the Kommandant's name before, but his wickedness and his fascination with photography had been impressed upon him by Raya. He shot a scowl at the Kommandant's frozen image and instantly shivered as a frosty breeze snaked up his spine. He looked over at the door and was surprised to see that it was closed.

He sat between Heydrich and Gerber's respective informational boards, keeping careful watch over the artifacts and occasionally hopping up to shoo away some kids who got too close and put their oily fingers on the glass.

Soon, however, the guests, polite and rude alike, skittered out of Barrack Four. One of Vilém's fellow guards stepped in to inform him that the Camp was closed.

"You good for the night?" he asked, and Vilém nodded.

"Good as ever," he replied.

"I'm locking up and leaving you with the ghosts, then. Night, Vilém."

"Night!" said Vilém, waving as his coworker exited the barrack. He perked up his ears and heard the Camp gate creak as it was shut.

"Well," Vilém sighed, patting his hands on his thighs and standing up, looking at the pictures of Heydrich and Gerber. "Looks like it's just you and me, guys. Fun times, huh?"

Obviously, neither Nazi said a thing.

"Right..." Vilém sighed. He exited Barrack Four to briefly patrol the rest of the Camp.

He returned after half an hour and instantly, a chill enveloped him. Not the chill he was accustomed to—the usual cold Czech air that sometimes passed through the thin wooden walls of the barracks. Yet it was still familiar. He had felt this before, even more strongly, when his fingers had brushed against the graffiti-clad wall of Barrack Five.

"Raya?" he whispered.

No familiar gentle voice replied, but the cold aura seemed to beckon him. He obeyed its wishes eagerly, thinking that perhaps Raya Pomnenka had returned to the campsite. He hoped that wasn't the case. The poor girl had seemingly moved on weeks ago, but her fractured memories might have hidden something from her. Perhaps she had remembered something and had returned to tell him before she faded for good.

"Raya? Raya, sweetie, is that you?"

The aura led him to one of the display cases in front of the Heydrich Exhibit.

His brow shot up. He was standing before a faded picture of a little boy. Some sort of notice. It was in German, and Vilém only knew a few words of German, so he couldn't quite tell what it said. The placard that accompanied it was not very helpful: *"Issue from Heydrich's Office, 1941."*

The aura continued to call to him, all but begging him to disobey Ms. Doubek and press his fingers against the glass. He sighed.

"Oh, you spirits are gonna get me fired," he muttered, but he obeyed nonetheless, letting his oily fingers smudge the display case.

He stood still for a moment, waiting, then, remembering how he had communicated with Raya before, he shut his eyes.

"Hello?" he called into the darkness.

A voice replied: *H...Hallo...*

Not Raya's voice. Stronger than that of the shy girl, but also much younger. The spirit speaking with him now must have been no older than eleven. He was partially relieved that Raya was truly at peace and hadn't returned, but at the same time he was astonished and saddened at the revelation that she was not the only restless spirit tarrying at the Camp.

He smiled softly, although he wasn't sure if such a gentle gesture would even register to the ghost.

"Hi, sweetie," he said. "Are you lost? Do you have something you need to tell me?"

J-ja...Ich...tut mir leid...Ich spreche...Ich...I don't...Czech...don't speak well...

Vilém grunted softly. Well, that was going to make things even more difficult. He would not give up just because of a language barrier, of course, but it would still make it harder than it had been when he'd helped Raya.

It was odd, however: what was a German child doing here, in a concentration camp that, as far as he knew, had been built to house Czech "undesirables"? Their little camp was hardly Auschwitz—not the sort of camp he could imagine the Nazis would go out of their way to ship Jews to if it was inconvenient. And it certainly wouldn't have been convenient to ship Jews from the Sudetenland or Germany to this particular camp when there were several other camps they could have otherwise been sent to that would have been closer.

Interrogating the girl as to why she was here likely wouldn't do any good. Or, at least, a verbal interrogation wouldn't do any good.

"*Alles ist gut, alles ist gut, kleine,*" Vilém assured the girl with what little German he knew. "*Ich kann dich hilfe, Ich will dich hilfe.*"

Danke...du...you...Raya...helped...

"*Ja. Du weisst Raya?*"

Raya, yes...knew her. Bad memory. Not so with me. Good memory...I...good memory...not as Raya.

"That's good. Very good. *Sehr gut.* Can you show me your memory? Show? Make me see? Like Raya? *Wie Raya?*"

Ein moment, bitte...ein moment...

Being pulled into this little girl's memory was like riding a bike for the first time after abandoning it for a year: strange, a tad uncomfortable, but familiar all the same. In fact, though the deceased Jew's embrace was icy, like Raya's had been, it was much less so. There was a hint of warmth, of hope, that morose Raya had lacked. Perhaps, Vilém thought, this child's story wouldn't be as tragic.

Of course, he couldn't let his hopes get too high. This *was* the Holocaust he was quite literally delving into.

The transition to the ghostly memory-world was sudden. One moment he was standing by the Heydrich Exhibit, his oily fingers touching the glass that kept him from the unreadable official notice, and the next...well, the next he was seeing the world as it had been a lifetime ago, through the eyes of a little Jewish girl.

The girl was running through a wooded area. She glanced to her side and Vilém saw another girl, a child with wavy blonde hair tied into two clumsy pigtails and shimmering emerald eyes, dressed in a very nice white blouse and a blue skirt. His heart ached for a moment. She reminded him of his sisters when they were younger. She was six, maybe seven if he was being generous.

My sister...my twin. That's my sister. My sister is Ilona. I'm Iveta.

Well, then at least he could get an idea of what the little spirit speaking to him looked like. He didn't have a mirror around this time, but it was probably safe to assume they'd be identical. Iveta glanced down and dusted herself off, and Vilém realized she and her sister were dressed exactly the same.

"Twins..." Vilém muttered. "I see...so you two were very close then? What year is...?"

S-sorry...sorry...still having trouble...not understanding well....maybe watch only?

"Oh! Oh, sorry..."

Well, he thought, *I hope these memories come with subtitles.*

Fortunately, he quickly discovered that he wouldn't need subtitles. Iveta started to fall behind in what was evidently becoming a race between the twins and cried out: "Sis! C'mon, slow down!"

And although she surely must have spoken in German, Vilém understood it clear as day, as though it had been uttered in his own native Czech. He marveled at this for a moment, wondering why he could now understand German-speakers in a memory. In Raya's memory, he hadn't been able to understand what the Germans had said.

Then again, he reasoned, *she was Czech and didn't speak German. Since I was in her memory, of course I'd only understand what she understood. Maybe it's the same here: this is Iveta's memory, so I'll hear words the way she did and understand them as much as she could. It's not the same thing as a recording or a movie.*

He breathed a sigh of relief for the small blessing. Comprehending this memory would still likely be tougher since he didn't have the benefit of a verbose narrator, but at the very least he would understand what the twins said to each other.

"Ilona, please!"

"Slowpoke!" giggled Ilona. Iveta stumbled and almost collapsed, and Vilém felt himself totter just as she did. Just like before, Vilém would feel whatever the little girl felt. The wind in her face, the sweet smell of the trees tickling her nose, all sensations Iveta had experienced so long ago.

Iveta barely summoned the coordination to keep herself from falling flat on her face. She took a moment to regain her balance and looked up to see that her sister was gone.

"Ilona?" she cried, and Vilém felt the little girl's heart skip several beats as she trudged on, her eyes shifting wildly about the woods, searching for a sign of her sister.

"Ilona!" she cried, louder, her frightened voice echoing out over the trees. In the distance, she heard her sister call to her, so far away that she couldn't even make out her words, only her teasing tone.

Vilém felt warm water build up behind Iveta's eyes, and as her eyes became foggy, he felt her heart palpitate. She couldn't see, couldn't see where her sister was. She was going to be trapped in the woods forever and starve and...

"Iva!"

Vilém felt a comforting little hand wrap around Iveta's wrist, and the sobbing girl (whose memories he could barely witness through the ocean of tears in her eyes) pliantly allowed her sister to lead her through the woods.

"You're so stupid, Iva!" sighed Ilona in an exasperated tone that made it clear this wasn't the first time this had happened.

"S-sorry..." hiccupped Iveta. They stopped and Vilém felt fondness warm his chest as Ilona reached up and wiped the tears from the corners of her twin's eyes with her thumb. Just like him and his little sisters: they could argue as often as they liked, tease each other until tears blinded their eyes, but they loved each other. He could feel that love nestled in Iveta's chest when her vision cleared and she saw her sister pouting in front of her.

"Damn it, Iveta," sighed Ilona. "You know if I wasn't around, you'd never survive these woods. You would'a been eaten by a wolf."

"P-probably..." muttered Iveta.

"And then what? The Star Shack would just go to waste!" Ilona laughed, grabbing her sister's hand and dragging her out of the bushes.

Vilém wasn't sure what he had been expecting the girls to be running towards, but nonetheless he was surprised when Iveta blinked the tears from her eyes enough to view her surroundings.

They were in the midst of what looked like a long-abandoned wheat field. Shriveled stalks of grain wafted about in the breeze. A railroad track split the gray field in half and continued on into the woods, but it was so old—with tracks beginning to come up and metal bits rendered copper with rust twisting here and there—that Vilém suspected there hadn't been a train rolling on those tracks for years. Perhaps the First World War had disconnected the track from the rest of civilization.

Iveta's eyes only lingered on the tracks for a second before they shifted to their true destination.

At the edge of the dead field stood a watchtower, the sort that Vilém always saw near farmland, the sort hired hands rested in while guarding the crop. Vilém shivered when he saw it. He had once found such structures innocuous, but working at the Camp had soured his perception of watchtowers.

Ilona grabbed her sister's hand and the twins jovially skipped towards the foreboding structure. Vilém realized that there was a sign hanging on the door, painted in a childish script that, even if the memory had given him the ability to read and comprehend German, likely would have been beyond his ability to decipher.

They entered the old watchtower, and Vilém almost chuckled when he realized the twins had transformed the abandoned building into some sort of clubhouse. They had placed pink cushions on the splintery wooden chairs, two violet sleeping beds lay on the floor, an army of stuffed animals was lined up on a desk, and the walls were decorated with their drawings.

Iveta inhaled deeply, and Vilém was grateful when she did so as he got to enjoy the most wonderful scent. Iveta turned towards a mountain of sacks stacked high in one corner of the hideaway. Although he didn't speak German, Vilém knew the word for "sugar", which was plastered all over a third of the bags. Sugar, flour, marshmallows, cookies. The girls had a stock of sweets fit for the apocalypse.

"Are we bringing anything back?" Ilona asked, darting to the stack of sugar sacks. "Flour? Sugar? What?"

"Nothin' this time," Iveta said, snatching a box of cookies and a blanket from the corner. "Mama said she's good for the week."

Iveta's spirit clumsily attempted to explain: *Ah...Mother...did...bakery...we keep things here for safety....many....much stealing in village...but nobody knows about clubhouse of Ilona and I.*

"I get it," Vilém said, though he could only barely comprehend what the girl was trying to tell him. He kept watching as Iveta gathered some books into her arms, catching a glimpse at the covers. Although he couldn't read the German, he could tell from the pictures of stars and celestial bodies on the front of the hardbacks that they were about astronomy.

"C'mon! The sun's gonna go down pretty soon!" Ilona yelled at her sister, causing Iveta's heart to race. She looked over her shoulder so swiftly that her own pigtails smacked her in the eye and she yelped in pain, causing her twin to giggle.

"Klutz, you can hurt yourself with anything!" Ilona laughed.

Iveta mumbled something so quietly that even Vilém—despite being inside the girl's skull—couldn't decipher her words.

She grabbed a small pile of papers and three freshly-sharpened pencils before bolting up the barebones spiral staircase. Vilém could feel Iveta's thudding heart quicken its pace as she felt the stairs, half devoured by age and termites, creak loudly beneath her feet. To Vilém, it was a familiar nervousness, one that he had possessed when he was a boy climbing up the shaky rope ladder to Erik's treehouse. Frightened that today would be the day it broke, but having trusted it to bear the burden of his body so many times that doing so was practically instinct.

Iveta clambered eagerly through the trapdoor to the top floor of the watchtower, which her sister, seemingly without an iota of fear, had thrust open so roughly that the whole watchtower trembled.

"Ilona!" squeaked cautious Iveta. Ilona, unfazed, grabbed the books from her sister and flung herself onto a well-worn sleeping mat laid out beneath a hole in the watchtower's roof.

"Don't be such a baby, sis. C'mon, I wanna see Taurus!" Ilona said, holding a pencil in her teeth and flipping to a particular page in one hardback. Iveta heaved a disgruntled sigh, but Vilém felt forgiveness wash over the little girl's heart as she took a seat beside her sister.

Vilém, who had failed astronomy, could barely understand what the girls discussed with such breathless amazement for the rest of the night. Iveta would gesture to the stars and point out shapes and ancient figures that Vilém couldn't see. But even though he couldn't discern the figures in the sky, he felt sparks of fascination light up Iveta's mind. He felt her love for her sister, the joy she felt spending time with her, and a slight spark of pride. A spark whose presence could perhaps be explained by the fact that it seemed astronomy was Iveta's area of expertise.

"Trace it out, Ilona!" Iveta said, gesturing to the stars above, and Ilona happily complied, sketching out Taurus. For a young child, she had an older artist's hand.

The girls both laid back once their stargazing had tired their eyes out.

"Hey...Ilona..." Iveta muttered, and Vilém felt the girl's heart sink. "What're we gonna do when we're older and I go to college?"

Iveta's ghost spoke again. *Sister was good...with the cakes...the bakery...wanted to own as adult, not me, not good with art or icing, me. Wanted to astro....student, student be.*

Ilona, unperturbed, shrugged her twin's question off. "We'll still see each other," she assured her.

"There's no college in the village, Illa. I'm gonna have to go away..."

"We walk all the way out here every other night, Iva! I'm sure I'll be able to get to you. I'll make those cookies shaped like stars you like and deliver 'em. Maybe I'll go to college. Baking college or art college. Dunno, but don't worry, I won't abandon you. Can't. You'd die if I did, klutz."

Ilona gave her sister what Vilém could tell was meant to be a light slap on the arm, but to delicate Iveta it felt like a boxer had punched her. She yelped and tears filled her eyes, clouding her vision, blinding her and Vilém.

Her vision suddenly cleared and Vilém was startled when he saw that the memory had shifted. No longer was Iveta in the watchtower; she was standing in a kitchen, sweat and tears covering her face. A woman knelt before her, scowling and shaking her head as she held out a hand.

"Let's see it," the woman said, and Iveta offered her arm, which was sporting a minor burn. The woman, presumably the twins' mother, clicked her tongue in disapproval.

"Silly girl, this is why I tell you to let Ilona handle the oven," she said.

"I was trying to make a surprise for her..." mumbled Iveta as her mother marched over to a cabinet and pulled out a roll of bandage tape. Iveta averted her gaze as her mother dressed her injury, her eyes falling upon her failed creation: a burnt cake that sat on a counter, surrounded by cans of icing. She must have burned herself taking it out of the oven: she hadn't been able to decorate it.

"I'm sure she'll appreciate you staying safe more than any cake, Iva," said the twins' mother, tightening the bandage and making her daughter squeal. Iveta's mother chuckled, reaching out with a flour-covered hand and pinching her daughter's cheek. Vilém could feel sticky batter cling to Iveta's face.

There was a *ring* from outside the kitchen, a telltale sign that someone had entered the bakery.

"Mama, it happened again!" Ilona's voice, filled with distress, rose above the slam of a door. Iveta's mother swore.

"Again...?" mumbled Iveta, and Vilém felt her heart tumble to the bottom of her stomach.

Her mother marched out of the kitchen like a hurricane and Iveta scuttled after her, running so quickly that Vilém only barely caught a glimpse of the family bakery: small, quaint, only enough space for two tables and a booth. The walls had been decorated with paper cut-outs of stars and planets, no doubt contributed by the little artist and the little astronomer.

"Let's go," huffed the twins' mother, slamming the door behind her, the bell jingling viciously in her wake. Ilona grabbed her sister's hand and the two stayed close to their mother, Iveta's heart pounding as they shuffled through the village. She looked side to side, earning scowls from her neighbors and rude gestures from a gaggle of teens.

Only Jews in town we were, the ghost explained. *Some fine with this, many not. My father...killed on way home from work...Jew-haters did...when very tiny me and Ilona were.*

"I'm so sorry..." Vilém muttered, watching as the family

rounded a corner and arrived at a graveyard by a church. It didn't surprise him that the girls' father was buried in a church cemetery: their village was so tiny, and if they were the only Jews, there was no other place he could have been laid to rest.

He felt his anger spike when he saw where the Jewish man's grave was located: in a muddy corner far from where the gentiles were buried, as though the Christians of the village hadn't even wanted their dead to associate with a member of the Jewish race.

"I guess the Nazis didn't bring any new ideas here..." Vilém muttered, and he sensed bitter agreement emanating from Iveta's spirit.

As they got close to the isolated plot, Vilém realized what had "happened again." Someone had painted graffiti all over the head-stone. It stood at an odd angle, as though the vandals had initially tried to knock it over and, upon being foiled, opted to deface it. Vilém couldn't read the graffiti, and when Iveta chose to read it aloud, he almost wished he had remained ignorant.

"'One Jew Down, Three to Go!'" the girl whimpered, and he felt her spine tingle as though a serpent had started slithering up her back.

Ilona's grip on her sister's hand tightened, a reassuring action that Vilém sensed Iveta appreciated.

"Childish nonsense, probably some teens," Iveta's mother said, squatting before her husband's grave and brushing her thumb over his name. "Don't you girls worry about it, not one bit..."

"They got Papa..." Iveta pointed out, her morose observation causing a cloud of fear to descend upon the family. The cloud parted, however, when Ilona hooked arms with her twin.

"I'll protect Iva!" Ilona volunteered. Their mother smiled.

"That's my brave girl...Iveta, don't worry, Ilona's got you. Nothing messes with Ilona."

"Hm..." muttered Iveta, looking towards her father's grave, her gut roiling as though she had eaten an expired pastry.

But suddenly, Ilona dangled a shiny something-or-other in front of her face. Iveta winced, but Vilém felt her fear transform into gratitude when her eyes focused on the object and she realized it was a bracelet.

"Surprise!" Ilona declared, grabbing her sister's arm. "Happy birthday! I made it for you, took me some time...I was just showing Papa. It's my best work, I think, even better than the cakes."

Ilona slipped the bracelet onto her sister's wrist and Iveta lifted her arm, holding the bracelet up to the sun. Golden star-shaped beads shimmered in the light, and a bead painted to look like the earth rested calmly beneath her thumb.

"Hey, what happened to your arm, sis?" Ilona queried, and Vilém felt Iveta's face heat up.

"Erm...I was trying to make your birthday present and I got burned...I didn't get to finish it...sorry..." muttered Iveta, fiddling with the beads on her birthday bracelet.

Ilona giggled. "You're silly! You don't know how to use the oven, you klutz! Next time for our birthday, just don't get hurt, okay? That's a good present."

"I was trying..." sighed Iveta.

"Well...that's good!" Ilona said, leaning forward and kissing her sister's cheek. Their mother smiled with fond sorrow at their affectionate display and then commanded Ilona to take her sister home while she handled the graffiti.

"See you back at the bakery, Mama!" Ilona cried, leading her sister away from the graveyard. But despite all of Ilona's attempts to comfort and distract her sister, Iveta looked back, looked at the dire warning on her father's grave. Her head started spinning, her heart trembling, fear rushing through her veins. Tears blinded her again.

"Ilona, get away from the window!"

The memory shifted once more. Iveta and her mother were ducking behind the counter, peeking out just enough to see Ilona crouching by the front of the store. A yellow word, '*Jude*', had been painted on the bakery's window. Outside, a thick crowd had gathered. Had Vilém not known his history, he would have had no clue what the hubbub was about.

But the nearby calendar showed that it was October 1938. The Munich Betrayal had just happened. The Sudetenland belonged to Hitler, and the anti-Semites of Ilona and Iveta's hometown must have been welcoming the Nazi troops.

Iveta's mother crept out of her hiding place, wrapping her arm around her too-brave daughter's waist and slowly pulling her away from the window. Iveta watched. It seemed as though she was in a trance: her eyes were glazed over, her mouth ajar.

CRASH!

A hunk of brick shattered the thick glass and snapped Iveta out of her dreamlike state. Ilona screamed and clung to her mother. Shards stabbed their flesh and Vilém could feel Iveta's fear paralyze her.

Everything happened too fast. Before the glass could even strike the floor, Iveta's mother ran to her other daughter and grabbed her hand. A mob pursued, screaming and hissing. Iveta's mother slammed the kitchen door shut and blocked it with a table. It wouldn't give her much time. Vilém knew that, and evidently so did Iveta's mother. She took her girls and dragged them to the closest hiding place: a massive oven. Vilém felt his heart sink at the irony. The scent of char and ash assaulted Iveta's sinuses as she and her sister were pushed in.

"Stay quiet!" their mother warned them, slamming the door,

and Ilona slapped a hand over Iveta's mouth. Vilém could tell that such a gesture was unnecessary. Iveta was too frightened to move or make a noise.

She sat there, the grate digging into her hands and bottom, listening to her sister's quiet, hopeless assurances that everything would be okay. She saw nothing, but heard everything. The door flying open. Her mother pleading for mercy. "Dirty Jew," being screeched by the neighbors. She heard her mother call out names, perhaps recognizing formerly friendly faces in the mob, but all masks had been pulled off and there was no mercy.

She heard her mother screaming. She heard laughing. She smelled skin burn.

And when there was finally silence, they lingered in the oven. They waited and waited until they could stand it no more. Iveta stretched her foot out and nudged the oven door open. Cautiously, the girls crawled out.

Iveta let her eyes flit to and fro. The bakery was in ruins, looted to the point where only a few rusty pots and pans and some baking supplies were left behind.

"Mama...?" Ilona whispered, and the twins searched for their mother.

Iveta peeked behind an upturned table and screamed. Vilém felt horror strangle her soul when she saw what had become of her mother.

A burned mound of flesh and tattered fabrics covered in blackened blood was all that remained. At first it seemed she was dead, and Vilém would have thought it better if that were true, but her chest rose and fell. Though her eyes had been pulled from her head, her fingernails torn off, her skin scorched, and though all she could do was blindly twitch, she lived. The mob had stopped just short of murder. Perhaps they thought it better to let her die blind, slow, in agony, alone.

She wasn't alone, but her daughter couldn't look at her. Iveta turned away and vomited all over the bloodstained floor. Ilona approached, and Iveta, still heaving and sobbing, barely saw her sister's expression shift from horror to sorrow before it settled on a frightening stoniness.

"She's alive..." Ilona muttered, walking to her mother's side. "Mama, can you hear me?"

Her mother did not indicate that she could. Iveta dared look at what remained of her mother once more, and Vilém could sense that she was grateful for the tears obscuring her view of the almost-corpse.

"We...we've gotta get her help, a doctor..." whimpered Iveta, and Ilona's eyes, full of fire, narrowed at her sister.

"The doctors are the ones who did this to her," Ilona said. "We're on our own. Nobody's gonna help us. Nobody cares."

Straightening up, Ilona stepped away from her mother, tip-toeing over glass and bricks until she reached a drawer. She opened it.

"They didn't take everything, good." She drew two sharp, shiny knives from the drawer and offered one to her sister. Iveta gingerly took it, staring inquisitively up at her severe sister.

"Ilona...?"

"We're alone, Iva," Ilona said. "We'll have to run for the Star Shack."

"And...then what?"

"Grow up, and then we'll come back and kill everyone here, everyone who did this to Mama," Ilona declared, one trembling hand twirling the knife, gently stabbing at the air, as though she was imagining their tormentors before her, as though the empty space was their flesh.

A sob choked Iveta. "I don't wanna kill anyone!" she insisted, but her sister ignored her. Ilona, whose eyes seemed to have aged fifty years, turned her gaze towards what remained of their mother.

"We gotta, though…" Ilona muttered, and although Vilém immediately knew what she was talking about, he felt confusion bubble up in Iveta's brain.

"W…wha…?"

"Mama…we can't leave her like this."

"Illa…no…"

"There's nobody to help her, she's hurting…"

"No, no, ***no!***"

"Shhh, Iva, keep your voice down or they'll hear us! They'll come back! They'll do it to us too!" hissed Ilona, towering over her sister. Iveta sobbed, shook her head, and dropped the knife. It clattered to the ground, landing in a puddle of blood and splashing a few droplets onto Ilona's ankles.

"I can't, I can't…" whimpered Iveta, feeling as though she was going to vomit again.

"You're not brave enough, I know…" whispered Ilona. "It's fine. I'll be brave for both of us. Give her a kiss goodbye."

Iveta glanced at her mother's peeling onyx skin, and Vilém could feel her stomach churn at the thought. He could feel guilt slash at her gut, attacking her for being so disgusted by her own mother, but she couldn't help it. She shook her head and hid her face in her hands.

"It's fine…." whispered Ilona again. "Fine, you're not brave enough. I'll be brave for you, Iva."

Iveta was crying so much that even if she had looked up, she likely wouldn't have been able to see through her tears. But she heard Ilona's footsteps daintily march towards the half-dead woman. She heard her twin whisper her final goodbyes and declarations of love to their mother. She heard her plant a bold kiss on her mother's cheek.

Iveta dared to look up, dared to let her tear-filled eyes fall upon her sister as she raised the knife.

Something wrong, someone here...

The ghost interrupted, and just as Ilona plunged the knife downwards, Vilém suddenly found himself back in Barrack Four, falling backwards, as though he had been shoved out of the spirit's memories.

Vilém yelped as he landed hard on the dusty barrack floor, but he wasn't a weak man and it would take more than a fall to stun him. He immediately hopped back to his feet and slapped his hand on the display case, nearly knocking it over in his haste.

"Iveta?! Iveta, what happened? Are you still there, are you all right?!"

A chilly gust of wind tickled his ear, but he didn't hear the girl's voice. He set about touching every object in the Heydrich Exhibit, but nothing summoned the ghost once more.

By the time he had touched every inch of Barrack Four, day broke and a coworker came in to relieve him of his shift.

"Jesus, man, you okay?" the day guard asked as he shooed Vilém out of the barrack and saw the worry spilling from his coworker's eyes. "Ya' look like you saw a ghost."

FOR THE NEXT FEW DAYS, Vilém didn't see or hear any ghosts, and he never would have thought that an absence of paranormal activity would distress him so greatly.

That Ms. Doubek didn't fire him after he left a criminology database's worth of fingerprints all over absolutely everything in the Heydrich Exhibit demonstrated that she had more mercy in her old, shriveled heart than she let on. Still, she warned him to stop touching everything.

"Don't know why you'd want to anyway...." she grumbled. "All this shit from the Butcher...even *I* don't want to get near it, much less touch it."

But he kept at it, night after night, the silence of Barrack Four tormenting him. He searched the other barracks, but he could find no sign of either Iveta or the entity that had frightened her.

Perhaps it was his latent paternal instincts kicking in, but he couldn't get the poor girl out of his head. So little and frightened and stuck in that damn camp for God knows how long. He could barely eat, barely sleep, and going out with Erik or planning something fun with Jana...he couldn't. The idea of going out and having fun and living when that poor child was still suffering made guilt tie his stomach into knots.

He looked up everything he could about ghosts, doing his best to separate the bull from what sounded like potential truth. Unsurprisingly, there was a lot of bull, and soon he gave up on the internet and decided there was nothing he could do.

He felt like he had when he was a little boy and his cat would tarry on her daily hunts. He would be at home waiting by the door, knowing there was nothing he could do, but too worried to do anything but sit on the porch and wait.

A week of hermitude went by, and one day, he got a text.

Erik: Hey bro, you ok?

He sighed and decided not to leave his friend hanging.

Vilém: Yeah, man. Just kinda in one of those moods.

Erik: Y'know that Jana girl's been texting you. I met her at the bar the other day and she said you won't answer.

Vilém felt guilt prick his soul. He liked Jana, and he would have been content to text her all day and night, but that was the problem. It would have made him content. He felt so spoiled, having the option to go out and have fun while Iveta languished. He was privileged enough to live in a time where he would never have to dream of mercy killing his own mother. Why did he deserve such a cozy, happy life when little Iveta didn't even get a peaceful death?

He chewed on his lip and considered lying to his friend, but he felt like his chest would explode if he kept holding everything in and decided to be reasonably earnest.

Vilém: We got a new exhibit at the Camp. I don't know, man, I think that place is getting to me again. I'm seeing these little kids dying and stuff every night and then I feel guilty wanting to go out and just have fun. It's like...if they didn't get a chance at that, why do I deserve it?

Vilém: Sorry, rambling.

Erik: Hey bro, believe it or not, I totally know where you're coming from. You remember my mom?

Vilém shuddered. He knew Erik would never bring up his mother unless it was a genuine friend emergency. Erik's mother had been an absolute nightmare, a soul without a drop of humor, even worse than Ms. Doubek. Vilém had never seen her smile.

Vilém: How could I forget?

Erik: You remember what she used to say to me whenever we got into trouble or I got a bad grade?

Vilém: "Your grandma didn't survive Auschwitz just for her only grandson to _______"

Erik: Lol, yup. But you know my grandma, she was the best. And I always kind of wondered, "Why is it that my grandma is literally awesome and enjoys life even after going through Auschwitz, but my mom, who didn't have to deal with any of that, acts like the whole world's a cesspit?"

Vilém: And what's your hypothesis?

Erik: Same thing you're going through right now. It's like a weird generational survivor's guilt. Grandma went through hell, she lost everything, and I bet every

time Mom tried to do anything, she had Auschwitz on the mind.

Erik: My mom loved Grandma, and I bet she was always thinking, "Why do I deserve to have fun and be a kid if my mom had to go through Auschwitz?" And then after I was born, same thing got foisted onto me. And you know my mom was never happy about anything, and you know my grandma hated that. She tried to give Mom a good life after what she went through, and Mom appreciated it in the wrong way.

Erik: I guess what I'm kinda trying to say is: don't be like my mom, man. You're great, and all those good people you feel guilty for, they wouldn't want ya' to make yourself miserable because they were miserable. Like my grandma. They'd want you to appreciate what they went through and be happy on their behalf.

Erik: Like my grandma used to say: every time a Czech or Jew smiles, Hitler turns in his grave.

Erik: So what I'm basically saying is: text Jana, you fuck, or I'm gonna steal her.

Vilém laughed, his heart lighter than it had been in a week.

Vilém: Ok, I'll text her right now. Thanks, bro, I knew there was a reason I'm still your friend.

Erik: Well, I DO still have those pictures from Christmas.

Vilém: Delete those. Now.

Erik: Fuck no, you know too much about me. I need blackmail material of my own.

Vilém: Fine, but I reserve the right to tell the slug story if those pictures ever leak.

Erik. That's mutually assured destruction, dude. That's what friendship is.

Vilém: TTYL, bro, I've gotta write an apology novel to Jana. Wanna do something stupid next weekend?

Erik: Prague?

Vilém: Prague.

Erik: Prague next weekend. Plan made.

Vilém switched to Jana's number. After he apologized for ghosting her and she forgave him, they made a plan to meet on Saturday. They exchanged some goofy texts and by the time Vilém set off for work, he was wearing the biggest, dumbest grin in the world. It felt like he had cast off a heavy weight. He felt happy, and even better, he didn't feel bad for feeling happy.

He got to the Camp, received his nightly lecture from Ms. Doubek, and then returned to Barrack Four with a newfound sense of hope. The Camp cleared out, and almost as soon as he was alone, he felt a familiar presence lingering by the poster in the Heydrich Exhibit. His heart somersaulted and he slammed his hand against the display case.

"Iveta?" he yelled, squeezing his eyes shut.

Seem...happier, you are...very good! The girl's spirit sounded much more cheerful than he would have expected given the circumstances. *Very no happy you were, all week. Thought you felt it too.*

"Felt what?"

Bad spirit somewhere here, can sense. Nazi maybe? Cannot tell, cannot find, but you must...careful, very careful be...don't want you to hurt.

"I'll be careful," he assured the girl, sounding much braver than he was. A Nazi spirit? He supposed it only made sense: if a Jew could linger, so could a Nazi. He remembered being in Prague and sensing an angry presence near the spot where Heydrich had died.

Perhaps Heydrich had attached himself to one of his old possessions. Vilém grunted. Fantastic, just what he *didn't* need: the ghost of the Architect of the Holocaust trouncing about his workstation.

He decided he would have to deal with one ghost at a time, however, and smiled at the invisible presence.

"Don't worry about me, Iva, whatever it is. Let's focus on you: what happened to you after the Bakery Incident?"

Ilona and I ran to Star Shack. Had food. Survived okay for very long. Nobody find for long time until one day...

Vilém felt his stomach lurch once more, like a roller coaster had taken off, and before he knew it, he was once again in Iveta's memories.

"Iva, there's a boy outside."

Iveta's eyes, bleary from sleep, slowly opened. Ilona was standing above her, three years older than she had been on that day in the bakery. Even though she was a mere ten years old, she had the eyes of a woman. Her clothes were much more ragged compared to what Iveta was wearing, indicating that she braved the outside world more often than her sister. Behind her, a mountain of flour and sugar still stood. It seemed that the stock had been serving the girls well for the duration of the occupation.

Iveta raised her hand up to rub her eyes, the star bracelet shimmering on her wrist as she did so. She hadn't been doing much for her own personal hygiene, but she must have made certain to clean that bracelet every day.

"...A...what...?"

"Boy. He's blonde. Looks like a gentile." Ilona held up the knife she had used on their mother. Rust-colored stains clung to the once shimmering surface of the blade. "I'm gonna go kill him."

That woke Iveta up. She sprung to her feet and grabbed her twin's wrist. "Wait! Illa, what if he's a Jew?"

"Don't look like one..."

"Neither do we! Where is he?"

"Lyin' on the tracks outside."

"The tracks?"

"Come up," Ilona commanded, and Iveta obeyed, cautiously

following her sister up the unstable spiral staircase and shoving her way into the tower.

She looked down at the dead field. Indeed, on the abandoned tracks, she could see a tiny figure, a little boy. It was difficult to discern very much from so far away, but she saw golden hair, and when she squinted she saw something yellow on his shirt. Vilém knew what that meant, and fortunately the girls had not isolated themselves so thoroughly that they didn't.

"I think he's wearing one of those yellow star thingies," Iveta said. "Like we saw when we snuck into the village. We saw that order, they're making the Jews wear them."

"Hm..." Ilona pursed her lips together in a thin, suspicious line.

"It'd be nice, y'know," Iveta muttered. "To know another Jew. We've only ever had each other."

"What's wrong with that?" Ilona snapped.

"Nothin', but more friends would be nice."

"Another mouth to feed."

"Another soldier," Iveta said, and Vilém almost chuckled. It seemed that Iveta knew exactly how to appeal to her vengeful twin. Ilona's eyes brightened.

"I guess...a boy may be useful."

"I'll go talk to him. You'll scare him if you march up to him with a knife."

"You *are* the friendly one," Ilona conceded, at last allowing a smile to tug at her lip. "I'll keep watch. But take your knife with you."

"All right..." sighed Iveta. She carefully maneuvered back downstairs, pausing by her cot to grab her knife, which was shiny and unused. She tucked it into her pocket and ran outside, slowing her jog as she drew close to the tracks.

The boy, whom Vilém immediately realized was the same

child from the poster in the Heydrich Exhibit, looked worse for wear. About nine years old, with golden hair and aquamarine eyes that shimmered with somber thoughtfulness. Well-fed, though even from a moderate distance she could hear his stomach rumbling. His pale skin was marred with dirt and bruises. His black sweater, which looked lovingly hand-knitted, was torn and stained. A big, yellow six-pointed star bearing a crudely drawn word, '*JUDE*', was proudly sewn onto his chest. It looked like he'd made it himself.

"Uhm..." Iveta started to say, and the boy winced, sitting up. He made no attempt to run, but the fear that spewed from his eyes when they fell upon the skinny wastrel that was Iveta was so palpable it was practically contagious. Iveta felt a shiver go up her spine, but nonetheless she attempted to smile.

"Uh...what're you doing out here?" she asked. The boy took in a deep breath and fell back onto the tracks, facing the sky with a scowl, as though something about his current circumstance had made him mad at the heavens.

"Killing myself," he replied in a tone that would not have been inappropriate for a bored pupil describing his least favorite class.

"Oh..." Iveta replied, playing with her bracelet to distract herself from the uncomfortableness of this encounter. The boy stretched his hand out towards the sky and wiggled his fingers, letting the light strike his face in different spots.

"Sorry," he said, purposefully letting the sun attack his eyes. "I didn't know anyone else was out here. I'll move..."

"It doesn't really matter anyway," Iveta said. She pointed down the train tracks, which disappeared into the foliage, and explained, "The train tracks end down there; trains don't come through here anymore. You're not gonna get hit by anything."

The boy sat upright and looked down the tracks, pricking his ears up as though he hoped to hear the roar of an engine. The only noise that greeted him, however, was the twitter of birds. He groaned, slapped his hands over his face, and fell onto his side.

"Damn..." the child hissed. Iveta stepped over the metal edge of the train tracks and sat beside the boy, her hand hovering above his blonde head. Vilém sensed her empathetic hesitancy: it was as though she would have liked to comfort him, but wasn't sure if he would reject her touch.

She heard a snarl that made her wince, and she smiled when she realized it was merely the boy's stomach.

"You don't have to kill yourself, y'know. That won't make anything better," Iveta said. "My sister and me, we're Jews too, and we lost our family. If you're alone and your family's dead, you should come with us and one day we can all get our revenge together."

The boy laughed, and Vilém had never heard a child laugh the way he did. Bitter as a rotten apple, that laugh. It wasn't a laugh that should have come from an innocent boy.

But he laughed and laughed until he was crying. Iveta slowly stood, and Vilém could sense her concern. She must have thought he was mad, and Vilém wouldn't have blamed her one bit for assuming that.

Finally, the boy stopped laughing. He wiped the tears from his face and stood up. He must have been weak from not eating for God-knows-how-long; he stood with all the grace of a newborn goat, legs wobbling and almost collapsing beneath him. Iveta swooped in and saved him from falling, draping his arm over her shoulders.

"You need to come inside! We can give ya' something to eat," she said.

"I don't wanna steal your food," the boy said, helplessly stumbling along as the girl dragged him back towards her safehouse.

"We have tons of food, it's no big deal," Iveta assured him.

"My sis and I have been out here for years. Don't worry about us. You look almost dead."

"That's the idea..." mumbled the boy.

"It's a bad idea, that's just what the gentiles want," Iveta said. "They want us to be hungry and miserable and dead! Don't do their job for 'em!"

"You're nice," the boy said, smiling at her, his eyes clouded. "You don't deserve to be out here all alone..."

"Not alone! Ilona, the boy's sick and hungry, get him something!"

Iveta nudged the door to the Star Shack open with her foot and called to her sister. Ilona came rushing down the stairs so fast that Vilém was surprised they didn't crumble under her feet. Iveta lay the boy down on her sleeping mat and ran to grab him something to eat. She smirked when she heard Ilona interrogating him.

"You have any friends?"

"I thought I did, but I think I was wrong," the boy replied, tugging on a loose thread on the mat. Iveta knelt by his side and offered him a loaf of bread, observing his angry fidgeting with a gentle smile.

"Our neighbors all betrayed us too, don't feel bad," Iveta said. Ilona shushed her.

"What's your name?" she asked. The boy nibbled on the bread, his blue eyes brightening.

"Klaus," he answered. He held up the loaf. "This is good!"

"We made it," Iveta said proudly, gesturing to the stock of wheat and flour behind them. "Not easy without an oven, but we manage!"

"Any siblings? Where's your mother? Where's your father?" Ilona asked. Klaus almost coughed up his bread at the word "father."

"My dad's gone," he said, and Iveta looked towards her sister, silently pleading for her to offer empathy. She was grateful when Ilona's stony eyes softened.

"Ours too, and our mom," Ilona said. "Eat something. You can stay here if you want."

Klaus offered Ilona what was left of his bread.

"I'm not hungry," he insisted weakly.

"Yes, you are. Eat," Ilona commanded, and after being harangued by both sisters for the better part of an hour, Klaus finally finished the one little piece of bread.

"If you're smart, you'll stay here," Ilona said. "You're welcome to. If you still wanna kill yourself, fine, but don't do it here or you may lead some Nazis right to us. Get your strength back and then go far, far away, and if you're captured, die and don't say anything about where we are. Got it?"

Klaus nodded, and Vilém could feel Iveta's heart plunge at the notion of letting the boy go off to his death. Vilém felt a wave of affection wash over him: poor Iveta was a sweetheart despite everything, caring so much for a boy she didn't even know.

Ilona announced that Klaus could do as he liked and climbed back up to keep watch, no doubt making sure the boy hadn't been followed. Iveta stayed by their exhausted guest's bedside, chatting with him. Klaus, perhaps unsurprisingly, wasn't in the mood for small talk, but he listened with a smile as Iveta explained how she and her sister had been living independently for so long.

"You two are really brave, living out here by yourselves," he said. Iveta fiddled with her star bracelet and shook her head.

"Ilona's the brave one. I'm just...here. I'm lucky to have her."

"You walked out to see me, that was pretty brave," Klaus pointed out, at last offering her a genuine, wide smile. He had one of the nicest smiles Vilém had ever seen, dimples decorating his rosy cheeks. Iveta tried and failed to suppress a blush.

"Nice one, Klaus, getting older girls..." Vilém joked, and Iveta's spirit laughed.

Liked him very much, Klaus. Klaus was very nice. Stayed for two weeks, hoped I...hoped he would stay forever...

"So...what happened to him?" Vilém asked, and although the Iveta of the past was chipper as she spoke to a smiling Klaus, the memory became cloudy and warped, as though the spirit herself was crying. When it cleared, the memory had once again shifted.

"Iva, get up, it snowed!"

Iveta evidently wasn't used to being roused with such enthusiasm. She screamed, and Vilém felt the word "Gestapo!" escape her lips before she sat up and realized it was only Klaus. The beaming boy had clumps of snow clinging to his shoulders and golden hair, but when his cheerful announcement was met with instinctual fear, his sweet smile turned sour.

"Sorry..." Klaus said. "Just wanted to let ya' know it snowed...Ilona's not really...uhm..."

He looked at Iveta's twin, who was fiddling with a box of matches. Ilona scoffed and lit the fireplace.

"Klaus, you need to quit being such a kid," Ilona sighed, and Vilém felt a dagger of sorrow strike his heart. What a thing for a ten-year-old to say.

"Hey, y'know...if you guys just...sit around and act miserable all day...well, that's just what the Nazis want. Miserable Jews," Klaus reasoned. He offered Iveta a hand, and Vilém could feel the shy girl's soul stir with eagerness as she grabbed it and let him drag her towards the door.

"Let's go play! Bet I could beat you in a snowball fight!" Klaus dared her, a mischievous glow conquering his aquamarine eyes.

Iveta hesitated only long enough to look towards Ilona. Her twin obviously thought it foolish, to go out and possibly get sick just for the sake of play, but she nonetheless waved for Iveta to go and have fun.

Vilém had never enjoyed a Holocaust memory so much. He remembered being a child, running around the woods and losing snowball fights to Erik. He had always wished he could experience those memories again, and through Iveta, for a short time, he did. Klaus was a brutal snowball fighter, showing no mercy despite his opponent being a girl. He defeated her, but he was a gracious victor, shaking hands over their snow peace treaty and even letting her keep half her territory.

Neither of them were dressed for the snow, but they stayed out, building a faceless snowman, creating snow angels, trying to knock icicles off the Star Shack. They played for hours, and Vilém almost forgot where he was. Iveta was so happy that the warmth in her heart made her feel toasty even as her fingers turned blue.

They finally became too tired to play anymore, but they didn't go back inside. Vilém could sense guilt growing in Iveta's chest, and though he didn't know the cause, he could assume she didn't want to return to her too-grown-up twin. She wanted to be a child, even if only for a few hours, and felt guilty about abandoning her sister for fun. She fiddled with her star bracelet and looked at Klaus, who was building a small, odd-shaped figure in the snow.

"What's that, Klaus?" asked Iveta. She looked at her friend's face and Vilém felt a sting in the girl's heart when she saw his forlorn expression.

"A bear..." Klaus answered. He smiled wistfully, his eyes becoming misty with nostalgia. "I had a white teddy bear...my papa got it for me. He took me skiing once, just him and me and my uncle. We played in the snow and he helped me ski...and when it was all over, he bought me a bear at the gift shop. I named it Heldi."

"'Hero'?" Iveta helpfully translated.

"I named it after Papa. He always picked me up if I hurt, but he didn't treat me like a baby. He let me get up myself..."

He stared down at the snow teddy bear for a moment, tears trailing down his ice-nipped cheeks.

"He really was my hero..." Klaus whispered.

"I'm sorry, Klaus..."

"Don't be...it's not your fault." He smiled at her, wiping his tears away with his snow-coated sleeve. "I know about your mom, but what about your dad?"

"He was Czech, I know that. He died before the Nazis came. Someone in the village killed him for being a Jew. I was little...I don't remember him much. I think Ilona remembers him better. He used to smoke a pipe...I remember the smell. And...I remember he'd do this thing where he held us both under his arms and he'd twirl us around and we'd pretend we were airplanes..."

Klaus laughed, but as he laughed, he seemed to cry as well. Tears rolled down his face, hiccups rocked his little body. His laughs died away and he sobbed.

"Papa did the same thing with me and my brother...the same thing," Klaus whimpered. "I don't understand...I don't understand...it doesn't make sense..."

"No...it doesn't," Iveta agreed. They sat still for a moment, sobs wracking the little boy's body. But suddenly, Klaus stood up, red-rimmed eyes wide, ears pricked up like a deer that had just heard a wolf howl.

"Klaus, what?"

"They're here...damn, I knew I shouldn't have stayed this long."

"Klaus...?"

"Shhh! Get down!"

He grabbed her by one of her pigtails, and Vilém was impressed that despite the sudden, painful tug on her hair, Iveta managed to keep herself from crying out as Klaus pulled her behind one of their snow forts. Klaus poked a small peephole in the icy structure and peeked at the woods.

"Shit..." the boy whispered, leaning away from the hole and gritting his teeth. Iveta shoved her eye into the hole and whimpered when she saw dark figures emerging from the thicket.

"Nazis..." she whimpered.

"SS," Klaus clarified. "They're combing the woods, looking for Jews. Iveta..."

He grabbed her by the shoulders and spun her around, forcing her to look into his eyes. His irises were colder and more intense than a blizzard. There was something strange about the child's eyes right then, something familiar.

"Run back to the watchtower! I'll lead them away from this place. I never should have stayed this long..."

"Klaus, no!" Iveta hissed, grabbing his hand as he started to stand and pulling him back down to safety. "They'll kill you, Klaus!"

"Good," Klaus said, and Vilém had never seen a nine-year-old with such a grim expression. There was no sign of sadness, however. Just acceptance, almost eagerness, as though he was about to give an old bully a kick to the balls.

"Klaus..."

"It's okay, Iveta." He offered her a smile. "It was nice to meet you. I wasn't wrong. You guys don't deserve any of this."

"Wha...?" Vilém felt confusion whirl through Iveta's brain, but before she could ask a question, Klaus leapt over the snow fort like a WWI soldier vaulting into No-Man's-Land. He screamed and waved his arms, and the Nazis rushed towards him. He led them away from the Star Shack.

Iveta squatted behind the snow fort for a moment, shell-shocked, but Klaus' sacrificial cry rang in her ears. She skittered back to the Star Shack, kicking down the door and slamming it shut behind her.

"Ilona! Ilona! Put the fire out! The Nazis are here!" she shouted. Ilona cursed and stomped the fire into cinders. Iveta was sobbing uncontrollably, covering her face with both hands, desperately trying to silence herself.

"Where's the boy?" snapped Ilona, kneeling by the window and stealing a peek at the outdoors. Iveta lingered by the door. Her conscience begged her to be brave and stay by her sister, but her twisting throat and churning gut kept her frozen in place, muffling her own sobs with her fist.

"Klaus...led them...away..." she sobbed. Ilona scowled, holding her knife and waiting. Iveta stood still, staring at her sister, admiration blooming in her chest. Brave Ilona. Where would she be without her? She felt ashamed of herself right then. *Coward.* She was a coward. Always depending on Ilona to save her. Letting Klaus rush to his death for her.

Coward. Vilém could feel the word pounding against Iveta's ears even as her sister announced that the Nazis were approaching the Shack.

Coward. It echoed in her eardrums as her sister grabbed her hand and started dragging her up the stairs, vowing that they would be fine. She would surprise the Nazis. She would slit their throats. She would protect Iveta.

Coward. Iveta felt her sister's hand. It was trembling. Ilona was quaking. She was terrified.

Coward. They were almost at the top of the stairs when the word in her mind became a dare. Ilona was terrified, and still she acted brave. Iveta was only a coward because she did nothing.

Coward. Coward. Stop letting everyone else sacrifice for you. Coward...

"I'm not gonna be a coward anymore..."

"What...?"

"Ilona..." Iveta stopped and pulled her hand away once Ilona was safely off the unstable spiral staircase and in the observation deck. She stepped back and her twin gazed down at her with confused exasperation.

"Smile, please, Illa..." Iveta begged. "I miss your smile."

Ilona blinked in surprise and tightened her lips as though to resist the request, but it seemed to dawn on her that this odd desire was innocent and dire. She obeyed, forcing her lips upwards into a cruel mockery of what had once been a lovely smile.

"Keep smiling, Illa," Iveta begged.

"Iveta, wha...?"

But before Ilona could complete her query, Iveta leapt into the air.

"IVETA, NO!"

Too late. Iveta came down hard on the staircase, and the rotting wood crumbled. She crashed through stair after stair, obliterating the path to her sister as she fell.

CRASH!

Vilém fell back, yelping as he almost smashed right into Reinhard Heydrich's old fencing saber. He steadied himself as the pain from Iveta's memory sent him tumbling into the real world. His every bone felt phantom aches, and he took a moment to recover before standing up and valiantly pressing his hand against the glass once more.

"Sorry," he said to the spirit. "That was...a lot. I guess it didn't kill you, though."

No, no kill. Ilona was safe, though. Nazis not bother with broken stairs for one Jew only. That made me happy. But Nazis got me and Klaus...

"Klaus survived too?" Vilém exclaimed. "Lucky kid."

Nazis almost kill him, but...well...lucky...maybe not...

Vilém felt bitter tears sting his eyes. In the blink of an eye, he found himself in a new memory. Klaus was squatting in front of Iveta, his face barren as he signed his name on her cast-bound leg. For having been apprehended by the Nazis, he was in fairly good condition. Only a few cuts on his face and a slightly swollen eye. He drew a small heart on Iveta's cast right next to his name.

"There..." sighed Klaus. He and Iveta were sitting in what must have been the coziest jail cell in all the Third Reich: a couch, a cot, a little table with a platter of untouched food. A Nazi soldier stood by the door, scowling at the children. Klaus stood up and tossed the marker at the SS officer.

"I'm done with this," he announced. The Nazi grumbled and stooped down, picking up the marker.

"Little shit," Iveta heard the Nazi hiss. If Klaus heard that remark, he chose to ignore it, instead staring down at his friend's cast.

"Are you feeling any better?" Klaus asked. Iveta shrugged.

"I'm confused," Iveta said. "Maybe the Nazis are not as bad as we thought?"

"Not as bad, sure..." sneered Klaus, sarcasm dripping from his voice. He strutted towards the Nazi guard, crossing his hands behind his back and holding his head up imperiously.

"I'm thirsty," Klaus said.

"Good for you," snarled the Nazi.

"Go get me something to drink, you ugly idiot," the boy commanded, and Iveta's jaw dropped. Was he mad?

"And something for my friend too. I think hot chocolate would be nice," Klaus added, gesturing to the injured girl. The guard scoffed.

"You really think we're going to waste chocolate on a little Jewess?"

"What's your name?" Klaus queried, and Iveta's head spun with wonder when she saw sweat break out on the Nazi's brow. A small standoff ensued between the tiny boy and the Aryan soldier, Klaus' river-blue eyes freezing into icy pools as he stared the SS man into submission.

"With marshmallows?" the Nazi queried.

Klaus smirked. "Lots," he said, and Iveta could only sit there, completely baffled, as the Nazi left and brought back two mugs of marshmallow-filled hot chocolate. Klaus snatched them from the SS man and sat beside Iveta, giving her a mug. It smelled divine: she almost burned her tongue, she was so desperate to taste chocolate again.

"Klaus, why'd he listen to you?" Iveta whispered.

"He's afraid," Klaus replied, not drinking his own hot chocolate. He stared at the steam that rose from the cup, his eyes watering.

"Afraid of you? You're just a Jew, Klaus, why would he be afraid of you?"

"You'll see..." the boy whispered. The children sat in silence for some time. Iveta finished her hot chocolate and Klaus gave her his and took her empty mug, hugging it to his chest. Just as Iveta was lapping up the last drop of Klaus' drink, she heard chaos erupt in the hall outside their cell.

"Reichsprotektor's here!" one Nazi shouted, and the SS soldier guarding the children started shaking in his jackboots. Vilém felt Iveta's heart sink. She must have heard all about the Reichsprotektor, the Blonde Beast, and what he did to her people.

"Heydrich..." she whimpered. Klaus inhaled deeply, wiping the tears from his eyes and slowly setting the empty mug on the floor. He stood up, straightening the yellow star on his chest.

Their guard threw open the door and thrust his arm into the air. "Heil Hitler!" he barked.

Reinhard Heydrich entered, not bothering to greet the guard. Seeing the Blonde Beast in color was strange for Vilém, who had only ever seen him in pictures, in black-and-white like the monsters in old classic movies. But there he was, alive, real, clad head-to-toe in Nazi regalia, hair golden, eyes river-blue, his face...

Vilém and Iveta both felt confusion in unison. The Blonde Beast was wont, in pictures at least, to wear a wintry expression, at most an arrogant sneer. But standing before her right then, he looked like he had just narrowly dodged a bullet and was almost finished counting his lucky stars. Fear and relief gushed from Heydrich's eyes as they fell upon little Klaus.

Vilém realized before Iveta did that the Blonde Beast and the boy in the yellow star had the same eyes. Klaus bowed his head towards the war criminal, his eyes downcast, as though looking at the Butcher of Prague hurt his heart.

"Hello, Papa..." he whispered, and Vilém could feel Iveta's shock. It struck her like a bolt of electricity and she dropped the mug. The empty cup shattered beside her broken foot.

Heydrich senior didn't even look at her. He exhaled like he'd been holding his breath for weeks and fell upon his son, wrapping his arms around little Klaus. Iveta could see happy tears shining in the monster's eyes.

"Klaus, my boy!" he cried. "You've had me worried to death! What were you thinking? Are you okay? Your eye!"

Heydrich cupped his child's face in his hands, examining the boy's minor injuries. His eyes became cold. There. There was the Blonde Beast Vilém knew.

"I'll get the names of the men who did that," Heydrich vowed. "Klaus, what were you thinking, running around with this?!" He jabbed his finger at the yellow star on his child's chest. "You could have been killed!"

"That's the point!" Klaus screeched, smacking his father's hand away. Iveta felt her heart leap, but Heydrich didn't chastise his son for the blatant disrespect. He looked down at the boy, his icy eyes melting.

"What...?" the Blonde Beast said. Klaus inhaled sharply and stepped away from his father, clutching the yellow star.

"Grandmother told me the Bible stories, the one from Exodus," the child explained clumsily. "The one with the Pharaoh and the Jews. I thought if I died like in the last plague, you'd change your heart."

"What? Klaus, you're not making any sense."

"You murdered Jan's parents!" Klaus snapped, at last lifting his eyes and meeting his father's befuddled gaze.

"Jan? Your little friend from the village? Oh, I knew we shouldn't have let you and your brother associate with Czech vermin..."

"Jan's not vermin, and he's not my friend!" Klaus cried. "He was only being nice to me because he was scared of you! Everyone's scared of you! And you sent his parents to a camp and he hates me!"

"So the Czech boy provoked this," Heydrich mumbled, standing up, a murderous shadow crossing his face. "I'll have to speak to him..."

"No, no you won't! Don't murder any more kids!" Klaus screamed. "Jan told me what you did and I didn't believe him! I thought I knew you better..."

Klaus' anger abated and sorrow took its place. His shoulders slumped and he wrapped his arms around himself, squeezing as though his favorite teddy bear was nestled against his chest. "I thought you were a hero..."

"Klaus..." Heydrich muttered, stepping towards his son, but Klaus retreated from his father's comfort.

"I looked on your desk and I saw *everything*," Klaus cried. Iveta's gaze shifted to Heydrich. The Butcher's eyes widened for but a moment before hardening.

"Klaus, I've taught you better than this. I never should have let your grandmother fill your head with old Jew fairytales. I *certainly* never should've let you befriend undesirables. You can't understand now, but everything I do, I do so you can live in a better world one day."

"A world without Jews?" Klaus spat.

"Correct, son."

"You're a liar!" cried Klaus, "You lied to me about where the Jews go, you lied to me about the Czechs, you lied to me about everything! I don't trust you about anything anymore! You're a liar and a murderer! And I just want you to stop or else you're gonna burn in Hell forever!"

"Klaus, enough of this!" Heydrich snapped. He glanced at Iveta and Vilém could feel the girl's soul congeal as those pitiless icy eyes examined her.

"This," Heydrich declared, pointing to Iveta, "is the problem. You associate with them, you pity them, and you become weak and put yourself in danger."

"Don't hurt Iveta, she didn't do anything wrong!" Klaus snapped, grabbing his father by the belt and tugging, trying to pull his father's attention off the Jewish girl.

"She's filled your head with Jewish nonsense! She's fooled you! Klaus, I will not abide by my own son sympathizing with Jews, I'm your father and I..."

"I'd rather have a Jew for a father than you!" Klaus screeched, and the Blonde Beast's eyes erupted with anger. He raised a flat hand up, ready to slap his child across the face. Klaus seemed surprised by the concept of being struck, but only for a moment before he gritted his teeth and offered his cheek to his father.

Klaus' demonstration of bravery seemed to stir something in Heydrich. Vilém almost couldn't believe his—or, rather, Iveta's—eyes when he saw fear on the Butcher of Prague's face. The Nazi's cold eyes flitted to his own upraised hand and horror filled his features—the man could sign away a million lives, but the realization that he had even considered hitting his child horrified him. Vilém almost wanted to laugh at the absurdity.

Heydrich dropped his hand, trembling as though he had just aimed a loaded gun at his beloved boy. For a moment, there was complete silence. Iveta stared, waiting for the Butcher of Prague to decide her fate. Klaus glared at his father, tears in his eyes, and Heydrich looked from his son to his own hand, completely lost.

Finally, Heydrich let his gaze settle on his own black-gloved hand and he spoke. "We're going home, Klaus..."

"I'll run away again if you don't stop," Klaus declared. "You know I will, even if you get guards."

Heydrich chuckled. An odd sound, like a goat's bleat. "Yes...you take after me like that."

He looked down at his steely-eyed boy and commented, "Hopefully...you don't take after me in too many other ways."

"Hopefully," Klaus agreed, and Heydrich winced as though his son had buried a dagger in his heart.

"Klaus...please come home. You know I can't just quit my job. It's far too late for that."

Klaus' fists trembled and the tears he had been restraining started streaming down his face. "I know," he whimpered.

"I won't harm your friend, your little Jew friend," Heydrich said, gesturing towards Iveta. "Come home and be safe, and I'll keep her safe. As long as you're safe, she'll be safe. Deal?"

"Promise?" Klaus prodded.

"I swear to God..."

"No!" Klaus snapped, and Heydrich smirked.

"Smart boy. I swear to the Führer."

Klaus scowled and shook his head. Heydrich chuckled.

"You know me too well. I swear to you, how about that? No more lying."

Klaus looked towards Iveta. The boy wavered for a moment, as though he was tempted to resist this deal and insist that the Hangman quit, but he must have realized that he wouldn't be saving the Jews of Europe from his father anytime soon. He could, at most, save one.

"I want to be able to see her."

"Klaus..."

"I want to see her and write to her! That's the deal!"

Klaus shoved his hand towards his father, a demand for an agreement. Vilém saw a familiar smirk on Heydrich's face. That arrogant smirk he wore in the pictures Vilém saw in the exhibit, the look of a predator that had just caught a rabbit. He shook his son's hand, claiming a minor victory. The child would obey him. His little Jew friend would pay if he didn't.

Klaus yanked his hand away as soon as his father shook it, wiping his palm against his pant leg as though he had just touched dog shit. Heydrich's haughty expression shifted into sadness. He had won, but at a cost. His son would never look at him the same way again. Vilém hummed with surprise when he saw tears twinkle in the Hangman's eyes. It appeared that even for the loyal Nazi, that was a high price. Monster though he was, he seemed to love the boy.

Heydrich offered the boy his hand, this time as a father instead of a negotiator, but Klaus brushed right past him. The child ran to Iveta and hugged her.

"I'm sorry..." he whispered. Heydrich gave the little Jewish girl a venomous scowl, and all the fear, sadness, and confusion that had filled Iveta's soul boiled over and made tears attack her eyes, blinding her.

"Tell Heydrich this isn't a fucking kindergarten."

"The Reichsprotektor says..."

"Reinhard can say anything he wants, I don't care! I have enough bullshit to deal with! Just because we used to fence together doesn't mean I'm going to cover up for him!"

"I mean...he *is* your boss..."

"And I doubt *his* boss would appreciate the idea! Himmler's godson having a long-distance pet Jew...even Reinhard doesn't have enough blackmail material to get the Reichsführer to accept this!"

Vilém felt Iveta's heart tremble. She lifted her wrist to her face and wiped her tears away, clearing her vision enough for Vilém to see that the memory had shifted. They were on familiar ground: in the Camp, in the Kommandant's office. Vilém scrutinized the Nazi, hatred burning in his soul. Raya's old boss. He saw a familiar camera sitting on the Nazi's desk, polished and pretty. Several rolls of film sat nearby, waiting for a developer.

The Nazi soldier that Klaus had been ordering around before was standing beside Iveta, fear shining in his eyes. He must have expected (and hoped) that this would be a simple drop-off mission, but Kommandant Gerber was very brave and very stupid.

The Kommandant waved his hand. "Tell you what—she can stay, but she stays with the rest of the Jews and Czechs, in the barrack..."

"General Heydrich said she is to be separated and...kept comfortable," Iveta's escort declared.

"Fucking where? All the barracks are full, my men barely have any space! What does he expect me to do, let her sleep at the foot of my bed? Give her a little collar and call her Fido?"

"Kommandant, General Heydrich asks that you consider your old friendship...and he also reminds you that you're only a Kommandant because of his generosity."

"That piece of—!" the Kommandant shouted, but he stopped himself from cursing his old "friend." He pursed his lips together, sunk down into his chair, and rubbed his forehead.

"Fine, goddamnit, I guess I'll come up with something. She can be a little toy for Martin..." he mumbled. "Maybe the company will do him some good."

The Kommandant looked at the Jewish girl, peering into her eyes and making the girl's blood chill. "She looks Aryan...say, Fido, could you pretend to be German? I wouldn't want my boy to...get any ideas or become a bleeding-heart Jew-lover like Heydrich's son."

"I..." Iveta hesitated, and Vilém could feel disgust bubble up in her gut at the thought of denying her heritage. After everything she had been through because of it, to abandon it, hide it...the mere idea of doing so felt like swallowing a live slug.

"That wasn't a request, Fido. Come," the Kommandant declared, standing, strutting towards the girl, and grabbing her by one of her pigtails.

"Sir, General Heydrich said not to harm her!" Iveta's guard yelped, but the Kommandant ignored the soldier's plea and painfully yanked the girl towards the window, forcing her face against the glass.

"See that barrack over there, Barrack Four?" he sneered. Iveta barely could through the icy glass and her own tears, but she saw the wooden structure looming in the distance. She saw Nazi guards screaming and beating children with truncheons as they rushed out for roll call. She saw the young prisoners wearing rags, trembling in the cold. She saw how thin they were. She saw one little boy collapse. She saw a Nazi press a gun to the exhausted child's skull.

"That's where we put useless brats like you," the Kommandant declared as a gunshot echoed out across the Camp. Iveta whimpered, glad for her tears and the foggy glass, glad that she could barely see the boy's body.

"We sort you out from the useful workers, and little drains like you get shut in there until we send you off to be put down. Get it?"

Iveta nodded, causing the Kommandant to tug on her hair. Pain shot through her scalp.

"Good Jew. The second you become useless, more trouble than you're worth, you go to Barrack Four, then you go away. To Chelmno, to Auschwitz, or maybe you end up just like that boy and you die right here. Doesn't matter to me, but for now it matters to Heydrich. You'd better be a good, quiet little Jew, and you'd better pray for Heydrich's safety. The Butcher of Prague just became your guardian angel."

The Nazi slammed the child's head against the glass, and as tears consumed Iveta's eyes, the memory shifted once more.

So I...playmate to Kommandant son. Son was good, though very quiet. Not fun like Klaus, no smiles.

"Heydrich...your guardian angel..." scoffed Vilém in disbelief.

Heydrich evil, yes, but did love Klaus. Did protect me for Klaus. Klaus wrote every week, and...I was safe...

"But...the assassination...Anthropoid..." Vilém muttered, and Iveta's vision cleared at last, revealing the new memory. A plush environment, a lavish nursery. Soft carpets, mountains of stuffed animals, a little desk, a bed with a swastika-emblazoned blanket, and so many books. Enough books to put Vilém's local library to shame. The walls were lined with ceiling-high bookshelves. The Kommandant must have truly wanted his son to be well-educated.

The boy, Little Martin, a seven-year-old with golden, carefully gelled hair, was kneeling in a corner, covering his face with his hands, counting down. "....Nine...eight....seven..."

A game of hide-and-seek. It should have been fun, but Vilém could feel that Iveta wasn't enjoying herself. She was anxious. Not playfully anxious like he remembered being when he and Erik had played hide-and-seek as children. She was waiting for something. Something bad.

She bolted out of the nursery. The Kommandant's little home was quaint, if not luxurious. Well-furnished with stolen art and Hitlerian trappings, but small. It didn't take long for Iveta to stumble across a familiar face.

"Raya..." Vilém mumbled as Iveta ducked into the developing room, shutting the door behind her. The teenage prisoner was standing by the window, massaging her burned hands.

"Fido, be careful! Don't burst in or you'll ruin the Kommandant's...pictures," Raya warned. She gestured towards a hanging line and Iveta let her eyes flit towards it for one involuntary second. The girl briefly glimpsed the images of skeletal corpses and bodies tangled in the electrified wire fence. She shivered and her eyes returned to Raya.

"He likes the ones where they're on the wire, hm? Wouldn't wanna ruin those," grumbled Iveta. "Are you okay?"

"As ever. Hide and seek?"

"Yeah."

"Little Martin won't follow you in here, he's too nice. I don't know how he and that horrible Nazi are related."

"I always say that about Klaus."

Raya's slight smile died, and Vilém knew why. Raya had been interred in the Camp during the *Heydrichiáda*—the period of repression and violent reprisals that had followed Heydrich's assassination. Iveta's so-called guardian angel was dead. Her fate was uncertain.

"Has Klaus written you?" Raya asked, and Iveta slowly shook her head.

"His father's dead."

"His father deserved worse!" hissed Raya.

"Yeah, he did, but Klaus may be sad."

"He shouldn't be..." Raya muttered.

"But he may be," Iveta sighed, fiddling with her bracelet and idly letting her eyes wander to the pictures of men tangled in the wire, her stomach roiling. No doubt she was wondering if and when a picture of her body would end up in Raya's developing room.

A noise made Iveta's heart stop. The slam of a door.

"He's back," Raya whispered. "You...you should hide..."

"No," Iveta said, squeezing her wrist, pressing the star beads on her bracelet into her skin. "Enough hiding. If he's gonna kill me, hidin' won't matter."

She smiled at Raya, offered her a hand, and the two prisoners clung to one another for a moment.

"Bye, Raya, sorry I didn't know ya' very long. Please remember me."

"I will," Raya vowed, and Vilém felt his heart crack.

Iveta marched out of the developing room, still clutching her bracelet, squeezing it so hard that the beads bore into her skin and it hurt. She accepted the pain and strutted towards the front door with her head held high.

The Kommandant was dressed in full regalia, his medals glistening on his breast as he stumbled into his home, exhausted. He took off his hat and tossed it at a hook without looking, grumbling when it fell to the floor, but evidently deciding he was too tired to give a shit about his uniform and leaving it where it was. He looked towards Iveta, initially smiling, perhaps mistaking her for his son, but when he saw her his smile became a sneer.

"Fido," he said with a nod.

"How was the funeral?"

"How was the funeral...?" The Kommandant strode towards her, annoyance shining in his eyes.

"How was the funeral, Kommandant Gerber?" Iveta growled through clenched teeth, and the Kommandant petted her head like she was a hound that had just learned to roll over.

"Good Jew. The funeral was fine, but I'm going to assume you don't care about the glitz and glamor. Heydrich got what he deserved."

Iveta barely suppressed a snort. The Kommandant scowled at her, but seemed to decide that defending his dead "friend" wasn't worth the effort.

"Buried with honors, all that. But you're just upset because your guardian's dead. Worried about going to Barrack Four, aren't you?"

Iveta looked down at her bracelet.

"Well?" the Kommandant prodded.

"I guess..." the girl answered.

"Well, you're lucky Heydrich's boy is such a pain-in-the-ass. Came up to me at his own father's funeral to threaten me if I laid a hand on you. Little shit wasn't even crying. Kinda makes me feel bad for Heydrich."

Gerber waltzed into the kitchen and poured himself a drink. Iveta followed slowly, eyeing the nearby knife rack with hesitant desire. She thought about stealing one of the blades and stabbing the wicked Nazi when his back was turned, but her gut objected, her mind summoned an image of Ilona mercy-killing their mother, and she dismised the notion. She didn't have the strength, the stomach, or the nerve for it. Besides, it wouldn't do anyone any good. They would find another monster to replace him and she would be sent to the Pit.

There were two chairs at the kitchen table, and nearby was a dirty red dog bowl labelled, "Fido." Vilém felt ill. The Kommandant had refrained from physically harming Klaus' friend, but he still insisted on dehumanizing her.

"Since Heydrich's a martyr now, Himmler and the Führer will be extra nice to his children," Gerber said, downing a shot. "So congratulations, Fido: you get to stay until the boy gets bored with you. Or until he chokes on his silver spoon, whichever comes first. Speaking of which..."

The Kommandant reached into his pocket and pulled out a balled-up envelope. "The Heydrich boy wanted me to give you this. I have a feeling it wouldn't make it past the censors. Go to your house and read it, then burn it."

She nodded, grabbing the crumpled paper and running out of the kitchen, then out the front door. The Kommandant's "home" was, in fact, a refurbished barrack. He must have previously lived off-site and then decided to bring his home closer to work. Vilém saw a small plaque hidden beneath the white paint, partially obscured by a flowerpot. "BARRACK 1."

Iveta walked along the raised flowerbed, avoiding the carefully kept lawn and the cornflowers. Behind the former barrack, on a corner of the property full of weeds, was an old doghouse barely suitable for an animal. There was a hole in the roof, mold feeding on the wood, and sopping blankets lining the hard floor. She crawled in and carefully tore the envelope open.

It was a drawing, and Vilém could see why Klaus had felt the need to dodge the censors. The drawing was sloppy and (because the Kommandant had crumpled it up) hard to see, but Iveta could make it out. A land of fire, a smiling demon, a gate with a blazing warning: "Abandon All Hope Ye Who Enter Here."

And Reinhard Heydrich, helpfully labeled "Papa", was boiling in a cauldron full of blood while Satan stirred the pot with a pitchfork. Above the scene of Hell, Klaus had drawn a line to symbolize the divide between the underworld and earth, and above the line he had drawn himself, standing before a gravestone labeled "Papa", holding a rose, crying.

Iveta laughed, laughed and laughed until her sides ached. She fell against the wall of her doghouse and splinters stabbed her skin. She laughed even as it hurt, even as tears flooded her eyes.

"Hey..." A timid voice interrupted her cackling. She looked up and saw Little Martin kneeling in front of the doghouse. She could hardly see him through her tears.

"Found you..." the boy whimpered, and the memory shifted.

"Iveta!"

"Klaus?!"

Vilém felt a hurricane of emotions tear through Iveta's head. Joy, surprise, and relief, perhaps because she hadn't heard her true name in so long. Iveta cried with happiness as Klaus ran into the Kommandant's house and wrapped his arms around his friend, twirling her around.

"You look good!" Klaus cried, tugging on the straps of a brown box-shaped satchel that hung from his shoulders. "They've been feeding you? Taking good care of you?"

"Anything for the son of a German hero," the Kommandant mumbled. He grabbed Little Martin's hand and dragged him into the kitchen, shutting the door behind him and leaving Klaus alone with the Jewish girl.

"How's he, really?" Klaus asked, his expression becoming severe. Iveta chewed on her lip and fiddled with her bracelet.

"He's awful, but he could be worse," she sighed.

"He could be my dad," grumbled Klaus, but he shook his head, banishing his father from his brain and brightening up again. "Wanna go outside and play? Look what I brought!"

He swung his satchel off his shoulder and dropped it on the

ground. Vilém was surprised the little boy had been able to lift it so easily: judging by the *thud* it made upon striking the ground, it was hefty. The satchel popped open, revealing that it was stuffed to the brim with toys. Iveta grinned, grabbed a toy dagger, and a battle began.

Iveta and Klaus took the satchel and ran outside. They spent the next hour playing with toy daggers, planes, and cars. They had a marvelous time; Iveta's soul was light as a balloon. When weariness finally forced her to rest, she sat beside Klaus on the raised flowerbed, smiling so wide her face hurt.

"I'm happy you came, I haven't seen you in so long," Iveta said. Klaus dug around his now almost-empty satchel and took out a small toy dog.

"For you!" he said. "I wanted to get you a doll, but I dunno if you like them and my little sister probably would'a stole it."

"Haha! Thanks..." mumbled Iveta, and Vilém felt a pang in her heart. Her eyes shifted towards her doghouse. Klaus had no idea, and Vilém sensed that Iveta didn't want to tell him just how bad she had it. He had already done all he could.

She set the dog next to her and rubbed her bracelet between her fingers. "Have you and your family been doing...okay?"

"Yeah," Klaus sighed. "Godfather Hein...err, Reichsführer Himmler has been very...nice...he sent us a lot of gifts. He's coming to Prague to visit soon. My little sister's really upset. Papa was always sweet to her, and she's really little and doesn't understand..."

"And you?"

Klaus laughed. "I think I understand too much. So does Mama."

A shadow fell upon Klaus' face. "I think she knew. I had trouble getting her permission to come here, had to threaten to tell everyone in my Hitler Youth battalion about the camps. Mama doesn't like me talking to Jews....ha! She ended up dragging some Jews from the Terezin Ghetto to our house. They're building us a new pool."

He grabbed his satchel and looked into it, a feeble attempt to avoid Iveta's eyes. "I don't even wanna pool."

"The Jews...?"

"They live in a shed. I keep trying to sneak them some food, but Mama catches me. Look."

He rolled up his sleeve, showing off four welts on his pale skin. Vilém didn't feel a surge of shock fill Iveta's mind upon seeing the injuries, and he could only assume that was because of the era. Corporal punishment must have been relatively universal.

"Gotta get used to it," Klaus sighed. "Since Papa's gone."

"He didn't hit you?" Iveta queried, raising an eyebrow.

"Never, and he never let Mama hit us either, no matter what we did. Believe it or not, Papa was the one who let us get away with everything. Mama's the strict one. I remember one time...we were all in Berlin at this party thing for all the important people in the Reich and my brother and I got into the fireworks. I ended up settin' em off...what a mess! Almost killed the Führer...almost killed my dad too...and Mama wanted to thrash my ass...but Papa just laughed it off..."

Before Klaus could say another word, he spotted something at the bottom of his satchel. Slowly, the boy pulled out a white teddy bear.

"Heldi...?" Iveta queried. Klaus didn't answer. He let the satchel slip from his grasp and held the teddy bear close to his face, staring into its black button eyes.

"I should have..." he whispered. "I wish I'd killed 'em back then...everything would be fine if he died back then!"

He stood up and threw the bear. The stuffed animal landed in the mud beside Iveta's doghouse. Iveta looked up at the boy, fear flowing through her veins. His face was twisted in anger, his eyes flaring. Klaus Heydrich looked too much like his father right then.

But the moment was short lived, and although the boy still looked angry, tears fell from his eyes and he regained his innocence. He plopped back down, wrapping his arms around himself.

Iveta recognized what he needed right away. Without hesitation, she threw her arms around the boy. She felt Klaus resist instinctively for a moment—perhaps a small part of him was still trained to fear a Jew's touch, or perhaps he thought he didn't deserve her affection. Either way, he stiffened for only a moment before sinking into the hug.

"I cried when he died..." the boy confessed. "Is...is that okay?"

"Yes, Klaus, that's okay," Iveta assured him, hugging him tighter.

"I miss him...is that okay?"

"I think that's okay, Klaus..." Iveta released him, keeping one hand on his shoulder and making sure he looked into her eyes as she smiled at him. She stood, ran to where the bear had fallen, and picked it up.

A shudder went up her spine. Reinhard Heydrich had bought that bear with money he earned by slaughtering her people. Heydrich and his murderous hands had touched that bear. It almost felt cursed, but she ignored the squeamish sensation that filled her as she held the toy and carried it back to Klaus. The boy hugged Heldi close to his heart, wiping his tears on the bear's head.

"I wanna go ice skating," Klaus whimpered. "Or ride my bike....but it's not fair if I do that while you're in here, it's not fair."

"It's not fair," Iveta agreed. "But I don't want you to be miserable, Klaus. You're nice and...you tried your best."

Klaus sniffed, wiped his face on his sleeve, and smiled up at his

Jewish friend. "You're the nice one. He was really wrong about you people."

"We're just people."

"Exactly..." Klaus sighed. The memory shifted, but not by much. Klaus' visit was almost at its end. He stood by a black car. Iveta approached to say goodbye, hugging the toy dog he had given her.

"Bye, Iva," Klaus said, wrapping his arms around her neck. He made sure his lips were close to her ear, casting a nervous eye towards his guard.

"Listen to me," he whispered. "I looked at more of my papa's notes, and I peeked at some of Himmler's. The other camps are so, so much worse. They do horrid things to children, especially twins and Jews that look too Aryan. Whatever you do, don't let them take you to any other camp, especially not Auschwitz. Okay? Whatever you do, don't let them take you there."

"Okay," she squeaked, and Vilém felt anxiety swarm her heart. "Goodbye, Klaus. Go have fun, please. Have fun for me."

"Promise," he vowed. He stepped back, glanced at the Kommandant, and suddenly leaned forward and gave Iveta a small kiss on the cheek.

"Sorry, just wanna break some laws. You know kissing Jews is illegal," he said, his eyes glistening with mischief, and Vilém could feel Iveta's cheeks heat up.

"You're horrible," she giggled.

"It's in my blood. Bye, bye, Iveta! Please stay safe!"

He climbed into the car, smirking at his guard, who gave the children a look of disgust as he slammed the door behind the Aryan boy. Iveta watched as Klaus' car zoomed away. Once it disappeared, she looked down at the toy dog. She smiled, took off her star bracelet, and put it around her new stuffed animal's neck, giving it a star-studded collar. She sighed sorrowfully, stroking the stuffed animal's head. A single reminder of her two best friends.

Iveta's ghost interjected somberly: *Klaus died three days after.*

"What?!" Vilém exclaimed.

Riding bike. Was hit by bus...I...hope he was...having fun. Hope he...was happy.

"He...that's...he didn't deserve that."

No.

"He was just a kid....he seemed nice...not his fault his dad was a shithead..."

Nobody's fault but the Nazis, yes.

"And...once he was gone..."

Kommandant decided he did not need pet Jew.

"And that's how you got here."

Yes.

"If...you don't mind me asking...how did you die?"

Months later, rumor...Barrack Four was...to Auschwitz...to go to Auschwitz. Trains come to take us to Auschwitz. Klaus warn me. I...have good memory. Did not want to see Auschwitz.

"Oh, Iveta..." Vilém said. The memory shifted. It was so dark that Vilém could barely make out what was going on, but he felt the girl roll off her wooden bunk and crawl to the middle of the barrack. She carried the stuffed dog under her arm: either the Kommandant had let her keep it or she had been clever enough to smuggle it with her into Barrack Four. Either way, she pried a loose floorboard upwards. The star bracelet around the dog's neck shimmered slightly in what little light the barrack allowed in. Iveta kissed the gift from her sister.

"Bye, Ilona..." she whispered, shoving the bracelet-clad toy beneath the floorboards. "Sorry I wasn't brave enough."

She stood, took a deep breath, and everything that happened next happened so quickly that Vilém barely felt a thing: Iveta sprinted towards the door and her tiny body broke the flimsy lock. Guards shouted, dogs barked, a shot was fired.

She ran for the electrified fence, leapt upon it. There was pain only for a moment, the smell of burned skin, and then everything went dark.

Vilém opened his eyes and once more he found himself in Barrack Four. He could feel the little hairs on his arms and legs standing erect, as though an electric current had really gone through his body. He took a moment to breathe deeply and let his soul recover from experiencing death again before he reached out and touched the glass display.

"So...Iveta...thank you for showing me what happened to you. It must have been hard. You're a brave girl."

Danke...

"I really wanna help you, help you move on. What can I do to help you finish your business on earth?"

Iveta answered, and Vilém felt his heartbeat stall.

"Oh..." he sighed, smiling. "That'll get me fired. Let's do it."

Sladký's Sweets rarely had an early customer. Occasionally, some children would pop in on their way to school or a husband would run in desperate for a last-minute anniversary gift, but most of their clientele didn't arrive until the afternoon. Jana usually spent the morning making candies and restocking the shelves.

She was surprised, then, when she emerged from the stockroom lugging a box full of taffy and saw a young man leaning against the display case. She smiled at him, concern filling her heart when she saw the bags under his eyes. It looked like he hadn't slept for a week.

"You're not getting anything for free, Vilém," she teased. Before Vilém could even think of retorting, his stomach did so for him, snarling like a starved bear.

"No breakfast?" Jana guessed, and Vilém nodded. She plopped the box of taffy down by a table laden with jars and started refilling the glass containers. "Oh, all right: take a brownie. Not nutritious, but it'll tide you over!"

"You're an angel!" Vilém chuckled, swiping a brownie and devouring it in two bites. With his stomach somewhat sated, he marched towards Jana and grabbed a handful of watermelon-flavored taffy, shoving it into the appropriate jar.

"Thanks! I hate restocking, especially the taffy," Jana said.

"No problem. Hey, Jana, remember how you said your grandma could kick my ass?"

"Yup! You wanna challenge her? She's upstairs," Jana said, pointing towards the roof. "She lives right above the shop."

"I actually wanted to talk to her. I think I found something...someone, actually. Your grandma survived the war?"

"No, she died," snickered Jana, and Vilém grabbed the now empty box and bopped her on the shoulder.

"I'm being serious, Jana," he said, though he couldn't suppress a smile. "While I was at the Camp the other day, I...well, I think I found something your grandmother would really appreciate. Your grandma's name's Ilona, right?"

"Yup!"

"And she was born in the Sudetenland?"

"Jesus...you really did your homework."

"I had some inside help."

"Y'know, most girls would find this a little creepy," Jana said, offering him a bottle of hand sanitizer.

"Trust me, I was just as surprised as you are. More, actually. Just really good timing, I guess. It's actually about her twin sister..."

Jana slammed her hand on the pump, sending a stream of sanitizer into her palm. She cursed and Vilém grabbed some napkins, helping her clean up the mess of gel.

"Sorry...I didn't know my grandma had a twin..." mumbled Jana, wrinkling her nose as the store's pervasive scent of sugar was overpowered by the odor of alcohol. "She, uh...she doesn't like talking about the war. I'm warning you, you might get your ass kicked."

"I'll survive," Vilém said. "Is it okay if I go up and talk to her?"

"Yeah, please...and when you're done, if you're still alive, I wanna hear everything," Jana said, a glimmer in her eyes. She looked at him with appreciation, as though the little grain of information about her family was a precious treasure he had gifted her. He almost wanted to kiss her right then, but he held back, instead running to the staircase and blowing her a kiss.

"It's a long story, I'll tell you over dinner!" he declared, and Jana laughed. A musical sound. He would need to make her laugh more often.

Vilém darted up to the second story and after knocking on a few doors, an aged voice called out, "Jana, sweet-love, what in God's name are you doing out there?"

"Ms. Sladký?" Vilém cried. "I'm a friend of Jana's, my name's Vilém..."

"Oh, come in, you asshole! I was wondering when I'd get a chance to put you through the wringer!"

Vilém chuckled and entered. Ilona Sladký sat in a wheelchair, watching as two little zebra finches flitted about in a cage by the window, tousling over twine. She looked good for her age: her blonde pigtails had been replaced with a gray bun, and her blue eyes burned with a fire only slightly less intense than the inferno they had held as a child. Merely from her appearance, Vilém could tell Jana had been right—she could kick his ass.

"Sit, sit!" she cried, waving towards a red couch. He obeyed and sat across from her. A black Chihuahua snarled at him from the floor, but remembered its training and didn't lunge for his ankles.

"Bayaya doesn't like you, that's bad news!" Ilona cried. "Jana seems to, though. Won't shut up about you, ha! Bless that girl, but she has such a terrible taste in men. I hope you're not another mistake."

"I hope so too. Has she really been talking about me that much?"

"Non-stop! She was so upset when you wouldn't answer her texts! I was about to hunt you down, but then when you called her back, she was bouncing off the walls! I've never seen her so excited! She said you were gorgeous."

"Your verdict?" Vilém queried, and Ilona roared with laughter.

"Oh, I like you! So what brings you into the lion's den this early?"

"It actually doesn't have anything to do with Jana," Vilém said, reaching into his pocket. "Has Jana told you I work at the Camp a few miles outside town? I'm the night security."

"Ah..." Ilona's entire body stiffened, and Bayaya seemed to sense his master's discomfort. The tiny dog leapt into the old woman's lap and started licking her shaking, liver-stained hands.

"I hope this isn't another attempt at...at getting me to give a testimonial for some little exhibit...I'm not interested. I'd like to die without being pitied, I don't want to be an artifact..."

"Far from it, Ilona...."

"Ha! Are we on a first name basis, son?"

"No, sorry, it's just a force of habit. By any chance, Ms. Sladký, do you believe in ghosts?"

"I don't believe in anything I can't see with my own two eyes, and even then, I try to be skeptical."

"I don't blame you, and I know this will sound crazy, but...for the last couple of nights, I've been speaking with your sister, Iveta."

The old woman's eyes widened and she hugged her dog so tightly it yipped and fought back, tumbling off her lap and retreating under the couch. Vilém hoped he hadn't given the old woman a heart attack: Ilona must have known right then that something was amiss. If even her granddaughter didn't know about Iveta, Jana's new boyfriend shouldn't have had the slightest clue.

"Have you people been...digging into my family? There's no way you could know about her unless you started looking into...documents or birth records..."

"I'm not a historian, Ms. Sladký. Wouldn't know the first thing about archives. I only know what I've been told."

"And...what have you been told?" whispered Ilona, forcing her eyes off the man, staring at the finches and tightening her jaw. One of the birds had won the battle. The victor nibbled on the thread while the loser sat at the bottom of the cage, despondent.

"I know you two were twins. On your birthday, she tried to make you a cake and burned it, and you made her a bracelet with star beads. I know you two loved astronomy. She wanted to go to college, you just wanted to stay close to her. You two used to play together in an old watchtower you guys called the Star Shack..."

Every unknowable fact made Ilona's eyes bulge wider and wider. Her slight trembling became quaking.

"You can't know all this..." she whispered, keeping her gaze locked onto the cage, on the defeated finch.

"Are you okay? Should I...?"

"I've survived worse than the truth!" Ilona snapped, finally facing him again. Tears shimmered in her eyes.

"I know you did what you had to for your mother," Vilém said gently. "You don't have anything to be afraid of, Ilona. I'm not here to judge you."

Ilona covered her mouth with her hands, muffling a sob. Her mother. She must have forced herself to forget that day.

"God almighty, Iveta's at the Camp...?" whimpered Ilona. "She's still here..."

"She's been here for decades."

"Why? W-what happened to her?! Did she say what happened to her?!"

"Yes...you, uh...you know the boy, Klaus, you know he was Reinhard Heydrich's son..."

"I know...I found out after the war..." Ilona whispered, rolling the word "war" on her tongue. She must have spent a lifetime avoiding that word. It must have felt so strange to utter it at last. "He was the reason I never went back to our village and burned it to the ground. By the time it was all over and I gave up looking for Iva, all the monsters who...hurt us...and our mother...they were dead. Only their children remained, and if Iveta could love the Blonde Beast's son...what else could I do but...nothing? Let it all go...like a coward..."

"You're not a coward, Ilona," Vilém assured her, repressing a smile. It seemed Klaus had saved some lives after all. If he bumped into the boy's ghost, he would have to tell him that.

"Don't tell me I'm brave for surviving, surviving doesn't take bravery! Iveta was ten times braver than me!" hissed Ilona, digging her nails into the armrest of her wheelchair.

"She was brave, very brave right untill the end," Vilém said. He told Ilona everything that had happened to Iveta after they were separated. Ilona listened, glowering down at Bayaya's toys as Vilém told her about Iveta's status as a pet Jew.

"I knew she died at the Camp. I found one of the pictures the Kommandant took of her...her on the wire...I didn't know she lived with the Kommandant...a doghouse..." Ilona shook her head, looked into Vilém's eyes with morose tenderness and said, "Thank you, young man...for telling me this, but...I don't understand why she didn't speak to me the last time I was at the Camp. After the war, I went there, I found out she had died there..."

"And then you never went back," Vilém said. "You settled here, lived your life, and you've felt guilty about it every day. Every day, you think you should have been the one to break down those stairs. Iveta read you like a book, Ilona. She knows what you're feeling."

Ilona pulled her headscarf over her mouth and nose, sobbing into the soft fabric. "I should have been the one to jump!" she cried. "I was a coward, and then I gave up and did nothing!"

"You lived. You married. You had children. You started a business. You did everything she wanted you to, Ilona..." Vilém stood, walked to the old woman, and knelt before her, putting a hand on her wrist. "She just wants you to see that. She doesn't want you to run from the past, and she doesn't want you to be miserable. She wants you to go to the Camp and smile for her. She says she's missed your smile so much...she doesn't want to go to Heaven until she sees it again."

Vilém pulled out the treasure he had hidden in his pocket: a toy dog, still wearing the bracelet. Its time beneath Barrack Four had been harsh: holes marred its soft body, dirt had turned it brown, but still it held itself together. The star bracelet, carefully cleaned by Vilém, shimmered at Ilona.

He set the dog in her lap. For a moment, he was afraid she would toss it away, but her shaking hands reached out, lifted the little toy to her heart, and she hugged it with all the gusto of a little girl.

"REHOR, YOU HAVE SOME EXPLAINING to do!"

"Ow, ow, ow!" Vilém cried. He had stepped into Barrack Four and was immediately assaulted by his boss. Ms. Doubek grabbed him by the collar and dragged him towards the Heydrich Exhibit.

"WHAT IS THIS?!" Doubek screamed, pointing to Vilém's handiwork: the display case where Klaus Heydrich's wanted poster had been resting was knocked over, the floorboard of the barrack partially torn up.

"You not only almost destroyed a historical artifact!" Doubek screamed, gesturing towards the poster. Klaus smiled weakly up at them, and Vilém could practically sense the boy's spirit apologizing for all the ruckus on his behalf.

"But you damaged the Camp's foundation! You're fired and you'll be lucky if I don't get you arrested for damaging protected historical—!"

"Oh, pipe down, you!"

Ilona's voice came, so sharp that it shut up Ms. Doubek (no small feat.) Jana helped her grandmother into the barrack, nervousness oozing from her every pore. Vilém felt too sorry for his almost-girlfriend: her first visit to a concentration camp and she had to deal with all this craziness!

Jana walked her grandmother to the upturned display case. "Here, Grandma?" she asked. Ilona nodded and Jana sunk to her knees, letting her grandmother sit on the floor.

"Ma'am, please don't sit on the..." Ms. Doubek started to say, but Ilona gave her a withering glare and the museum director clammed up.

"Oh, quiet! My sister died here, I'll sit where I want! And this young man found a valuable and meaningful *artifact!*" She spat the word as though it were a curse, pulling the bracelet-clad toy dog from her pocket and placing it in front of the broken floorboard.

"If you fire him, you'll be firing a kind soul who helps Holocaust survivors!" Ilona decreed. "Vilém, don't you worry about that witch! Come, sit next to me!"

Vilém, whose collar was still firmly in Ms. Doubek's grasp, shot a pleading gaze at his boss. The last thing anyone needed was two septuagenarians going to war in the middle of the Camp. Ms. Doubek scowled at her employee and released him.

"You're lucky," she said, pointing towards Ilona. "I like her more than I like Heydrich's kids."

She marched out of the barrack, muttering about phone calls and lawsuits, leaving Vilém and the Sladkýs to themselves.

"This is so crazy..." Jana whispered.

"You always pick the crazies," Ilona said, pinching her granddaughter's cheek. Jana snickered.

"I wouldn't have believed you, Vil, but my grandma never trusts anyone and you somehow convinced her to come here," Jana said. "That's enough for me."

Vilém blushed, but before he could say a word, Ilona snapped her fingers right in front of his nose. "No flirting right now! Iveta first!"

"Okay...everyone put your hand on the dog and close your eyes..." Vilém instructed. In sync, the three reached out and touched the fake fur, shutting their eyes.

"Iveta?" Vilém cried. "I brought her here."

Danke, Vilém!

"Oh my God...Iva..." whimpered Ilona. Jana bit her bottom lip. She hadn't heard a thing, but she decided not to say anything. Whatever was happening, her grandma's voice was cracking. With happiness, with sorrow, with everything.

Hi, sis, Iveta said, switching to her native German and cutting Vilém out of their conversation.

"I...Iveta...I'm so sorry..." Ilona sobbed.

You don't have to be sorry, sis!

"But you're in here and I...I..."

That's your granddaughter?! She's so pretty! I hope she and Vilém stay together. He's been so nice, listening to me even when he didn't want to. He's a wonderful man. He told you everything?

"Yes...I can't believe you had to go through that. Iva, why did you jump that day?"

For you! To be brave like you. I love you and you always protected me. I just wanted to make sure you could live and...you did! But I thought you would come to the Camp and maybe bring your family. You never did.

"I'm sorry, Iva..." sobbed Ilona. "You were the brave one after all. I was too scared and guilty to come here, to remember how...unfair everything was. I didn't even tell my children about you. I felt like...if I avoided you, didn't talk about you or any of it...maybe the brick on my heart would go away. It's so unfair! I got my sweet shop like I always wanted and a nice wedding and beautiful children...and you never got to study the stars."

I'll see them up close very soon. But I wanted to see you and make sure you were happy. You are happy, right? Please be happy for me, not despite me. I want you to come here all the time and remember me, then go out and laugh and eat lots of candy. I want you to come here and smile for me, okay?

"Yes...I'll smile for you, Iva..."

I love you, sis. I'll kiss Mama for you. Goodbye.

And with that, Vilém and Ilona felt Iveta's presence dissipate as she pranced into the unknown.

"What happened? What'd she say?" Jana asked. She opened her eyes and looked at her companions. Vilém wore a somewhat befuddled expression of contentment.

And Ilona...Jana felt her heart flutter. The most beautiful smile in existence bloomed upon the face of Ilona Sladký.

BARRACK THREE

"Here we are."

"Jesus...I can see how a kid would get killed here."

Vilém Řehor nodded as he pulled in front of a rusted gate that defended a dilapidated manor. He stopped the car and glanced at his girlfriend.

"Got the dog?" he queried. Jana Sladký nodded, holding up a small stuffed animal, a toy that had been a gift to her great-aunt from the son of a monster. She looked down into its black eyes. A small part of her, the part that still heard Ms. Doubek's screeches about historical artifacts ringing in her ears, didn't like the idea of abandoning something so old, so meaningful. But Iveta Sladký had made her wishes clear via Vilém, and Jana would destroy a thousand precious pieces of history if it meant making her happy.

She was so caught up in her thoughts that she didn't see or hear her boyfriend get out of the car. He ran to the passenger side and threw her door open.

"M'lady," Vilém said, bowing and offering her a hand.

"I'm gonna smack you," Jana warned, but she nonetheless took his hand and let him pull her out of the car. She pecked his cheek and stepped into the road, framing the old manor with her fingers.

"Finally here!" she sighed. "Can't believe it took so long for you to get a week off."

"Doubek's been after my head ever since I ruined Klaus' poster. I'm just grateful I still have a job."

"Me too...I mean, I kinda wish I could see you more during the day...awake...not drooling on your pillow...but I'm afraid there may be more ghosts at the Camp."

She laughed and shook her head. "I sound fuckin' insane."

"The world's fuckin' insane, babe. Even without the...y'know...ghosts."

"You haven't seen any more ghosts at the Camp, have you?"

"Not yet, but it's only a matter of time...anyway, let's get this over with. We've gotta get going so you can meet my folks!"

Jana smiled. "Y'know, I've never met anyone who's *this* eager to introduce his girlfriend to his mom."

"My mom's the best, and my dad too. And you're the best. So what's not to look forward to?"

Jana giggled, but before she could say a word, Vilém suddenly grabbed her arm and pulled her out of the road, slamming her against the outer gate of the manor. A car zoomed past, barely missing the couple.

"Jackass!" Vilém shouted, waving a pointed index finger at the car as it sped away. "Didn't even stop!"

"I can *definitely* see why Klaus got killed out here..." sighed Jana. She made sure the dog was all right, then followed her boyfriend towards the gate, hugging the wall all the while lest another car suddenly come around the bend and flatten her.

Reinhard Heydrich, the Butcher of Prague and the Architect of the Holocaust, had once called this manor his home. A property that had once been fit for an Aryan hero was abandoned and neglected: the plaster on the outer walls had crumbled away, revealing the bricks beneath. The gate was rusted. When Vilém peered past the bars and looked onto the property, he could see litter and debris marring what must have once been a pristine environment.

Two stone statues guarded the gate, chipped and fractured: on the left was a wild boar, on the right a bear. Vilém stared at the bear's ancient, weathered face for a moment, remembering Klaus' little white teddy bear. He reached out and touched the bear, shutting his eyes.

"He's not here, right?" Jana asked, squeezing the stuffed animal. "Heydrich?"

"The innocent kid Heydrich or the mass murderer Heydrich?"

"Either," muttered Jana, biting her thumbnail nervously. She hated the idea that poor, sweet little Klaus Heydrich, who had tried so hard to save her great-aunt, could still be here, stewing over a crime that wasn't his fault. The only worse scenario would be his wicked father lingering on earth. So far, the ghosts Vilém had encountered hardly seemed able to affect the living, but if Raya could carve her name onto a wall, Jana didn't want to think about what the Butcher of Prague's ghost could do.

"I don't sense anything...and so far, every spirit I've encountered tends to stick close to the place where they died. I think I felt Heydrich Senior somewhere near the spot where the assassination happened, but I'm not eager to talk to him. Klaus, though...I think Klaus moved on."

"Good," sighed Jana. "Then...should we *not* leave the dog? He's gone and someone else may take it..."

"Iveta said to leave it no matter what. She wants someone else to pick it up and get joy out of it. She said she doesn't want it to sit in a museum for a hundred years and make people cry. Ilona has the bracelet, so...it's not like we're giving up every piece of her."

"All right...here?"

"Yeah, I think that's good..." Vilém said, watching with a bitter smile tugging at his lips as his girlfriend placed the stuffed animal beneath the stone bear. Jana stepped back and grabbed Vilém's hand. For a moment, they looked at their handiwork. There was silence except for the soft songs of the birds.

BEEP BEEP!

"Get outta the road, you weirdos!"

"We weren't in the fucking road, you asshat!" Vilém screamed as a convertible practically brushed against their heels. Jana laughed bitterly. Heydrich probably should have picked a different castle.

With Iveta's final wish fulfilled, Vilém and Jana clambered back into their car. Vilém's parents lived relatively close to the village of Panenské Březany, where Heydrich's manor stood. They were just outside of Prague.

"So how'd you end up in my neck of the woods if your parents are from Prague?" Jana queried.

"We're not *from* Prague. We moved around a lot when I was a kid. Mom and Pa liked to change things up, see new sights and get new jobs. I lived in the village for a few years when I was little; that's how me and Erik became friends. After I turned sixteen and dropped outta school, I decided to move in with Erik since I really missed him. We only lasted a week as room-mates...ha! I love him, but he's such a slob! I couldn't take it! But I stuck around for him, cheap rent, and because the town has family history. The Camp's where my grandpa was held during the war."

"Oh, Vilém..."

"He was really little, barely remembers it. And his whole family survived, even my great uncle...and he was just a baby! You know Sergeant Klammer?"

"Why wouldn't I? The sweet shop's on Klammer Street!" Jana reminded him.

"Oh, right! Well, I'm here thanks to him," Vilém explained. Sergeant Joseph Klammer was the Camp's poster boy: a young Nazi guard whose conscience hadn't allowed him to be a cog in the genocidal machine of the Third Reich. He had conspired against the Nazis, rerouting a train that had been bound for Auschwitz and saving four-hundred people.

The valiant act had cost him his life: the Nazis had hanged him as a traitor, but history and the Czech people had given him all the honor and praise he deserved. The Camp had a whole exhibit devoted to him in Barrack Three. Streets were dedicated to him, children were named after him, flowers were always left by his exhibit, and even all of this didn't seem like enough. Hundreds of people owed their lives to him. Vilém owed Joseph Klammer his very existence.

"You haven't heard from Sergeant Klammer, have you?" asked Jana. Vilém shook his head.

"I hope you never do," Jana sighed. "He deserves to be at peace after all he did."

"Yeah," Vilém agreed. He smiled at Jana. "Anyway, I got a job at the Camp and I'm a dumbass dropout, so good paying jobs are hard to come by. Pay's good at the Camp, I'm close to Erik, not far from my folks, and...well, now I've got you, so I'm pretty settled."

He let go of the wheel just long enough to tenderly touch her hair. Jana giggled, teasingly smacking his hand away.

"You're gonna make me puke," she said. "The Camp's made you sentimental."

"I guess..." sighed Vilém. "I've just learned to appreciate what I have."

"Well, I'm glad you ended up in the village, and I'm glad you got a job at the Camp. Grandma's so much happier now, and you made Iveta and Raya happy. You basically saved them from being stuck in the barracks. You're kind of a hero."

Vilém felt blood rush to his cheeks and he gripped the steering wheel tightly. He didn't want to outright deny such a statement since he knew Jana would merely continue to insist that he was a hero, but he knew he wasn't. The idea of using that word to describe himself in a world where people like Joseph Klammer existed...he shook his head. No, he wasn't a hero. He was just a janitor, trying to clean up the mess that the actual heroes and villains had left behind.

"*Vil-Vil!*"

They pulled in front of the Rehor residence and Lida Rehor ran out of the house, waving both arms. Vilém opened the car door and his mother tugged him into a tight embrace.

"Hey, Mama!" he laughed, kissing Lida's cheeks. Perhaps it was a side effect of being friends with Erik and knowing how horrible some mothers could be, but he had never been shy about being a Mama's Boy. The day he didn't kiss his mother and call her "Mama" was the day he lost his soul.

"Oh, I wish you were wearing your guard uniform!" Lida cried. "I saw that picture you posted on the Facebook! You're so handsome!"

"Mama, I wear that uniform too much," chuckled Vilém as Lida pinched his cheeks and examined him to make sure he was sufficiently fed.

"Have you...?"

"Been eating?" he snickered.

"Not just microwave dinners!" Lida said, wagging her finger in his face.

"Yes, Mama, and very well thanks to..."

"Jana!" Lida shrieked as Jana ventured from the car. Vilém

laughed as his mother engulfed his girlfriend in a bone-shattering hug.

"Goodness, you're even lovelier in person!" Lida cried.

"Thank you, Mrs. Rehor," Jana choked, already overwhelmed by the Rehors' friendliess. Lida pushed Vilém and Jana into the house, drowning Jana in compliments all the while.

"Oh, cactuses!" Jana exclaimed when she entered the Rehors' family room and saw an army of cacti standing guard: five cacti on the windowsill, a cactus on every tabletop, there were even a few small succulents perched on top of the television. An older man, Tomas Rehor, was sitting before the cactus-clad TV, watching soccer.

"Hey, old man!" Vilém said, clapping his father on the shoulder and kissing his forehead. "How's the game?"

"Horrible as ever," Tomas said, standing up, stretching, and grinning at Jana. Tomas Rehor looked good for his age; muscular and tall, with an impressive handlebar moustache perched above his thin lips.

"Vilém, for God's sake, I've told ya' to stop blackmailing pretty girls into datin' ya!" joked Tomas, shaking Jana's hand. "C'mon, she's way out of your league! You don't expect me to believe she actually *wants* to date your ugly arse, do ya?"

"Get his phone off him, I'll delete the pictures," Jana whispered. Tomas laughed and winked at his son, a silent statement of approval. He liked her already. Vilém winked back before letting his eyes wander about the room, examining the cacti.

"Hey, where's Steve?" Vilém asked.

"Oh, Vil-Vil, Steve died..." sighed Lida, and Vilém gasped as though she had just announced the demise of his childhood dog.

"Not Steve!" he cried. Jana, confused, scrutinized the cacti, realizing right then that every plant had a name painted onto its pot.

"Uhhh...should I ask about the cactuses?" Jana said. Vilém and Lida both laughed while Tomas threw up his hands.

"Oh, God, you opened Pandora's Box, Jana!" he cried. "Lida-love, explain the cactuses!"

Lida took Jana by the hand and led her to the staircase. The Rehors had carefully hung up a plethora of pictures. The youngest members hung above the bottom steps while Vilém's forefathers were displayed above the top stair.

Jana paused to admire a picture of eight-year-old Vilém making a face like a dying fish as Tomas held him in a headlock. Much to Vilém's relief, however, Lida didn't allow her to linger by her boyfriend's old pictures and stock up on blackmail material. She led Jana to the top of the staircase, pointing to a black-and-white family photograph. A woman and a man, both sporting curly black hair and wide smiles. The woman held a toddler in her arms while a grinning eleven-year-old sat on the man's shoulders.

"This is from the end of the war, when they were finally free. My grandmother, Rebecca," Lida gestured to the woman. "She ran a flower shop before the war, and my grandpa Sam—he was friends with Sergeant Joseph Klammer! He was a gardener by trade and the Nazis made him tend their grounds, but Sergeant Klammer was always kind to him."

"We were just talking on the way here," Jana said, smiling at her boyfriend. "Vilém said he was on Klammer's Train."

"Him, Rebecca, my uncle Daniel." Lida pointed to the youngest child. "And my father, Fabian."

She tapped the image of the smiling older boy with her finger and said, "Now my grandma and grandpa and Uncle Danny, all of them had green thumbs, loved plants. But poor Dad—he loved plants, but he killed everything he touched! The only plant that could survive him were cactuses, and he loved them. I grew up with cactuses everywhere and I like to carry on the tradition now that he's gone."

"His wife, my grandma, she was allergic to pretty much everything," Vilém explained. "And since they lived with us when I was little, that meant I could never get a dog or indoor cat or...well, anything with fur. Only pet I ever had was this tabby, and he was half feral and could only live in the garage. Loved him, but it wasn't the same. Grandpa felt bad about it, so he'd let me and my sisters name the cactuses and keep them as pets. We'd paint their names on their pots, it was a lot of fun. We still name the new ones we get. It's a tradition now, a tradition to honor him."

"That's so sweet!" Jana chirped. She looked at the pictures and pointed to an image of a curly-haired man in a white lab coat. "Is this Fabian?"

"No, that's Danny! They both have the curly hair, haha!" Lida said. She gestured to a photo of a bespectacled man dressed in paint-stained overalls. He held a paint roller aloft like a knight wielding a mighty sword and grinned as he repainted the walls of a synagogue.

"This is him! Danny was the ambitious one, went the doctor route, but Dad was a quiet guy. Painted for a living, painted when he retired. Never stopped painting things."

"I've still got all the birdhouses we painted in my room," Vilém said.

"Never get rid of them," Jana commanded. "Or the cactuses. Poor Steve..."

"Steve was strong, but it was his time to go..." Lida sighed. "I say we toast in his honor. Tomas, get dinner started, I'm getting wine!"

The Rehors spoiled Jana with wine, food, and embarrassing stories to hold over Vilém's head. They stayed up stupidly late, laughing and drinking until Lida finally corked the wine and escorted Jana to Vilém's little sister's room.

"Emma won't mind if you mess with her stuff!" Vilém assured his girlfriend, pecking her cheek.

"I'll try not to anyway," Jana promised.

"Oh, please, dear, make yourself comfortable," Lida said. "You're a positively wonderful girl! Vilém is lucky to have found someone so special."

"Oh, trust me, Mrs. Rehor," Jana said, grasping her boyfriend's hand and smirking. "Vilém's the special one."

IN THE EARLY HOURS, before the sun had even considered awakening, Jana found herself possessed by an urge for a well-past-midnight snack. She slipped out of Emma's room and crept towards the staircase only to find her path impeded: Vilém was sitting on the top step, gazing up at the frozen visage of his grandfather.

"Hey, dummy, trouble sleeping?" Jana said, tapping him on the shoulder and plopping down beside him. Vilém smiled gently and shook his head.

"Nah...just hanging with my grandpa," he laughed, and she realized right away that he was upset. Without asking any probing questions, she wrapped her arms around his neck, gently hugging him, offering a silent assurance that she would listen if he wished to talk and wouldn't be offended if he didn't.

He opted to speak. "He was really great. I love all my grandparents, but he was like a big teddy bear. There when you needed him, quiet and just...there. Never helped me with my homework, didn't really give big gifts like Great-Uncle Danny, but...he kinda didn't have to. He was just super happy all the time, and he was always ready to paint stuff or listen to me blab about school."

He sighed and picked at the peeling paint on the wall. "I dunno. There's a little selfish part of me that wishes he had some unfinished business. I was an asshole teenager when he died..."

"You didn't...like...*argue* before he died, did you?" Jana asked, and Vilém shook his head.

"No, no, I was just, y'know, an asshole teenager. I just feel like I didn't...say enough, do enough to show him I loved him. I feel like now I kinda...feel more and I wanna show it. I appreciate everything he went through and I appreciate how happy he was despite it all and I appreciate the great life he gave me. I feel like I could say goodbye better than I did, but..."

He looked at his girlfriend, smiling bitterly as he said, "I know he died like he lived. He died happy, so he's...gone."

Jana kissed her boyfriend's nose and slid her hand into his, resting her head on his shoulder. "Vilém, he's looking down on you and smiling," she assured him. "I meant it when I said you were special. You see ghosts and you don't...run to make a buck, you try to help them. You're a hero. He'd be so proud of you."

Vilém smiled at her even as that word—*hero*—grated on his soul. He looked up at his grandfather's smiling face and winced. He knew he didn't have to do anything to make his grandpa proud. Fabian would have been proud of him even if he were a normal security guard at a camp without ghosts. As long as Vilém was a good and happy man, Fabian Svoboda would be smiling upon him.

But that moniker that Jana was so determined to attach to him...it didn't feel right. Appropriating that word made him feel like a thief. All he did was listen to stories. His sweet grandfather, who had lived through the Camp's torments as a mere child, deserved the title far more than he.

"You're *late*, Rehor."

"Sorry, ma'am..."

"If Ms. Sladký weren't so invested in your welfare..."

"I'd be out on my ass, ma'am. Yes, I know..." Vilém sighed, adjusting his uniform as he walked beneath the entrance gate and into the concentration camp. Ms. Doubek emerged from the swarm of historians and students, ready and raring to chew him out. Since he had nearly destroyed the Heydrich Exhibit (a crime which, thankfully, Heydrich's surviving children had chosen not to hold against him), Ms. Doubek had taken every opportunity to lay into him. Ilona defended him as often as she could, but she couldn't save him from every barb.

"I don't like employing incompetent workers. I especially don't like employing *lazy* workers," Doubek continued. She scowled and leaned forward, taking a great big whiff of his breath and snarling.

"Are you drunk? I smell alcohol!"

"Ma'am, I was in Prague," sighed Vilém.

"Partying like some hooligan college student?!"

"Ma'am, I was with my best friend and my girlfriend..." Vilém grumbled, his chest bubbling with ire. He wanted to tell her that what he did on his weekend off was none of her damn business, but he remained mum. He smirked at his own cowardice. Jana would certainly retract her "hero" label if she saw him now, nodding along as Ms. Doubek tore him to shreds.

When visitors started giving her looks and recording videos, Doubek finally dismissed him. Vilém darted into the nearest barrack, Barrack Three. Sergeant Klammer smiled at him from beyond time: a huge picture of the hero in full SS regalia stood as the centerpiece of the exhibit.

Klammer, with his blonde hair and bright blue eyes, looked like the star of a Goebbels film. He looked like the perfect Nazi, yet the exhibit boasted that he was a "Hero German." Bouquets had been laid at his feet, smooth stones had been left by Jewish admirers, and some people, lacking more expensive offerings, had framed Klammer's image with notes that expressed their gratitude. Vilém smiled when he saw the sweetest offering of them all: a little girl's drawing of her entire family, fifty people who would have never existed were it not for Klammer's heroism.

One of Vilém's coworkers, who had been watching the ordeal with Doubek through the foggy windows of the barrack, offered him a low whistle.

"Damn, the Kommandant's not showin' you any mercy," he said. Vilém looked away from Klammer's memorial, his smile wilting.

"Does she ever?" he grunted.

"Y'know if she sees you again, you'll get another lecture," his coworker said. He gestured towards one of the large placards devoted to Joseph Klammer's exploits and suggested, "Hide behind there 'till the Camp closes. Here!"

He threw his flashlight and Vilém caught it, thanked him, and took his advice, crawling behind the placard and curling into a little ball.

He hoped he would only need to wait there for a few minutes, but the local school must have been doing a field trip or something. He kept peeking under the placard, but an endless stream of feet continued to parade into the barrack. Even as the sun set, the visitors kept pouring in.

He yawned. He wasn't precisely drunk, but he was still coming down from a buzz. After driving all day to get back from

Prague, he could use a nap. He would have normally never dreamed of falling asleep in the concentration camp, but perhaps encountering two ghosts and experiencing their stories had made him less squeamish about his environment. He leaned against the barrack wall. His eyes drooped, his head lulled...

Hey there...

And suddenly, he was sitting up, yelping in surprise. The Camp was completely dark, void of visitors. He sighed. He must have fallen asleep.

He pursed his lips. Asleep. Sure.

He leaned back again and shut his eyes. "Hello?" he called out.

Sorry. Didn't think I'd spook ya'. Figured at this point you'd be used to this shit.

Vilém chuckled. The spirit's voice was male this time, male and young, maybe slightly younger than him. Given the exhibit he was sitting in, Vilém could take an educated guess at the specter's identity.

"Sergeant Klammer?" he assumed, and the ghost chuckled.

Yep!

"Damn...y'know, my girlfriend and I were just talking about you the other day."

There's a coincidence. What were ya' talkin' about?

"How you saved my mom's side of the family. How you should be in Heaven right now instead of...being stuck in this shithole."

The spirit let out a bitter laugh. *Well, that's just the issue...where I should be. I don't think I'm nearly as noble as you've been led to believe.*

"You're gonna have a hard time convincing me of that, Sergeant. I wouldn't be here to have this conversation if it weren't for you. My great-grandpa was your gardener, Samuel Svoboda..."

Vilém felt the spirit's energy spike, as though he had nearly leapt out of the barrack's wall from shock. *Holy shit, that explains a lot...*

"A lot of what?"

If you're Sam's great-grandson...well, you're way more important than you know. Hm...I guess you kinda look like him. Hair's not as curly, though. And no offense, but you're not as handsome.

Vilém snorted. "I take after my pa."

Klammer laughed once more, and Vilém could feel the spirit's bitter joy. Affection seeped off the old wooden wall and filled Vilém's heart with warmth. Klammer must have truly valued Sam's friendship.

Yeah...yeah, I can see Sam in you. Well, how about it? I'll tell my story, you'll learn some of yours.

"Let's do it," Vilém volunteered, and once again he felt himself being tugged into another soul's memory. This time it wasn't sudden or dizzying. It felt like the spirit took him by the hand and gently led him into another world. He opened his eyes and suddenly he was seeing everything from the point of view of Joseph Klammer.

Well, here we are! Klammer's ghost declared. Vilém could feel the pulse of young Joseph Klammer quickening with excitement. He was standing in a somewhat bare living room. An older woman that Vilém assumed was the soon-to-be-hero's mother knelt before her teenage son, helping him adjust the swastika band on his arm.

"There, you look perfect!" Klammer's mother declared, kissing his cheek. "Now get out there and show our men some love!"

"Yes, ma'am!" Joseph said, offering her a hasty Hitler salute before rushing out the door. The streets were crowded with celebrating Germans. Swastika-shaped confetti fell from the windows, flowers were tossed at SS men, children waved little Nazi flags and licked lollipops decorated with the crooked cross. Vilém could feel enthusiasm and pride filling Joseph's chest like helium in a balloon, and experiencing such affection for swastikas, even if it was someone else's affection, made Vilém feel foul.

"Is this Germany?" Vilém asked.

Nope. Sudetenland, 1938. Small village. Everyone here loved Hitler, and so I did too. We hated the Czechs, and Jews...well, I had never seen a Jew in my life...

The young Klammer walked past a pack of little boys. The children had dressed up some sacks of flour with horsehair and a hat. One of them had drawn a giant nose on the flour-dummy's "face" and a yellow Star-of-David on its "belly." Klammer paused to watch, chuckling with amusement as the children pelted the Jew effigy with stones. Vilém could feel righteous fury stir in Joseph's heart, the same sort he felt whenever he read about the Nazis' crimes.

"Jesus..." he whispered.

I apologize if you feel a little racist right now, Vilém. I promise that's all me.

Vilém chuckled, though he felt no joy right then. "It's...weird. I've always wondered what the Nazis were thinking the whole time and...I guess I kinda know now. You really thought you were the victims."

I did. Can't speak for all my old comrades. We were all bullies, but bullies come in all different sorts. Some, like me, really believed the lies. Others...others just wanted someone they could beat up. But I, well, I'd been told my whole childhood that the Czechs took us away from our homeland, that the Jews were our misfortune, and I believed every word. So when the Munich Agreement happened and Hitler took us back, I wanted to repay him.

Joseph marched towards an old bakery, where a battalion of SS men were being treated to cakes and coffee on the house. Joseph's eyes fell upon their commander, a dashing dark-haired man with multiple medals twinkling on his chest.

Vilém felt a blush invade Joseph's cheeks as an alien-yet-familiar feeling took over. When Joseph looked upon the man and felt the same rush of admiration Vilém felt whenever he gazed upon a beautiful woman, it was, to Vilém, as uncomfortable as it was surprising.

"I didn't know you were gay," Vilém said.

Amazing what the history books will leave out! If anyone bothered to read through my journals, they would have figured out I was an absolute queer. I guess that would have ruined my nice, clean image, though. You wanna leave now? I assure you it's only going to get more uncomfortable.

"Mr. Klammer, I can put up with feeling a little gay if it means finding out my family's backstory."

Klammer's ghost cackled. *Oh, yeah, you're definitely Sam's descendant! You're spirited.*

"Thanks! I am a little...puzzled. Why would you join the Nazis if you were gay? They weren't exactly known for...*tolerance* in that regard."

I was in denial for most of my life, Vilém. I thought it was something horrible and shameful, but fixable. I thought if I acted like a perfect Aryan man, I could really become one.

"I'm guessing it didn't work?"

Not for lack of trying, though I guess hanging around a bunch of muscular men didn't help matters. Now hush! You really are just like Sam, you never stop asking questions!

"Yes, sir..." mumbled Vilém. He felt Joseph's pulse quicken with eager anxiety. Klammer stepped towards the medal-clad commander and thrust his hand into the air.

"Heil Hitler, sir!" he cried. The Nazi Commander looked up, smiling as he gave the youth a once-over with his eyes. No doubt Joseph's impeccably Aryan appearance impressed him.

"Heil Hitler, young man," he said, gesturing for Joseph to

come closer. With as much grace as he could muster, Joseph marched towards him. Vilém could feel the young man desperately attempting to force the blush off his face.

"Enjoying the celebrations?" the Commander asked.

"Very much, sir!"

"You came over with a purpose, I can tell."

"I'd like to join the SS, sir!" Joseph proclaimed.

"Doesn't everyone? How old are you, young man?"

"Seventeen, sir!"

"Good. I assume there's a reason you're telling me this instead of filling out the official forms. I realize we just got here, but..."

Joseph's heart did a gymnastic feat against his chest. He must have been expecting and dreading that question.

"My mother had a degenerate youth before the Führer opened her eyes to the value of her race," Joseph explained. "While she never knowingly had relations with a Czech or any other undesirable, we do not have any records of my father's side of the family, and therefore..."

"Therefore you couldn't submit a family tree, I get it...here, let me get a look at ya'."

The Commander stood and grabbed Joseph by the chin, and the battle Joseph had been waging against the blush on his cheeks became a humiliating defeat. He clenched his jaw and made his blue eyes as wide as he could, staring at the Commander's face. Vilém realized that Joseph was focusing a bit too much on the Commander's lips, and he felt a volcano of shame erupt in the closeted man's belly.

"Well, young man, I realize that blonde Jews exist," chuckled the Commander, releasing Joseph. "But if you're an undesirable, I'll throw myself in Dachau. Not to worry: I think I can work some magic."

An explosion of gratitude went off in Joseph's brain, and he could only barely resist the urge to yank the Commander into a hug.

The memory shifted to darkness, and Vilém sensed that Klammer was drifting.

"Mr. Klammer?" he called out.

Still here. Don't worry, I'm not leaving...I was just thinking. You won't see it, but that man, Commander Weber...he got caught stealing gold from the Jews we "processed." The Nazis sent him to die on the Eastern Front, threw him right where the fighting was worst. It was fine for us to steal from those filthy Jews, but how dare he steal from thieves?

"The Nazis are expert hypocrites."

Ha! Don't I know that! Commander Weber worked his magic all right, and I became a good, loyal, hypocritical Nazi.

"I vow to you, Adolf Hitler, as Führer and Chancellor of the German Reich, absolute loyalty and bravery..."

Joseph stood in a single-file, oppressively constructed line of black-garbed men, offering a three-finger salute to a massive portrait of his Führer. He let his eyes flit away from Hitler's visage for but a moment, looking to the sidelines. His mother's face peeked out of a small cluster of onlookers. She was glowing with pride.

Vilém felt the ghost's energy become icy.

"You okay, Klammer?" he queried.

The other children in the village used to mock me...called me a whore's son...which I was, ha! But...I joined the Nazis and suddenly I was more than that. Not just some accident, not a piece of filth...a perfect human. She was so proud.

"I vow to you and the leaders you have set forth for me...absolute loyalty unto death." Young Klammer continued the oath, though Vilém sensed he was no longer directing it towards Hitler. His eyes shifted from his mother to the proudly grinning

Commander Weber. The Commander realized he was being watched and offered the boy a wink. There was a proud gleam in his green eyes.

"So help me God!" Joseph completed the oath, and the SS man who had been swearing in the fresh recruits slammed the book he had been reading from shut.

"Welcome, all of you, to the SS! You are the Fatherland's heart and soul, the shield of the Reich against the undesirable forces within and without. Do your nation proud!"

He clapped, and the rest of the Nazis followed suit. Joseph looked at his mother and laughed when he realized her applause was the most enthusiastic. When the lines broke apart and the new SS men went to greet their families, Joseph's mother let out an excited shriek.

She ran to him, holding a potted plant under her arm. She hugged him with her one free arm, pressing his cheek against hers. He felt that her face was moist with tears.

"Mama!" he laughed. "Please calm down!"

"I'm calm! I couldn't be calmer! I'm so, so proud! My handsome boy! You're the handsomest recruit! Oh, you're going to be the best SS man! You'll get a handshake from the Führer for sure!"

"Hopefully, he'll get that handshake on stage and not in a field hospital," Commander Weber chuckled, clapping Joseph on the shoulder. He must have learned to control his infatuation after being under the handsome Commander's wing for so long.

"Thankfully, your battalion's getting trained for a simple job," the Commander said. "I made sure you wouldn't get sent anywhere uncomfortable. Worked my magic."

"I need to learn that magic," Joseph joked.

"You will, my boy! You learn fast in the SS. You're not going to be digging ditches, though—or, God forbid, dealing with the

Russians! I made sure you got an honorable post. You'll be helping us solve the Jewish Question."

Vilém wanted to retch, and his disgust doubled when he felt young Joseph's heart soar at the notion. The idea of murdering an entire race excited Joseph Klammer. The new SS recruit glanced at his mother, who was biting her nails.

"Oh, Christoph, are you sure about that? Dealing with those *creatures* when he's so young..."

"Mama, I'm eighteen!" sighed Joseph. His eyes shifted to his superior and he saluted. "What's my first post, Commander?"

"Your enthusiasm never wanes, Joseph, my boy! I could tell from the moment I saw you—I could tell you'd be a star if you could get a chance! Frau Klammer, there's nothing to worry about. He'll be guarding a ghetto, helping to keep the Jews tame."

"I don't think there's such a thing as a *tame* Jew, Commander," muttered Joseph's mother, clenching her jaw, and Vilém wanted to wince at the inferno of hatred flaring in her eyes.

"Oh, madam, any animal can be made tame with sufficient force. Wolves, lions, even filthy rats. Yes, even Jews can be tamed, and it will be Joseph's job to keep them in line until we can figure out a humane way to deal with them."

"Humane!" spat Vilém, and yet he could feel that young Joseph Klammer didn't disagree with a word of this.

I told you, didn't I? Klammer's spirit mumbled. *I was a loyal Nazi. I really thought Jews were rats. Dirty animals...less than animals.*

"So what changed your mind?" Vilém asked.

See that flower? Klammer's ghost queried. Joseph's mother pushed the potted plant into her son's arms. It was a beautiful sapphire cornflower. Vilém felt Joseph's heart plummet.

"Oh, Mama, you know I'll kill it," Joseph laughed.

"It's the Reich's flower! I want you to have something to brighten your dorm and remind you of me!"

"I'll think of you every day, Mama! I don't need a flower!" laughed Joseph, cradling the plant. "All right, but I know it'll only last a week."

"Hm...well, since that's the Reich's national flower, you'd better take good care of it," Commander Weber joked. "Or else I may have to kick you out for defacing a symbol of German nationalism."

Joseph chuckled, looked down at the blue flower, and in the blink of an eye, the memory changed. Joseph was standing in what must have been his dorm room at the SS barracks. He tarried by the windowsill, staring down at the now almost-dead cornflower.

"Shit..." Joseph mumbled, gingerly gripping a petal between his fingers, accidently tearing it from the plant as he did so. He let the dead petal fall into the dry dirt and sighed, looking past the plant and gazing at the Ghetto in the distance.

A forest of barbed wire surrounded the Ghetto, cutting it off from the rest of the town. Dark smoke from the factories spewed into the sky. Joseph grunted, and Vilém could feel disgust rear up in the young man's heart. Even from far away, the Jewish Quarter smelled vile. Vilém knew that was the Nazis' fault: bodies were rotting in the Ghetto streets, trash and feces weren't getting cleaned up. Letting the Ghetto become unlivably filthy was part of the Nazis' grand scheme to solve the Jewish Question. The more Jews that dropped dead from disease, the less money the SS would have to waste on bullets and gas.

But Joseph...well, Vilém could tell from the anger burning in Joseph's chest that he blamed the Jews for the rank odor.

Joseph turned his attention to the dorm building's idyllic property. A well-kept lawn, flagpoles bearing swastikas and SS lightning bolts, and a lovely garden right beneath Joseph's second-story bedroom.

Joseph leaned over, looking down at the garden and noticing a man kneeling by the flowerbed, tending the plants. A gardener, and evidently an unfamiliar one since Vilém felt a spark of surprise flare in Joseph's brain. The young Nazi glanced from the faraway figure to the almost dead plant. His eyes wandered to his roommate's empty bed and Vilém felt a stab of loneliness strike the Nazi's heart.

The SS was supposed to be a brotherhood, but the dorms were very competitive, everyone trying to out-Nazi each other. I think many of my "comrades" were jealous that they, with their flawless family trees, didn't carry as much favor as me, the whore's son who got lucky. I didn't have any friends, and when I saw the gardener down there...I was hoping to make one...or at least save my little flower friend.

Joseph grabbed the cornflower and bolted out of his room, down the stairs, and out the door. He approached the gardener with more nervousness than an Aryan superman should have.

When Joseph got close enough to actually see what the gardener looked like, Vilém recognized him right away. Dark curly hair, soft eyes. It was his great-grandfather. Sam Svoboda was patting manure into place. He was covered in dirt, his overalls were torn, and a brown jacket lay beside a heap of tools. He wasn't wearing the mandatory yellow star. Vilém assumed that the Nazis either didn't yet know he was a Jew, or his star was sewn onto the jacket he had dared to take off while he worked.

Vilém's great-grandfather was decently handsome, certainly no Adonis. Yet when Joseph got a good look at the gardener, a wave of wonder washed over him. Vilém loved Jana with all his heart. As far as he was concerned, she was the most gorgeous woman in the entire world. The way Joseph felt right then as he gazed at Sam was identical to how he felt whenever he saw his girl-friend: pure awe.

"U-Uhm..." Joseph stuttered. Sam looked up, and while Joseph's cheeks must have been red as the Nazi flags fluttering nearby, the gardener's face became placid.

"H-Heil, Herr..." Sam mumbled, keeping his eyes downcast. Joseph, standing there in all of his Aryan glory, must have been a terrifying sight for the young Jew. If he were watching this situation from a different point of view, Vilém might have feared for Sam's safety.

But experiencing this moment through Joseph's eyes, he could feel the SS officer's knees wobbling, his tongue tying itself into knots, and the deep, terrible shame he felt for swooning over a man. Vilém felt Joseph's brain attack his heart with insults. Degenerate. Dirty. Undesirable.

Joseph's roiling stomach urged him to flee, to return to the house and pretend he had never seen the handsome gardener. But somehow, he ignored his impulses and summoned the strength to offer Sam his dying cornflower.

"I...don't mean to interrupt you, Herr Gardener..." he choked. "But...my little friend could use your...green thumb."

A splash of color returned to Sam's face. He hesitated for only a moment before something—either his love of plants or fear of what the Nazi would do to him if he refused—convinced him to nod. "Give it here," Sam said, and hearing the voice of his great-grandfather made a bubble of happiness form in Vilém's heart.

"He has a nice voice..." Vilém observed as Joseph sat in the dirt beside Sam and handed him the plant. Sam scrutinized it like a doctor might a critical patient.

Musical, and once he started talking, he wouldn't stop...but I didn't mind. I loved to listen to his voice. He just...glowed whenever he talked about the things he loved. His plants, his wife, his baby. It was like watching a flower bloom.

In the blink of an eye, the memory changed, though not by much. Joseph was holding the potted cornflower, which was livelier than it had ever been, glistening proudly in the sunlight. Klammer trotted to the garden, and evidently enough time had passed for Sam to regard the SS man with a bright smile.

"How's your baby?" Sam asked. Joseph sat on the raised flowerbed, setting the plant down in front of the gardener. Sam brushed his fingers against the flower's soft petals.

"He looks good!" Sam announced, his eyes dancing with pride.

"Thanks to you!" said Joseph. "How about your baby?"

"He said 'Papa'!"

"Finally!" laughed Joseph. "If he kept on refusing to say anything but 'Mama', I think you would have had grounds to disown him."

"Ha! He'll never know how frustrating he was....but...all things considered, he's doing well." Sam shoved his trowel into the dirt, his smile tapering into a worried grimace.

"Listen," Joseph murmured, and Vilém could feel fear shoot through the Nazi's body as he spoke. "If...you or your kid need anything...I know you're Czech, but you're...I...appreciate your company. I'd like to help, if you need it. I can get away with a lot. I could...well, I could work some magic."

Sam snorted, lifting the full trowel and slowly letting the dirt fall, watching as it rained down on his already-filthy shoes. "I think you'd have to be a genie to help me."

"Try me," Joseph said. Sam chewed on his bottom lip, dropped his trowel, and covered his face with his hands.

"He keeps getting sick, my boy," Sam said, his voice cracking. "And I can't get him to a doctor, I can't even get him cough drops..."

Without a second of hesitation, Joseph hopped to his feet. He darted to his room, affection practically giving him super-speed. He ran to his dresser and pulled out a small rectangular tin. Vilém couldn't read the German on it, but judging by the little illustration of cherries on the front, it was probably a tin of cough drops. Smiling victoriously, Joseph returned to the garden, kneeling before Sam and offering him the tin.

"He won't like the taste, but they'll help," Joseph said. "And I can get you more."

"Private Klammer, you may get in trouble, giving me Reich resources..." Sam whispered. Joseph grasped Sam by the hand and felt as though a bolt of electricity had struck him. Love burned in the young Nazi's chest so intensely that Vilém could tell he was barely suppressing the urge to yank Sam into a kiss. He resisted, however, and instead pressed the tin into the gardener's palm.

"Joseph, please, just call me Joseph," he insisted, folding Sam's fingers over the tin and pushing it towards the gardener's dirt-stained chest. "I value your friendship, Sam. I enjoy sitting with you, talking to you. I'd like to make sure you're secure and...well, as happy as you can be, given the circumstances."

Sam glanced down at the little tin before looking into Joseph's eyes and smiling. Joseph's heart fluttered. He must have thought Samuel Svoboda had the world's loveliest smile.

"Thank you...Joseph...."

"Joseph!"

In the blink of an eye, the memory shifted. No longer was Joseph sitting in the lovely garden with his handsome friend by his side. He was leaning against a wooden post, half asleep. He snapped to attention as Commander Weber marched up to him and gave him a light smack on the cheek.

"Wakey, wakey, Private!" the Commander cried, an affectionate smirk masking his annoyance. "We've got Jews to ship out! You need to guard the gate!"

"Yes, sir!" yawned Joseph.

"Stop staying up all night, Private!" Commander Weber ordered. "I don't care if you're reading *Das Arbeiter*! If you don't sleep, the Jews get out and run amok!"

"Sorry, sir!" Joseph said. He rubbed his eyes, adjusted his gun, and skittered to his new post. There was a small booth set up which blocked the exit to the Ghetto. Several trucks were parked outside the barriers, and Vilém shivered when he saw skulls decorating the sides of the vehicles. Two German words that even Vilém could recognize were painted right below the death's heads: "Live Animals." It seemed that the Nazis had commandeered some glue-factory trucks to transport the Jews. To the train stations? Probably, and from there, to Auschwitz, Treblinka, Chelmno.

"Move, Jews, quickly!"

A crooked line of people formed in front of the booth: elderly Jews were collecting their bags and passports, waving goodbye to their younger family members. Vilém almost retched. They were cleaning out the Ghetto, sending the old to the death camps.

"Please remain calm!" Commander Weber screeched into a microphone. "All Jews above the age of sixty must evacuate the Ghetto for their own safety. Elderly Jews who cannot work are to be relocated to an elders' camp. Rest assured: you will be taken care of."

He locked eyes with Joseph and snickered. Vilém's disgusted reaction clashed terribly with Joseph Klammer's amusement. Joseph knew they were lying. He knew, and he thought it was hilarious.

I warned you...I was an unpleasant human being, Klammer's

ghost said. *Fuck, "human being" is giving me too much credit. I was a goddamn monster.*

"No," Vilém argued. "I'm feeling everything you did...you thought you were right. You thought this was okay...justified..."

And that makes it better?

"It makes you human," Vilém said. The ghost scoffed.

Don't speak too soon. Watch...

Most of the elderly Jews seemed to trust the Commander—or perhaps they didn't, but their situation was hopeless and all they could do was force themselves to believe he was telling the truth, that they would all be okay. They stayed in line, showing their passports to the Nazis and climbing into the glue trucks, urged on by truncheon-waving SS soldiers. It was all orderly.

Until one man, older than almost anyone there, limped out of the line, clutching his cane. His family begged him to stop, but his ancient eyes were flaring and he refused to yield. He marched up to the Commander and wagged his cane in the Nazi's face.

"You're lying!" he accused, and the Commander was too surprised by the old man's gall to respond. The old man faced his people and cried out, pointing his cane at Weber. "He lies! They're all lying! You think they'll let us live? Have you heard what they've said about us? I've lived long enough to see this sort of thing happen again and again! Our gentile neighbors turn on us, butcher us! They're doing it again!"

"Papa!" The old man's daughter, keeping her distance and clinging to her children, watched his bold display with horror. "Papa, please, stop!"

"They'll kill us wherever they take us! They starve us here, they'll starve us there! They'll shoot all of us!"

"We don't have any intention of shooting you, sir," Commander Weber declared, and Vilém once again felt amusement rise up in Joseph Klammer's heart. Vilém almost choked. No, of course. The Nazis wouldn't waste bullets on dirty Jews. They would only get gas.

"Please don't trust them!" the old man begged. "They'll kill us, and then they'll kill our children and our grandchildren!"

The old man's speech started to cause a stir. A few Jews tried to sneak away, but they were brutally forced back into the queue by the Nazis. Commander Weber saw that seeds of doubt were being sewn and looked towards Joseph.

"Get rid of him," he mouthed, nudging his head to indicate the old man. Joseph nodded, and Vilém felt adrenaline shoot through Joseph's body as he approached the old Jew. It was the feeling of a hunter approaching his prey.

No, not a hunter. Vilém had once dealt with a horrid cockroach infestation in his apartment, and the sensation that Joseph Klammer felt as he marched towards the old man was identical to the feeling Vilém had experienced when he was just about to crush one of the disgusting little creatures under his boot.

"Sir, you're hysterical. Please follow me..." Klammer grabbed the old man by the arm, trying to tug him towards a building, away from the eyes of the populace where he could be properly "dealt with." The old man, who wasn't nearly as frail as he looked, put up an admirable fight, grabbing his cane and striking at the Nazi's crotch. He missed Joseph's balls by a mere centimeter, and the anger that coursed through Joseph was blinding.

"Stupid fucking Jew!" he snarled, throwing the old man to the ground. He started smashing the helpless Jew's face in with the butt of his rifle. Vilém wanted to leave, he didn't want to feel this, to feel like he was crushing cockroaches as Joseph pummeled the old man.

"Stop, stop, please!" The old man's daughter ran at Joseph, grabbing his arm and trying to pull him off her father. The old man wasn't moving.

"Do *not* touch me, you dirty Jewess!" Joseph snarled, grasping a handful of her dark hair and throwing her down beside her father. He kicked her in the stomach. Her children started screaming and crying. He raised his gun. The thrill that went through him as he put his finger on the trigger...he felt like a God.

"JOSEPH!"

But a familiar voice brought him back down to earth. He looked up and saw Sam Svoboda. A yellow Star-of-David was sewn onto the gardener's chest.

"Sam...?" Disbelief and horror consumed Joseph's soul. For a moment, the two men stood in the midst of the now-chaotic deportation, Joseph staring slack-jawed at his scowling crush. Even as Nazis screeched at Jews and the woman beneath the barrel of his gun screamed for her children to stay away, Joseph was deaf to everything except Samuel's labored, nervous breathing.

"Sam, what are you doing? Get back in here!"

A woman in a nearby apartment complex shoved her head out the window. Vilém recognized her as his great-grandmother right away. Rebecca looked down at her husband in horror, but Sam refused to flee. He opened his arms wide and beckoned with his fingers, daring Joseph to shoot him.

Joseph, paralyzed from the realization that he was in love with a Jew, didn't move for what felt like a full minute. Slowly, however, his blood started pumping and his heart began pounding. He looked to and fro to make sure he wasn't being watched. Once he was certain that all his comrades were distracted, he abandoned the old Jew's daughter and ran at Sam.

"No!" Rebecca shrieked, and Sam inhaled sharply as the Nazi grabbed his arm, no doubt ready for his so-called friend to betray him. Joseph dragged Sam to the gardener's apartment building. He shoved Sam into the stairwell and slammed the door behind him, waiting for a moment to make sure nobody had followed them before turning to his friend.

"You're a Jew," Klammer hissed, hiding his shock behind a scowl. Sam grunted and tugged on the collar of his jacket.

"I take this thing off when I work," Sam said, turning to show off his yellow star. "So you never saw this thing."

"That's illegal...you're supposed to always have it on..." Joseph growled, gripping his rifle with shaking hands. "God fucking damn it, Sam, why are you working at the SS dorms?!"

"Because you fuckers made me!" Sam snapped. "Your commander came into the Ghetto, asked for gardeners, and yanked me out of line! I go to work for you assholes for free, keep your lawn nice and pretty, and since my wife and son are here I don't think of escaping! I'm a slave, Joseph! *Your* slave!"

"You...you should have told me before..."

"Before fucking what?" cried Sam. "Before you talked to me like a human being instead of a rat? Before we became 'friends'? Ha! Well, we're not really friends, are we?"

"Because you were using me!" Joseph accused, and Vilém felt the young Nazi's brain racing in desperate circles, trying to twist this madness into something that made sense, trying to shove this round peg into his worldview's square hole. "I get it! Act all sweet and innocent and then convince me to..."

"To *what*, Joseph?" Sam snarled, jabbing his finger into the Nazi's chest. "*I* never asked *you* for anything! *You* kept coming to *me* for your little flower friend! *You* offered *me* help! And what would I have asked for? Medicine for my child? How nefarious! What a monster I am! Well, if you want to take everything back, then here!"

He pulled the little cough drop tin Joseph had given him out of his pocket and offered it to the Nazi. "Take it! Take it and go back to beating up old men!"

"I..." Joseph looked down at the cherry-red tin and felt bile rise in his throat. He felt ill. Ill and yet, when he looked at Sam and saw the gardener's fire, his bravery, he felt more infatuated than ever.

"You don't...get it! You can't understand!" Joseph shouted, turning away from the Jew and slamming his head against the concrete wall so hard he almost knocked himself out. There was a slight clinking noise as Sam shoved the cough drops back into his pocket.

For a few seconds, there was silence save for the muffled screams emanating from outside. Eventually, Sam spoke.

"So...am I under arrest?"

Joseph turned, glaring. Hatred and love battled in his soul as he looked at the young Jew. He hated him for his silent lies, for daring to be a Jew, for all the horrible self-hatred he was feeling again. But...

"Of course not!" Joseph submitted to the love in his heart even as Hitler's fury-filled voice echoed about his skull. He smiled ever so slightly as he accepted his internal Führer's ire. There. He was a dirty Jew lover. Worse than a Jew. An eager race-traitor.

He looked at Sam, smiling as though he had just heard the most wretched dead baby joke in creation and found it hilarious. He laughed.

"What's...wrong with you?" Sam asked as Joseph leaned against the wall, hugging his gun, laughing so hard it hurt.

"Because I'm a dirty whore's son and my only friend's a Jew, you ass!" Joseph howled. "And look at me! Look at me! It's funny, isn't it? Imagine if Hitler shook my hand and then found out I'm a dirty whore's son who gives Reich resources to Jews! Haha!"

"I...don't know if any of this is funny, Joseph..." Sam muttered even as a small smile grew on his lips.

"It's hilarious!" Joseph insisted. "Oh, you don't get it. You Jews have no sense of humor."

"What?! We have a marvelous sense of humor!"

"I've never met a Jew that's made me laugh!" Joseph giggled, sliding down to the floor and smiling up at Sam. "Well...I guess you make me laugh."

"I...didn't intend to. I'm...sorry?"

"You sound so uncertain. That 'sorry' wasn't a real sorry."

"Well, sorry! But...you were beating that old man and you almost killed that girl. I...I don't know what to think right now."

"How do you think I feel?" scoffed Joseph. "Five minutes ago all Jews were dirty rats and now..."

"Now it's different? Just like that?" Sam snapped his fingers. "God, send me to Berlin, I'll just help Hitler save some flowers and all this foolishness will end."

"I know you're joking, but...I don't know. Maybe you're just...the exception to the rule. You know, Himmler says everyone in Germany has their one good Jew. I guess you're mine."

"Well, if that old man had saved your little flower," Sam said, gesturing towards the door, "then he'd be your good Jew. Get it?"

"Oh...don't ask me to think too hard right now, Sam, my head's spinning," Joseph sighed, pressing his skull against his gun, comforted by the cool metal that soothed his feverish forehead.

"I just...I didn't even think *one* of you was good. But you're good, I know you're good, I thought you were just a Czech...a salvageable Czech, maybe even a little German...ha! I was gonna ask for your family tree because I was sure you had to be part German...you're too good to be an undesirable. But...you are, you are an undesirable and I still lo...like you. But you're not...different, are you? You're just a Jew like all the rest. And if you hadn't talked to me in the garden, I would have shot you just now."

The very thought of murdering Sam made Joseph's heart

clench up. "And...maybe I've shot you before. Maybe I've shot seven Sams. Maybe they were all good Jews."

He felt ill enough to vomit, but he lifted his chin, facing the gardener as he quietly queried, "Am I a murderer, Sam?"

"I...maybe a manslaughterer. I don't think you're evil, Joseph. You're just...a dumb kid..."

"Dumb kids kill kittens, not people," Joseph argued.

"Well...we're rats, aren't we?" Sam countered sarcastically.

"I hope so..." Joseph whispered, gazing down at the swastika on his arm. "I'd rather be an exterminator than a monster. I want you to be wrong so bad, Sam, I..."

"Sam!"

But before Joseph could say another word, a pair of footsteps and a scream interrupted him. Rebecca appeared at the top of the stairwell, holding a two-year-old child in her arms. The little boy had dark curls so long they almost covered his eyes. Vilém could only assume that was his beloved Grandpa Fabian as a baby.

"Oh...he's so cute," Vilém said as he looked at the little boy. He could certainly see why Sam was so worried about his son's health: had Vilém not known that Fabian would live, he wouldn't have given the boy a month. The toddler was pale, skeletal, and when he coughed a horrid gag emerged from his throat, as though he had just tried to smoke a cigarette for the first time.

Rebecca hugged her sick son to her chest, gazing down at her husband with saucer-sized eyes. She obviously wanted to run to him, to protect him, but her little baby needed her. Both Vilém and Joseph realized that she was pregnant, just starting to show.

"Becca, it's okay," Sam assured her, motioning for her to come down and meet Joseph. "This is the German I told you about before, from the SS garden."

"Is he...?" Rebecca said hesitantly, covering her son's face with her hands. The boy let out a sneeze so loud that it was a wonder the Nazis outside didn't hear it.

"God bless you, little one," Joseph mumbled, and Vilém could feel horror rise in his chest once more.

I might have killed that kid...and you wouldn't be here.

"Who...did you kill before this happened?" Vilém queried.

Escapees, healthy adults. Sams.

"You didn't show me that, you killing anyone."

Should I? I don't think you'd like the feeling of being a murderer. Even if you're not the one killing, trust me, it's a feeling that will never go away. Besides, I...would rather not relive those moments.

"No...you're right. That...out there...with the old man and the woman...that was enough."

The people I killed were not as memorable, I hate to say. I only saw them as little dots running from the Ghetto. I didn't look into their eyes or hear their children scream. It was just like...killing little gnats.

"How many?" Vilém asked.

Seven.

"But you saved four hundred!"

Murder isn't a goddamn balancing scale, Vilém. Saving a million people wouldn't make what I did before better.

"It means you learned!" Vilém argued, and the spirit chuckled.

You really are Sam's great-grandson.

Sam looked at Joseph and offered him a smile that made Joseph's heart roil. "Don't worry," the gardener said. "He's not like the rest of them."

"The rest..." Joseph leapt to his feet. "The rest! The rest will be wondering where I am! Here!" He shoved his rifle into Sam's arms.

"Take this!" he insisted, and Sam jumped back, recoiling from the firearm as though it were a venomous snake.

"Joseph, are you insane?" Sam cried. "We're not supposed to have weapons in the Ghetto!"

"You're not supposed to take your star off either!" Joseph pointed out. "Take it! I may not always be here to protect you! And listen...no matter what, you can't allow them to take your child out of this Ghetto. Trust me."

He looked towards the coughing little boy and said, "You have no idea what they'll do to him at a camp."

"I can imagine..." murmured Sam, slowly accepting the gift of the gun.

"I won't be able to smuggle anything else like this to you," Joseph said. "So only use it when you absolutely must. And whatever you do, don't let them deport you. That old man...he was right."

Joseph saw fear shine in Sam's bright eyes and he wanted nothing more than to pull him into a hug. He resisted, however, and turned away from the Jewish man. Without another word, he opened the door...

And the memory changed. Joseph, clutching a small sack, was opening the front door of his dorm building. He ran to the garden and found Sam, now sporting his yellow star. Sam greeted him with a hug, and Joseph's heart almost exploded with joy as he buried his face into the gardener's neck.

They sat, chatted, and everything seemed wonderful. But Vilém could feel a cocktail of fear and excitement swirling in Joseph's chest.

It was thrilling, you know...breaking the law. Just hugging a Jew was against the law. To love him? To give him gifts?

Joseph handed the sack to Sam. "I scavenged what I could, but the Commander's getting particular about supplies. He's apparently under investigation for something-or-other. But there's chocolate! Your boy should appreciate that, should help the medicine go down!"

"He's better about medicine than I was at his age! I'd always spit it into the nearest potted plant. Didn't care if I died, just didn't wanna taste it."

"How's he doing?"

"He appreciates your gifts, but...I think he just needs a doctor and the Nazis took all the Jewish doctors away."

"Of course," mumbled Joseph. "We wouldn't want you rats saving each other. I'm sorry, Sam. I don't think I can smuggle a doctor into the Ghetto."

"It's okay..." chuckled Sam, reaching out and grabbing Joseph's hand, provoking an eruption in Joseph's heart. "You're doing enough."

Joseph looked down at Sam's hand and squeezed it. He allowed himself a moment of bliss, to enjoy the small sin, before he pulled away. "No..." he sighed. "No, I'm not."

The memory faded. Joseph was standing before his Commander. Weber's eyes were moist. His smile, once natural and wide, was forced.

"I'm sorry to see you go, my boy," he said. "But I don't think I can magic my way out of this one, and I'd hate for you to get wrapped up in my nonsense. You'll be a fantastic camp guard. Gerber will be pleased with your record. You'll do our nation proud...do me proud."

"Y-yes, sir..." Joseph stuttered, a host of feelings clashing in his soul. Pride—what little lingered—battled against anger and affection. He still admired the Commander even though he now knew what he was. Weber had been his friend and mentor for far too long. Joseph couldn't hate him, and the knowledge that he was betraying him...it hurt.

The Commander pulled Joseph into a hug. Joseph hesitated for a moment, but then he carefully put his hands on Weber's shoulders, an imitation of a hug. He pushed the Commander away and offered him a bitter smile.

"I'll get my things..." he muttered. He turned, glancing over his shoulder and stealing one last look at his mentor. Weber sunk into his chair and let out a long, exhausted exhale. He covered his face with his hands, and if those hands hadn't had so much blood on them, Vilém may have felt bad for the Nazi Commander.

Don't hate him too much, Vilém. If you don't hate me, you can't hate him. He was just as misled.

"He didn't change," Vilém argued.

Perhaps he would have...if he had a Sam of his own.

Joseph ran to his room, but not to pack. He found his precious sapphire cornflower. Vilém observed with confused distress as the young Nazi plucked the gorgeous flower from the pot, tearing it from its roots. Joseph ran to his drawer and pulled out a few pieces of parchment paper. He then scurried to the laundry room. Vilém watched with mild fascination as Klammer placed the precious flower between two pieces of parchment and pressed it with a hot iron.

A little trick from Sam...well, really from Rebecca, but Sam told me about it, said she was always pressing flowers.

"Ha!" laughed Vilém. "Yeah, I think my mom keeps all the family artifacts up in the attic in this old trunk. I remember going through it once. There were pages and pages of pressed flowers."

I wanted Sam to have the flower...to remember me. I figured it would be easier to press it...more permanent, and easier to smuggle into the Ghetto. And I...well...I figured I would give it to him and...confess. I figured once I left, I would never see him again. I wanted him to know how much I loved him, just in case...

Once the flower was pressed, Joseph hugged it to his chest and darted out of the dorm building, running to the garden. Sam was kneeling by the tulips, his head bowed. He had pulled a blue tulip from the dirt and was twirling it between his fingers.

"Sam, I...I have something to tell you!" Joseph said.

"Please go away..." Sam hissed, sadness lacing his voice. Vilém bit his lip. Fabian must have been getting worse.

"He survived, though. The little boy, my grandfather, and Sam and Rebecca and my great-uncle Daniel, too. All of them survived."

I'm glad I know that now...I feared the worst. But that's all hindsight. At the time, it seemed like that child was as good as dead.

"I..." Joseph dropped the pressed flower, forgetting about his confession and approaching the gardener with concern. "Sam, are you okay? I just wanted to..."

Sam raised his head, glaring at Joseph with all the hatred a Nazi deserved, and screamed, "GO AWAY!"

And right as he screamed, something struck Vilém in the chest. At first he thought Sam's anger was so painful to Joseph that it felt like a physical punch to the gut, but then he found himself lying on the floor of Barrack Three. His chest ached, the wind was knocked out of him.

"The fuck...? Klammer?" Vilém gasped once he recovered enough to speak. He sat up. Sunlight was beginning to spill into the barrack. He looked around, inhaling sharply. He couldn't sense Klammer's powerful spirit, but there was definitely something nearby. Something different. Something evil.

Vilém rose to his feet and stumbled to the front of the Klammer exhibit, cautiously trying to figure out where the dark energy was coming from. But just as quickly as he felt it, it vanished. He pursed his lips together and looked towards the door. A part of him wanted to run right then. This was becoming far more intense than he had imagined. Listening to stories was one thing, but getting attacked...

He grabbed his still-throbbing chest and looked back at Joseph Klammer's picture. Seeing the young hero's severe continence made bravery stir in Vilém's chest. He shook his head. No. He would not run. He needed to listen, to see—he needed to help the man who had helped so many.

He went back behind the panel, shut his eyes, and touched the wall. "Klammer?" he called out.

Goddamn, are you okay?

"Felt like someone punched me in the chest. Did you see anything?"

No. We actually can't see each other, just...feel. We're not physically here anymore. There's nothing to see, I guess.

"I think I've sensed Heydrich's spirit before, in Prague."

If I can stay behind this long, he could. And I couldn't see who or...whatever hit you, but it definitely felt familiar.

"Familiar bad I assume?"

It kinda reminded me of Kommandant Gerber. I didn't know him very well, so I may be wrong...

"I think you're on point. He spooked Iveta back in Barrack Four. Maybe he's got something to hide and he's worried I'm gonna figure it out."

He doesn't exactly have a sterling reputation to uphold. Why would he care?

"Dunno. Depends on what he's hiding. Maybe he likes being remembered as an asshole pure Nazi...maybe he wasn't as perfect a Nazi as the history books say."

That still doesn't explain how he was able to hurt you. We're all dead, we shouldn't be able to do anything like that.

"Raya Pomnenka was so determined to be remembered that she ruined Barrack Five, scratched her name onto the wall. I think if Gerber's determined enough, he can do some damage too. Maybe not to walls, but to me."

Okay, this isn't safe. You need to leave.

"I thought about it, but I'm not gonna. I dunno why, maybe it's just luck, but I can see and hear you guys. I'm not just gonna leave you here to rot."

I'm not going to let anything bad happen to Sam's great-grandson, Vilém. I'm not asking you, I'm telling you to leave.

"Sorry, Sergeant. War's over: I'm not obligated to obey a German's command," Vilém declared, smiling cheekily. The spirit chuckled.

Fuck, fine. I guess there's really nothing I can do except get this story over with so you can get out. Just...please be careful. I don't think Sam would forgive me if I just watched and let you get hurt.

"No offense, but you're a little too dead to do much. I think Great-Grandpa Sam would understand."

Ha! True, I suppose. Believe me, if I could smack the Kommandant, I would. Well, no use dwelling on it right now, let's finish this as quickly as possible. Where were we?

"You were getting reassigned..."

Ah, right! Well, I ended up leaving without saying goodbye to Samuel. I was sent to this camp, to guard it. I couldn't stop thinking about Sam...but there was no way to write to him, nothing to do except...follow orders.

"Klammer!"

A new memory formed. Joseph was standing in a guard tower, gazing down at a mass of people clustered on the Selection Platform. Kommandant Gerber was clutching a camera and snapping a few pictures of one particular new prisoner, who was bound and gagged, kneeling at the Nazi's feet.

"Klammer, come down! Schwartz, you too!"

Joseph looked towards the second watchtower, watching as the other guard, a baby-faced SS officer who couldn't have been a day older than sixteen, eagerly bolted from his station and ran to the Kommandant.

"Heil Hitler!" the baby-faced Nazi, Schwartz, screeched as he shoved his arm into the air. His enthusiasm was rewarded with a scoff from the Kommandant. Joseph took his sweet time, lazily sauntering up to Gerber, not even bothering with a proper Nazi greeting and instead offering his boss a curt nod. Gerber didn't seem bothered by Klammer's lack of Nazi fervor: he greeted his soldier with a small smirk.

"See this Czech rat?" the Kommandant said. He grabbed the bound prisoner he had been photographing by his bloodstained hair and tugged his head up so both watchtower guards could get a good look at his bruised face.

"Yes, sir!" barked Schwartz.

"He's resistance?" Joseph assumed, and Kommandant Gerber nodded.

"Good guess, Klammer. He's tied to the Czech rats who murdered our *beloved* Reichsprotektor Heydrich."

"*Beloved*, of course," Klammer said, offering the Kommandant a wink.

The Kommandant was evidently friends with Heydrich, but he wouldn't stop complaining about him. Heydrich would come here with his son every once in a while, apparently some kind of father-son learn-how-to-be-a-Nazi trip.

"No..." Vilém muttered. "Klaus...err, Heydrich's son came here to visit Iveta."

Iveta, that was the last...dead person you spoke to, yes? Hm...why was he visiting her?

"Long story: she was a Jew, she and Klaus were friends."

A Jew! Her!? Wow...that's not what Little Martin said.

"Little Martin? The Kommandant's son? You knew him?"

Watch.

The Kommandant shoved the Czech's face into the dirt and pressed his jackboot down on the resistance fighter's spine. "This one was...a little *too* easy to catch, if you know what I mean. We suspect he may have gotten captured on purpose to spy on our operation and report about it to the outside world." He laughed, and Vilém had never wanted to punch a memory so hard.

"Not that the world will or should care about what we do to these Jews, but we'd rather not cause a panic. So be on the lookout: if he escapes, it will be trouble. You see him anywhere near the gate, you shoot to kill."

"Yes, sir!" Schwartz said, Nazi-saluting again and almost dropping his gun as he did so. Joseph chuckled at the younger Nazi's clumsy gusto and nodded.

"Going back to my post," Joseph said, turning on his heel and starting towards the watchtower.

But a familiar face appeared in the crowd of frightened Jews, making him stop in his tracks. Sam, sporting a black eye, stood on the Platform, the only Jew who wasn't carrying luggage. Instead of a suitcase, he held a little boy in his arms. Vilém at first thought the child was Fabian, but he realized the two-year-old was too young to be his grandfather. It was his great-uncle, Daniel, who looked to be in good health despite the circumstances.

Joseph moved so fast that Vilém almost didn't see what happened. One moment he was standing on the Selection Platform, frozen, staring at his beloved Sam, and the next he was running.

"You there, Jew!" he bellowed, grabbing Sam by the arm and pulling him into the closest empty cattle car. A few Nazis laughed as Joseph yanked Sam out of sight.

"You show him, Joseph!" Schwartz cheered. Joseph pushed Sam into a corner of the cattle car and gave the side of the car a harsh kick, so harsh that it felt like the whole train trembled. Sam cowered, shielding his baby with his battered body.

"Sam, it's me!" Joseph hissed. "It's me, Joseph!"

"Joseph...?" gasped Sam, wincing as Joseph kicked the wall once more.

"Don't talk! Pretend like I'm beating you! Scream!"

Sam let out a scream so convincing that it wouldn't have surprised Vilém if his great-grandfather had been holding it in since the Holocaust had started. Baby Daniel, startled by his father's apparent distress, started wailing.

"Where's Rebecca? Say it quickly!" Joseph demanded.

"Not here, she got away, the gun you gave me..."

"Hey, Klammer, need some help in there?" Schwartz called to his comrade from the Platform.

"N-no, I've got him! Leave me be, I'm having fun!" Joseph kicked the cattle car and Sam let out another terrible cry.

"Listen, we have no time. The baby can't be here. He's too young, too much trouble. He'll be taken from you and killed."

Sam clutched the sobbing toddler to his chest and shook his head. "Then I'll die with him..." he whispered.

"Neither of you are dying! Give me the baby, I'll take him to my dorm and hide him. You need to go to the Kommandant and *beg* for a job. Tell him you're the best damn gardener in all of Europe. Tell him you'll do whatever he asks. Name drop me if you must, get on your knees if you must, but you *have* to work for him. I'll protect your boy, give him to me."

Joseph reached out, arms open, but Sam recoiled, his eyes pinned to the swastika on his friend's arm.

"Sam...please, I need you to trust me. You have nothing to lose. I would never hurt you or your child. Please trust me, I know I don't deserve it..."

"I trust you..." Sam kissed Daniel's forehand and handed him to the Nazi. While Sam continued to scream as though he was being beaten, Joseph took off his coat and wrapped the sobbing, confused child in the black tunic.

"Papa!" whined Daniel.

"My boy, be quiet. We're playing the quiet game now, you have to be quiet no matter what. If you win, we'll both get to see Mama again."

The boy was too young to fully understand and continued to sob, shoving his little fist into his mouth to muffle himself, a valiant and desperate effort to win the quiet game. Joseph held the coat-swathed child under his arm and, with his heart hammering like a drum at an SS parade, he emerged from the cattle car.

"Jesus, Klammer, you kicked the shit outta that one! What'd he do?" laughed Schwartz.

"Pretended he wasn't a Jew rat," Joseph said, fighting to maintain a casual tone. "My coat's covered in Jew blood, gonna go clean it. Cover for me."

"Gotcha!" Schwartz said, winking at his co-worker and making his way back towards the watchtowers. Smuggling the sobbing baby Daniel Svoboda away from the Selection Platform was relatively simple. Though the boy cried, he didn't struggle, and his sobs easily melded with those of the other children who screamed for their parents, with those of the babies who were ripped from the arms of their mothers.

Vilém had read enough of the Camp's grim placards to know what happened to the babies. Their parents would be assured that they were going to a nursery to be taken care of, and they would be brought to a far corner of the Camp. The Camp was too small to have its own gas chamber, but they did have one gassing van. All of the children Daniel's age would be tossed into the back of the van and suffocated with carbon monoxide. Their bodies would be thrown into a great Pit, burned into ashes.

Joseph rushed past the little wrought-iron gate that separated the Nazis' residences from the rest of the Camp. His barrack was situated behind the Kommandant's cozy abode. He almost made it, but here, far from the Selection and the screaming babies, Daniel's sobs were piercing.

"What are you doing?"

A child's gentle voice made Joseph freeze. He turned to face a boy with curly golden hair that Vilém recognized as Little Martin, Iveta's former playmate.

"I...Heil Hitler, little one..." Joseph stuttered. Martin looked at the Nazi with wide eyes before glancing at the sobbing bundle in his arms. The child was wise enough to figure out what was happening right away.

"Baby?" he assumed. Joseph felt as though he was going to keel over right then. His heart was beating, beating...

"Come on, quickly, and be quiet!" Martin hissed, running to the front door of the Kommandant's house. "His little spy'll see!"

The boy gestured towards the other side of the house. Vilém was confused for a moment before he realized Martin was trying to point at Iveta's doghouse.

"Spy...?" Vilém muttered as Joseph decided he had no choice and followed Little Martin into the Lion's Den.

Little Martin didn't have any clue that Iveta was a Jew.

"The Kommandant made her keep it a secret, he said he didn't want her to give his son any liberal ideas about race."

Well, that little secret backfired terribly. Martin never trusted her. He thought she was there to spy on him.

"Why would Gerber spy on his own son?" Vilém queried. Before the spirit could answer, Martin ushered Joseph and Daniel into the nursery, his big blue eyes shifting to and fro as he did so, no doubt worried that Iveta was watching.

"This way," Martin whispered, pushing Klammer through a door inside the nursery labeled, "Emergency."

Joseph stumbled into a small infirmary. There was a bed, enough medical equipment to put a field hospital to shame, and even a doctor, an older man with a full beard dressed in black-and-white prison garb.

"Doctor Rabbi!" Little Martin yelped, slamming the door shut and blocking it with a chair. Joseph unwrapped Daniel and put him down on the bed. The Doctor, baffled, sat frozen for a moment before he hopped up and knelt before Little Martin.

"Boychik, what in God's name is wrong with you?" he whispered. Joseph faced little Daniel and patted his curly locks.

"Hush, little one, please..." he begged.

"It's okay," Martin assured him. "The guards in the barracks would'a heard him, but he won't be found here. The walls are all cushioned, it'll muffle him. The Kommandant never comes in the infirmary, I think it makes him feel weird. Besides, I always cry, so he can cry and the Kommandant won't notice. The spy's not even allowed in here."

"Boychik..." the Doctor started to say, but Martin held up a hand to silence him.

"He's doing a mitzvah, Doctor Rabbi!" the boy argued. "We *have* to help him!"

The Doctor-Rabbi offered a hollow smile, as though even he didn't fully believe in the pillars of his religion anymore but didn't want to crush the boy's heart. Joseph stole some candy from the Doctor's desk and handed little Daniel a lollipop, which successfully shut him up for a moment. With the toddler's wailing temporarily silenced, Joseph turned to the Doctor, questions buzzing in his mind.

"Doctor Rabbi?" repeated the Sergeant, and the Doctor gave him a slight smile.

"I'm both, he can never decide what to call me," the Rabbi explained, gesturing to Little Martin. The blonde boy plodded over to baby Daniel and sat beside him, gently comforting the younger child.

"What are you doing here?" Joseph asked.

"I could ask you the same thing, Sergeant! Why do you have a Jewish baby with you?"

"I'm a two!" argued little Daniel, holding up two fingers, and Martin giggled.

"I'm an eight!" he countered, holding up both hands and wiggling eight of his digits. Joseph smiled at the cute display, but then remembered how dire the situation was and let his smile die.

"It's a long story," he said. "I'm friends with his father and…it's just a long story! Point is: I can't let him die."

"I see…" sighed the Rabbi. "Well, a secret for a secret, then. The boychik here is a hemophiliac."

"Hemo…what?"

"I bleed a lot when I get a little bump," Martin answered, tapping the cushioned floor with his foot. "I could die if I get even a little cut."

"Ah," said Joseph, feigning understanding even though Vilém could feel that he was still confused.

"My grandpa had that," Vilém said. Klammer's spirit let out an affirmative grunt.

Guess that may explain why he was sick all the time, your grandpa.

"I made a deal with the Kommandant," the Doctor explained. "I keep the boy alive, he keeps my daughter alive."

"A son for a daughter," Joseph said with a nod, but Martin let out a noise like an angry kitten.

"He's *not* my father!" Martin screeched. "I hate him, he stole me! He killed my mama and he stole me!"

"Stole...?" muttered Joseph in confusion, and Vilém, recalling all of his high school history lessons about Czech children during the Second World War, interrupted the memory once more.

"Stole?"

Martin told me later on that he arrived at the Camp and the Kommandant took him from his mother. Sent her to die and then...well, I guess "adopted" wouldn't be the best word. But the Kommandant always had us guards believe Martin was his son. I still don't know why he stole him.

"We learned about this in class once," Vilém said. "The Nazis used to think that some Czechs who looked 'Aryan' enough were salvageable, that they could be trained to be German."

Ha! I thought that of Samuel before I knew he was a Jew.

"Yeah, but a lot of 'em took it a step further. If they saw a Czech kid who had blonde hair, blue eyes, looked Aryan...they grabbed him, stole him from his parents, tried to brainwash him into thinking he was German. Poor boy."

I wish I'd known that...stealing one's life is terrible enough, but to strip him of his whole identity...that's like killing his soul.

"So...Great-Uncle Danny hid with Martin and the Rabbi."

Yes, and Sam tended to the Kommandant's garden. He stayed in Barrack Three with the rest of the useful workers. Unfortunately, I wasn't assigned to guard his barrack. I rarely got to see Sam or Danny, but I sometimes managed to exchange a word...or sneak Sam some food.

The memory shifted to the dead of night. Joseph was squatting inside Barrack Three, placing a little bag of food beside a sleeping Sam.

Sam lay on a wooden bunk. His curly locks had been shaved off. He didn't look like himself anymore: thin, bald, broken. But Joseph looked down at him with just as much love as ever, wanting desperately to kiss the exhausted prisoner, but refraining. He was already breaking enough rules.

"Stay safe..." he whispered. He exited the barrack.

"Hello, Sergeant!"

He winced when he saw the Doctor-Rabbi emerge from Barrack Two, grinding his teeth when the old Jew greeted him with sardonic cheer. Private Schwartz stood nearby. Schwartz looked from the Jew to his coworker with a question in his eyes.

"Sergeant..." Schwartz mumbled. Joseph marched up to his fellow Nazi, grabbing the Rabbi's arm and roughly tugging him out of the Private's grasp.

"There you are, and with Little Martin's Jew too! I thought you went to Barrack Three!" Joseph lied. "You have to keep your eye on the Jews at all times, Schwartz. Don't let them have a private moment! Shame on you!"

"I...I'm so sorry, Sergeant! I'll do better!" the Private squeaked, and Joseph had to suppress a satisfied smirk.

"Back to your post, Schwartz! I'll escort this Jew back to the Kommandant's home!"

"Y-yes, of course! Heil Hitler!"

"Heil Hitler!" grunted Joseph, watching smugly as the younger Nazi scampered away like a frightened rabbit.

"You're lucky," the Rabbi observed. "That boy's too enthralled with everything Nazi to question anything you do or say."

"He can't imagine why anyone would disagree with Hitler," Joseph said. He pointed at Barrack Two. "That's the barrack for working women, why is your daughter there?"

"Barrack Four is worse. Dirtier, and they clear it out too often. She may get caught in a deportation if she stays in Barrack Four, but here...she's...well, not safe, but not dead. Same as Danny's father, I suppose. Favored, pliant Jews can only expect so much privilege."

"I'm worried about Sam," sighed Joseph. "Typhus outbreaks keep happening and he looks sick…"

"Everyone here is sick, Sergeant Klammer. The prisoners, the guards, everyone except little Danny. He's fortunate. He still doesn't know…"

A terrible stench struck Joseph's nose, terrible and, to the Nazi, familiar. Vilém didn't recognize it right away, but he recalled his paternal grandmother's cremation and shivered.

"That's…" he muttered. Joseph's eyes flitted towards a far corner of the Camp. A vast pit was glowing orange, like a portal right to hell. Plumes of smoke rose from the Pit, coating the cloudy sky in gray.

"The babies…the children…" the Rabbi whispered. Joseph nodded.

"Joseph…that could be Danny," the Rabbi said. "In a week, that *will* be Samuel. What is the difference? Why save one and damn another?"

"Selfishness, Rabbi," Joseph answered, covering his nose with his sleeve in a futile attempt to keep the smell of burning bodies at bay.

"At least *you're* honest…but do you really believe in this Nazi nonsense anymore? Do you think *that* is okay?" The Rabbi pointed towards the Pit. Joseph Klammer, trembling, shook his head.

"I don't, but what am I supposed to do? Quit and leave Sam and Danny helpless? Refuse to work and get kicked out, sent to the Eastern Front to die in a pointless battle?"

"Those aren't your only two choices, Joseph."

"If you have another suggestion, I'd love to hear it!" hissed Joseph, pushing the Rabbi through the gates to the Kommandant's property. He heard Iveta in her doghouse, whimpering in her sleep.

"Fido's having nightmares again," the Rabbi observed. "Perhaps it's the Pit."

"Who cares?" snapped Joseph, sneaking the Rabbi back into the house and shoving him towards the nursery.

"Who indeed..." sighed the Rabbi, looking down at Martin's bed with a raised eyebrow. The boy was gone. He opened the door to the infirmary.

"Boychik?"

"Daniel!"

"Unca!" Daniel's sweet voice drifted up from beneath the table. Joseph and the Rabbi squatted down and saw both boys sitting together. Martin had shoved two cotton balls in his nostrils and Daniel was sporting an oversized gas mask.

"Stink, yuck!" Daniel said, waving his hand in front of the nozzle covering his nose. Joseph covered his mouth with his hand, muffling himself as he laughed, then cried.

"Yeah..." he sobbed. "Yeah, Danny, it stinks..."

I hope Danny didn't remember any of this...he was a sweet kid.

"I don't think he did, he never really talked about it. Neither did my grandpa, don't even know what he went through," Vilém sighed.

I'm sorry I can't give you those answers.

"You're giving a lot already. I'm wondering, though: what made you finally decide to step up?"

Oh, it's simple. The war started to go downhill, and the Kommandant received orders from Himmler. The Camp was to be liquidated. The Russians were getting closer and Himmler didn't want the Jews falling into the hands of the Allies. He didn't want the world to know what we had done. At a time when we should have been devoting our resources to the boys on the front, Hitler focused on his war against the Jews. We were ordered to clear out Barracks Two through Five, to ship all the Jews to Auschwitz.

"Including Sam…"

Including Sam. Of course, I couldn't let that happen, but there was no way to get Sam and Daniel out. If I wanted to save them, I had to save everyone.

"I've read about how you did it. Pretty impressive."

Whatever you read, I'm sure it gave me too much credit. I never could have done it by myself.

"So what did you do?"

Step one: free the Czech partisan and get him to help me. During my shift guarding him, I made an arrangement: I would let him go, he would return to his comrades, and they would meet me at a rendezvous point, help me steal the train. They would take the Jews, guard them, keep them safe.

The memory shifted. Sirens were screeching, dogs were barking, Joseph was standing up in the guard tower, watching as the Czech partisan ran from his work unit. The partisan made it out of the gate.

"I've got him!" Schwartz yelped from the other watchtower.

"No! Stand down, I've got him!" Joseph commanded, and nervous, eager-to-please Schwartz complied, lowering his gun and letting Joseph take the shot.

Joseph moved slowly, giving the Czech a generous head start. The Nazis on the ground, not wanting to face friendly fire, stayed behind the wire, waiting…

Joseph aimed, fired, and missed.

"Whoops…" he muttered, smirking as the resistance fighter vanished into the thicket.

Step two: the Czechs' job was to take the train off my hands, my job was to deliver it. I made sure I would be one of the guards on the Auschwitz Transport. But I wasn't going to be the only guard, and if I wanted to steal the train and change its course, I would need a distraction.

"Sam?"

No. The distraction's job would be to leap from the train, feign an escape attempt to get everyone's attention on him. It was essentially a suicide mission, but...thankfully, I knew someone who had something to die for.

"It's time..."

Joseph stood in the infirmary, gripping his rifle. The Rabbi sat with Daniel in his lap, quietly praying.

"I'll be a moment, Joseph."

"Not that I don't want to give you all the time you need, Rabbi, but I have to return Danny to his father."

"It will be better if I take him, Sergeant. We don't want to risk someone spotting him in Barrack Three and tossing him into the Pit," the Rabbi said. "I'll give him to Sam tomorrow...before I say goodbye to my daughter."

The Rabbi chewed on his thumbnail, his eyes becoming cloudy. Seeing his sacrificial lamb so worried—about his own mortality, about his daughter's fate without him, or perhaps he feared that their mission would fail and all of his people would be doomed—Joseph felt guilt strike at his soul. He placed a comforting hand on the Doctor's shoulder.

"You're saving her life, Rabbi," Joseph assured him. "You are a hero. She'll be proud of you. They'll all be proud of you."

"I'm sure..." the Rabbi whispered, raising his emerald eyes, which shimmered with pride as he gazed at the SS officer. "God be with you, Joseph."

"Just this once..." Klammer sighed. He looked down at Danny, who was fiddling with the Rabbi's striped cap, and patted the boy's cheek.

"Be good, okay?" he pleaded. "You're gonna see Papa again, but only if you win the quiet game."

"Okay!" Daniel said with radiant enthusiasm, still blissfully ignorant of all that was going on. Joseph pinched the toddler's cheek, then looked down at Little Martin, who was glaring into the button eyes of a toy cat. He held the ratty stuffed animal by its neck, squeezing its throat, futilely trying to throttle the toy and rid himself of whatever awful feelings it inspired within him.

"I'm sorry," Joseph said. "I don't want to take your doctor from you...at least he's here for your birthday."

"Doctor Rabbi's doing a mitzvah," replied Martin with a shrug. "So it's okay. Besides, it's not my birthday today. It's the day the Kommandant stole me...he just says it's my birthday."

"Oh..." Klammer whispered. "I...well...I guess it's a good thing I didn't buy you a present."

Martin giggled, looking up from his stuffed animal. "It's okay. I've been a good little Nazi, so the Kommandant probably got me something big, a big stolen toy. The other guards probably got me...socks with little swastikas on them."

"Come now, Martin: the guards here are evil, but none of them are *that* evil," joked Joseph, earning another giggle from the child. Little Martin looked at him, his eyes twinkling, and Joseph felt a pool of pride form in his chest. He had made the miserable boy smile on his not-birthday.

That kid never smiled...not really. He smiled when he was with Danny and the Rabbi, but everywhere else, when the Kommandant paraded him around and the guards gave him candy, he just had dead eyes. I hated leaving him there to be miserable, but if the Kommandant woke up and his "son" was gone, the whole operation could fail. He seemed to understand...he didn't make a fuss.

"Thanks for being nice, Sergeant Klammer," Little Martin said. "Please don't die."

"I'll try my best," snorted Joseph. He knelt down and offered the boy his hand, which Martin eagerly grabbed. The Nazi and the kidnapped Czech shook hands, and Vilém was surprised by the strength of the sick little boy's grasp.

Joseph left the infirmary, exited the Kommandant's property, and ventured back into the camp area. A terrible, familiar smell drew his attention to the electrified fence. The Kommandant was snapping a picture of a twisted, tiny body that hung from the barbed wire.

"Iveta..." whispered Vilém, barely able to recognize the burnt remains of Jana's great aunt. "Oh no, she missed the Freedom Train by a day..."

Poor kid...wish I'd known. Wish Little Martin had known, he would have fought to keep her in the house if he had...

"Klammer!" the Kommandant cried. "Where you off to?"

"I was just wishing Little Martin a happy birthday and I saw that your gardener left a mess," lied Joseph, cracking his knuckles. "I want to teach him a lesson."

"Got it!" chuckled the Kommandant. "Don't be *too* harsh, though. We don't want any trouble."

"Right. No trouble..." muttered Joseph, letting his eyes dart to Iveta's body and barely holding in the urge to gag as he slipped into Barrack Three. Most of the prisoners who normally slept in the barrack were out working, making guns and assembling trucks for the Nazis. The only Jews that remained were those too sick to move, those left to die alone.

"Sam!" Joseph whispered, kneeling beside the gardener's bunk. Sam, still terribly ill, hardly stirred.

"Sam, please get up! Listen to me: you have to leave with the others tomorrow. Even if you feel like you're going to die if you move, you *must* move. I'm going to free you and your boy, but you must get on the train tomorrow."

"Train, what train...?" mumbled Sam, sleepily sitting up on his elbow.

"You're going to be deported..."

"To where?"

"Doesn't matter, I *will* free you and every other Jew on the train. You need to meet up with a man named Rabbi Yosef. He will have your boy. Find him on the Platform, get your boy, and survive."

"You're going to save us all?" Sam asked, hope seemingly giving him strength. Joseph reached out, cupping Sam's gaunt face in his hands.

"Listen to me, Samuel Svoboda," Joseph said, almost nose-to-nose with the gardener, his heart throbbing painfully against his chest. "If anything happens tomorrow, I want you and everyone else to know that I'm doing this for you. Not for glory, God, not for the Jews and not because I'm good. I'm doing this for you. Because I love you."

He started to pull Sam close.

Er! Uhm!

But Klammer's spirit forced the memory to vanish into blackness before Vilém could have the extremely uncomfortable experience of knowing what kissing his great-grandfather felt like.

Er, sorry...I...well...you get the point and...uh...yeah, that's your relative...so...sorry.

"Ha! Thanks!" chuckled Vilém. "I can die happy without living through that. Uhm...did he kiss back, though?"

...Yes.

"He really loved you."

Maybe if things had been different, I could have been a home-wrecker in addition to all my other bad qualities.

"Haha! You were always so nice to Rebecca and Sam's kids, though."

Whatever he may have felt for me, he loved them. I would have never asked him to destroy his life on my behalf. They made him happy. It wasn't their fault I could have never done as much.

"You still saved his life. Speaking of which..."

Ah. The train. Well, the operation almost went down flawlessly.

"Almost?" Vilém dared to ask, and a new memory started up.

"Hey, that Jew's getting away!"

Joseph was standing on top of the train, on the cattle car closest to the engine. His blonde hair whipped in his face as he watched Doctor Yosef leap from the Auschwitz Train and bolt towards the woods. The Doctor was wise enough to run in a zigzag, but every one of Joseph's comrades gathered on the caboose.

We used to get extra rations and a day off if we shot an escapee, Joseph's spirit explained as the Nazis eagerly took aim at the running Jew. *I knew they couldn't resist.*

Joseph acted quickly, raising his gun and opening fire on his comrades. He was too late, however, and one of the SS men fired off a shot that toppled the Doctor. Joseph heard a girl scream. The Rabbi's daughter had seen everything.

"What the...?" Schwartz yelped, turning towards the source of the apparent friendly fire. Joseph hesitated only for a moment before he emptied his gun into the young Nazi's chest. Schwartz and the other SS soldiers tumbled off the train, and with the guards neutralized, Joseph struggled against the wind, climbing into the engineer's compartment.

"What happened?" the conductor cried, but Joseph didn't dare offer him an answer. He jabbed the barrel of his gun into the Nazi's heart.

"Would you like to change the train's course, or should I?" he offered, and the conductor, evidently not eager to die for his country, squeaked and nodded pliantly.

"Where to?" the conductor asked, and Joseph commanded

him to switch tracks. The conductor obeyed, and the train chugged along for a few more miles until it arrived at the rendezvous point. Joseph ordered the conductor to stop the train and he obeyed, yanking on the lever. The train screeched to a halt, and once it stopped, Joseph grabbed the conductor and tossed him out of the compartment. The Czech partisans emerged from the woods, lunging at the German conductor, kicking him fiercely before tying his wrists together.

"He'll make a good hostage!" one partisan, whom Vilém recognized as the one Klammer had let escape, yelled to the Sergeant. Joseph jumped down and shook the Czech's hand.

"I'm impressed, Klammer!" the Czech cried. "Half of us didn't think you were actually gonna manage this! The other half thought this was a trap."

"I had a good motivation..." Joseph said. His eyes flitted to the cattle cars and he watched with joyous relief as the Czechs released the baffled Jews.

"You're all free!" the Czechs announced. "The spy freed you!"

"Spy...?" chortled Joseph, and the Jews looked towards their savior, some with suspicion, some with smiles. He tried to find Sam's smile, but he didn't see the gardener. He wanted to find him, to kiss him again, to see him as a free man for the first time...but his heart was hastily reminding him of one last obligation.

"One of the Jews jumped off the train to distract the guards, a Rabbi," Joseph said, opening his arms towards the Czechs and begging, "Do you have a car to spare? Or a bike? I have to go back for him."

"You're sure?" the Czech leader said, clenching his jaw.

"He may still be alive, I *have* to."

"We have a bike, you can take it...but we're going. We can't stay here. If you go back for him and he's alive, you'll have to figure out what to do with him yourself."

"That's fine...just please keep the Jews safe."

"Jews, gentiles. They're all Czechs. We'll protect our people," the partisan assured him. Another Czech pushed a motorcycle towards Joseph, a sputtering machine that more resembled a heap of rusted scraps than a reliable means of transportation. Joseph felt his blood pressure spike at the mere sight of the barely-functioning vehicle, but he huffed, decided that beggars couldn't be choosers, and hopped on.

He sped off, daring to glance over his shoulder, desperate for one last look at Sam.

"Joseph!"

His heart fluttered. Sam had climbed on top of the Freedom Train. He stood there, hugging Daniel. Still gaunt, still sick, but he was free and he knew it. He smiled a smile so radiant it all but burned Joseph's corneas.

Sam waved to him, and though Joseph didn't dare to wave back as taking one hand off the old cycle could have very well sent it careening into a tree, he grinned so widely that Sam must have been able to see it even a mile away.

Klammer rode until he couldn't see the train anymore, following the tracks and finally coming across the bodies. He jumped off the bike and ran to the Doctor's side. Almost-dry blood stained the Rabbi's black-and-white uniform. He wasn't breathing, and when Joseph knelt down and tried to find a pulse, there was merely silence.

"I'm sorry..." he muttered, leaning down and gently shutting the Doctor's eyes. "I wish I knew a Jewish prayer, but..."

Before he could say another word to his deceased partner, a groan made him leap to his feet and pull out his gun. He aimed at the fallen Nazis and discovered that one of his former comrades was stirring.

"Schwartz..." he hissed. He chewed on his lip and Vilém could feel hesitation tugging at his heart. His fingers gingerly touched the trigger. It would be easy to put the teenager out of his misery and run back to Sam, to freedom. It would be easy and it was so, so tempting.

"Fuck me..." But something stopped him. Vilém felt guilt and self-hatred take hold of Klammer and force him to lower his gun. He shoved the weapon back into its holster and carefully approached the young Nazi. Joseph grabbed the injured teen's gun and tossed it into the bushes before slinging the boy's arm over his shoulder and carrying him towards the bike.

"You...you shot me..." groaned Schwartz as Joseph sat him on the bike, which almost crumbled beneath their shared weight.

"And now I'm saving you," Joseph huffed, as though doing so was a chore.

"Why...?"

"Why did I shoot you? Because you deserved it. Why am I saving you? Because I do too. You're a Nazi and so am I..."

"You're not a National Socialist, you're a traitor to the Führer and our people..." mumbled Schwartz, and Joseph let out a bitter laugh.

"Even half-dead you still spit propaganda! Goebbels would be proud," the Sergeant chuckled. "You're a stupid kid that's grown up in a stupid world, and I hope you live long enough to realize that."

"You're gonna get shot..." Schwartz growled.

"Oh, I doubt it," Joseph sighed. "I just unleashed a plague of Jews upon the Fatherland. They'll do far worse to me. It was worth it, though. And you...I hope you can make this worth it."

Slowly as possible, he rode back towards the Camp. The memory shifted to darkness.

I couldn't just let him die...

"You could have lived if you had," Vilém muttered. "Do you know what happened to him?"

No idea. Never saw him again after that day. He didn't even attend my execution. Oh, speaking of which, he was right. I got back to the Camp, he spilled his guts, and I was arrested. Once a proud Aryan superman, now a traitor. I didn't have a fun time...especially since the Kommandant was in a nasty mood. Turns out Little Martin snuck onto the Freedom Train. Kommandant lost his little project.

"I hope he found his family...whatever was left of it," sighed Vilém.

I hope he learned to be a Czech again. I hope he never spoke a word of German again for as long as he lived.

"And you...?"

No regrets, except...

A new memory formed. Vilém shivered. Every inch of Joseph Klammer's body was aching. He had been stripped of his SS regalia and shoved into thin, black-and-white striped garb. He had been beaten, he was starving, and it was so cold. He sat on a small mound of hay in a tiny concrete cell. No bed, no chair, only a bucket for a toilet (which, thankfully, it appeared he hadn't used yet, though perhaps that was because he'd been given nothing to eat or drink.)

There was a *clang* from somewhere nearby and the sound of footsteps echoed throughout the cell block: one set of jackboots and one set of heels.

"Visitor," a Nazi guard grunted, standing near the cell as Joseph's mother approached the bars. Joseph stood too quickly and almost fell over; his legs felt like pudding, but through pure willpower he managed to stumble towards his mother, collapsing before her, clutching the bars.

"Mama..." he sighed, finally allowing some weakness to show

as he looked up at her face, hungry for the smallest smidgeon of affection.

But she scowled at her son like he was a diseased worm. Frau Klammer inhaled deeply and then spat right in Joseph's face. He yelped and recoiled, rubbing the spittle out of his eyes and seething when he heard the Nazi guard snicker.

"You're no son of mine," Frau Klammer declared. "You're a traitor to the Führer and the nation. You are a filthy little nothing and you will die alone."

Joseph scowled, peering into his mother's eyes, trying to find a sign that she was lying, that she was only saying this because she was scared, because she was forced to, because she *had* to.

But there was nothing. The mother that had once kissed his cheek and called him her pride looked upon him with eyes of ice. She meant it. She loved Hitler more than her own son.

Vilém had always thought of his mother as one of his best friends, and had often, during his low points, been afraid of disappointing her. On those terrible occasions when he had fucked up enough to earn her ire, he had felt like a boot was being laid upon his back, crushing him like a bug. But Lida Rehor had always lifted that weight right off his shoulders. She had always assured him that she would love him no matter what.

He would need to visit Lida again after this, to give her a hug, to see the love pouring from her eyes. Feeling Joseph's soul shatter beneath his mother's boot felt almost as bad as any death he had experienced in a memory. Frau Klammer turned and marched away with a slight bounce in her step, as though she had just done something truly brave.

I wish she would have let me talk.

"I...I'm sorry, Sergeant, I don't think I could arrange a reunion," Vilém sighed as the memory shifted. Joseph was standing on a platform above a small crowd of Nazis. Neither

Schwartz nor Frau Klammer were anywhere to be seen. Joseph searched the sneering onlookers, but found no familiar face to latch onto.

"Was it worth it, Klammer?" the Kommandant's arrogant voice sneered in his ear. Joseph glanced at his former boss. Gerber was leaning against a post with a noose.

"Absolutely," Klammer proclaimed, forcing his face to remain expressionless even as his eyes frantically darted here and there, trying to find a comforting thing to look at while he died.

But there was nothing. Barbed wire, watchtowers, barracks, and swastikas. The forest was distant and enshrouded in shadow, and there were no more flowers decorating the Kommandant's home.

The Kommandant reached up and tugged on the noose. "Piano wire," he said. "Traitors don't get a rope."

"I get it, it's gonna hurt," grunted Joseph. "I have many regrets, Kommandant, but I'll never regret freeing those people."

"*People!*" scoffed the Kommandant. "You *are* gone."

"I was..." sighed Joseph. With nothing else to look at, he turned his gaze towards Barrack Three, which was wonderfully, mercifully empty. He smiled even as the noose was wrapped around his neck, even as the wire sliced into his skin, even as the executioner lifted him up and he dangled by his neck, his body convulsing...

Enough!

And suddenly, it was over, and Vilém was back in Barrack Three. Klammer had kicked him out of his final memory. Grunting with ire, Vilém shut his eyes and touched the wall once more.

"Why'd you do that?" he asked.

You get the picture. I died. It lasted a while. It hurt. I don't want you to experience it, there's no need.

"I...thanks, I guess...the feeling of dying is never...pleasant..." muttered Vilém, rubbing his neck and inhaling deeply, enjoying the cool and assuring sensation of air sweeping into his lungs.

"So," Vilém said. "Thank you for showing me all that, and thanks for being honest. It's...nice to know a little more about what happened to my family. It's...different from what I was told...not that I was told much...but it's...good to know, it gives me perspective. I owe you a lot, and I want to help you however I can, Sergeant Klammer. Why are you still here? What's your unfinished business?"

Isn't it obvious?

"Is it your mom? I'm sorry, but I really don't think I can help you with that."

No! It's this! This whole exhibit! Don't you get it? It's all a lie! I'm not a hero! Doctor Yosef is! He died for his people, I only tried to save someone I loved! That doesn't make me a hero! I was selfish and stupid and I don't deserve any of this! I want the truth to get out there! I want everyone to know that I'm not a hero!

"But you *are* a hero, Sergeant!" Vilém argued.

I am not! All of these streets named for me, these memorials, they should all be taken down and redone. I want Rabbi Yosef to be honored instead of me! He deserves all of this love, he was truly brave, not a selfish piece of shit like me...

"Rabbi Yosef died for *his* daughter, for *his* people," Vilém pointed out. "Does that make *him* selfish?"

Of course not!

"Well, you're not selfish for doing what you did to save someone you loved, then!" Vilém proclaimed. "You did it, and you did it for a good reason. That doesn't mean the terrible things you did before are just...erased, but it does mean you're not the same Joseph Klammer who did those things."

But...

"Shut up, you've talked all night, now let me talk!" Vilém exclaimed. "I'm proof that you're a hero. Do you know how many people are here because of what you did? Those four hundred Jews and all of their children and their children's children. Entire generations are going to exist because of you."

I told you before, it's not about the numbers! One murder does not equal one saved life! The seven people I shot? The hundreds I helped deport? What about them? What about their families and descendants that aren't going to exist now?

"They matter too, they matter, Joseph. I'm not telling you to stop feeling guilty about the crimes you actually committed. But...you need to have some perspective. You were a stupid kid. I know that's no excuse, I know other stupid kids like Schwartz never learned, and maybe you just got lucky by meeting Sam. Maybe if you hadn't met him, you would have lived and died a Nazi. But all of those what ifs and comparisons are pointless."

I...

"You're a hero because of *what you did* when push came to shove. You're not just a hero because we respect you, you're a hero because you saw the truth and you did something. There were so many horrible choices you could have made that would have made your life easier, but in the end, you made more good choices than bad. You're a good person. Know how I can tell?"

I'm afraid to ask.

"My great-grandpa liked you and my family is made up of geniuses," joked Vilém. "But seriously: you went back for Schwartz, you saved him even though you *knew* he'd turn you in. Because you're not arrogant. Because you have empathy. Because you *are* a hero."

Vilém sighed. "And I get it, we kinda turned you into a...non-person, just a flawless hero, and you're not flawless. But nobody is. In those days everyone made mistakes, and back then mistakes destroyed lives. If you want, right after I'm done writing about Raya, I'll write a book about you and include all your dirty laundry. But I'm still gonna call you a hero. You sacrificed your own happiness and comfort, you risked your life and you did the right thing. You are a hero."

You are Sam's descendant.

"I'll take that as a compliment."

You should. I...I really want Doctor Yosef to get the credit he deserves.

"I'll start hunting down documents and testimony," Vilém promised. "He'll get his own exhibit if I have to build it myself."

Ha! All right. But...I'm...scared. I don't know what'll happen if I leave. I don't know what the...standards are. I just...if I were God, I wouldn't let me into Heaven. I just...I don't think I deserve it.

"And that," Vilém said, "is why you're a good person. You're humble, you're good, and you really regret all of the horrible things you did. You're going to Heaven, Joseph Klammer. If you don't get in, nobody gets in."

You're being too nice. I...I'd really like to see Sam again.

"Then go."

I'm just...

"Get outta here, ghost! Go! You've done enough down here! Go on! Go be a homewrecker in Heaven!"

Klammer's spirit laughed. *Fine, Jesus, I'll do whatever you want, just stop nagging me!*

"Do me a favor," Vilém said. "Say hi to my grandpa for me."

I will. I'll give Sam and David a big hug for you. Bye, Vilém. Thanks for listening.

Vilém raised an eyebrow, but forced his mouth to stay shut, not wanting to keep the valiant spirit there for one more minute. He felt a wave of affection wash over him, and suddenly, the ghost was gone.

Vilém stood, stretched, and walked to the front of the exhibit, staring at Joseph Klammer's image. Terribly flawed, terribly brave, terribly human in all the best ways. He smiled and saluted the stalwart Sergeant.

"Bye, hero. Hope you drown in love up there," he said. He fiddled with his flashlight, gazing into Klammer's frozen eyes and cursing his rotten luck. Despite offering him so many answers, Klammer had left him with a question more intense than any little query he had possessed before.

"Who's David?"

BARRACK TWO

"I'm pregnant."

The announcement struck Vilém Rehor like a sledge-hammer to the gut. He stood before his girlfriend, who cradled her not-yet-showing belly and pronounced her pregnancy with restrained fear. He had treated her well tonight: dinner, a walk in the park, and now they stood by a water fountain, Jana grimacing, Vilém gawking at her.

He gave her a moment to declare that she was just kidding. When she didn't, he clenched his jaw. A whirlwind of emotions went through him. Happiness, love, nervousness, excitement...it all hit at once and he was shocked when his body still managed to move.

"Well...I guess this is appropriate, then," he said. He reached into his pocket and pulled out a small box, dropping to one knee. The atmosphere changed immediately: Jana lit up like a star and Vilém grinned.

"Oh, you asshole!" Jana screamed. She heard laughter nearby

and looked towards the bushes. Erik, Vilém's best friend, was hiding in the thicket, recording the proposal on his phone.

"Now, I warn you: I'm too broke to buy a ring, so..." Vilém opened the box, revealing a sapphire flower, pressed and preserved in a little glass oval. Jana realized what it was right away: Klammer's flower, the one he had given Vilém's great-grandfather.

"How...?" she whispered.

"Good question! I think Rebecca had it. I looked through the attic at Mom's house and recognized the tin," Vilém said. Jana looked at the box again and realized it wasn't a box, but an almost century-old tin. She could barely make out a duo of cherries printed on the front. An ancient cough-drop tin. Sam had saved it, stored the precious flower in it, and now Vilém was offering it to his beloved.

"Vilém, I can't take this!"

"You can if you become my wife!" Vilém said. "By the way, wanna be my wife?"

"Yes, I wanna be your wife, dummy! I love you!" she cried, lunging at him. The now-engaged couple toppled to the sidewalk.

"Congrats, buddy!" Erik laughed. "Jana, be careful, don't kill him before the wedding!"

"I'll try!" giggled Jana, rolling off her fiancée. She grabbed his hand and kissed his knuckles, and Vilém had never felt so happy.

Jana hugged the cough-drop tin and the preserved cornflower close to her heart, tears falling from her eyes. She squealed as though she had just won the lottery.

"Oh, I'm gonna be a wife!" she cried, grasping her fiancé's hand and pressing it to her belly. "I'm gonna be a wife and you're gonna be a daddy!"

And then there was that. That...well, *that* he hadn't been expecting, but Vilém wasn't disappointed. Not in the least. His old life as an immature young adult was over, and now...now he was going to have a little bundle of responsibilities.

"I'm *so* not ready!" he laughed as he pulled his wife-to-be into a hug. "I'm so not ready, this is gonna be crazy! I'm gonna be a dad!"

He stood up with a hoot, announcing to the smiling onlookers and everyone else in earshot, "I'm gonna be a dad!"

"So lemme guess: 'I forgot a condom just one time.'"

"Oh, shut up, Erik."

"Am I wrong? C'mon, man, I know ya'."

"...Twice."

"Lucky you! Ha!" Erik smacked his friend on the shoulder. Jana had gone back to the sweet shop to tell her grandmother that she was engaged. Erik, meanwhile, had dragged Vilém to the bar to celebrate the merry occasion.

"Happy accident!" Vilém said, taking a swig of beer. "Jesus Christ, I'm like...happy and I feel like I'm back in school about to take a pop quiz! It's a totally alien feeling, I can't even really describe it. I'm gonna be married and a dad! Wow..."

He grinned at his friend and said, "I'm an adult now!"

Erik snickered, clinking his mug against Vilém's. "Always knew you'd mature before me. I'm gonna be best man, right? And godfather?"

"Jana's probably gonna wanna raise the little one Jewish, Erik, and I'm deferring to her."

"Damn it!"

"Look, considering where I work, if I can bring a brand-new little Jew into the world, I'll feel a little better."

"Ha! Every new baby Jew makes Hitler spin in his grave. Oh, speaking of your job, though: I didn't wanna bring this up since you're celebrating, but I got some info that may help you complete your mission."

Vilém shoved his mug away and forced his jubilant spirit to settle. For months, he had been struggling to fulfill Joseph Klammer's last wish and give Doctor Yosef the recognition he deserved. Unfortunately, Vilém still didn't know the Doctor's full name, and even combing through the Camp's archives had yielded nothing. Kommandant Gerber had covered his tracks well. There was nothing about Raya, Iveta, Little Martin, or the Doctor-Rabbi. The Nazi Regime's power to destroy so much information, to annihilate lives physically and in writing, was almost as impressive as it was frightening. It was a small miracle that historians knew as much about the Holocaust as they did given the lengths the SS had gone to covering it up.

"So," Erik said, pulling out a small piece of paper. "I get a call to fix a toilet at the hotel. I go in and the room's guest is this old guy, like really old, older than Granny Illa. German guy, but y'know, there are Germans who live here, not a big red flag. We end up chatting and I ask him why he's in town. He says he comes once a year to leave flowers for Sergeant Klammer, says the guy saved his life. Not a big deal, y'know, must be one of the Jews from the Freedom Train, but he ends up leaving a tip for me with his credit card and look..."

Erik pulled out the receipt and pushed it towards Vilém. The name of the customer was printed in bold at the bottom of the paper: Helmut Schwartz.

"You're kidding..." whispered Vilém. Schwartz, the young

Nazi that Joseph had gone back for, the foolish child who had been unquestioningly loyal to the Nazis.

"I mean, I know Schwartz isn't an uncommon name, but it's a little...much," said Erik.

"If it *is* him, he's taking a risk coming here every year," Vilém observed, scowling at the former Nazi's name. "He may have been young back then, but he's still a war criminal. He must have a warrant on his head."

"He must...but he's old. Maybe at this point he doesn't care if he dies in a cell."

"Well," said Vilém, leaning back and smirking as he curled the receipt around his finger. "It would be a shame if someone *happened* to turn him in. Unless he has some good info or could give a statement."

"Vil, you're becoming a history vigilante. I love it. Let's get to the hotel before he drops dead."

"Hey, Herr Schwartz, can I come back in? I'm the plumber from earlier."

Vilém scowled as the old man opened the door to his suite and invited Erik and his "associate" inside. SS Private Helmut Schwartz had not aged gracefully: liver spots covered his bald head, his Aryan blue eyes had weakened to the point where he needed inch-thick glasses to see, and he had developed a Quasimodo-like hunch. He smiled at the two Czechs with such sweetness that nobody would have suspected he once considered their race undesirable.

"Oh, I'm sorry, I've tried not to use it," Schwartz said, scooting towards the restroom, but stopping halfway and taking a seat on the foot of his bed. "This happens every time I come here, something breaks, but it *is* the only hotel in town so...can't be picky."

"I imagine you've experienced worse in your lifetime," Vilém said. "Private Schwartz."

It was a miracle the old Nazi didn't keel over of a heart attack right then. He froze, his weary eyes flitting from Vilém to Erik.

Erik retreated into the bathroom to let Vilém do his work. Vilém leaned against the door, blocking off the Nazi's only escape.

"Am...I under arrest?" Schwartz asked.

"You should be," Vilém snarled. "You should have been arrested decades ago."

"Yes...you're right," sighed Schwartz, looking down at his gnarled hands. "I should have. If I were a good man, I would have turned myself in after I realized what I was, but...I only have one life, and I didn't feel like spending it in prison."

"Those Jews only had one life too," Vilém accused, pointing in the direction of the Camp. "You and your comrades took that from them. And here you are...old. Must be nice. Do your kids know?"

"I have none."

"Good," scoffed Vilém, pleased that Schwartz never had and never would feel the explosion of uncertain joy that came with becoming a father. "So you're here for Klammer?"

"I can explain..."

"You don't have to," Vilém said. "I know you were on Klammer's Train, and I know he shot you, then saved you. I know he took you back to the Camp and you sold him out. I know it's *your* fault he's dead."

What little color still clung to the old man's face faded. "H-how could you possibly know that?"

"I know a lot," Vilém said with a dismissive wave of his wrist.

"But the Kommandant told everyone *I* captured Klammer! N-nobody knows what really happened except for me!"

"That so?" Vilém said. "I don't suppose there are more tidbits of history that *only you* know..."

Schwartz folded his hands on his lap, trembling. "So am I under arrest? Is this an interrogation?"

"In a way. You come here every year to honor Klammer, so I assume you've had something of a change of heart."

"Of course!" exclaimed Schwartz. "Listen, I know I'm a terrible person. I've tried my best all my life to make up for what I did as a boy. I've worked, I've given to charity, I've given my time and my blood...I've tried, and I think I've done better outside of jail than I would have inside. I know I can't make up for what I did to Sergeant Klammer and those people during the war..."

"*People*," Vilém repeated, rolling the word on his tongue and nodding slowly. "All right, I guess you *have* changed. And you're right: there's nothing you can do to make up for it, but I'm not going to have you arrested. That's not my job, and I don't know you well enough to decide how much you've really repented. All I know is you're here, and you owe Klammer. So do I, and I'm trying to help him settle an old wish."

"Wish...?"

"Long story short: Klammer had help organizing the capture of the Auschwitz Train, a man named Doctor Yosef who used to work for the Kommandant's...'son.'"

"Little Martin?"

"That's the one. The Doctor distracted the Nazis while Klammer shot you assholes in the back."

"Oh...he was the man who jumped..." Schwartz whispered.

"Precisely, and Klammer wanted to make sure he went down as a hero."

"How do you know that? Did Klammer keep a diary or something? He didn't speak much after we got back to the Camp, and his mother..."

"My great-grandpa Sam was his closest friend," Vilém explained, not precisely lying, but also avoiding the topic of ghosts all together. He didn't have time to explain the afterlife to the old Nazi.

"Oh...I see..." Schwartz mumbled. "Well, I *do* know who you're talking about. What do you need to know?"

"His full name, firstly."

"Oh! Right! I forgot Little Martin just called him 'Doctor Rabbi.' It was Yosef Doubek, he was from a little Jewish village in the south."

"What?"

Erik voiced Vilém's thoughts perfectly as he burst out of the bathroom, his eyes bulging.

"Doubek?" he cried, gawking at Vilém. "Like your crazy boss Doubek? *That* Doubek?!"

"Doubek's a common enough last name, it may be a coincidence," Vilém muttered, trying to maintain a calm facade even as shock almost made his jaw drop. "Did the Rabbi have a daughter?"

"He did, yes. We weren't allowed to touch her, that was the deal he had with Kommandant Gerber. I think her name was Alica."

"Yep...that's Ms. Doubek's first name," sighed Vilém, running a hand through his messy dark hair. "That doesn't make any sense...if his daughter's the museum's director, why was it so impossible to find anything about him?"

"If it were *my* dad, I would'a made an exhibit just for him," said Erik. Vilém chewed on his thumbnail, pondering this revelation. Ms. Doubek might have been a bitch, but if she really was the Rabbi's daughter, she could be helpful. She could offer trustworthy testimony about what her father had done, and then it would be easy to fulfill Klammer's wish.

"Listen," Vilém said, gesturing for Erik to take out his phone and start recording. "We're not going to have you arrested, but Joseph Klammer wanted the world to know the truth. I need you to give me your testimony. Can you do that? For him?"

Schwartz clutched the bedspread with trembling hands, shaking his head. But he looked out the window, towards the Camp, and Vilém could see guilt chew at the ex-Nazi's soul until he had no choice but to consent.

"For him, of course. I'll tell you anything you want to know."

"Good," said Vilém, grabbing a chair from a nearby desk and sitting across from the former SS officer. "First question: do you know who 'David' is?"

Private Schwartz did not know who 'David' was. In fact, he could hardly be called a well of knowledge. As a mere Private, he had not been privy to most of the Kommandant's grand secrets, but he was able to testify that Doctor Doubek had existed, that he had worked for Sergeant Klammer, and that he had helped save those four hundred people on the Auschwitz Train.

With a copy of the footage in hand, Vilém went to work. He weaved through the crowds of students, mourners, and amateur historians.

"Hey!" he shouted at the day guard. "You know where Doubek is?"

"The Kommandant?" snickered the day guard. "Barrack Two, women's exhibit."

"Thanks," sighed Vilém, rolling his eyes at the nickname. Though Ms. Doubek had certainly earned the derision of her employees, after everything he had experienced and after getting to know just how evil the real Kommandant had been, that epithet made Vilém's gut churn.

He trudged into Barrack Two, which was a barrack he tended to avoid. The barrack, which had once housed over a hundred women, now featured an exhibit on women's experiences during the Holocaust. As mothers, as daughters, as survivors.

Vilém shivered and averted his eyes from one placard that offered an article about sexual assault in the Camp. Since the prisoners had by and large been "dirty Jews", it had been rare, but not unheard of, for the guards to take advantage of the denizens of Barrack Two. Several SS officers had been arrested for offenses against female prisoners. Not because they committed rape, of course, but because they betrayed their pure German blood, forcing themselves on undesirables. To the Nazi Regime, raping a Jew was equivalent to bestiality.

Vilém inhaled sharply and forced himself to look at the pictures of the shaved, skinny women. Fire rose up in his chest when he saw images of little girls being pulled from their mothers' arms. He looked at the formerly faceless women and saw Jana. He looked at the sobbing little girls and a paternal flare consumed his heart as he imagined his potential daughter amongst them.

He bit his bottom lip, looking into the women's eyes, trying to find a young Ms. Doubek.

"Rehor! What are you staring at?"

Vilém whirled around. Ms. Doubek had snuck up behind him. She looked as angry with life as ever, but for once Vilém didn't scoff at her attitude. If she was the very same Alica Doubek who had lived in this horrid barrack during the Holocaust, he was impressed. If he had lived through what she had, he wouldn't have been able to work at the Camp.

"Hello, Ms. Doubek," he said. The old woman raised an unkept eyebrow and snorted.

"Don't try to soften me up, I know what happened," huffed his boss. "Ms. Sladký called me earlier and bitched my ear off, told me to be nice to you because you're going to be her grandson-in-law soon, and you're apparently giving her a great-grandchild."

She jabbed at him with a pencil. "I always figured you were the irresponsible sort. I hope you don't expect me to give you time off for a wedding *and* paternity leave. I'm not going to pay for your bad decisions."

"'Bad decisions'?" repeated Vilém with a smirk, more amused than offended. Doubek snarled and pressed her pencil into his chest so forcefully he could feel the lead stabbing into his skin.

"Bad! Decisions!" she snapped, emphasizing each word with a stab. "And you'd better not even think of dragging little Dumbass Junior to the Camp and have him or her or it pitch a fit and ruin the atmosphere!"

"I'm not gonna bring my *baby* to a concentration camp, ma'am...who does that?"

"Irresponsible morons who have children before they can afford a babysitter, that's who!" Doubek declared, tapping her pencil against his chest one last time before tucking it back into her suit pocket. "I see them every day. One of these days, I'm gonna give you the day shift, Rehor. Then you can see the shit I have to put up with from the general public."

"I'm sure I have it easy at night, ma'am," chuckled Vilém.

"Was that sarcasm?"

"Honestly, no, I don't think you're wrong," Vilém said. "But Ms. Doubek, my personal life's really not important."

"Precisely: that's why I'm warning you not to bother me about it. Also, please tell your fiancée's grandma to stop calling the Camp! I know her sister died here, but that doesn't give her the right to tell me how to do my job!"

"Uhm...sure, ma'am. I'll get on that. But actually, I wanted to talk to you about *your* family. You see," Vilém pulled the flash drive out of his pocket and offered it to the director. "I've been doing a bit of independent research and collecting some testimonies, and I found some info about a man that I think is your father, Rabbi-Doctor Yosef Doubek. He helped Sergeant Klammer save the Jews on..."

Before he could say another word, Ms. Doubek grabbed the drive and threw it to the floor. Vilém yelped in shock as she brought her boot down on the drive, shattering it with a single stomp.

"What the Hell?!" cried Vilém, and a few visitors gawked at the altercation, some pulling their phones out of their pockets and snagging a video.

"*Come here,*" Ms. Doubek snarled, grabbing her employee by the arm and dragging him out of Barrack Two. She pulled him behind the wooden structure and shoved him against the outer wall.

"Listen," she growled, shoving her finger in his face. "And listen well: my father lived as a fool, he died as a fool, and he deserves to be remembered as a fool. I've done him a favor by making sure he's forgotten. I've put up with your weird shit too long, boy. If you start digging into my life, I will fire you, and I will make sure you and your new little family starve. Understood?"

Vilém might have been intimidated a year ago, but experiencing the lives of Holocaust victims had hardened him to such relatively meager threats. He squinted down at his boss. Behind the anger, behind the seething, behind the clenched teeth, there was something else: sadness.

Of course, probing would do no good. Better to wait. Wait and hope that someone long gone would offer him answers tonight.

"Understood, ma'am. I'm sorry."

"Good," she huffed, straightening up and combing her fingers through her gray hair. "Now enough playing amateur historian. Get your flashlight and get ready for work! And if I even suspect that you've gone anywhere near my office…"

"I'll stick to the barracks, ma'am. Don't worry."

Ms. Doubek grunted. Her dark eyes darted to Barrack Two and Vilém saw a slight shiver wrack her body before she turned and stomped over to a group of day guards, screeching at them for lollygagging.

Vilém waited behind the barrack to make sure Ms. Doubek was busy harassing the other employees before he snuck back into Barrack Two. Since the ghosts typically showed up in a barrack that held some significance to them, he assumed Barrack Two would yield something.

"C'mon, Doctor," he whispered as the sun set and the Camp became empty once more. "Give me something here…."

Once the gates were locked, the lights were off, and Vilém was seemingly left alone, he started wandering around Barrack Two with his eyes closed, touching every corner, every artifact, every picture.

Right when he was about to give up, his hands found a cluster of pictures displayed near the back of the barrack. He sensed something, though just barely. While the other spirits had been eager to chat, this one seemed intent on making himself scarce. Vilém smiled and sunk to his knees, getting comfortable before calling out.

"Doctor Doubek?"

He heard the spirit unleash a sigh so heavy he might have been holding it since the war.

I guess it's my turn.

"So do you ghosts talk to each other...?"

Never, but I knew Joseph was still here. I never talked to him, though. I tried, but I couldn't. It seems you have a gift.

"Somehow," sighed Vilém. "I guess Ilona spoke to Iveta, but I can talk to ghosts I don't have any connection to. It's...weird, but I hope I'm putting this 'gift' to good use. Speaking of good...y'know, it's kinda funny, you and Klammer. Joseph and Yosef. The same name, but very different people. And yet...you're both heroes."

A chill struck Vilém's heart, and he could practically feel the ghost shake its ethereal head.

I'm no hero. I'm many things, but I'm no hero.

"Don't tell me I'm gonna have to give you the same speech I gave Klammer."

Oh, boychik, you have no idea what I did. Joseph's sins were all committed with the best of intentions. He always did what he thought was noble. Me? No. There's a reason my daughter despises me.

"Enlighten me, please, Rabbi," Vilém begged.

I'm...not sure you'd understand. And...I don't want to be judged.

"Sir, whatever you did, you did it during the Holocaust. I can't promise I won't judge you, but I'll take the circumstances into account."

Are you a father, young man?

Vilém smiled, that now almost-familiar feeling of uncertain joy filling his soul. "I will be very soon."

Mazel tov! Well, then maybe you will understand. Very well, but please do not become as angry as my little Alica.

"I can promise that, I don't think that'd be physically possible," Vilém vowed. The

Rabbi's ghost chuckled softly.

Very well...hm...I think this all began when Alica was born.

Vilém felt as though he had been gently pushed. He fell and fell until finally, he found himself sitting in a dimly-lit synagogue sanctuary.

He was seeing the world through the Rabbi's eyes, feeling what he had felt a lifetime ago, and the intense clash of emotions that the Rabbi was experiencing was dizzying. Pain beyond measure...and love so overwhelming he felt like his chest might implode. The Rabbi was sitting on a small staircase that led to a clear glass arc, holding a little bundle in his arms.

He pulled back a bit of the blanket, revealing a baby's face. Ms. Alica Doubek. Only a few hours old.

It was a wonderful day...and a terrible day. My little Alica came at the cost of her mother.

"Oh...I'm sorry." Vilém shivered at the notion, mentally thanking God for letting him live in an era where death during childbirth was so rare. He couldn't imagine what he would do without Jana, with the baby...he was already certain he was going to fuck up being a father, being a single father would destroy him.

It was more than a lifetime ago, boychik. I've come to terms with it. But it meant that Alica was to be my only child, all I had left in the world.

The Rabbi leaned down and kissed his newborn baby's forehead. "I'll always protect you, Alica, my little sunshine."

Vilém might have laughed under different circumstances. "Little sunshine?"

I always called her that, and when she was little, she was. Even without her mother, Alica was a little ray of light. In the community, I was known for being somewhat liberal. I was a man of science and God, a doctor and a Rabbi. I believed that knowledge should flow freely, to boys and girls alike, and while many Rabbis reserved their classrooms for boys only, I taught any child who wanted to learn about our faith. My little Alica was my best student.

"Children!" A new memory started. Rabbi Doubek was clapping his hands together, sending chalk dust flying into his face. He let out an exaggerated cough, causing the children that sat before him to giggle. Boys in kippahs, sporting sidelocks, sat beside little girls wearing head coverings. They all held notebooks and pencils. Rabbi Doubek's eyes fell upon a little girl in the front row, a little girl with curly brown hair, chocolate-colored eyes, and a smile that made the Rabbi's heart melt.

"Aww...she was cute," Vilém confessed as the Rabbi tenderly gazed at seven-year-old Alica Doubek.

The Rabbi turned to look at an illustration he had made on the blackboard. A picture of a woman standing atop a wall, throwing a goofily-drawn severed head down to a waiting soldier. The head had X's for eyes and a tongue sticking out the side of his mouth, somewhat alleviating the morbidity of the drawing.

"Now!" the Rabbi said. "For today's lesson, we are going to discuss the permissibility of..."

"Cutting someone's head off?" one little boy interrupted. A wave of giggles went through the little classroom and the Rabbi shook his head.

"Close, but no, Chassed. Today we will discuss the incident of Sheva Ben Bichri and what his story teaches us about sacrifices. Now, since I assume you all read your Tanakh passage for class today..."

The Rabbi shot an accusatory glare towards one particular nose-picker, who blushed and hid his face behind his Bible.

With a chuckle, the Rabbi continued. "I'll keep it short: Sheva Ben Bichri rebelled against King David, and when David's forces tried to capture him, he hid in the city of Abel. This is where we learn the story of the Wise Woman of Abel. When King David's forces started to sack the city, threatening to destroy it, she took it upon herself to make a deal with David's commander to save the city and all within. She convinced the people of Abel to behead Sheva Ben Bichri, and they tossed his head over the wall. Thus, Abel was saved."

The Rabbi pointed with a ruler towards the picture he had drawn. "Now, what we must ask ourselves is: was this a mitzvah or a sin? Are we permitted to give up one for the lives of many? The Talmud teaches us that should someone say to us, 'Go kill so-and-so or I will kill you', we are not permitted to do so. One man's blood is just as red as another's, and it is not permissible for us, as humans, to say that we are more worthy of life than another human. Only God, in all of His wisdom, may decide that."

"Papa...err, Rabbi!" Alica chirped, shoving her hand into the air. The Rabbi beamed at his daughter's enthusiasm and gestured for her to speak.

"So, Papa, the Talmud says we have to *shev ve'al ta'aseh*—sit and do nothing—if that happens. If a gentile comes and says, 'Give us two Jews', we're not allowed to do that even if they threaten all the Jews. So...we all just have to sit and do nothing and let more people die?"

"In a way, Alica."

"Well, I'm confused, then: why didn't God punish the city of Abel for killing the rebel?"

"A very good question, Alica, and you're right. The Talmud teaches us that we must not cast lots to choose who lives and who dies. Now, Abel's situation is different. We learn from Maimonides in the *Code of Jewish Law* that if, say, a group of Jews is traveling and come across a group of gentiles, and the gentiles say, 'Give us one of you, or you will all die', then all must die, for we, as men and Jews, cannot decide whose life is worth more."

"But," he continued, "if they come upon the Jews and say,

'Give So-And-So or we will kill you all', then it is permissible to give that specified person over, for then we are not deciding who is more worthy of life, but we are like the Wise Woman of Abel. And if we are the one singled out in such a situation, we are obliged to die for the community, for the greater number of Jews. But it is never permissible to kill for numbers."

The pupils nodded and scribbled down the teaching. Alica finished her notes fastest, smiling up at her father once she was done. She looked at him like he was Moses, like he was the greatest man who had ever lived.

I know she's a very different woman now, but when she was a girl, Alica was happy. She loved school, loved life...loved me. She adored me. I really was her hero.

A dust cloud of chalk whisked the memory away, and a new one took its place. Doctor Doubek was kneeling before a young boy, tending to the child's broken arm while his mother hovered nearby.

"Papa!" Alica's voice cut through the Doctor's focus. He turned and saw that his daughter was standing in the doorway, sporting a black eye.

"Alica, who did that?" he cried, and Vilém almost tumbled out of the memory. The fear and anger that the father felt upon seeing his child hurt was so intense it was almost painful.

The Doctor barely heard the injured boy's mother snap at him. He ignored her harsh plea and abandoned his patient, kneeling before his daughter and cupping her face in his hands. Alica laughed.

"Papa, I just fell off my bike!" the girl cried, pointing to the little boy. "David needs your help!"

Vilém's heart somersaulted at the name, but he reminded himself that he was looking into the memories of a Rabbi from a Jewish village. There were probably a dozen Davids that had nothing to do with Klammer. Broken-Armed David's face was slightly foggy. The Rabbi's attention had been so focused on Alica that everything else seemed cloudy by comparison.

"R-right…" muttered the Rabbi, and he turned his attention back to David, listening with a hammering heart as his wounded daughter skipped away, humming happily.

Nothing seemed to trouble Alica. She was always singing, always bouncing, always dancing…oh, she had two left feet, but she danced like she was possessed and it was so lovely to watch. She loved American music even though she couldn't understand a word of it. This one song, sung by Billy Cotton, it went, "Smile darn ya smile!" It was her favorite, she loved it! Every time it came on the radio…

"Oh, Papa, it's the song!"

A new memory formed from the darkness: the Rabbi was resting in what must have been his study, reading a Hebrew book and sitting in a cozy chair beside a crackling radio. A bouncy American tune filled the whole house and Alica bolted into the study, pushing his book aside.

"Oh, sunshine, you'll make me lose my spot!" the Rabbi complained, though he couldn't repress a small smile as she grabbed his hands and pulled him to his feet.

"Dance, Papa, c'mon!" she laughed as Cotton's voice urged her on.

"Smile darn ya smile!
Y'know this great world is a good world after all!"

Vilém could hardly believe his eyes as he watched little Ms. Doubek move like she was made of water, swaying and spinning and kicking her legs into the air. The Rabbi tried his best to keep up with her enthusiastic movements, but he was no match for his little sunshine.

"C'mere, you crazy girl!" he cried, grabbing her waist and lifting her into the air, spinning her around and around.

"Papaaa, I'm dizzy!" she squealed. He set her back on the ground and she grabbed his hand once more, twirling around and kicking her leg up.

"Things are never black as they are painted
Time for you and joy to get acquainted...
So make life worthwhile,
Come on and smile, darn ya—KKKHHHHHHHHHT!"

But just as Alica was finishing her dance with another kick, she spun too close to the radio and ended up kicking the machine right off the tabletop. It fell to the ground, and the jazzy beat became terrible static.

"Oh, Alica!" sighed the Rabbi. "Look what you did, you crazy girl!"

"Whoops..." muttered Alica sheepishly, and even though she had destroyed what must have been the 1930s equivalent of a giant television, she refused to stop following the song's directive. She still smiled.

We were very happy...at least at first. We lived amongst our own. No gentiles in town, and when gentiles did come to visit, they were always sent right to me. I had spent my youth in Prague, learning medicine, learning about the gentile world. I learned Czech and German, and I learned how to please the gentiles.

"Errr...sorry," Vilém squeaked, suddenly weighed down by gentile guilt.

You're not Jewish?

"One-fourth, my grandfather was a Jew. I'm gonna marry a

Jew and my kid's gonna be a Jew...but, uhm, I don't really believe in anything."

I don't blame you one bit.

A new memory appeared. The Rabbi sat across from a blonde couple, obvious gentiles, in the midst of what must have been his kitchen. His eyes flitted to the nearby living room, where Alica was playing with the gentiles' daughter.

In contrast to the Rabbi's study, his entertaining area was a synagogue of science: every bookshelf boasted medical tomes, every painting featured plants and animals, and statues of eminent doctors and scientists decorated the tabletops. A silver Newton's Cradle sat on a coffee table in the living room. The Rabbi had been very careful not to let his Jewishness show in the spaces where gentile guests were wont to trod, instead opting to make himself look as cultured and Western as possible.

"Doctor...or, Rabbi," the gentile man said. The Rabbi chuckled.

"Yosef will do, Herr Muller!"

"Yosef," Herr Muller said, gesturing to the scientific finery around the room. "I have to say, I never thought that a Jew in such a...primitive community could be so civilized."

"Oh, Herr Muller, I promise I'm not the only one," the Rabbi said. "I know from my travels that even in the great cities, not everyone is privileged with adequate schooling. Such is the case with many Jews. But my people, we are known for our curiosity. We thirst for knowledge even when it seems to contradict our faith."

"You may be better than the Catholics, then," chuckled the German woman. "Thank you for inviting us into your home, I feel like we've learned a lot. Oh, it makes all the silliness going on in the Fatherland seem so much worse, though."

"Silliness?" the Rabbi queried.

"Oh, you haven't heard?" Herr Muller said with surprise.

"I'm afraid news travels slowly, and my radio has been on the fritz for weeks thanks to my lovely daughter!" Doctor Doubek gestured towards Alica, smiling fondly. Little Ms. Doubek blushed and giggled.

"It was an accident!" she squeaked, and Herr Muller snickered.

"Oh, how many times have I heard *that* one?" he cried, winking at his daughter. "In all seriousness: our leader, the Führer, he won't be satisfied until we take back everything that was stolen from us."

"'Stolen'?" the Rabbi repeated, his voice an octave too high pitched. Herr Muller took a slow, thoughtful sip from his wine glass.

"Well, I agree with the Führer where that is concerned," he said. "These lands belonged to us Germans, we ruled them well and justly...and I think it's our right to rule them again."

"Oh, love, please!" Muller's wife groaned. "I was having fun, a fun cultural exchange without politics..."

"Politics *is* culture, my dear," Muller said, and the Rabbi nodded.

"Truth be told, Herr Muller, our village has been here so long, under so many different figureheads," Doctor Doubek said. "If this Hitler fellow is a decent leader and he wants to rule over us, we likely won't notice or mind."

"Unfortunately, the Führer, for all of his brilliance, has let silly race-baiting cloud his judgment," Herr Muller explained. "He cares about the German people, but instead of focusing on the French and the Brits, he's honed in on the Jews. We came here because we wanted to see if he was correct about your people, and happily I've found that he's mistaken...but..."

The German clenched his jaw and glanced at the cheerful,

ignorant children. He beckoned for the Rabbi to lean close. When he did, Muller whispered, "I fear that your people would not do well if we took over. And I know we will...so please, be careful."

"Listen," Muller continued after a moment of contemplation. "If you or your daughter need help, drop my name. Dietrich Muller, brother of SS Lieutenant Alois Muller. My brother isn't nearly as intellectually curious as me, believes everything he's told, but he loves me and respects me...and he still owes me for breaking my wrist when we were children. He's good friends with Himmler, the Führer's right-hand man. Used to sell that crackpot laying hens when he was just a chicken farmer. If you need a favor, ask, and I'll do my best to pay you back for your hospitality."

"I...thank you, Herr Muller," whispered the Rabbi, looking at his daughter and watching her play dollhouse with the German child, dread welling up in his chest like a balloon.

I should have packed Alica up and left that night, but I didn't want to abandon my people. I thought that if and when Hitler came, it would be better if I was there to help, to cash in Herr Muller's favor for my community.

"And when they came...?"

I tried to get by at first, but it was hard. Our village was transformed into a ghetto, and Jews from all over the nation were crammed in. Food became scarce, everything became scarce. For me, for my congregation...for my daughter.

"Papa, look, I found an apple!"

The Rabbi was once again sitting in his study, but it looked completely different. The books and fineries had been stripped away, either stolen by the Nazis or sold for necessities. The Rabbi was scowling at an old medical tome, perhaps looking for a way to treat his patients when supplies were so scarce.

He looked up at his daughter. Alica, a few years older, looked too terrible to be smiling. Her hair was matted and filthy, her dress torn, her cheeks hollow and placid. Nevertheless, she smiled, holding up a half-eaten apple.

"An apple!" she cried happily. "I think one of the Germans threw it out before he finished. Do you wanna bite?"

"Alica..."

The Rabbi watched in despair as his pathetic, precious daughter bit into the apple, and Vilém prayed that he never felt as terrible about his own parenting skills. The horrible sensation that struck the Rabbi right then, the sensation that he was failing his daughter...panic and guilt weighed him down. It felt like there was a brick in his gut.

"Papa, why are you crying? It tastes fine, Papa!" Alica insisted, offering the filthy fruit to her father. "Please have a bite, Papa..."

Tears blinded the Rabbi, and the memory faded into darkness.

That...that...seeing her do that, I knew I had to call in the favor...even if it meant kissing Himmler's bloody boots.

"Don't feel bad...she's your daughter..." Vilém said. "You had to protect her."

I had many obligations, boychik. To my daughter, to my congregation...I had hoped that Herr Muller's brother could help me take care of all of them. I was terribly naïve. Still...Herr Muller did what he could, and he wasn't lying when he said his brother had friends in high places.

"Come on, Jew. If you embarrass me, I'll kill you and then I'll kill my brother."

Vilém felt the Rabbi bite down on his tongue. The weary, starving Rabbi trudged behind a man who was almost identical to Herr Muller save for his relative youth and haggard appearance. Alois Muller marched through the Ghetto gates, and the Rabbi felt his heart flutter as he stepped out of the Ghetto for what must have been the first time in years.

"This way! You're lucky he's here, I would *not* have the

patience to drag you all the way to Prague," Alois grunted, leading the Rabbi past several sneering SS soldiers, towards a small tent.

Before Vilém could even begin to wonder who "he" was, Alois entered the tent and the Rabbi followed at his heels. Vilém felt his heart somersault. Inside the tent was a gaggle of Nazis sitting around a table that boasted a map of the Ghetto. Towering above all the SS men was a familiar snake-like face.

"Heil Hitler, General Heydrich!" Alois barked, shoving his hand into the air.

"Fuck, not him..." muttered Vilém. Heydrich stood up, his already narrow eyes becoming even thinner as he scowled at the Rabbi. Vilém felt uncertainty rise in the Rabbi's chest, perhaps because he didn't know how to greet the Nazi General. Surely a Hitler-salute would be seen as an insult.

Heydrich grunted, and a teeny smirk played on the edge of his lips when he sensed the Jew's fear. "This is the one who is willing to cooperate?" he said, looking towards Alois. Vilém felt the urge to snicker but suppressed it. Heydrich's squeaky voice would never sound natural, especially when he was trying to be intimidating.

"Yes, Reichsprotektor," Alois said. "My brother said he was pliant. He knows German, and he is relatively cultured compared to the rest of the Jews in this area."

"Oh, that's not always a positive," Heydrich mused, folding his hands behind his back and approaching the Rabbi. He gazed down at the Doctor as though he were a cockroach that had just skittered onto the countertop. "The so-called *cultured* ones are the biggest problem. Our people are fooled by them, and they blend in too well."

His icy blue eyes scanned the Rabbi and he shrugged. "Well, this one's too obvious to fool anyone. You're a doctor, Jew?"

"He is, sir..."

"I wasn't talking to you, Muller," snapped Heydrich, nodding for the Rabbi to speak. The Rabbi felt his tongue twist itself into a knot, and for a moment he couldn't say a word.

"Yes..." he finally said, adding hastily, "Yes, Reichsprotektor."

Heydrich, evidently pleased with the frightened correction, nodded. "While I normally wouldn't want to associate with someone who contributes to the longevity of the Jewish Race, I think you may have an appropriate mindset. Tell me, Jew: if a patient comes to you with an infected limb and you have no good options, what do you do to the limb?"

"Cut it off to save the body, Herr Reichsprotektor."

"Very good!" Heydrich said, clapping his gloved hands together. "You'll be used to making the sort of...decisions I need you to make. Come!" Heydrich pushed past the Jew, and his aggressive touch made the Rabbi squirm. The Doctor swallowed his pride and followed, no doubt thinking of Alica even as he trailed the Nazi like a loyal dog.

"You see," Heydrich said, rolling his eyes as every single SS man who saw him saluted like their lives depended on their gusto. "I want to show Hans Frank that my Czechs are far more productive than his Poles. I want this Ghetto to be the new Lodz. Smaller, obviously, but with just as much output. No waste whatsoever. It would please the Führer, and..."

He turned, smirking a wicked smirk. "It would give me an opportunity to be generous. You should know, Herr Doctor, that I'm fully aware that not all Jews *must* be eradicated. Some, perhaps, but the more pliant ones...the ones who demonstrate that they, unlike the rest, are not a threat to our people..."

"Herr Heydrich, we're not a threat!" the Rabbi interjected, perhaps seeing Heydrich's little proclamation as a sign that his mind could be changed. Heydrich turned, a blizzard spewing from his eyes, and the Rabbi timidly bowed his head.

"W-what I meant to say was..."

"Do not..." Heydrich hissed. "Do not speak unless you're told to, Jew. *That* is the behavior I'm talking about. Aberrant, rebellious, but...Jews who can learn their place, they may be granted certain privileges."

The Rabbi lifted a brow, but kept his lips shut. Heydrich observed his silence for a moment before smiling like a dog owner whose pet had just learned a new trick.

"You may speak your mind, Doctor," he said.

"What precisely do you want me to do, Herr Reichsprotektor?"

"Simple! It's very hard to get the Jews to fall in line. They don't like to take orders from gentiles, they distrust us...not that I blame them. But it makes my job harder, and it means we waste time and resources...and it also means that Jews who may otherwise be productive and pliant suffer..."

He patted his sidearm. "So what we've done in Poland—and what I would like to start doing here—is we have a designated Jewish Council made up of obedient Jews, Jews who know their place and are willing to enforce our rules for the betterment of their people and ours. They make sure the Jews in the factories keep up with quotas, they make sure the weaker Jews who cannot work are not wasting valuable Ghetto resources..."

"Uhm..." the Rabbi started to say before covering his mouth, and Heydrich snickered.

"You're doing so well already!" the Hangman chirped. "Go on, Doctor."

"What would happen to those...weaker Jews, Herr Heydrich?"

"For now? Resettlement. But we're coming up with a more permanent solution." the Blonde Beast leaned down, his smirk vanishing. "Now listen, Herr Doctor, for you I won't use euphemisms: it will not be pleasant. Humane, of course, we

Germans are well known for treating animals humanely. But not pleasant...no..."

Heydrich's eyes suddenly flitted upwards, as though he expected to see the eyes of God scowling down at him. Both the Rabbi and Vilém were surprised to see a flash of fear dart across the Hangman's face. Whatever he was looking for did not manifest, however, and with a relieved exhale, Heydrich continued.

"Don't harbor any childish illusions. Your community is sick, and the only way it will survive is via amputation. If you are not willing to assist in the operation, you may very well find yourself hacked off...you, and those you care for. Would you prefer to be a limb, Doctor?"

The Rabbi covered his mouth with his hands, shaking. He must have known before he even called in his favor that the Nazis were planning on a massive pogrom; Vilém didn't feel surprise course through the Doctor's body. Just guilt. Guilt and love, love for Alica. He inhaled deeply and made his Faustian bargain.

"I'll do what you want...if you can promise me that no child will be harmed."

"I can't promise that," Heydrich said, his voice becoming quiet, almost contemplative. "I can promise that my men will not choose who is to live and who is to die...within reason. You will be the head of the *Judenrat*, you will make those decisions, and you may spare whoever is most worthy of being spared. If you do this and you do it well, I will procure supplies and the Ghetto will flourish. If you do not...it will starve."

The Rabbi clutched at his heart, which hammered as though to protest. He ignored its pleas and bowed his head to the murderer.

"We'll be very productive, Reichsprotektor," he promised, and Heydrich beamed at his petty victory.

"Salute properly, please," the Butcher of Prague sneered. "You work for me now, I insist."

Revulsion boiled in the Rabbi's chest, but what very little pride he had clung to evaporated as he obeyed, raising one hand into the air and whispering, "Heil Hitler..."

The memory faded into darkness, and Vilém blurted out, "Do *not* feel bad about anything that *monster* made you do! He was *beyond* evil! He gave you false hope, he *lied* to you..."

No, he didn't. He never lied about anything. I accepted it...because I wanted to save Alica.

"She was your daughter! Of course you would kiss that fuckhead's boots if it meant saving her!"

Yes...and I did. I ran the Judenrat like a good little pet, and Heydrich...well, he always favored the carrot and stick method.

"Doctor!"

The Rabbi was being escorted out of the Ghetto, along with a small group of elderly men and women. The old Jews were pushed into the back of a gray truck, and the Rabbi watched, guilt throttling his heart.

But his focus was diverted to a motorcycle that roared to a halt close by. Heydrich, looking arrogant as ever, hopped off the vehicle and gestured for the Rabbi to come. Doctor Doubek skittered to the Blonde Beast's side.

"Look!" Heydrich said, gingerly prodding the motorcycle with the toe of his jackboot. "Runs well, and it was made in this Ghetto. Production has soared, and with far fewer instances of sabotage."

"My congregation trusts me," the Rabbi confessed. Heydrich looked like he might have laughed, but he refrained.

"I'm very pleased," said the Butcher of Prague. "Your Ghetto will receive double rations..."

Heydrich's high-pitched voice faded as the Rabbi heard a yelp of pain. He looked towards the trucks. An old woman had fallen trying to get on. Another man tried to stoop down and help her, but the Nazis smacked him with their batons.

"Move it, Jew! Step over it!" snapped one SS officer, and one by one the Jews were forced onto the truck, forced to trample the woman. She cried out over and over and the Rabbi...the Rabbi watched, he listened, he heard her screams and wanted so desperately to help her.

"Doctor!" But Heydrich's goat-like bleat, laced with ire at being ignored, broke through the haze. Heydrich looked at the fallen old woman, whose cries had finally been silenced. She was covered in blood, but the Rabbi could see her twitch. She was still breathing.

The Hangman rolled his eyes. "How typical..." he muttered, eyes flitting upwards once more. He leaned down, grunting as though he had been pushed, hovering above the Rabbi's shoulder.

"Doctor," he said. "I just said I'm giving your people extra rations and the Sabbath off. I think a 'thank you' is in order."

A Nazi walked over to the fallen woman, stepping on top of her and slamming the truck door shut. He knocked on the back of the van twice and it drove off, leaving the broken woman behind. The Nazi looked down, nudged her with his heel, then pulled out his gun.

"Well?" Heydrich growled. The Rabbi shut his eyes.

"Thank you, Herr Heydrich..." he whispered, and a gunshot echoed across the Ghetto.

When the Rabbi opened his eyes again, he found himself standing in the synagogue. The Jews were sitting cheek-to-jowl, some on the benches, some on the floor. Only the young and healthy remained. Some children played in the middle aisle. Alica was with them, throwing jacks across the wooden floor. She was much healthier than before: full rosy cheeks, clean clothes, washed hair...but her smile was gone.

My bargain with Heydrich seemed to...succeed for some time. We worked for the Nazis, none of us were deported except the old and sick...and I thought...I hoped we wouldn't have to sacrifice more. But one day Heydrich gave me a new order, a terrible order. He wanted more space in the Ghetto for more workers...more food for workers...and the children...

"Oh no..." whispered Vilém, watching through the Rabbi's tear-obscured eyes as he stood before the congregation.

"I come to you today with a heavy heart," he announced. "For the past few weeks, our willingness to cooperate has allowed us relative prosperity..."

"Rabbi, my mother's gone!" one woman retorted. "I don't feel very prosperous!"

"My dear, your mother is much happier where she is, in another ghetto...have you not received a letter from her yet?" queried the Rabbi.

"I have, but..." the woman said, plucking a small postcard from her dress pocket and holding it up. "It feels...wrong, Rabbi, like it wasn't written by her hand. It's like...like someone else wrote it."

"Oh, my dear, please..." the Rabbi begged, guilt battering his spirit. "For all of their gusto, the Germans have not burned our synagogue. They're far more cultured than any other gentile force we have had to deal with in the past. Are you going to believe some wild conspiracy theory?"

"I...suppose not..." whispered the woman, sinking down into her seat and staring at the forged postcard.

Heydrich had it all planned out so well. He really was an evil genius. He made sure they signed a paper before they were shipped off to die, and then he had an entire team of prisoners write post-cards to the living family members, to keep them calm and ignorant.

"Shitface," snarled Vilém, overwhelmed by the urge to drive

over to Prague and kick Heydrich's ghost square in his ethereal face.

"I want to assure you," the Rabbi lied, every word tasting foul on his tongue. "Your mothers and fathers and grandparents are fine. The Reichsprotektor merely wants to turn our village into a model of productivity, and sadly that means we must be separated from our loved ones for some time, until we have reached our quotas. Life will get better! We will be reunited and the hard times will be a distant memory."

The congregation tensed, as though they had heard this speech one too many times and knew that a fresh deportation was about to begin.

"But we must continue to cooperate if we are to get through this as a community. Believe me, my people, I wish there were another way, but it is better to cooperate than to rebel and die. And so...I must ask you to cooperate with me. I have received another order from Reichsprotektor Heydrich..."

"We've already deported all of our elders, there's nobody left to deport!" one Jew argued.

"Alas, there are many. Heydrich has ordered that one hundred children under the age of fourteen must be deported..."

The outcry was instant. Men shouted, women howled and held their children, and little boys and girls clung to their families, screaming that they didn't want to go. Alica stared at her father, eyes wide, mouth agape.

"Please! Please!" the Rabbi cried. "Your children will be taken to the same old-age ghetto as your elders, they will be given schooling and..."

"Why can't they get that here?!" one woman yelled, hugging her toddler to her breast.

"Any mother who does not wish to be separated from her child is welcome to go with them, though I do not recommend it as Herr

Heydrich wants as many workers to remain here as possible!" the Rabbi said. "Herr Heydrich is plotting out a humane way for us to coexist, but the war is raging and he wants the Ghetto to be exclusively devoted to production! Your children will be fine, but we must obey the quota..."

"What about *your* daughter?!" one man shouted, pointing at Alica. The Rabbi's daughter winced as all eyes fell upon her. She looked up at her father, her head tilting inquisitively to the side, as though to silently ask, "Yes, what about me?"

"There will be a raffle, a fair raffle," the Rabbi announced. "One hundred names will be chosen out of a hat, excluding babies too young to be separated from their mothers. It will be fair, and my daughter's name will be in there as well. And if she is sent away, I will not shed a tear. I promise you, our children will be safe! They will be safer at the other ghetto than they will be here! If my daughter's name is called, God be blessed!"

The congregation, somewhat calmed by the Rabbi's proclamation of equality, let their screams morph into whispers, clinging to their babies, their eyes flitting between Doctor Doubek and Alica. The Rabbi's daughter smiled at her father, but it wasn't the same sunny smile she had once possessed. It was a half-smile, chillingly similar to Heydrich's. A smile that spelled trouble.

The Rabbi blinked, and the memory shifted even as the location stayed the same. The Jews were sitting in the synagogue, but a few fresh faces had joined the crowd. Nazi guards stood by the exit, their eyes trained on the Rabbi, who stood before the frightened congregation, clutching a hat filled with little slips of paper. He glanced at his daughter, who was sitting up front, leaning forward as though she were at a magic show and he was about to pull a rabbit from the hat.

"Please stay calm..." the Rabbi begged the Jews before him as he reached in and chose the first paper. He unfolded it.

Alica Doubek

He bit his lip, but didn't hesitate for one moment. "Chaim Nagel."

Chaim's mother screamed. The boy cried and clung to her. His father stood up, prepared to fight for his son, but a Nazi smacked him with a baton and grabbed the child, yanking him out of the synagogue. His screams rung in the Rabbi's ears.

Doctor Doubek tore up his daughter's name and pulled out another paper.

Alica Doubek

His eyes widened and he stole a glance at his daughter. Her little hands were balled into fists, clutching the ribbon on her dress. There was a dare in her eyes.

"Rivka Orten..."

And on and on it went, the Rabbi pulling out his daughter's name one hundred times, the Rabbi lying one hundred times, Alica's smile dying one hundred times as one hundred families were destroyed.

When they were done, Alica stood, tears in her eyes, and ran from the synagogue. The Rabbi's heart almost stopped, and he moved without a single thought, barreling past furious, mourning parents and chasing his distraught daughter into the street.

Alica was watching as the other children were tossed onto the trucks. She watched as they were driven off, driven to their deaths. She watched, and Vilém saw a piece of her wither away right then. The sunshine in her soul vanished with her friends.

"Alica, come..." the Rabbi begged, grabbing her arm. She pulled away.

"Don't touch me!" she shrieked, shoving him and running away. He cursed and followed her all the way back to their home.

"Alica!" he gasped as he burst into their house, collapsing to his knees and trying to catch his breath. She was standing in the living room, hugging one hundred pieces of paper. She tossed them in her father's face and he winced as the names of all the Jewish children fell on him like snow.

"You...you replaced the papers, then...why?" the Rabbi asked. Alica, who now truly looked like the furious Ms. Doubek that Vilém knew too well, snarled.

"You're a liar and a hypocrite!" she accused. "You've been working with the Nazis all this time and lying for them! And if you lied about sending me off, that means they're gonna die!"

Alica choked, tears streaming down her face as she looked at the papers covering her living room floor. "You just murdered all my friends..."

"Alica, I didn't murder them, please, listen..." the Rabbi begged, crawling towards his daughter and reaching out to hold her face in his hands. "They would have killed every single one of us, they would have killed you too..."

"What happened to sit and do nothing, huh?" Alica screeched, slapping his hands away. She grabbed the corner of his *tallit* prayer scarf and shoved it in front of his eyes. "What about this? What about the Talmud and the Torah? What about God's laws? What about everything you ever told me?"

"Alica!" the Rabbi yelped as she pulled the holy garment right off of him and tossed it to the ground.

"It was all just a lie wasn't it? Just a lie to make me feel better about Mother and everything else in this stupid, horrible world!"

"Alica, it wasn't all a lie, this is...our people have dealt with such cruelty before..."

"Our people have never *betrayed* each other!" Alica screamed. "Our people didn't sacrifice children to Molech! Our Rabbis didn't *lie* to us! Our Rabbis were not selfish *traitors!*"

"Alica, please! I love God, and I love our people, but I love you more!" the Rabbi cried, standing up and trying to put a hand on his child's shoulder.

"Get away from me, I hate you!" Alica screamed. She ran up the stairs and slammed her bedroom door shut. The Rabbi, sobbing, knelt on the names of the children he had damned, and Vilém hoped to never feel the way Doctor Doubek did right then.

Tears filled his eyes, blinding him, and...

"Doctor?"

A familiar voice spoke in an unfamiliar tone as a new memory formed. The Doctor was sitting in front of Heydrich, who had made himself at home in the Rabbi's living room. The Hangman of Prague was sitting on the couch and clutching a folder labeled "*Ghetto 15 Output*." He must have been so pleased with Rabbi Doubek's cooperation that he had stopped by for a house call.

The Rabbi hastily blinked away his tears and rigidly stood at attention. Heydrich let out a noise like a teenager that had just been spoken to like a toddler.

"Oh, for Heaven's sake, enough of this dance!" huffed the Blonde Beast. "Just talk!"

Heydrich winced as though the invisible hand of Hitler had just smacked him for straying even slightly from Nazi protocol, but he seemed to recover quickly and waved for the Rabbi to speak. Vilém felt a lump of hesitation form in the Rabbi's throat as his mind buzzed with potential excuses, but he decided to tell the truth.

"Some of my daughter's friends were deported and she...put two and two together, Herr Reichsprotektor."

"Ah. Clever girl. More clever than half of Europe...or maybe just brave enough to speak the obvious."

"She's...upset with me for cooperating with you, Reichsprotektor. She thinks it is a betrayal of my religious values."

Heydrich gave the Rabbi a studious look, as though he were a rat that had just performed a feat of acrobatics.

"Is it?" the Butcher asked.

"...I...suppose," the Rabbi whispered.

Heydrich leaned forward and pulled back one end of the Newton's Cradle that still rested on the coffee table. His light blue eyes flitted back and forth as the balls clicked and clacked against one another, sending the metal orbs at the ends of the cradle flying.

"It seems your role as a doctor and a Rabbi are in conflict," Heydrich observed, keeping his eyes fixed on the silver cradle.

"She said she hates me," sighed the Rabbi. "Even after I did all of this for her."

Heydrich's thin eyes widened. Vilém saw his hand flit towards his back pocket. Perhaps he had his wallet there. Perhaps he had a picture of Klaus inside. Perhaps the Nazi was recalling his own son's words. Heydrich reached forward and cupped the clacking Newton's Cradle with both hands, forcing it to become still once more.

"I know how that feels..." the Hangman whispered, slowly leaning back, staring at the still-trembling Newton's Cradle. Vilém almost couldn't believe his ears when he heard empathy in the Nazi's tone. Heydrich winced again, as though an unseeable force had punished him once more for daring to sympathize with a Jew. He scowled upwards, and the possibly-imaginary being that kept striking him seemed to slacken its grip on his soul.

"Children are far too simple and innocent for their own good," he said, staring at the multiple distorted little Reinhard Heydrichs that the orbs of the Newton's Cradle reflected. "They so rarely recognize that occasionally...painful and terrible as it may be...we must...do things that are wrong so they can be safe..."

He glanced down at his own gloved hand and shook his head, looking up at the Rabbi with a small, genuine smile.

"I'll continue to give you and your child what you deserve," Heydrich vowed. "You're very different from the rest of the Jews, Doctor. Almost human. In fact...I don't think we're very different at all."

Heydrich winced again, as though that confession had hurt his very soul, and with a brusque farewell he grabbed his things and scurried out of the Rabbi's home.

"So..." Alica's voice drifted into the Rabbi's ear. He looked towards the staircase. Alica was there, her hair unbrushed, frowning deeply.

"Not so different," she sneered. "I guess you're not."

She turned around and marched back upstairs, and the Rabbi, weighted down by guilt and disgust, collapsed onto the couch, covering his face with his hands as though he wanted to hide from the very face of God.

So...still think I should get my own exhibit?

Vilém, who had been prepared for a lot but certainly not this sort of moral dilemma, huffed. "This is *not* your fault, Rabbi! I'm no historian, but I've read enough to know that yarn Heydrich spun about sparing *some* Jews was bull. He lied to you..."

And I lied to my people.

"What else were you supposed to do? Sit and die?"

That is what the Talmud instructs. That is what I spent my life preaching.

"I'm not a Jew, but I don't think God would be angry at someone who genuinely tried to save lives."

By damning others to death...

"Rabbi, they were all dead from the moment the Nazis marched into Czechoslovakia!" Vilém argued. "Perhaps your actions saved a few of them..."

And perhaps not. Perhaps they would have escaped, lived. Perhaps I should have told my people to fight back.

"With what, sticks and stones?" Vilém exclaimed. "You had nothing, you were helpless! You shouldn't have *had* to even *consider* fighting back against an army! Rabbi, there is no shame in making mistakes when there's a gun pointed at your head!"

Perhaps not, but there is shame in shoving someone else in front of the bullet.

"Maybe, but shoving someone else in front of your child...I don't know, Rabbi," Vilém sighed. "I'm not even a dad yet, but I feel like I'd commit a thousand sins so my kid could live. I'd do a million terrible things..."

Well, that's precisely what Heydrich thought he was doing. A million terrible things. Six million, more specifically.

"Well, he can think he was doing the right thing as much as he wants, but he wasn't, and he had plenty of opportunities to see that! You weren't given the same choices he was! Don't compare yourself to him!" Vilém snapped.

I truly appreciate your words, Vilém. Nonetheless, can you blame Alica for despising me?

"Well..." muttered Vilém. "I can't pretend like I've ever been in her shoes. The only thing me and my old man ever really argued about was my curfew, and I said I hated him too...but I didn't. I bet she doesn't either. She's just...upset."

She has a right to be. I really tried to protect her, but I failed.

"Failed? She's alive!"

Alive, certainly, but that doesn't mean I didn't fail her. That conversation with Heydrich was the last one we had before he was assassinated. Suddenly, our terrible benefactor was gone and Hitler was seething. Hitler demanded reprisals, and we were swept up. My daughter, what was left of our congregation, and myself.

"And that's how you got to the Camp?"

Correct. But fortunately, once we arrived and the Selection started, the Nazis asked for doctors to step out of line. And there I was again, making a bargain with a demon.

"This is her?"

"Yes, Herr Kommandant."

"Get off of me!" Alica demanded, trying and failing to free herself from the grasp of the Nazi guard who dragged her into a familiar office. Vilém grunted. Kommandant Gerber's office again. The Kommandant sat at his desk, as usual, though all aggravation and arrogance had abandoned him. He wore a neutral expression as he allowed his bright blue eyes to dart from Alica to the Doctor, finally settling on the trembling Rabbi.

"So…" sighed the Kommandant, standing up. "We have an agreement, then."

"Where's the boy?" the Doctor asked.

"He has his own nursery," the Kommandant said, crossing his arms behind his back and sauntering towards the window. "You will stay in the infirmary. You'll be on call at all times. If Martin has an accident, you will drop everything to take care of him."

"And my daughter…?" the Rabbi said. Alica snarled.

"I can't believe you're making *another* deal with them!" she cried.

"Shut her up, please, I can't handle the screeching," snapped the Kommandant, and his soldier covered the girl's mouth with his hand. The Rabbi didn't seem to notice—or if he did, he forced himself to ignore it—but Vilém saw a wolf-like smirk form on the Nazi's face as he muffled the girl's cries, as if this was a familiar, pleasant motion.

"Fuckhead," whispered Vilém, but the Kommandant spoke again before Vilém could let out any more curses.

"I would offer your daughter the spare room, but we've converted it into a developing room," he said, gesturing to the camera that rested on his desk. "And I already have a Jewess staying there. Besides, your daughter's...feisty. I don't think I want her near Martin."

Alica kicked and let out a muffled howl.

"My point precisely," the Kommandant said, flourishing his hand to indicate the thrashing girl. "She's...how old now?"

"Thirteen, Kommandant."

"Thirteen, fine," the Kommandant said, jabbing his thumb towards the window, gesturing to Barrack Two. "She'd normally be placed in the children's barrack, but the women's barrack will be safer. I'll give my men orders not to touch her, and she can have double rations under-the-table. I can't offer much more: too much favoritism will make her a target to the other prisoners. We've had some...race-mixing difficulties with some soldiers and believe me...the Jewesses in those cases never fared well."

The Rabbi shuddered and glanced at Alica. She looked at him with fire in her eyes, as though he was nothing more than another Nazi, no better than the Kommandant.

"Very well, Herr Kommandant," Doctor Doubek agreed. "As long as she's safe and I get a chance to see her."

"Good, good!" the Kommandant said. "Then take the Jewess to Barrack Two and be sure to give her a special armband so the rest of the men know not to touch her."

"Yes, sir," the Nazi guard snickered, and with that he carried the writhing Alica Doubek out of the office, slamming the door behind him.

And well...you sort of know what happened after that. I lived in the infirmary. I worked for Little Martin Gerber...a sweet boy. He didn't speak much, but believe it or not, he was a Jew by faith.

"You're kidding!" Vilém cried. "I thought he was a Czech!"

Half Czech, half German, and I suspect his mother was a convert to Judaism. For some reason—and Martin never told me why, maybe even he didn't know—but for some reason, the

Kommandant was determined to mold Martin into a good little Nazi. Gerber made it clear to me that if I taught the boy about Judaism or encouraged him to be a Jew, I would be in trouble.

"And...?"

Well...Martin was very persuasive.

"Doctor Rabbi, do you know what day it is?"

"It's hard to keep track of the days, boychik, please hold still..." The Rabbi was tending to Little Martin, who was pale as a corpse save for his knee, which boasted a huge, ugly black bruise.

"It's Yom Kippur!" the boy announced. The Rabbi felt his heart plummet. He winced when the child's stomach snarled.

"Boychik, you will get us both in trouble. You *must* eat. Did you injure yourself on purpose again?" whispered the Rabbi. Little Martin smiled, and something about that smile made Vilém's heart flutter.

"Maybe," the child said cheekily. "I wanted to sing Kol Nidre."

"I have a terrible voice, boychik. Please do not bump yourself on purpose, you could die."

"Fine," huffed Martin, glowering at the bandage the Rabbi wrapped around his bruised leg. "Then the Kommandant could get a new pet."

"You really should call him Father, boychik, you know he..."

"He's not my father, I don't have a father!" the boy insisted. Martin's eyes shifted to the ceiling and he added, "Except God. But...maybe He's gone too."

The Rabbi felt a rush of agreement, followed by a stab of shame for his own lack of faith. He gently patted the boy's cheek. "Boychik, don't speak that way. One day we will be free and you will find your papa."

Martin let out a shuddering breath, as though the mere mention of his biological father lit a fire in his belly. He slowly shook his head and muttered, "I just wanna sing Kol Nidre...please, Doctor Rabbi?"

The Rabbi's eyes darted anxiously to the door, as though he expected the Kommandant to burst in at any moment and execute him for merely entertaining the notion. He looked up at the white ceiling, waiting for a divine sign that didn't come.

He bit his lip, and a rebellious spirit took hold of him as he pulled the boy into a hug and sang in his ear, so quietly that only God could have heard.

"Kol Nidre...Ve'esarei...Ush'vuei..."

How could I refuse? My daughter despised me, but Martin still looked to me as a man of God, as a savior, as a hero...to the point where he trusted me when he came across a real hero.

"Doctor Rabbi!"

Vilém watched with fascination as a familiar memory played out, this time from the Doctor's point of view: Little Martin burst in with Joseph Klammer in tow, Joseph revealed little Daniel Svoboda, Klammer and the Rabbi traded vague explanations.

It was strange, to feel it all in another body, to see it all with a new pair of eyes. In Joseph's memory, the Rabbi had seemed so calm. In reality, a war raged within the Doctor's soul as he looked down at Danny. Fear pulled him towards the Kommandant's office. He would probably be rewarded for turning the traitorous Nazi in. He would be known as a good, obedient Jew who knew his place. He would be safe. His daughter would be safe.

But guilt, guilt for all the children he had already betrayed, forced him to proclaim that he would hide the boy.

And for once, I didn't betray my people. I let little Danny stay in the infirmary. Thankfully, the Kommandant let me be, and Fido the Spy never intervened.

"Iveta wasn't a spy, and Daniel's my great-uncle," Vilém said. "You saved him."

Klammer saved him. I just didn't betray him the way I betrayed everyone else.

"Did Alica know?"

She didn't. Martin usually brought Danny food, but sometimes he just couldn't get us anything, not without making the Kommandant suspicious. When that happened, I had to split my rations with Daniel. If Alica had known, she would have given him her food as well. I didn't want her to go without, but...she often did.

"Alica, sunshine, you're thin." A new memory formed, so dark that it took a moment for Vilém to realize it: the Rabbi was inside the women's barrack, sitting on a straw-covered bunk beside his daughter.

If Alica was getting special privileges, it was hard to tell. She looked just as emaciated, just as tired, and just as hopeless as the rest of the women. The only difference was that her head hadn't been shaved.

She played with her hair, picking at the mats, trying to loosen the knots.

"Alica, do you need a comb?" the Rabbi asked. The girl pretended as though she couldn't hear him, staring at her lap, her eyes empty. Vilém could barely tell that this was the same girl who had once possessed a blindingly sunny smile.

"Alic..."

"I don't have anyone to look pretty for," Alica hissed, tugging a knot out of her hair and wincing from the pain. The Rabbi bit his lip.

"Have the guards been...hurting you?"

"Who cares?" she whispered.

"You know I care, I..."

"It makes no difference. If they don't hurt me, they hurt another girl in Barrack Two."

"Have you been giving your rations to the other women in the barrack, Alica?"

Alica didn't answer, but her picking at her hair became frantic. A silent "yes."

"Alica, my brave girl, you're very sweet, but you must think of yourself first. An extra bite offered to everyone else will do them no good, it will not save their lives, but it will cost you yours."

"You don't understand anything," Alica insisted, hugging her knees to her chest and lying down, turning away from her father. "I'm tired."

"All right, but please, if you have something to tell me, just...I'll do whatever I can to help you."

"I know you will..." Alica whispered, and it sounded as though knowing that made her ill. The Rabbi stood above his daughter, and Vilém felt a tug in the Doctor's chest. The Rabbi wanted to kiss his daughter goodbye, but cowardice made him flee from the barrack before he could dare.

A familiar face was waiting outside Barrack Two: none other than Private Helmut Schwartz. Vilém chuckled. Then that meant...

The Rabbi looked up and saw a distressed Joseph Klammer exit Barrack Three. Ah, familiarity.

"Hello, Sergeant!" the Rabbi cried, and again the same memory played out: Joseph took the Rabbi from Schwartz and started leading him back towards Barrack One. The Pit started burning...the smell made the Rabbi's gut writhe.

"That could be Danny..." the Rabbi said. "In a week, it will be Samuel. What is the difference? Why save one and damn another?"

Vilém was surprised how different this conversation felt from the Rabbi's point of view. In Joseph's mind, the holy man had been offering him a moral lesson. But Vilém felt bitterness settle on the

Rabbi's tongue and he realized that Doctor Doubek was talking to himself more than he was talking to Joseph.

"Selfishness, Rabbi..." Joseph said, and Vilém felt empathy rise up in the Rabbi's chest.

"At least *you're* honest," the Rabbi sighed, and even as Joseph tried to cover his nose, the Rabbi inhaled deeply, fanning the flames of his guilt, reminding himself of the fate he had consigned so many Jewish babies to.

You see now? Joseph didn't understand one bit. He thought he was the one who needed redemption.

"Joseph's a hero, but he *did* kill people before he figured out that the Nazi worldview was bullshit," Vilém said. "You made mistakes, but you saved Danny...and you saved the rest of the Jews, you helped Joseph!"

Ah, yes, the Freedom Train. Well, Joseph was very convincing. He told me that if I didn't help him, all the women in Barrack Two would perish, including my daughter. At first, I thought my daughter might be spared...we did have our deal, the Kommandant and I.

"But...?"

But the Kommandant never said a word about the deportation. Never warned me, never did anything to save my daughter. Perhaps he forgot all about her. I have a feeling he wanted to replace me, though: Martin had been acting like a good little Nazi, perhaps Gerber decided to get him a less undesirable doctor. Regardless, my daughter was evidently going to be treated just like every other Jew. She was going to die...and I couldn't let that happen. I let Sergeant Klammer think I did it for my people, but I actually did it for her.

"You're saving her life, Doctor." They were back in the infirmary, the day before the Freedom Train left the station. Joseph placed a hand on the Rabbi's shoulder. The Rabbi looked into the young Aryan's eyes and saw a familiar flame, a flame of guilt burning in Klammer's irises.

"You as well…" Doctor Doubek said, forcing his eyes to burrow into Joseph's, perhaps hoping that Klammer would see the inferno of guilt in the Rabbi's soul and realize that he was the better man. "God be with you, Joseph."

"Just this once…" Joseph sighed. He said his farewells to the children and scurried off to Barrack Three. As soon as he was gone, Little Martin dropped the ratty toy cat he was holding and ran to Danny, planting a determined kiss on the toddler's cheek.

"I'm not staying!" Little Martin vowed. The Rabbi winced.

"Martin…"

"I'm not staying! I hate Gerber! I want to go with you and Danny!" Martin yelped, pointing to the door and adding, "The little spy's gone now, so he won't notice I'm gone if I leave last-minute!"

"Martin!" the Rabbi hissed, shushing Danny as the toddler squealed joyously at the notion of his friend coming along and playing the quiet game. "Martin, I know you've been through a lot, but if you leave, the Kommandant may hunt us down to the ends of the earth…"

"I know it's selfish, Rabbi, but I can't stand it anymore!" Martin cried. "I'd rather die a Jew than live like this for another second! I hate this! I'm so sorry, but please let me be selfish! Please let me come with you! Please…it's my birthday!"

The Rabbi almost laughed at the boy's invocation of his not-birthday, but Little Martin wasn't joking. He fell at the Doctor's feet, his brilliant eyes wide and pleading, tears cascading down his cheeks. Danny started crying, reaching for Martin.

"No leave! No!" Danny cried. The Rabbi's ears buzzed, the screams and pleas of both children summoning the ghosts of old sins.

"All right...all right, you can come, but you must disguise yourself..." the Rabbi said, finally allowing an authentic smile to bloom on his face as the two boys shrieked with happiness and hugged one another.

How could I refuse? Those boys loved each other, and after everything he went through, Martin had more of a right to be selfish than I did. He deserved to be free, to be a Jew, to keep that little spark of innocence alive. The day came and...haha! Well, he definitely disguised himself.

"Doctor Rabbi, look!"

A hectic memory formed. Jews, unaware that they would be free in a few hours, wailed and tried to say their last goodbyes to their loved ones as the Nazis shoved them onto the Auschwitz Train. The Rabbi had been holding a half-asleep Danny and staring at the top of the train. Schwartz and a few others were getting into position atop the cattle cars. Klammer was nowhere to be seen.

The Rabbi looked down at Little Martin and almost burst into laughter. The boy had shorn his curly blonde locks and stolen a dress. Vilém chuckled. He must have snatched one of Iveta's spares some time ago, just in case he was eventually given this kind of opportunity.

"See? I look like a girl!" Martin whispered, his eyes dancing as he ran a hand over the stubble on his head. "I look like all the other Jews!"

He sounded so happy. The little boy had been stripped of his Jewishness for so long that being shaved, dirty, and despised made him giddy. He hadn't been lying when he said that he would rather die as a Jew than keep living as the Kommandant's project.

"Ah, ah!" Little Daniel woke up and saw his cross-dressing friend, recognizing his voice. The toddler reached down, softly crying for Martin.

"Give him to me," Martin volunteered. "I can take him to his papa. You find Alica and we'll all meet after this is over."

"Ah...yes, after..." mumbled the Rabbi. He felt his heart sink as he gazed at the cheerfully smiling and terribly ignorant little boy. He knelt before Martin, setting little Daniel on his back and kissing the older boy's almost-bald head.

"Go, and God bless you. If anything happens to me, find my daughter. She'll take care of you."

"Nothing will happen to you, Rabbi! God's watching!" Martin said confidently. "This is a mitzvah, He'll protect you!"

"Of course He will..." the Rabbi whispered. He kissed both boys once more and watched as Martin piggy-backed Daniel towards the crowd of former Barrack Three occupants.

I never saw him again. I hope he stayed safe. He was a good boy.

"I'll look into him," Vilém vowed. "Maybe Ms. Doubek knows where he went and—UNGH!"

All of a sudden, an invisible force assaulted Vilém. Not a mere kick to the gut: it felt like someone had jabbed their thumbs right into his eyes. He fell back into Barrack Two, writhing on the wooden floor, clutching his face.

"Fuck, fuck, fuck!" he yelped, and for a few moments he feared that the wicked spirit had blinded him, but slowly he managed to open his eyes a sliver. He was barely able to see, but he knew he still had his sight, and that was enough to keep him from rushing to the hospital. He reached out and touched the panel once more, shutting his injured eyes.

Mr. Rehor, are you all right? You have a black eye...you have two black eyes! And that presence...

"Kommandant Gerber?" Vilém assumed.

I'd recognize that...coldness anywhere. It seems he still holds a grudge. I suppose I did steal his "son."

"And it looks like he's lashing out at me," Vilém huffed.

You are bringing up some old wounds, I suppose. Perhaps he was content so long as we were all stuck here together. I doubt he wants to be alone in his misery.

"Too bad," Vilém grunted. "Let's finish this. Tell me what happened with Ms. Doubek."

Vilém, you're hurt, and he may come back...and I don't want anyone else getting hurt on my account.

"And I don't want that shithead Gerber to win," Vilém countered. "Tell me what happened, Rabbi, please."

Very well, but then you have to go to the hospital. If you want me to have peace, that won't happen if you go blind. You deserve to see your baby.

Vilém smiled fondly, and the thought of his future child granted him a surge of strength. He was going to be a dad. He was going to have a baby. He needed to be good, to be brave, to be the sort of man his child could look at with adoring eyes.

Well...where were we? Oh, yes...

"Alica!"

Rabbi Doubek spotted his daughter among the frightened women: easy enough since she was the only one who still had her hair. In one swift motion, he grabbed her and wrapped Danny's blanket around her head.

"Stop! What are you doing?" she huffed.

"You mustn't let them see you," he whispered, pulling his daughter close. She tried to wriggle away, but sacrificing her double rations had made her weak.

"I'm going with everyone else!" she argued. "Enough deals!"

"Enough deals," the Rabbi agreed. "We're leaving with the others. I'm going too."

Alica ceased her struggling, looking up at her father with inquisitiveness. Before she could even open her mouth to question him, however, a familiar voice snapped at the father and daughter.

"Move it, Jews!" Joseph Klammer appeared behind them, grabbing the Rabbi and Alica. Alica froze when the man laid a hand on her, and the Rabbi, seeing his daughter's panic, whispered to Joseph.

"Gentle, please, my friend," he begged. Alica shot a glare at her father.

"No more deals," she spat, dragging her feet as Joseph, feigning forcefulness, led them to the train and opened the rearmost cattle car.

"Hey, Sergeant Klammer, it's crowded back there!" one of the Nazis on top of the train warned. Joseph smiled up at him.

"Five Marks says I can fit them both in!" he dared, and Vilém saw the bitterness in the reformed Nazi's eyes.

"You're on!" laughed Joseph's "comrade." Joseph threw Alica in first, then her father, making sure he would be near the door.

"Wait until we're far..." Joseph whispered, sliding the door shut and pretending to lock it.

"There! Five Marks, Dietrich!" he cried, and the Rabbi heard him climb on top of the train.

"Goddammit," hissed the losing Nazi. "Fucking Jews..."

"Don't be mad, Dietrich," Schwartz chuckled. "You can get even when we get to Auschwitz."

"Auschwitz..." whispered Alica. The Rabbi tried to look down at his daughter, but the train car was so crowded that he couldn't even turn to face her. He reached out and put a hand on top of her head. She pushed him away.

"Get off," she hissed. The train took off with a roar and the Jews inside cried out in fear.

"Can I sit, please?" one exhausted Jew beside the Rabbi begged.

"Nobody can sit!" another prisoner whimpered.

"Lean against me," the Rabbi offered. "Stay strong."

"Bless you..." the man sighed, leaning his body against the Rabbi. Alica grunted. For what felt like an eternity, but must have only been an hour at most, they chugged along. The Rabbi peeked through the holes in the wooden cattle car, making sure that the Camp had disappeared into the distance.

"Sir, please stand!" Doctor Doubek begged the exhausted Jew who was leaning his scant weight against him.

"I can't, sir..." the Jew moaned.

"Please, somebody take him!" the Rabbi cried. "We're going to escape! We're not going to Auschwitz!"

"What...?" muttered Alica as another Jew, eager to help the Rabbi free his people, let the ill prisoner lean against him.

"Alica, my dear, I love you," Doctor Doubek cried, forcing his body to contort so he could see his daughter one last time. "Smile, please, sunshine..."

Her face, partially concealed by the darkness, glowed with confusion for a moment before the scowl that Vilém knew her for conquered her countenance.

"I don't want to," she said. "I don't trust you."

Sorrow drowned the Rabbi's soul. He reached out, touched her cheek, and his hand burned when she pulled away. The final rejection solidified his will to go, and without the slightest bit of hesitation, he threw open the door and jumped.

Alica evidently hadn't been expecting that. "Papa!" she shrieked, but adrenaline didn't allow him to look back at her. He ran, ran, ran...

BAM!

A bullet struck him in the chest. It hurt, but not worse than Alica's hatred. He fell to the dirt, barely able to raise his head enough to look up, barely able to hear the cries of the Nazis as Joseph shot them in the back.

All he heard was Alica, screaming. "PAPA!"

He saw the train speed off, he saw it vanish...a small fleck of happiness settled on his soul. Not enough to suppress the woe of knowing that his daughter despised him, but enough that he could press his face into the dirt and let out a satisfied sigh. She hated him, but she was safe. She would live.

He was alone. With only himself, the seemingly dead Nazis, and whatever God was watching over him.

"*Sh'ma...Yisrael...*" he tried, even as the life drained from him, to give an almost empty proclamation of his faith, but he couldn't. He wasn't strong enough.

He lay there, alone, silent, and eventually, everything went dark.

It was a slow death, and Vilém hoped that he wouldn't die that way. He pulled his hands away from the panel and opened his injured eyes.

A face, once one in a hundred, emerged from the crowd in the picture he had been touching. A face that had once made the Rabbi's heart sing, a face that had refused to smile for him. Alica Doubek, barely a dot among the Jews, sat in the back of Barrack Two, staring at the camera, her face drooping like a dead flower.

"Oh, Rabbi..." whispered Vilém. He shut his eyes again and touched the image of little Alica.

I miss her smile...but I know I don't deserve it. She was right about me. I was a fool...and a traitor.

"Depends on the definition of 'traitor,'" Vilém argued. "As far as I know, a man's first obligation is to his child. Above everything else. Not all selfishness is evil, and if protecting your child is selfishness, then everyone is selfish. Joseph only did what he did because he loved Sam, you did what you did because you loved your daughter..."

And that makes it all right?

"I don't know, Rabbi!" huffed Vilém. "I'm not God! And I'm

not you, either! God willing, I'll never find myself in the same position you found yourself in...and if I do, I don't know what I'd do! A thousand children for my child? I don't know...maybe it is wrong, maybe it is evil, but...well, I'm not casting stones. It's not my place. How can I damn you for making an impossible choice? And anyone who would call you a monster, they have no right! And that includes Ms. Doubek!"

Alica suffered horribly...

"Alica was a kid. She didn't have to make the same choices you did. What if she had been forced to choose between her friend and a stranger? Or choose between letting you live or letting a hundred strangers live? Yes, the choice you made was against your religious laws, but if I remember the Bible correctly, even great men sin. The greater the man, the greater the sin. David!"

He clapped his hands together. "King David! He let a man die, he knowingly sent a man to die for horribly selfish reasons, for reasons far worse than what you did, and God still gave him a kingdom!"

I appreciate that you're trying to comfort me with my faith, Vilém, but...I'm not so sure about those stories anymore.

"Real or not, stories have a point, and the point is that even godly men can be hypocrites. Life is more than just...following rules. I can see why Alica didn't put you in an exhibit...maybe you don't deserve an exhibit. But you deserve to see your daughter's smile..."

Vilém shakily stood up, announcing confidently, "And I think I know how to revive it."

Alica Doubek was not in a good mood, which was not in and of itself unusual. Alica Doubek was rarely in a good mood. Even when she was, even when everything was going perfectly, even when none of her employees were calling her "Kommandant" behind her back, even when dreadful little teenagers weren't disrespecting the dead...even then, she would refuse to show it. Her smile was reserved for...well, nobody. She had never found anyone worthy enough. If her father had not deserved it, nobody did.

Least of all Vilém Řehor, who was working off the fumes of her patience. That irresponsible borderline-criminal had given her so many dreadful days and nights. The thought that he was going to have a child soon made Alica fear for the human race. One Vilém was too many—future generations didn't need to deal with his defective genetics.

She almost had to admire his determination to disobey her. She brought up her unwillingness to give him paternity leave, and he managed to wound both his eyes and secure paid time off for workplace injuries. She assumed he was lounging in bed with his fiancée, eating candy and being babied by Ilona Sladký.

She was surprised, then, when she entered her office one day and found a note sitting on her desk, written in Vilém's barely-legible handwriting.

Please meet me in Barrack Two after closing.

She grunted, but her annoyance gave way to curiosity. Vilém was a frustratingly strange character, but even when attempting to look at the world from his brain-dead point of view, she couldn't think of one reason he would want to see her after dark. She almost chuckled as the notion of assault flashed through her mind. Maybe once upon a time, but thankfully she wasn't pretty enough to worry about such things anymore.

Her frown deepened. At least she hoped that was the case.

Nevertheless, for as much as she didn't like Vilém, she thought he was stupid, not evil. She decided to oblige. Maybe he would finally give her a good excuse to fire him.

The day ended and she sent Vilém's replacement on a wild goose chase through the former guards' barracks. Ostensibly because she had seen a small child run that way, but really because she didn't want anyone to interrupt her verbal beating of Vilém Rehor. She grabbed a thick metal pointer just in case words weren't enough and a physical beating was required.

She marched into Barrack Two, which by now was too familiar to trigger any unpleasant memories. She found her employee sitting on the floor in front of a laptop, struggling to plug a small speaker into the device.

"Rehor, you're supposed to be on leave," Alica snapped. Vilém looked over his shoulder, showing off his two swollen eyes and a small smile.

"Oh, hello," he said, finally managing to plug the speaker in. "I figured it was about a fifty-fifty shot, you showing up. Glad you made this easy."

"Made *what* easy, Rehor?" huffed Alica, crossing her arms over her chest. "I'm not in the mood for this, I've been here all day."

"You're not running home to anyone, Ms. Doubek," Vilém sighed, and Alica felt a tsunami of fury crash over her.

"How dare you?" she snarled. "You have a lot of nerve, barging in, staying here *illegally* after hours, and then insulting me right to my face! You've gotten away with a lot of shit, Rehor, but I will not tolerate—!"

But Vilém pressed a button on the laptop, drowning her rant out with a song. A familiar song. A song she had tried her hardest to never hear again.

"Smile, darn ya' smile!
You know this great world is a good world after all..."

For a moment they stood there, Alica frozen, Vilém swaying slightly to the tune. He let it play for long enough that she knew without a doubt it was *that* song. The song she had broken the radio to. The song she had danced to when she still had a smile.

"Do you believe in ghosts, Ms. Doubek?" Vilém asked. She was so shocked that she could barely shake her head and force a scowl back onto her face.

"I don't believe in anything," she proclaimed.

"Not even love?"

Doubek rolled her eyes. "What is this, a fucking Disney film? I hope you're not trying to..."

"Not that kind of love, ma'am. The parent kind. The kind that would make someone do foolish, terrible things."

Alica's heart, which she had purposefully encased in frost long ago, started to hammer against its prison. "You...you read about my father."

"You know I didn't, ma'am. You already got rid of every trace of him. You didn't want anyone to know what he did...what he did for *you*."

Tears battered her corneas, but she refused to let them escape. She narrowed her eyes in a desperate attempt to keep the salty water imprisoned.

"You have no idea what you're talking about..."

"You don't have children, Ms. Doubek," Vilém said. "I don't know if that was just your preference or if you were scared...scared, maybe, that you'd understand why he did it..."

"There is no excuse for what he did!" Alica screamed, stomping her foot, sending a tremble through the old building. "And if you're trying to say that his ghost is here, waiting for me to say I'm sorry, waiting for me to say I still love him, he's got another thing coming!"

Tears broke through her barrier, dripping down her face as she cried out. "You hear that, Father? I'm still angry! I will never stop being angry at you!"

Vilém shook his head, his teensy smile vanishing. "Ms. Doubek, your father was many things, but y'know...he was a good father. That may not make him a good person, but he put you above everything. Even himself. Your emotions are yours, and he doesn't want you to stop being angry at him. He wants you to stop being angry at yourself."

She wiped her tears away with her sleeve, seething at Vilém. "I am *not* angry at myself, I am *not*!"

"You blame yourself for what he did. You think because he sacrificed your friends for you, that guilt is yours. That's why you gave your rations to the other girls in the barrack..."

"Shut up..."

"That's why you've never let yourself smile or dance or have fun, not once in your whole life..."

"*Shut! Up!*" She charged at him, wielding her pointer like a sword. Vilém was ready. As she raised her little weapon to smack him, he dodged and grabbed her hand. She screeched.

"Let go of me!"

"Sure thing, ma'am," Vilém said, pulling the pointer out of her grasp and releasing her. He stepped back and, holding the pointer behind his back, offered her a hand.

"May I have a dance?" he asked, bowing towards her. She looked at him as though he had just suggested the world was flat.

"Excuse me?" she gasped.

"You don't deserve to be miserable all the time, Alica. What happened wasn't your father's fault, and it wasn't your fault. Blame the Nazis be mad at your father for what he did, but please stop being so angry all the time. You deserve to smile."

She covered her mouth with her hands, her eyes betraying her, shimmering with want as she looked down at his outstretched hand. Her foot committed treason by daring to tap.

"I can't..." she whispered. Vilém shrugged.

"Fine! Then I'll dance alone!" he declared. He twirled the pointer like it was a cane and began to dance just like she had when she was a child: with no sense of step and no skill whatsoever, with reckless joy.

"Rehor, stop, stop, you're in a barrack! People died here!" Alica shrieked, and he grinned when he heard suppressed amusement in her voice. She pressed her hands against her lips, desperately trying to keep her long-gone smile from returning.

"And you lived! Isn't that great?" Vilém cried.

"No, no it is not!" Alica insisted, sobs starting to wrack her old body. "I didn't deserve it!"

"You *all* deserved to live and laugh and dance! The Nazis took that from all of you! Take it back!"

"You're so..." she started to say, but before she could accuse him of being stupid or irreverent or horrible, he danced right into his laptop. He stepped on the machine, cracking the keyboard, and jumped back, falling to the floor with a yelp.

"So make life worthwhile...
Come on and smile, darn ya', smile!"

Despite the terrible damage done to the computer, the old song continued to play. Vilém, dazed, rolled over and looked towards his laptop, his face turning red when he saw what he had done. He looked up at Alica, grinned, and shrugged.

"Whoops!" he cried, and the dam broke. Alica's hands flew from her mouth to her sides. She didn't just smile, she laughed. It was the strangest, most beautiful noise he had ever heard: an extinct laugh returning from the grave. Hoarse and clumsy like a child singing. She laughed so hard that she fell to her knees, so hard that tears conquered her eyes.

"Oh, you're so stupid!" she howled. She laughed and cried and smiled, and her smile was even lovelier than it had been when she was a child. It was a smile that had been waiting a lifetime to come out, and it was worth the wait.

Vilém sighed happily and collapsed to the floor, shutting his eyes.

"Mission accomplished," he whispered, and he heard the Rabbi's cracking voice echo from faraway.

You're a miracle, Vilém. You are an amazing man, and you will be an amazing father. Good luck...and thank you.

And with that, the Rabbi's spirit disappeared, and the only spirit left in Barrack Two was someone else, someone Vilém could sense was seething.

"Well..." Vilém sneered at Kommandant Gerber's furious ghost as Alica Doubek's melodious laughter drove the wicked phantom from Barrack Two. "You lose."

And the Jewish woman's laughter was so raucous that Vilém barely heard the Nazi's parting remark.

Not yet.

BARRACK ONE

"Vilém, we need to talk…"

"We probably do, but can we do it after *this asshole quits tailing me?!*"

Jana snickered and craned her neck to look behind her. They were on their way to visit Vilém's parents—since they were planning on having their wedding in Prague and Tomas Rehor had offered to pay for the ceremony, they had to go over all of their plans.

Jana was just hoping her fiancé would be able to get them there in one piece. Unfortunately, Vilém refused to let Jana go anywhere near the wheel while she was pregnant, insisting that she sit shotgun and hug a pillow to her chest while he drove. Which normally wouldn't have been a problem, but even though it had been weeks since the spirit of Kommandant Gerber had injured his eyes, Vilém's vision still hadn't fully recovered.

"Vil, he's not tailing us, you're blind," Jana sighed.

"He is *directly* on my butt! If he was any closer, I'd have to ask *him* to marry me," Vilém said with a smirk.

"Vilém!" laughed Jana, slapping his arm.

"Fuck it, I'm pulling over. Let's get something to eat and let this guy pass," Vilém suggested. He found a drive-thru and joined the line.

"Oh, come on!" Vilém cried as the driver behind him, evidently famished, followed him off the road. Jana shoved her face into her mandatory pillow in a desperate attempt to protect Vilém's pride as she laughed herself stupid.

"Oh, yes, laugh! Laugh at my misery!" Vilém teased. "All right, well, we're stuck between an indecisive orderer and a literal ass-kisser, so I guess we might as well talk."

"Okay..." Jana sighed, setting her pillow back in her lap and grabbing her fiancé's hand. "Listen, Vil...the Camp, I know it's a good job with good pay, and I know you do wonderful work there..."

"Oh, don't tell me you want me to quit!" Vilém cried, trying to achieve a joking tone but unable to stop genuine disappointment from slipping into his voice. "Ms. Doubek's finally bearable! She actually likes me now!"

"I know, honey," Jana said, tugging his hand towards her belly. "But I'm thinking about the baby and...I don't wanna have to raise her alone because some crazy Nazi ghost killed her daddy. I know you still wanna get rid of the Kommandant, but..."

"Jana," Vilém sighed, gently patting her stomach. "I'm thinking about the baby too, you know I am. If he can hurt me, he could hurt someone else...he could hurt her someday. I'm not gonna let her grow up with the same worries your grandma had."

"She's gonna be a Jew, Vilém. Ghost or no ghost, she's gonna have to grow up with some of those worries. You can't stop that."

"I can mitigate it. Look, nobody else has been able to see or hear Gerber or any other ghost. I've gotten rid of the last four..."

"They were good people, though. They weren't Nazis."

"Sweetie, Klammer," Vilém reminded her, and she threw up her hands.

"Fine, one ex-Nazi! Same difference! Oh, I'm just so worried...if he can hurt your eyes this bad..."

"Then he's gotta go," Vilém said. "He may be a Nazi, but he's still human. If I can figure out why he's still here, maybe I can force him to give it up and get out."

"Maybe. But for all you know, his unfinished business may be that he didn't kill enough Jews. Him and Heydrich are probably just angry the Final Solution wasn't final."

Vilém's eyes widened, but he didn't dare say a word. Heydrich! He had almost forgotten that the Hangman of Prague's ghost was almost certainly still lingering in Prague. Information on Kommandant Gerber had been nearly impossible to come by even with Ms. Doubek's enthusiastic assistance, but Kommandant Gerber and Heydrich *had* been "friends."

Perhaps the Blonde Beast could give him something besides grief for once.

The soon-to-be-newlyweds arrived at the Rehor residence in somewhat decent time despite Vilém's road rage almost leading to an all-out brawl ("Vilém, I can't believe you said that to him, you're lucky he didn't kill you!" "Maybe next time he won't sexually harass my car!")

Vilém hadn't even put the car in park when his mother appeared outside Jana's door. Squealing, Lida Rehor pulled her almost-daughter-in-law out of the vehicle and into an embrace so crushing that Jana was almost afraid for her baby.

"Hiya, Mrs. Rehor!" she cried.

"Oh, *stop,* you! When will you learn?" cried Lida, kissing Jana's cheek.

"My bad, Mama Lida!" giggled Jana, returning the greeting and pecking her future mother-in-law's cheek. Vilém stumbled out of the car and Tomas, showing much more enthusiasm than he normally would, darted from the porch and pulled his son into a half-hug.

"There he is!" laughed Tomas. Vilém grinned and teasingly shoved his father away.

"Hey, what kinda trick is this?" he cried.

"No tricks! I just love you!" Tomas decreed, ruffling Vilém's hair. Vilém pursed his lips together with derisive suspicion.

"Plus, I have to stay on your good side," Tomas joked. "You're about to give me my first grandchild, so for once I have to pretend you're the favorite!"

"Aha! I knew there was a twist!" Vilém cried, wagging an accusatory finger in his father's face. Lida and Tomas helped the couple take their bags into the house.

"Since you're going to be newlyweds, you two can share the same room now!" Lida declared, lifting Jana's hefty suitcase up to Vilém's old bedroom.

"It's not a sin anymore," Tomas chuckled.

"I think the real sin is asking us to share a twin bed," Vilém snickered, and Jana patted her stomach.

"Only room for two! Sorry, sweetie, you're on the floor," she declared.

"I'm sleeping down here with the cactuses," Vilém joked. He looked around at the menagerie of cacti that decorated his parents' living room, sparing a glance at the picture of his grinning Grandpa Fabian that rested among the plants. The cactuses always reminded him of his grandfather's less-than-green thumb and all the hours they had spent together, painting pots for the succulents.

His eyes flitted to the top of the TV and he was surprised to see a familiar plant sitting in a pot decorated with tiger stripes. The name 'STEVE' was painted on the rim.

"Mama, I thought Steve died!" he cried, stepping close to the imposter cactus and scowling down at it, realizing that although from the distance it was a dead-ringer for Steve, up close it looked subtly different.

"Oh, honey, I know, but Oda loves Steve and she's going to be down here for the wedding!" Lida cried from upstairs.

"Mamaaaa, that's pretty deceptive! There's only one Steve!" Vilém proclaimed, crossing his arms and glowering at Not-Steve. "Steve is irreplaceable."

"I wish I could have met Steve," Jana sighed wistfully, shaking her head and hugging her belly. "The baby could have used a godfather!"

"Hey, you said no godfathers! I already told Erik no!" Vilém laughed. "I mean, granted, Steve still would have been a better godfather than Erik..."

"Vil-Vil, if you're really upset, we can call that one Steve Junior," Lida said, trotting down the stairs and grabbing a sharpie from a nearby desk, tossing it to her son. Vilém nodded and drew a large, prominent "JR" next to the "STEVE."

"I guess Oda has to learn about death eventually," sighed Lida.

"Mama...Oda's twenty," Vilém pointed out.

"She's still my baby and so are you!" Lida cried, pinching her son's cheek. "Oh, speaking of babies...Jana! Come, me and Tomas went shopping and we bought the most adorable clothes for the baby! We kept everything purple, nice and gender-neutral."

Vilém followed his wife-to-be and mother into Emma's room, which was packed to the brim with purple baby clothes, toys, and even a cradle. He hung back, letting Jana and his mother have their fun, until he felt a tap on his shoulder.

"All joking aside," Tomas whispered in his son's ear. "I'm very proud of you!"

"Of what, Old Man?" snickered Vilém. "Jana's the one who's doing all the work!"

"I can see that look in your eyes. Same look I had when we were about to have you. You're stressed, and that's good! It means you're worried, and it means you're going to try your hardest. You grew into a good man and you're going to be an excellent father. I'm proud of you. And don't worry too much about the baby..."

"Pap, the baby may be the least of my worries right now," Vilém sighed.

Vilém did his best to keep Jana and his parents awake for as long as possible. He wanted them to sleep deeply. By 2 AM, everyone in the house was practically dead. He slipped into his old bedroom and kissed his snoozing fiancée's forehead.

"Don't freak out," he whispered. He tiptoed out of the room and down the stairs, pausing to smile affectionately at Fabian before darting out of the house and rushing to the car.

It probably would have been dangerous for anyone else to drive when they were as sleep-deprived as Vilém, but he was so used to adjusting and readjusting his sleep schedule that he managed a relatively lengthy drive without so much as a droopy eyelid.

He drove until he reached the corner of Kubišova Street. When Vilém had been young, there had been no memorial, but now a tall tower stood at the spot where two brave Czech partisans had assassinated the Butcher of Prague. Shaped like a triangle with three metal men poised at the top holding out their arms, as though they were preparing to take a bullet for their nation.

Vilém parked near the memorial. Thankfully, the street was

practically vacant at this early hour and only a few cars whizzed by. He hopped out of his car and approached the triangular tower, looking down at the flickering candles and vibrant flowers that grateful Czechs had left for the partisans.

"Well, he wouldn't be here..." Vilém muttered. He tried to remember where he had been standing when he had previously sensed Heydrich's spirit. He marched around, keeping his eyes as close to shut as possible without rendering himself blind. The last thing he wanted was to bumble right into traffic. He imagined Heydrich would find that amusing.

Vilém trudged through the trimmed grass until a freezing breeze struck him. He shuddered and opened his eyes, looking under his foot and realizing that there was a small triangle-shaped boulder jutting out of the dirt. He initially couldn't see why Heydrich would choose to cling to a tiny rock of all things, but he glanced from the boulder to the statue and chuckled when he realized what the Nazi's thought process must have been.

"Jealous asshole..." he whispered. Heydrich had chosen a rejected scrap from the memorial.

Vilém knelt down and rubbed his hands together. "All right, let's see if this works for evil ghosts."

He shut his eyes and pressed his hand against the tiny triangle.

"Hey, Reichsprotektor," he greeted the Nazi. A small wave of aggravation crashed against him.

Go away. Vilém recognized the squeaky voice right away. Definitely Heydrich.

"So what's keeping you here, Heydrich? Didn't burn enough babies to death?"

I have nothing to say to you.

"You don't seem to be very busy."

How did you see me?

"I followed the trail of blood," Vilém grumbled. "Listen, this isn't pleasant for me either, but I'm willing to trade information for information. I want info on Kommandant Hans Gerber. You give that to me, I'll give you something."

You don't have anything to offer me. We lost. That's all. I don't care about anything out there.

"Not even Klaus?" Vilém hissed, and he felt a small burst of sadness emanate from Heydrich's spirit at hearing the name of his beloved son.

No. No I do not.

"That's a lie. You're a monster, but not *that* much of a monster."

I'm not a monster. There's nothing you can tell me about Klaus. He's dead. He's gone.

"So what are you still doing here? I was kidding about the not enough burned babies thing, but..."

You're not even a real person! Heydrich's spirit had evidently had enough small-talk and sarcasm. Vilém winced as he felt a sharp pain in his hand, as though someone had dug their finger-nails into his flesh. He grunted. Intimidation? Well, Vilém wasn't about to run away.

He sat silently for a moment, gritting his teeth, his skin screaming for him to hurry up and think of something. Threatening a ghost wouldn't work, but he remembered reading about the Hangman's Achilles' Heel.

"Wow...you're really pathetic..." said Vilém, letting a grin take over his face. He suppressed a yelp of pain as the Nazi ghost punched his hand.

"Is *that* the best you've got?" Vilém giggled.

You're a very stupid Czech...

But Heydrich's ghost fell silent as Vilém started laughing, laughing as though he had heard the greatest joke in the universe, laughing so hard it hurt worse than anything the dead Nazi could do to him.

What...what's so funny?

"You, Billy-Goat! You and that voice, you sound like a lamb!"

I....

"And what are you doing right now? Stepping on my hand? Oh, how the mighty have fallen! What am I saying? You were never mighty! I heard your mom used to beat the shit outta you when you were a kid."

Enough...

"Did Mommy make you cry, Reini? Did Mommy say she didn't love you, so you decided to take it out on some helpless people? Did that make you feel big, Reini? Did killing Jews make you feel better about yourself, Reini?"

Enough, I said!

"Did it make you feel like a hero, Reini? Klaus said he thought you were a hero! Remember his face when he found out your secret? Oh, he was so disappointed. He thought you were a hero, and then he thought you were a monster. Oh, poor kid didn't even know! You're not a monster, you're just a pathetic little nobody. A dumb little goat that wanted to be a wolf. Bleat more, come on! Baaa! Baaa!"

Enough, enough, enough! Stop talking! Shut your mouth and don't talk about my son!

Heydrich's ghost attacked Vilém's hand, and Vilém could feel his fingers crack. But he kept laughing. He laughed and laughed and the ghost's anger morphed into desperation.

Stop laughing at me!

"Jesus, don't tell me anything about Gerber! I want an excuse to stay here and listen to you squeak! It's so funny!"

I'm not funny! I bathed the streets of Prague in Czech blood, I...

"'I bathed the streets of Prague in Czech Blood', ha!" Vilém cried, making his voice absurdly high-pitched as he teased the Blonde Beast.

Oh, you're as bad as...you know what? I'll tell you whatever you want to know about Gerber if you promise to leave me alone and never come here again!

"Not a problem, Reini," Vilém snickered, letting his raucous laughter fade. "I don't want to save your soul."

That seems to be a common sentiment around here...all right, you wanted to know about Gerber. What about him?

"His ghost is still at the Camp, and he's being a nuisance."

That sounds like Hans.

"I heard you two were friends."

I don't have any friends.

"Golly, I wonder why! You're so pleasant. All I wanna know is why he may still be there and how I could convince him to leave...short of 'finish the Holocaust.'"

I don't think you'll have to worry about that. Gerber was a National Socialist, but nowhere near as ardent as most. He never would have gotten as far in the Party as he did were it not for my kindness.

"His favorite hobby was taking pictures of dead Jews, how was he not 'ardent'?"

Oh, he hated Jews. More than me, actually. He hated everything about Judaism. But he had his...strayings.

"Not like you, you never strayed."

Czech, you should learn this: there was never a perfect National Socialist.

"Himmler and Hitler called *you* the perfect Nazi after you died."

Ha! Now that...that is funny. I'm sure Goebbels wrote a lovely script for my funeral...well, you don't care about me.

"Nobody does."

Yes...well, Gerber, then. He hated Jews for personal reasons. His father served in the First World War, Martin Gerber...

"Martin?" Vilém cried. "Martin was his...well, his so-called son's name, the name of the Jewish child he kidnapped..."

What?

"Guess he kept this from you...there was this little blonde Jewish kid, Gerber stole him from his parents and was trying to make him become 'Aryan.'"

I know exactly who you're talking about. Gerber and his lies— he told me the boy was his illegitimate child. But...Jews can't become Aryan. Are you sure the child wasn't a mischling?

"A what?"

Part-Jew, mixed race. If the boy only had one Jewish grand- parent or one Jewish parent...well, depending on how liberal Gerber became while I wasn't looking, he could have decided the boy wasn't a real Jew. The definition of "Jew" tended to vary from person to person in the Reich. Goering used to say he would decide who was Jewish, but even with the Nuremberg Laws, a lot of it became a matter of guesswork and preference.

"These rules seem arbitrary and stupid."

This isn't a debate, Czech. The point is: it doesn't make sense for Gerber to take in a random Jew...he must have known something about the boy.

"Such as...?"

Perhaps the boy's father. I was just about to talk about that. Gerber's father died in the Great War...er...the first one...not the one I was in, the one before that...

"World War One. I get it. What happened?"

He gave his gas mask to a young child, a Jew. Gave his life for a little Jew.

"Jesus, you're lying..."

I'm not. I don't know many of the details, but Gerber said that the Jew his father saved lived in his house throughout his childhood. Evidently the Jew was a nightmare, constantly in trouble...I believe his name was Isaac Goldstein. The details are really not important. Use what few brain cells you have, Czech: clearly the Jewish child Gerber "adopted" wasn't just an experiment. Perhaps he was the son of Isaac, and if so, he would have possessed sentimental value. Gerber might have truly cared for him.

"Which would mean that when Little Martin ran away from the Camp..." muttered Vilém. "That might be it...yeah..."

I said Gerber wasn't a truly ardent National Socialist for a reason: he cared less about his nation, less about the Cause, than he did about his own legacy. Everything he ever did was for his legacy. Our deeds are our legacy, but our children are as well. If he viewed Martin as a son, then the boy was his legacy.

"Legacy, hm...? Maybe he's not too happy with the legacy he has now. Maybe he wants a different legacy."

If you can communicate with me, you can communicate with Gerber. Bring up Isaac and his father, that should convince him to talk to you. Failing that, I suppose you could just annoy him into submission.

"If it comes to that," Vilém sneered. "So one more question before I leave, Heydrich: you said you weren't a perfect Nazi. If you're not still here because you're upset about not winning the war or killing all the Jews, why *are* you here?"

I have nowhere else to go.

"Too evil for Hell?"

Ha! I wish. Didn't you promise to leave me alone?

"Gladly. When you get the chance, please go to Hell..."

Already...

But Vilém removed his injured hand from the rock, refusing to let Heydrich have the last word. He stood up, hissed, and wiggled his fingers. Heydrich, even trying his hardest, hadn't broken Vilém's bones.

"Ha!" laughed Vilém, cradling his hand and glowering down at the little triangle. "You really *are* pathetic."

Vilém was lucky to be alive. Not because he had survived Heydrich's attack, but because Jana refrained from killing him when he called her from Bulovka Hospital. She took a taxi and stayed with him for the rest of the night. He was released by morning, and while Jana was merciful enough to spare his life, she was not merciful enough to leave his ears unharmed. Once they were away from the doctors and nurses, she started screaming at him and didn't stop until they pulled up to his parents' house.

"This is it, Vilém Rehor!" Jana shouted. "No more! You use the info Heydrich gave you! After that, no more! I can't do this..." She started to cry, clutching at her belly. He reached out and pulled her into an embrace.

"I know," he sighed. "I give. Just one try, and then nothing else."

"And if it looks like you'll get hurt..."

"I'll run," he promised, despising the notion of fleeing from a Nazi. Doing so would be a betrayal of his blood and pride, but Jana was right. He needed to stay safe for her, for his baby.

They spent the rest of the week with Lida and Tomas, planning the wedding and, in Vilém's case, coming up with increasingly stupid excuses for why his hand was bandaged ("I got attacked by lemurs on my way home from defending my fiancée's honor at the local distillery" quickly became Tomas' favorite).

When the week ended and Vilém was obligated to go home, he insisted that Jana stay with his folks.

"I love Ilona, but if something happens and I'm stuck at the Camp, I want someone to take care of you and the baby. I'm not sure she could handle that," Vilém said. "Oh, Mama! Speaking of which, I promised Ilona and Ms. Doubek I'd bring the album!"

"You remembered!" squealed Jana happily while Lida retrieved a small leather-bound book full of pictures.

"There! Everyone should be there! We haven't gone through them since Papa passed," Lida sighed. Vilém vowed to take good care of the old memories, kissed his mother and fiancée goodbye, and hugged his father.

"You look like you're about to go into battle, my boy," Tomas whispered into his son's ear.

"I guess I kinda am, Pap."

"Chin up. You're a tough boy. Whoever's pissing you off, give 'em Hell."

"So, Rehor, have you come up with a way to get rid of our little pest?"

"I think I have, though it may require some danger..." Vilém replied as he marched into his boss' office. Ms. Doubek was rifling through a small stack of pictures. She saw that he was holding a leather-bound book and held out her hand, offering him a smile. Vilém grinned and gave her the album. Ever since he had made her laugh in Barrack Two, Ms. Doubek had become much nicer. Not sweet as sugar, and she still didn't abide by nonsense, but she showed off her smile once a day now, usually reserving it for him.

"Thank you! You already showed Ilona?" Alica said, rifling through Vilém's family photos. He nodded.

"Uh huh, and digitized them, if you need digital copies…"

"I'll handle that, and I can restore them a bit," Ms. Doubek said, meeting the frozen eyes of little Fabian Svoboda and letting a lovely smile grace her wrinkled face. "These will do well! I think it's about time we gave the survivors some love."

"So the Heydrich Exhibit's going down and the Survivor Exhibit will be in Barrack Four, right? I wanted to take my mom, and if possible Ilona…"

"Oh, of course! I may need some quotes and statements from Ilona, and since your grandfather's passed maybe your mother could tell us a few things. Or you could!"

"I could, but my grandpa wasn't at the Camp…we always kind of assumed he was. But he never really talked much about the war, so we only really knew that Sam was on Klammer's Train. But, well, Klammer showed me his memories and Grandpa and Great-Grandma Rebecca weren't here. My great-uncle was here, though. I could tell you about him or I could call his kids."

"That would work…hm…I'm just wondering about aesthetics right now…" Ms. Doubek sighed and glanced out the window, peering at the few solemn visitors that remained at the Camp. "You think an exhibit like this will be…appropriate? I know the guests will like it, they hate leaving the Camp completely depressed, but it seems like…"

"The Holocaust isn't just about the dead, Alica," Vilém said, leaning over the desk and gesturing towards the image of Sam Svoboda. "If it was, we wouldn't have to talk about it so much. We should show how people lived after it…the fact that they lived on after it, that's a kick to the balls for Hitler and Heydrich, and Gerber too."

"Gerber! Yes, I almost forgot!" Alica cried, shuffling the papers and pictures into a neat stack and then twirling her finger impatiently at Vilém. "Come on, come on, tell me what you found! I want to get rid of this bastard as quickly as possible. I doubt he'll appreciate the Survivor Exhibit, and I don't want him making trouble."

"I found some info about his personal life, enough that I think if I can get to him, talk to him on my terms, then maybe I could get him out."

"That would require knowing where he stays. He goes to every barrack and never seems to linger for very long."

"True. But everyone else stayed where they had a reason to stay, and he has most reason to stay at..."

"His old house," sighed Alica, plopping her papers into an accordion folder and biting her bottom lip. "Barrack One."

"It's the only place we haven't checked."

"And it's the only place you can't get into," Alica said, trotting towards the window and parting the curtains enough that she could see a distant corner of the camp. An old building stood in the shadows, blocked off by yellow tape and thick wire fencing.

"I was hoping you could..." Vilém started to say, but Alica shook her head.

"Vilém, I don't own the Camp, and that building is supposed to be preserved for historical studies only. We're not supposed to let anyone go in there unless they're sent by the government for restoration. Amateur historians and students have to wait months to get permission to go in, and they have to be supervised to make sure they don't touch anything. If you went in there without the proper papers, I would *have* to fire you. It would be out of my hands...and you would never get permission to go 'conduct research' in there after dark."

"I understand, Ms. Doubek," Vilém sighed.

"I...would rather not fire you, Vilém," Ms. Doubek said,

releasing the curtain and facing him with her lips upturned. "You were going to be my employee of the month."

"You're joking!" laughed Vilém.

"Most of my employees just get drunk and lounge around all night, maybe chase some teenagers away. If I'd known you had to deal with all these ghosts, I may have paid you better."

"You could always give me a bonu—"

"No."

"Worth a shot," Vilém snickered. "In all seriousness, I'll take the risk."

"Vilém, you are about to have a child, I don't want to fire you and have you..."

"I won't starve. We'll still have the sweet shop. It'll be hard, but I'll live. This is important. You're right: he won't like the Survivor Exhibit, and I don't want anyone else getting hurt."

He gestured towards his eyes and Ms. Doubek's wrinkled hands curled into shaking fists. She nodded.

"Very well...I'll cover for you as much as I can, but we never had this conversation. If you can manage this without disturbing anything in Barrack One, all's well, but if you can't...I'm sorry."

"It's not your fault, Ms. Doubek," Vilém said, grabbing his family album and hugging it to his chest, trying to draw strength from the images of his ancestors. "This is all Gerber's fault. I'm gonna make sure he knows that."

Sneaking into Barrack One proved relatively easy. Ms. Doubek made sure to "accidentally" leave the key on her desk, and once he "stole" it, getting into the barrack was simply a matter of climbing over the tape, snipping some wire, and reaching the too-familiar front door.

He squeezed his family album. He had brought it with him just in case he needed ammunition against the Kommandant, to show him how thoroughly he had failed. Gripping the leather book like a child might a teddy bear, he looked up at the weathered building. The paint had chipped and fallen away, revealing the "Barrack One" plaque that Hans Gerber had been determined to hide.

Vilém took out the key and jabbed it into the rusted doorknob. The ancient door shrieked as he opened it, revealing a gloomy interior. The electricity must have been cut long ago, when the Communist government of Czechoslovakia had restricted access to the Kommandant's house. Why such a decision had been made was a mystery. Perhaps they hadn't wanted Fascists to turn the house into a memorial. Perhaps the Reds had not liked the notion of people entering the building and seeing little pieces of humanity. Perhaps they didn't like to be reminded of how similar they were to the Fascists they had fought.

Vilém tarried at the threshold of the forbidden property. The modern Czech government didn't want grubby gross men getting their grubby gross hands all over the little piece of frozen time. Touching anything was not only governmental grounds for dismissal, it was illegal. And though Vilém was willing to do almost anything to get rid of the Nazi, he didn't want to be a criminal. Ms. Doubek was right. He had a child to worry about.

But before he could let fear conquer his heart, he felt a warm burst of defiance. Where it came from he wasn't sure, but it felt like a gentle push, like someone had just grabbed his hand and promised him that he wasn't alone.

He stepped in, and although he could sense that the Kommandant's former residence was awash in a cold aura, whatever force stood by him kept it at bay, bathing him in comforting warmth and allowing him to journey through the house without shivering.

He peeked out a nearby window and saw that Iveta's old doghouse was gone, probably thrown out when she had been moved to Barrack Four. He wouldn't find the Kommandant there. He decided to check Gerber's old office. It was so identical to how it had looked a hundred years ago that it felt like stepping into a memory. The desk was the same, the Nazi books lining the shelves were all there, there was even a scowling bust of Hitler on the mantle. He touched everything he could, even poking the Hitler bust's moustache, but he found nothing.

He checked Raya's old developing room next, which was bare except for a few empty chemical tubs and the broken bits of the Kommandant's camera, which rested in a display case in the corner. Vilém scowled at the shattered camera lens, looking at his reflection in the foggy glass. He touched the display case, then lifted it and touched the camera. Nothing.

One more possibility. Vilém left the developing room and stumbled into the nursery. Most of Martin's toys had been preserved, though they sat behind glass now instead of laying hither and thither.

Vilém felt something right away, a pull towards one partic-ular toy: a ragged little stuffed cat with onyx button eyes. It rested separate from the others, lying outside of the glass on the little twin bed right beside the pillow. Vilém squinted at it. It looked familiar...yes, he remembered it from Klammer and Doctor Doubek's respective memories. Martin had been holding it on his not-birthday, the day before the Freedom Train left the Camp.

Vilém, not wanting to test the strength of the bed, sat on the ground and gingerly picked up the toy. He cradled it in his arms and closed his eyes.

"Heydrich told me about Isaac," he called out, and he felt a burst of surprise come from the malicious spirit.

Asshole.

"Enough with the menacing boom in your voice, Gerber, I've already figured you out. Your dad sacrificed his life for a Jew, and you blame all of them for that. It's simple."

Nothing is ever that simple, Czech.

"Would you care to enlighten me, then?"

Ha! Cute. Are you here to save my soul, Czech?

"Not really. I'm curious."

Ask that cat about curiosity.

"If I managed to squeeze info out of Heydrich, I'll squeeze it out of you, Gerber."

Heydrich was always weak. Sentimental.

Vilém snorted. "The Blonde Beast? Sentimental?"

Oh, he always droned on and on with excuses and justifications. He was always content to write orders for Jew deaths, but he never wanted to see it up close. Always got so squeamish when I showed him pictures. He always avoided the prisoners and the barracks when he came to the Camp. He was a glorified paper-pusher. He didn't have a warrior's heart.

"And you did? You liked making the Jews suffer?"

Is it so strange to enjoy an enemy's pain? Would you not indulge in my suffering, Czech?

"Yeah, but you're actually evil. You just decided that all Jews are evil because...well, because."

Because of many factors. Look at the world...look how they've corrupted your culture, look how they've...

"I didn't come for a Hitlerian sermon, Gerber, I came for a story. Your story."

Really? Hm...I am curious, how are you able to talk to us?

"I wouldn't know."

Don't lie, Czech! I know you've been working with the Jews, and I know you made it your mission to release them, to make them move on...

"I get it. You're upset I helped them. You wanted me to let them stay here forever. Miserable. With you."

They deserved it.

"You deserve it, they didn't. But I've been through the Camp a hundred times looking for you. I know you're the last one here. You lost. You're alone."

Yes...I suppose I am. There were a few seconds of bitter silence between the Czech and the Nazi as the Kommandant seemed to mull over this fact for the first time in weeks. Vilém felt the slightest twinge of sadness echo from the depths of the wicked soul.

I'd rather not be alone here, and there is one thing I need to know. And you...you may be able to help me.

"I don't wanna help you, I wanna get rid of you," Vilém hissed.

Same difference. I'm not leaving until I get what I want.

"Fine, but let's make this quick. I don't want to see too much from your point of view."

Pity, that, but I suppose you Czechs are ever so intellectually...uncurious.

"Said the man whose ideology is known for burning books," Vilém countered, earning a small chuckle from the Nazi spirit.

Well...fair point. If you help me, I'll refrain from attacking you again. How's that for a deal, Czech?

"And you'll leave?"

Hm...well, I'm not sure. I don't know what comes after this.

"Scared of Hell, Nazi?" Vilém teased, and the Kommandant scoffed.

If there is a God, and He is all merciful, then whatever Hell He designed is preferable to staying here and hearing ignorant lamenta-

tions and Jew crocodile tears from dawn till dusk. So...no, I'm not afraid of Hell.

"Good, I'm sure you have a reserved seat. Let's get you down there as fast as possible."

Don't rush me, Czech. I'm being rather generous, allowing a mutt like you to see my memories. They're precious, and you don't deserve them. But...you must look. Seeing may make all the difference. Now...I suppose we'll start with Martin. Senior, that is.

Vilém almost yelped as he was shoved into Gerber's memory: the Kommandant, unlike every other ghost, was forceful. It felt as though the Nazi had grabbed him by the throat and thrown him into a deep pit. When Vilém opened his eyes and found himself in the past, he was so dizzy that it took him a second to get his bearings and actually see through Gerber's eyes.

He settled into the body, which was that of a very young Hans Gerber. The picture of innocence so far: Vilém felt nothing but childish awe flowing through the little boy's body as he peered out his window and gawked at a marching troop. Vilém saw little spikes on the helmets of the German soldiers and realized they were off to WWI, off to die in the trenches.

Comfortable? The Kommandant's snide intrusion reminded Vilém of who he was occupying.

"For now. You're not evil yet."

Children are foolish, but adults were as well back then. They didn't realize how the Jews would rob them...they marched alongside the German-speaking Jews who infiltrated their ranks, genuinely believing they wouldn't stab them in the back...

"Pipe down, I'm not going to learn anything if you recite a passage from *Mein Kampf* every time a new memory starts."

So uncurious...fine. Well, you know what happened to my father, but at the time...well, he was invincible to me. I was only five. I didn't think anything could hurt him...

Vilém felt the child's eyes focus on one soldier in particular, a dead-ringer for the Aryan superman who marched behind one company, holding an Imperial German flag. Little Hans Gerber squealed and ran out of his nursery.

"Hansie, don't...!" A woman wearing a worried expression, presumably little Hans' mother, leapt from her seat at a grand piano and tried to stop her son. Vilém only got a brief look at the interior of Hans' house, but judging from the polished piano that lay in the finery-clad living room, the Gerbers were well off.

"Papie, Papie!" Hans squeaked as he burst out of the house and barreled towards the parade. A small crowd of onlookers stood in his way, waving flags and blowing kisses to their departing loved ones. Little Hans didn't let them stop him, however. He crawled towards the soldiers, weaving through the civilians' legs until he emerged on the other side of the throng. He found his father amongst the marching men and ran towards him, causing the onlookers to laugh and cry, "Aww!"

"Hansie, you little sneak!" Martin Senior laughed, scooping his child into one arm, making sure to hold the flag up high and proud. Hans wrapped his arms around his father's neck, giggling as the tassels on the flag tickled his nose.

"Mama wants to go to Paris, Papie!" Hans announced. "Can we go too? Are you sure we can't go? Papie, pleeeease?"

"Hans, by the time I come back, Germany will *own* Paris!" laughed Martin Senior. "We can go there whenever we want and we'll take lots of pictures!"

Ah...yes. When I was little, I loved picture books. Papa used to make them for me. We had a camera—something of a luxury back then! He would go places and take pictures and Mother would sew them into a little book for me.

"Hm...you really loved your father," Vilém observed.

He was a good man. He was never distant...always kind, loyal, and loving in a way many fathers were not back then. Any other father would have beaten me senseless for interrupting a parade. Not him.

"Apple fell far from the tree, then," grumbled Vilém. Little Hans kissed his father's cheek and Martin Senior put him down.

"Be good!" Martin Senior commanded. "Help your mother, don't be a leech!"

"Yes, sir!" Hans cried, saluting his father. Vilém could feel the child's heart swelling, and he could only hope that his child would feel the same overwhelming sense of adoration whenever they looked up at him.

In the blink of an eye, Martin Senior was gone and Hans, a year older, was in his living room, sitting beside his mother. Frau Gerber was unfolding a letter.

"Lemme see the pictures! Lemme see the pictures!" Hansie begged, reaching for the letter and whining when his mother refused to hand it over right away, insisting on reading it over before she let him see it. Hans threw an absolute tantrum at not getting what he wanted right away.

"Lemme see, lemme see!" he cried, smacking the chair so hard that his little fists ached. Vilém scoffed.

"You were a real spoiled brat," Vilém said. "Guess I can see where the entitlement came from."

That's a bit of a stretch. I admit to being spoiled as a child, but I don't see what that has to do with my eventual political views.

"You didn't get what you wanted when you were a kid, you threw a fit and punched furniture. You didn't get what you wanted as an adult, you threw a fit and killed Jews."

Hm. The Führer didn't have the cushy childhood I did, nor did Heydrich.

"Fine, you're not wrong. It's a factor, not the *only* reason."

I would argue it's not a factor at all, but that's beside the point.

"All right, all right, sweetie," Frau Gerber sighed, picking up her writhing son and plopping him on her lap. He settled as soon as he got what he wanted, grinning as she showed him the message. Martin Senior had formatted the letter carefully, pasting several pictures next to the paragraphs.

"Papa says he's made friends with all the men in his company. Papa's guarding a small border town in the Austro-Hungarian Empire," Frau Gerber explained, gesturing to a picture of a grinning Martin Senior standing in a trench, hugging a gas mask to his chest.

"He says he's made friends with a man named Friedrich, there they are..." A picture of Martin Senior and his grinning comrade sharing a chocolate bar.

"He also says the people in town are very nice and give them flowers all the time!"

She pointed to the last picture: Martin Senior was clutching a bouquet and patting a little boy on the head. The boy had curly ebony hair. His facial structure was familiar.

"That's him?" Vilém asked.

Isaac Goldstein. My age. He was a big fan of the military. Liked to give the soldiers treats and get a little too close to the trenches. But I don't think I can blame him too much for that. In the early days, the war was a fun affair. It was all about honor and glory, but then...things became worse. Pictures became more and more scarce, and one day...

The memory shifted in the blink of an eye. One moment little Hans was sitting in his mother's lap, staring at his smiling father's image, and the next he was older, hiding under the piano seat. He was lying with his cheek on the ground, hugging a bound book of pictures and staring at the front door. A German soldier was talking to a hysterical Frau Gerber, half-hugging her. Hans' ears were ringing, his heart was beating so loud he only heard little shreds of the soldier's speech.

"Hero...sacrificed...gas attack...village...this boy..."

The soldier gestured to his side, and Hans' eyes widened when he saw a tiny figure peeking out from behind the man's pant leg. A small child with curly dark hair. Isaac Goldstein lifted his eyes from his grime-covered shoes and sheepishly met Hans' gaze.

Well...the Allies attacked, the village got hit by gas while my father was there...he gave his gas mask to Isaac. He died to save Isaac's life.

"And you're bitter about that? Is that it?" Vilém queried.

Not precisely. My father was a hero...he died a hero, died to save this boy's life. Isaac's parents died in the gas attack, and my mother decided to take him in. We had the space, and we...didn't want my father to have died for nothing. I didn't mind the idea at first. It felt...nice to have him there. It was like he was a little piece of my father, like my father lived on through him.

"Isaac, catch!"

A new memory formed. Hans stood in the backyard of his sprawling home, heart racing, blood pumping. He hurled a ball at little Isaac, who had traded his scrappy peasant clothes for fine, soft garments. Isaac was prodding at the grass with a stick, drowning in his own thoughts.

"Isaac!" Hans cried, and the ball struck Isaac's head. The Jewish boy fell to the ground, clutching his skull.

"Oooowwww, Hans!" whined Isaac, rolling onto his back. Hans scurried to his friend's side and stood above him, smirking.

"I warned ya!" Hans giggled. Isaac grunted, grabbing a fistful of grass and yanking it out of the dirt.

"I was *thinking*, you ass!" the Jewish child snapped, tossing the grass at Hans, who squealed and reached down, pulling a mass of dirt, grass, and roots out of the ground.

"Dirty Jew!" Hans laughed, throwing the dirt at Isaac, who barely dodged his friend's assault. Isaac squatted on the damaged lawn, scowling at Hans even as a slight smile forced its way onto his solemn face.

"Don't call me that, that's not funny!" Isaac cried, tugging a chunk of the lawn from the ground and hurling it at Hans.

"You *are* a dirty Jew right now, look at you! You've got dirt on your ass!" Hans replied playfully.

"And you're a dirty goy!" Isaac retorted, ducking behind a tree and yanking a vine off the trunk, trying to use it as a makeshift whip to beat his brother. Hans found his own tree to hide behind, grabbing as much dirt and grass as his little fists could hold.

"Whoever gets dirtiest is the loser!" Hans dared. "Loser's gotta clean the winner's room!"

"You're on, but I get the first bath!" Isaac snickered, and Hans blew out an agitated breath.

"Damn it..." Hans muttered. The boys roared like soldiers as they charged at each other, flinging mud and rubbing grass into each other's clothes. By the time the battle was done and Isaac was declared the victor, the lawn was in ruins, both boys were coated in filth, and they were laughing themselves stupid. Right then, it seemed like they really were brothers.

It was good...for some time. When we were both little, we got along. I...cared for Isaac. He was a friend, a brother...it seemed to me that my father had died for a good reason, to let this boy live.

"...But?"

We grew, and he changed.

Hans blinked and the memory shifted. He and Isaac, now clean and pressed, were standing in front of a mirror. Frau Gerber was brushing Hans' hair, smiling down at her son. Vilém noticed that Isaac's satchel was worn down while Hans' looked brand new.

"Be good for your new teacher, Hansie," Frau Gerber cooed at her child.

"Yes, Mama!" Hans chirped.

Frau Gerber stepped behind Isaac and roughly ran her brush through his hair, grunting when his tangled curls offered resistance and giving up right away, handing Isaac the hairbrush.

"You'll have to manage it yourself, Isaac," she said. Isaac nodded slowly, reaching up and wincing as he combed his own hair. Vilém could see tears shining in his eyes.

"You need to try harder this year, Isaac," Frau Gerber commanded, standing over Isaac's shoulder and scowling at the Jewish child's reflection. "Your grades last year were not acceptable."

"Yes, ma'am," sighed Isaac, giving up on his hair and handing the brush back to Hans' mother.

"Wow, your mom definitely *didn't* pick favorites," Vilém muttered sarcastically as Frau Gerber snatched the brush out of Isaac's hand and sent the boys off, kissing Hans tenderly on the cheek and banishing Isaac with a dismissive wave.

Isaac was not her son. She had no obligation towards him. No obligation to treat him as her own. She didn't have to take him in, yet she did out of kindness. He should have appreciated that without demanding more.

"She took him in, she should have treated him the same as you. He didn't choose to lose his family, he didn't choose to be taken in by people who didn't love him."

We did love him!

"Taking someone in and making them feel bad for being alive constantly, treating them like a burden and telling them they should be grateful for scraps...that's not love."

You sound just like him...

"Try having some empathy for once, Gerber!" Vilém snapped,

watching as Hans walked two steps ahead of Isaac, occasionally glancing back at the Jewish boy. Isaac was dragging his feet, looking from his worn-down shoes to Hans' brand new boots.

"How would you feel?" Vilém asked. "If you lost your mother and father and everything else and suddenly found yourself in his situation, how would you feel?"

I would show gratitude and understand how troublesome I was. I'd understand the sacrifice the family had made and I'd never complain.

"I'm sure you'd *love* to be treated as second-class..." muttered Vilém.

At the time, we were second class. Germany's victory was stolen. We were betrayed, we were robbed, and our currency became worthless. We were the world's second-class citizens...

"Hey, Jew!"

Hans heard a grunt and Vilém felt the boy's heart cartwheel against his chest. Surprise, however, didn't strike him. Instead, it was a familiar sense of dread, the sort of feeling that Vilém had experienced whenever he had gone to class on test day knowing he had not studied, expecting to fail, expecting to be humiliated.

Hans turned just in time to see a small pack of hooligans surround Isaac. One of them, a dark-haired boy who might have passed for a stereotypical Jew himself, grabbed Isaac's satchel and dumped the heavy books on the Jewish boy's head.

Vilém felt Hans' cheeks flush. The young German scrambled inside the nearest shop, pressing his face against the glass, watching from the window as the boys tormented Isaac.

"Here, Jew, here! Have some money!" the pack leader sneered, and he and his comrades pulled little stacks of paper out of their bags and tossed it at the Jew. Vilém almost wanted to laugh when he realized they were attacking their victim with piles of Reichs-marks, rendered worthless by the post-war hyperinflation. The sight might have been funny if it weren't at the expense of the already-downtrodden boy. Isaac curled into a little ball, trying to cover his face. The boys laughed and the leader grabbed Isaac by his satchel, forcing him to his feet.

The big guy there is Derek. Lived on our block once, but the Depression ruined his family. We continued to have a somewhat cordial relationship, but he didn't like Isaac at all.

"Obviously," Vilém growled as Derek and his goons started shoving the worthless bills into Isaac's mouth, nearly choking the child with Marks.

Isaac was a Jew by blood alone. At our home, he never attempted to celebrate Jewish holidays. He attended church with us, celebrated Christmas with us...but he still insisted on calling himself a Jew. I wonder why.

"Pride?" Vilém suggested, and the Nazi spirit sneered.

Jews have nothing to be proud of.

Little Hans watched as Isaac was beaten and humiliated, and yet neither pity nor guilt entered the child's soul. He felt embarrassed, he felt irate, he tapped his foot as though this entire affair was a waste of *his* time. He never looked at his so-called brother's turmoil with empathy, and the impulse to go out and help was nonexistent.

"Wow..." Vilém whispered. "You really were a little bastard."

What was I supposed to do? Defend him?

"Uhm...yes."

I was already unpopular because of him. I suffered many indignities on his behalf because we were kind enough to take him in after my father gave his life for him. The least he could have done was handle some bullying with grace. I had no obligations towards him.

"With this kind of environment, I wonder what might have fucked him up," Vilém scoffed. "I bet I'd be mentally healthy if my so-called brother was refusing to help me and constantly guilting me for killing his father."

He DID kill my father! And all we ever asked of him was that he make something of himself, make it so that my father didn't die for nothing! But no! No, he had to be selfish! He had to act like a child!

"He *was* a child!" Vilém cried as the bullies grew tired of their quarry and dropped Isaac on the ground, giving him a few final kicks for good measure. They giggled and scattered, Derek pausing outside the window of the shop. He tapped on the glass in front of Hans' face, offering the German boy a small smile and gesturing towards Isaac.

"Hey, Gerber," Derek sneered. "You can have your Jew back."

"...Thanks..." Hans sighed, waving farewell as Derek darted off. Once he was sure that the bullies were gone, Hans exited the shop and slowly approached Isaac, who was sitting in a pile of Marks, crying.

"C'mon, Isaac," Hans said. "We're gonna be late for school."

"You go."

"Mama said..."

"I don't care what *your* mother said!" Isaac hissed, finally lifting his eyes. Hans jumped back as though he had just touched a hot stove, the furious fire in Isaac's irises shocking and upsetting him far more than Derek's attack had.

Anger jabbed at Hans' heart, and Vilém could hardly believe it. It seemed strange to him, that anyone could be so blind to how terrible they were, but Hans right then felt moral outrage, as though Isaac had beaten *him* up.

"Fine!" Hans hissed. "I don't wanna be seen with you anyway!"

Vilém felt a tiny, weak strike at Hans' soul. The part of him that loved Isaac, the part that wanted to go to school with him and be his brother, tried to assuage his pride and convince him to take that back. But Hans' ego was stronger. He turned, wiped his eyes...

And the memory shifted. Hans was a teenager now, his face covered with a fencer's mask. An eager, energetic rush filled his veins as he swung his saber at his opponent. With a dodge and a stab, he claimed victory, jabbing his opponent in the chest.

"Fuck!" his opponent cried, ripping off his mask and revealing himself to be Derek. Isaac's bully seemed sour for a moment, but the referee chastised him for being a poor sport and he seemed to remember his honor.

"Sorry, coach," Derek sighed. He reached out and grasped Hans' hand.

"I sometimes forget we're on the same team," Derek chuckled. "Just be sure to do that shit when we go up against Kiel."

"Will do!" Hans laughed, following his brother's bully back to the benches. They sat beside one another, chatting casually, and Vilém huffed.

"Reeeeal nice," he said. "Getting all buddy-buddy with someone who hates your brother."

Should I have cut contact? Refused Derek's friendship because of his views? Should I have lingered in the shadows with Isaac?

"Yes, Gerber! Yes, that is what you should have done! I can't believe you can't see this!" snapped Vilém. "You are *such* a shitty person and you don't even realize it! Good people don't betray people they claim to love! Good people stand by the victim, not the bully!"

Derek acted as a child would when he was younger. He knew about the wider Jewish Problem and behaved immaturely, but he mellowed over time.

"Ooooh, so he became a *polite* anti-Semite, I get it," sneered Vilém. "That makes it *so* much better!"

You're rather caustic.

"*You're* rather toxic," Vilém retorted as Derek left Hans on the benches, running outside for only a few seconds before darting back in with a vicious smirk on his face. He sat down beside Hans again and leaned close to his ear.

"Hey, Hans, your Jew is by the outhouse again."

"Shit, how big's the bottle?" Hans asked, and Derek held his hands a fair distance apart.

"Cover for me, please," Hans begged, and Derek nodded, still wearing an insufferable expression of giddiness even as his so-called "friend" ran from the gym with distress decorating his face.

Hans exited the building and glanced at the outhouses, spotting a figure sitting beside them. With an agitated huff, Hans approached Isaac, who was now sporting a patchy beard. Isaac's hair was long and unruly, as though he had completely given up trying to comb it, and he had almost finished off a tall bottle of what, based on the smell, Vilém assumed was either whisky or some kind of moonshine.

Around the time we turned sixteen, he started drinking. He stopped coming to school except to drink and loiter around the building...

"Can't imagine what might have driven him to drink..." Vilém hissed as young Hans knelt before his not-brother and reached out, trying to grab the bottle. Isaac, so drunk that he could barely move, moaned in agitation and hugged the bottle to his chest.

"Isaac, enough of this!" snapped Hans. "Mother said you're not allowed to drink anymore!"

"Well, she's not my mother, is she?" sneered Isaac, taking a defiant swig from the bottle. Hans used the opportunity to steal the alcohol from the Jewish teen, yanking it out of his weak grasp and emptying the bottle's contents into the grass.

"Jackass!" snarled Isaac, attempting to stand but immediately collapsing. Hans rolled his eyes and threw the empty bottle at Isaac's feet.

"This is pure foolishness, Isaac!" Hans sighed. "You're supposed to be in class!"

"Who cares about class? The fucking teacher'll fail me anyway," grumbled Isaac. "Even if they don't, I won't be able to focus. Your fencing friend will just steal my fucking notebook again and again..." Isaac sat up, swaying slightly as he scowled at Hans. "How're you enjoying fencing club?"

"Isaac, please, not this again..."

"Bet it's fun. You don't have to deal with any dirty Jews in there since they don't let us join. You don't have to be embarrassed about me existing..."

"I wouldn't be embarrassed by you if you would just shape up, Isaac!" shouted Hans, squatting down to Isaac's level and jabbing his not-brother in the chest with his index finger. "We ask very little of you, only that you try to make something of yourself!"

"I *am* making something of myself, Hansie," hissed Isaac, grabbing a handful of dirt and shoving it in Hans' face. Hans sputtered and recoiled, anger filling his every atom.

"You dirty Jew!" snapped Hans, and gone was the affectionate teasing that had been present when he had uttered those words as a child. His voice was filled with nothing but anger.

He lunged at Isaac, but the Jew grabbed the empty bottle and swung it, striking Hans on the shoulder. The glass shattered and the teenager tumbled to the ground. He lay there, stunned, breathing in brief spurts, and Isaac lay beside him, too drunk to run.

Hans stared up at the bright blue sky, fury and sorrow flooding him. He grabbed his throbbing head.

"I hate you..." Hans sniffled, failing to hold in a sob.

"Yeah...I know..." sighed Isaac.

"I wish Papa was alive and you were dead," Hans hiccupped, covering his face with his arm, shame attacking his soul. He must have looked terrible right then. Like a dirty weakling. Like a dirty Jew.

"I know..." Isaac whispered.

Hans wiped his tears away. "Please go to class, Isaac, please..."

"I didn't ask for this shit, Hansie," Isaac muttered, ignoring Hans' plea. "I didn't ask to be your Jew. I didn't wanna be with your family."

"'Your'?" Vilém repeated.

He was always a guest, Czech.

"You made him feel like a pest," Vilém accused.

Young Hans rolled over, facing Isaac. When he saw that the young Jew had pearls of salty water rolling down his cheeks, he finally allowed pity to fill his heart.

"If I quit fencing...will you go to class?" Hans asked. Isaac's lips quirked up into an almost-smile.

"Promise?" he asked, his voice bitter, as though he had been offered this very deal one too many times.

"Yeah...and you can borrow my notes for class...if you need them," Hans vowed. "Please, Isaac, don't make all of this pointless."

Isaac stared up at the sky for a few moments before turning to face Hans. He nodded once, wiping his face with his mud-covered hand and leaving a grimy streak on his cheek. Hans giggled.

"You...you *are* a dirty Jew!" he hiccupped, grabbing a handful of grass and shoving it in Isaac's face. The Jew snickered and rolled away.

"Ouch!" Isaac cried, lifting his palm, which had a shard of glass stuck in it. Hans started to stand, laughing.

"Serves you right, you drunk—OW!" Before he could truly tease Isaac for his injury, Hans cut himself on a piece of the broken bottle. The two teens looked at one another, glanced at each other's wounds, and both cackled.

"Hey, here!" Hans said, opening his injured palm towards Isaac. "Get some German blood in ya', maybe you'll do better in class."

"Get some Jew blood in you, maybe you'll be less of an ass," Isaac countered, and both boys shook hands, letting their blood mix.

Didn't I tell you? I gave him a chance...but he kept squandering it.

"Well...*did* you go back to fencing class?" Vilém queried.

Well, eventually, but...

"And did you keep speaking to Derek?"

I...

"And did your mother ever treat him like an equal?"

Well, she...

"Yes or no?"

No, but...

"Kinda funny. Heydrich said you used to describe Isaac as a nightmare. Really, though...you sound like the worst. I have four little sisters, and I can't *imagine* doing this kind of shit to them and then pretending to be the victim."

Your sisters are your blood!

"You made a blood pact with Isaac. You adopted him. You should have treated him like a brother, not a project."

Ha! Well, if Isaac was a project, he was a failed one. He dropped out of school at a young age...kept drinking...never managed to keep a job no matter what we did. Granted, at the time it was difficult for anyone to get a job.

"I'm very sorry, son, but we really don't need a photographer right now." A new memory formed. Hans, heart falling, stumbled out of a building, led by an old, kind-eyed man.

"If I get any openings, I'll call you...there are other newspapers in town, though! Talent like yours, you'll find something!" the old man declared.

"Thank you, sir..." muttered Hans, anger boiling in his blood. He hurried away from the editor as quickly as he could, ducking into an alleyway and slamming his fist against a wall. The petulant act made his hand ache, but he didn't care. He just wanted to punch the wall, punch something, punch someone...

"Hey! Hey, Hans!"

Hans turned to the mouth of the alley, shoving his fist into his pocket and repressing a pained expression. Vilém wasn't surprised to see Derek standing there, and he was even less surprised that the bully was sporting a swastika armband and a black SS uniform. Hans, however, evidently was surprised. He raised an eyebrow at Isaac's old foe.

"Derek, what's with the getup?" he asked. Derek glanced down at his SS uniform and grinned like a missionary that had just been asked a question about Jesus.

"SS! You haven't heard of it?"

"I've heard of the SA," Hans said, gesturing towards a candy shop across the street. "They got into a fight with some Reds a few days ago and nearly killed the shopkeeper."

"The SA are a bunch of degenerate brutes," Derek said with a nod. "Hitler shouldn't bother with them, and he won't bother with them for much longer."

"Hitler? Oh, Derek, you know his party's illegal right now..."

"But it won't be for much longer, it's been banned and unbanned five times!" Derek argued. "Besides, Hitler's blossoming into a real politician, he's not just a street-brawling ruffian anymore. He has a proper plan, and the SS is going to be his elite unit to combat the Reds and restore Germany's dignity!"

"You know I'm not very political, Derek," sighed Hans.

"Besides, I've heard what they have to say about Jews and...well...Isaac."

"Isaac, yes, but isn't Isaac sort of the...posterboy of those views?" Derek said. "Speaking of Isaac, though, he got caught again."

"Fuck! Again!" Hans snarled, barely repressing the urge to punch the bricks again. Derek nodded.

"Yep, he's lying in the alley behind the bar. Again. You may wanna grab him before the Brownshirts do. And listen...if you joined the SS, it would give you *and* Isaac security. You could protect him. He gets into so much trouble and...if the Führer wins, Jews like him will be dealt with harshly. I don't like him, but I know that would upset you..."

"Yes..." whispered Hans, pulling his throbbing hand from his pocket and wiggling his fingers, perhaps imagining what they would look like covered by a black glove.

"And we have a lot of extra programs! We're forming our own newspaper, so you could probably get a photography job! And there's even a fencing club! We take physical fitness very seriously!"

"All right, all right, I'll think about it!" laughed Hans. "Quit missionizing, I've gotta go get Isaac!"

"Fine, but let's get a beer later and talk about it more!" Derek suggested.

"If the barkeeper doesn't ban my whole family," grumbled Hans. He bade Derek farewell and rushed out of the alley, hurrying down the block. He found a small hole-in-the-wall bar situated beside an alley that looked ripe for mugging. Its dangerous appearance wasn't helped by the fact that when he looked, he saw a figure sitting beside the garbage cans. He scoffed and marched into the foreboding alley, grabbing a besodden Isaac by the arm and dragging him to his feet.

"Get up, asshole!" Hans commanded. "I've told you not to steal anymore! You're lucky he didn't kill you this time."

"How else am I supposed to get a damn drink around here?" slurred Isaac. Hans slung the Jew's arm over his shoulders.

"You shouldn't! You're not supposed to be drinking at all, we talked about this!" huffed Hans. "You never listen!"

"Frau Gerber gives *you* money every week and ya' don't have a job either."

"That's because *I* don't spend *my* money on booze, Isaac."

"I didn't get an allowance...even before I drank..." muttered Isaac. Hans rolled his eyes.

"Would it kill you to put the past behind you?" he snapped, and Isaac turned his cloudy eyes towards the German, hatred burning in his dark irises.

"Would it kill *you*?" he countered, and the memory faded.

His drunkenness...his inability to find work or be useful to society...all of that I could have dealt with. But the final straw came when my mother died. I waited and waited, but...he never showed up to the funeral.

"ISAAC!"

With a brutal kick to the front door of his home, Hans introduced a new memory. The Gerber household was a shadow of its former esteem: the furnishings must have been sold off, the fineries were gone. The home was bare save for the pictures decorating the walls and the piano that still sat in the foyer, which Hans evidently hadn't had the heart to sell.

Isaac was sitting at the piano, leafing through an old bound book of pictures with one hand while the other grasped a bottle. He looked up as Hans entered, smiling joylessly as he held up the book of pictures.

"This is cute..." he said. "Wish my papa had a camera when I was little. I don't even have any pictures 'a him."

"Put! That! Down!" Hans snarled, not giving Isaac time to comply as he marched up to the Jewish man and snatched the picture book from his hands. Hans examined it to make sure it wasn't damaged. Once he confirmed it was pristine, he set it aside and towered over his not-brother.

"You weren't there!" Hans growled, gesturing to the suit he wore. "You weren't there, after everything! After she took you in, protected you...you would be in an orphanage if it weren't for her kindness! You would be a dirty street urchin...and you couldn't even show up to her funeral and say goodbye!"

Hans blinked to keep the tears gathering at the corners of his eyes from escaping. Isaac started idly tapping at the piano keys, creating a sloppy little tune.

"As though she would have cared..." he muttered.

"She would have, Isaac! She would have cared that you sat on your ass and drank during her funeral..."

"Oh, I'm sure! And I'm sure if I'd gone, she would have said I look like a slob! I'm sure I would have gotten a nice suit like yours...oh, but maybe you could'a spared a suit. Maybe...if you'd worn *this* instead."

Isaac tossed the bottle aside, reached under the piano bench, and pulled out a wrinkled black tunic that hung on a hook, a tunic that boasted a swastika armband.

Vilém felt Hans' heart stop as he looked down at his own SS uniform, but embarrassment swiftly morphed into outrage. "You went through my closet!"

"Yeah, I looked through your closet because I was looking for a spare *suit!*" Isaac threw the uniform at Hans, who caught it clumsily. "Because I was gonna go to *your* mom's funeral. But *your mom* never bought *me* nice clothes, so I was scavenging like the dirty little Jew urchin I am. And you..."

Isaac scowled at the swastika. "You despise me anyway, so why bother going? Why bother with anything?"

"I don't...despise you, you don't understand..." Hans muttered.

"I understand perfectly!" Isaac snarled. "You didn't save me, you stole me! You stole me from my people, you trained me to hate myself, and you succeeded! Are you proud, Hansie? Are you proud of yourself?"

"I...yes, you know what, yes I am!" Hans hissed, grabbing the jacket off the hook and throwing the black SS garment on. He pointed to the swastika and announced. "I'm proud of my race, and I'm proud that my family was generous even to a dirty Jew like you! Even after everything *your* people have done to ours, even after everything *you've* done to me! And I'm proud to be a productive human rather than a waste of not just one, but *two* lives!"

"Proud, ha!" sneered Isaac. "Proud of being born wealthy? Proud of losing a war?"

"We didn't lose anything..."

"Proud of being the laughingstock of Europe?"

"Enough..."

"Oh, I'm sorry! I forgot, you're a Nazi now! Sorry, let me rephrase that...are you proud that you, the superior race...you apparently got trampled by a bunch of dirty Jews?"

"You're going too far!"

"Are you proud of being a loser, Hansie?"

"You need to be quiet..."

"Are you proud of being a Nazi, Hansie?"

"You. Need. To. Be..."

"I bet your dad would be *really* proud of you..."

Vilém had never in his life felt as angry as Hans felt right then. It was as though Isaac had lit a match and set him aflame. Hans, half donning the Nazi uniform, decked Isaac in the face, sending the Jew falling to the floor.

"You be quiet, you lousy Jew!" Hans screeched, leaping on top of Isaac and punching him, punching him over and over and over. "Don't you dare mention my father, you fucking Jew! It's your fault he's dead! It's all your fault!"

Isaac made no attempt to fight back. He lay there, hands at his sides, laughing. He laughed and laughed even as Hans knocked his teeth out, even as Hans broke his nose and covered his cheeks with bruises. Vilém felt a spike of adrenaline shoot through Hans' body with every punch he landed on Isaac, and the Czech guard felt sick. He had, on occasion, harbored animosity towards his sisters, but the feeling of doing this to someone, to someone that a small part of Hans still loved...and to enjoy it this much...

"Enough, enough!" Vilém yelped, and acting as though he had heard the command, young Hans finally ceased his attack. He looked down at Isaac, who was barely breathing. The young Jew could only take short, halting gasps. Vilém was surprised he could even do that. Isaac looked like he'd been hit by a car.

"Isaac...?" Hans muttered. Isaac made no sound to indicate he heard anything, and Vilém was befuddled when worry and guilt started clawing at the young Nazi's soul.

"Isaac! Isaac, you idiot, get up! Get up, you stupid fucking Jew! This is your fault!" Hans insisted, his voice becoming high pitched with panic. Isaac didn't move. Hans reached under Isaac's head, trying to lift him up and carry him to the couch, but he felt a splash of warm liquid as soon as he touched the back of Isaac's head. He pulled his hand out from under the Jew's skull and trembled. His hand was crimson.

"Fuck!" snarled Hans, laying Isaac's head down and rushing up the stairs. He grabbed a small first-aid kit out of a drawer in his room and ran to the phone, dialing the operator and ordering him to call the hospital for him.

"Have them send someone over, fast! My brother is injured!" he begged, hanging up before the operator could say a word and bolting back down to Isaac.

But when he ran into the foyer, all he found was the empty bottle of booze, the trousers of his SS uniform, and a puddle of blood staining the carpet. Isaac was gone, gone without a word.

"Isaac?" cried Hans. The German ran out the semi-ajar front door and looked down the street, in the garden, everywhere he could. He must have figured that the injured Isaac couldn't have gotten far, but search as he might, he couldn't find the Jew.

I never saw him again after that day, and believe me, I tried to find him. For as much as we argued, I didn't want him to die in the streets.

"Yeah, you didn't want your father 'wasting' his sacrifice," scoffed Vilém.

Precisely.

"Maybe this wouldn't have happened if you had treated him well for his sake instead of tolerating him for your father. Besides, you couldn't have tried *that* hard to find him. You were friends with Heydrich! Heydrich had a file on every Jew in the Reich."

Every Jew except Isaac, apparently. You think I put up with Heydrich because I liked him? Nobody liked Heydrich, and frankly Heydrich didn't like anyone. But time kept marching on, the SS grew in power, I rose through the ranks and learned more and more about the Jews and their...

"What did we say about quoting *Mein Kampf?*"

Uncurious as ever...fine. Point is, I learned how to live in the New Germany, and in the New Germany becoming friends with Heydrich was a benefit. While Heydrich was hardly a social butterfly, he enjoyed sport, especially fencing, and anyone who indulged him earned his respect, if not his affection. And if you earned that, you could get favors...that is, if you were willing to look bad. Heydrich hated to lose.

A new memory started, and Vilém felt Hans' pride screech in agony as the Nazi purposely performed a clumsy swing, leaving himself wide open. Judging by the sweat Vilém could feel on Hans' brow, he had been fencing with the Blonde Beast for some time. Long enough to satisfy the Hangman's thirst for battle, but not long enough to wound Heydrich's fragile ego.

Heydrich easily won the match, tearing off his mask as soon as he landed the final blow and grinning with all the satisfaction of a cat that had just dumped a dead mouse at his master's feet.

"Still undefeated, Gerber!" he sneered, and while Vilém never thought he would empathize with Hans Gerber, a knife of hatred stabbed him and Hans in unison. Gerber hesitated to take his mask off, perhaps afraid that he wouldn't be able to hide the disdain on his face.

"Good game, Herr Heydrich!" Gerber declared.

"You're one of my best sparring mates!" said Heydrich. "Too bad we won't be attending the Olympics anytime soon. If you and I could be on the team, we'd wipe the floor with the whole world."

"We'll have to kick their asses on the battlefield instead," Hans joked, and Heydrich's lip curled as though he would have liked to chuckle at that, but simply didn't possess enough humanity to allow himself to be seen laughing.

"Of course," the Blonde Beast said, grabbing a towel and wiping his neck. "Did I tell you the good news?"

Vilém felt Hans' heart skip. "Good news, Rein—err, General Heydrich?"

"You're being moved to a new department, directly under my authority. The war is going well, but the Führer wants to focus more on the internal war. The war against the undesirables in our midst. The Jews, the Communists...the traitors."

"Sir...?"

"That wasn't an accusation, Gerber. Trust me...I have my file on you, and while your association with Jews may be...*concerning*...you've been honest with me. And I understand. Everyone has their *Edeljude*. Even Hitler."

"*Edeljude?*" Vilém repeated.

Honorable Jew. Even a vile race is bound to produce a good apple every once in a while. None of us were simple enough to believe that no good Jews existed, it was simply a matter of scale.

"Ha!" laughed Hans. "Well, sir, Isaac Goldstein isn't precisely an honorable Jew. I merely would prefer it if he could have...a higher purpose, whatever higher purpose he may achieve within the Reich."

"A Jew with a higher purpose, hm...how funny..." Heydrich muttered. He winced as though someone had just stepped on his foot and scowled at the ceiling.

"Herr Heydrich?" muttered Hans.

"I'm fine, just a spasm," Heydrich blurted. "As I was saying: I understand your desire to retrieve the Jew Goldstein. Of course, in order to find him, much less be allowed to keep him, you must prove yourself worthy of my time and energy. Put simply: I will find your Jew, but you have to help me plug a leak."

"Leak, sir?"

"Our sources have uncovered a smuggling operation coming out of your hometown, and the contraband is Jews. German Jews are being taken from Gestapo custody, given false papers, and smuggled to Switzerland. And from there? Who knows what sort of damage they could do...who knows what *rumors* they could spread."

"Right...*rumors,*" said Hans with a small, grim smirk.

"This is unacceptable, and more so, it means we have a mole. The operation is too advanced to succeed without internal help," Heydrich said.

"SS help?"

"Precisely. Honestly, if I had been forced to dig up your relationship with the Jew Goldstein myself, you would have ended up being my prime suspect. But since you were honest, I believe you have nothing to do with it."

"I'm not fond of Jews, Herr Heydrich."

"No, but one doesn't need to be fond of them in order to be sympathetic. You may not be fond of rats, but if you see one squirming in a trap...well, sadly the German people are often too humane and virtuous for their own good."

"So...you want me to find the mole?"

"Correct, Gerber. Find the mole, plug the hole. We want to solve this Jewish Problem quickly, without interruption. If you can manage this, you'll have stopped perhaps hundreds of Jews from escaping, and I will consider your plea on behalf of the Jew Goldstein to be more than justifiable."

Vilém felt what remained of Hans' conscience object to this exchange, but the young Nazi muted it easily and finally removed his mask, a genuine smile lighting up his face.

"Thank you, sir," he said. "I won't disappoint."

And I didn't...

"Who was the mole?" asked Vilém, and the Nazi ghost snickered.

You'll be as surprised as I was...

A new memory started with a scream as Hans, kneeling before a cellar door, threw the hatch open and shined a flashlight down into the basement. Dozens of eyes shined back. At least fifty "undesirables", most of them children, were huddled together in the tight space. Vilém felt Hans' heart sink, but the Nazi forced it to become hard as iron.

"Gather them!" Hans snapped, and several SS officers obeyed his command, descending into the cellar and pulling out the children by their hair, by their wrists, by their ankles.

"Hans!" A familiar voice, drowning in distress, made Hans turn. Vilém was indeed surprised when he saw the mole. Derek. Isaac's old bully, restrained by two SS officers, watched with horror as the Nazis roughly collected the Jewish children.

"Now, now, Derek, I'm surprised at you!" Hans cried, strutting towards his quarry. The guards holding Derek forced him to kneel before their commander, and though Gerber wore a look of disdain as he towered over Isaac's old bully, Vilém could feel that Hans' chest was writhing.

"From what I remember, you were never a fan of Jewish brats," Hans said. Derek, whose eyes were alight with anger, spat on his old friend's boot.

"They're *children*, Hans!" he snarled, and Hans kicked his ex-friend in the ribs.

"Traitorous bastard," Gerber hissed. "Filthy hypocrite."

"I wanted to send the Jews out of Germany, to send them to Palestine or somewhere else...I *never* signed up to be a murderer!"

"Plans change," Hans said, letting his eyes flit towards one child, a little girl who had decided she would not go without a fight. She scratched and bit the SS officer who held her, acting like the rabid animal she had been labeled as.

"You've changed, Hans," Derek snapped.

"No...no, I really haven't, but *you* have," Hans insisted. "You've betrayed the Fatherland, you've sheltered enemies of the state..."

"They're just kids, Hans!"

"Jewish whelps will grow into full-grown Jews," Hans said. "They must be dealt with as one deals with newborn rats."

"You don't believe a word of that," sneered Derek. "I get how this works, Hans. You hand over these Jews and Heydrich spares yours. You loved Isaac even though you were always a coward, always too scared to stand up to me..."

Hans smacked Derek across the face, but the former bully laughed even as blood dripped from his split lip.

"Coward!" he cried. "You'll do anything to seem strong, but deep down you're just a stupid little boy still crying about his daddy's death!"

"Enough!" snarled Hans, kicking Derek in the groin. Derek grunted in pain and the two guards restraining him let him fall on his face. Hans slammed his boot on top of the former bully's head.

"Speak of my father again, I dare you..." hissed Hans.

"Your father died for nothing!" Derek sneered. "He died for a pointless war! He died for the enemy! He died for a Jew! And you're going to kill these children to save that one useless Jew!"

Hans put almost all his weight down on Derek's skull, but Derek refused to shut his mouth. "But you're a coward, you always were! You're a coward just like Heydrich! You don't have the guts to put your money where your mouth is!"

It felt like Hans was possessed by the devil. He pulled out his gun, jammed the barrel against Derek's ear. The sound of Derek's laughter was echoing, echoing, the sound of the children screaming, piercing, assaulting his brain. The eyes of the SS officers were watching, judging, ready to report everything. He wanted everyone to stop looking, he wanted everyone to shut up.

"OW!"

One little Jewish girl bit her captor's hand and tried to run to the door. Hans moved on instinct. Everything happened so fast.

Raising the gun, hearing Derek scream for him to stop, pulling the trigger and painting the door crimson.

Derek vomited, one guard swore, the children screamed, and Hans Gerber stood there for a moment, gawking at his gruesome handiwork. The echoes ceased and he heard nothing. He saw nothing. Nothing but red. His heart stopped, his hand trembled.

Guilt, his old foe, threatened to end him right then. It commanded him to shove the gun to his own forehead and pull the trigger, but his instincts and a little devilish voice that sounded too much like Hitler whispered that it was fine. It was fine. It had to be fine. It was no worse than stepping on a bug.

A bug. He looked at the little girl's remains and forced himself to see nothing but a squashed bug, blurring his own vision until there was nothing but a blob of dirty Jew blood.

"There..." he whispered, pressing the gun against Derek's forehead. "There's my conviction."

He pulled the trigger, and Vilém, quite literally unable to stomach another moment, threw the stuffed cat to the floor. He bolted out of the nursery, out of Barrack One, and vomited in the mud.

"Fuck..." he gagged. He understood now why Joseph Klammer had refrained from showing him his own killings. The sensation of being a murderer was horrific, and worse...the justifications. The fight that took place in the Nazi's soul, the feeling of evil winning.

Winning! Vilém cursed himself for running when he realized he had fallen right into the Nazi's trap. Gerber had wanted to scare him, to drive him away, to make him into a coward.

"Not happening..." Vilém snarled. He didn't care what horrific things the Nazi insisted on showing him. He would not run away. He would not give the Nazi the satisfaction of frightening an undesirable.

Vilém marched back inside, back into the nursery. He looked

down and saw that he had left his family album sitting open beside the toy cat. He saw little Fabian sitting on Sam's shoulders, grinning from ear to ear, and he wanted to sit and stare at that lovely image for hours, stare at it until the vision of the little girl vanished from his mind.

But no, no, that would be wrong. Ignoring her pain would be just as bad as forgetting Raya and all the rest.

Vilém sat down once more, cradling the cat in the crook of his arm and setting the album in his lap, bathing in Fabian's smile for only a moment before shutting his eyes.

You came back.

"You sound surprised, murderer."

I am not a murderer. Murder is killing a person...

"Isaac wasn't a person?"

People have pet rats.

"I felt what you felt back then, Hansie," said Vilém. "You can't pretend with me. Derek was right. You shot her because you were angry and afraid, afraid your little guards would tattle to Heydrich. And then when your conscience tried to guilt you into ending your pointless life, you freaked out and forced yourself to believe it. I bet you did that a thousand times until you actually started believing the bullshit."

It's not bullshit...but it was pointless.

"Hm?"

We lost, don't you get it? We did what we did for the greater good, we did...inhumane things...to better the world. And yet we lost. Everything we did was for nothing.

"Is that it, then? You just don't want all your murdering to be pointless?"

No...there's nothing else to be done. The war is over. The war against the Jews? Even if it continues in other forms, our cause is over. But...during the war...after what happened with Derek...I kept marching on, hoping that it would all be for a greater purpose, and hoping that I would find Isaac while doing this good work. But...well, you know that Heydrich eventually became the Reichsprotektor of Czechoslovakia. I could speak Czech, and therefore he took me with him.

"Well, Hans, I have good news and bad news."

Gerber strutted into a new memory, his chest weighed down with medals that Vilém could only assume he had received for shooting an appreciable amount of Jews.

Hans approached a large oaken desk that was covered in papers. He glanced at the reports and several words—*Transport, Solution, Effective*—leapt out at him, but most of it appeared to be bureaucratic blabber, albeit genocidal bureaucratic blabber.

Heydrich scribbled an untidy signature onto one document and plopped his pen into an inkwell, leaning back and cracking his knuckles as though the act of writing a death warrant was as taxing as beating an opponent.

"Good news first?" Hans pleaded, and Heydrich barely hid a smirk.

"You're getting a promotion. In fact, you're getting a new position," the Butcher of Prague declared. "We're streamlining the Final Solution, and since the plague is so spread out, we will need a precise network of camps and ghettos. We need a system to separate the Jews that can be put to work from the useless ones. The elderly, the sick...the children."

He paused for a moment, as though waiting for Hans to object to something he had said. When his underling remained complacently quiet, he gave a small nod of approval and continued.

"And since you've demonstrated your dedication to the Cause, I think you've earned an opportunity. You will command a transit camp. You will have full control over every undesirable that enters your grounds. Consider yourself the Führer of the

Camp. You've offered me loyalty, and therefore I will give you freedom."

"Thank you, Reichsprotektor!" said Hans. "I won't disappoint."

"I'm sure you won't," Heydrich muttered, picking up a folder and peeking at the contents therein with a small grimace.

"So...bad news now?" Heydrich said, looking at Hans like a father that had just hit the family dog with his car and wasn't sure how to explain himself. Gerber nodded and Heydrich leaned over the desk, offering the folder to his subordinate.

"I'm...sorry," the Hangman said, spitting out the words as though they stung his tongue. "It appears your *Edeljude* didn't survive. Died in a ghetto within the Sudetenland a year ago. Records were sparse, but we were able to confirm that this is...*was* him."

Hans' heart dropped to the bottom of his stomach, and he hesitated to open the folder. Morbid curiosity made him peek. There was a picture inside. Isaac Goldstein was indeed shown lying atop a pile of bodies, emaciated and filthy, his curly hair matted into a rat's nest, a stream of blood oozing from his lips.

Vilém had never felt someone's soul die so quickly. Whatever good there was within Hans Gerber perished right then, when he saw his almost-brother dead by Hitler's hands. His father's death had been for nothing.

Vilém felt bitter affection bloom in Hans' soul for a brief moment before it was beaten to death by his ego. He had loved Isaac, but Isaac was gone. There was nothing left except the Cause. Heydrich's Cause.

"He was only a dirty Jew," Hans said, tossing the folder back onto Heydrich's desk, and though Vilém expected Heydrich to approve of this sentiment, the Hangman of Prague raised a concerned eyebrow.

"You went through so much trouble to find him...*I* went through so much trouble to find him," Heydrich said. "He can't be that...disposable..."

But before Heydrich could say another word, he suddenly grunted and almost fell on top of his desk, as though something had kicked him square in the chest. Hans stepped back, and Vilém felt bewilderment buzz in the Nazi's brain.

"I don't suppose you believed in ghosts..." Vilém said.

I didn't believe in anything except the Cause.

"Well...I guess Heydrich probably had a lot of ghosts who wanted to kick his ass," Vilém remarked.

Perhaps. At the time, I just thought he was insane.

"He *was* insane," Vilém huffed, and insane though he may have been, Heydrich quickly recovered from whatever had made him spasm.

"Sorry...old injury acting up," Heydrich said, gesturing to his side. "What I *meant* to say was...don't...let this stand between you and your work. I would hate for you to go the way of that Derek fellow."

"I won't, Herr Heydrich, though I am curious...by any chance, did he leave behind a family? Children? I haven't seen him since 1930, he may have..."

"Fortunately, your *Edeljude* did not bring any more of his kind into the world," Heydrich sneered. "It appears he died as he lived: a worthless drunk."

Hans curled his hands into fists and nodded. "Very well."

"Understand, Gerber: your father's death in the Great War will not be meaningless. The work we are doing now, that work will avenge him. That work will make all the deaths in that war *and* this war worthwhile. We will make the world a utopia. *You* will. You will become your father's legacy. Work hard, get married, have plenty of Aryan children...let this Jew's death be your liberation, and continue to help us liberate the rest of the world."

Heydrich chuckled. "Sorry...I'm not as good at speeches as the Führer or Herr Goebbels, but...I do mean it."

"Thank you, Herr Heydrich," said Hans, his heart swelling with purpose. "You're completely correct...and if I may say, more persuasive than Herr Goebbels."

"Oh, get out of here!" Heydrich chuckled, waving for Hans to leave. "I'll have no bootlicking in my office. Go, go see your new kingdom."

"Yes, sir!" cried Hans, clicking his heels together, pulling his heart back into its proper place, and throwing his arm into the air. "Heil Hitler!"

And from that day on...well, I tried my hardest to live by Heydrich's words. But women were boring to me...

"Uhm..."

Not like that. I simply had no interest in being married, no lustful fantasies. I suppose I've always been practical. I didn't want to be a father either. Children are so...unpredictable. Look at Klaus Heydrich: his father was the Man with the Iron Heart, and he became a soft-hearted Jew-lover.

"God forbid your child have humanity," grumbled Vilém.

Regardless, I didn't like the odds. Instead, I threw myself into my work, the Cause. It went well, all things considered. The Camp you stand in was a model of efficiency for years. I was very hands-on, working from dawn 'till dusk, sorting Jews and making sure production was always at peak.

Eventually, I decided to move to the Camp, refurbishing the barrack you stand in for my own personal use. I even took up my old photography hobby once more. I was hoping that one day, when the Reich ruled over Europe and the Jews were an extinct race...well, I hoped that my pictures would show future generations how it was done. The iron will that was required. I hoped they would end up in a museum.

"Well...you got that much," Vilém snarked.

Yes, well...the world we sought to build never formed, but at the time I thought it was a certainty. We would win. We...we had to win. To make it all worth it, as Heydrich said. All of it...the Jews, their children, even my father. But although my work for the Cause consumed my life, I couldn't help but continue to think of Isaac.

"Need more albums..." A new memory formed. Kommandant Gerber sat at his desk with an enormous pile of leather albums sorted before him and a small stack of what appeared to be freshly developed photographs waiting to be catalogued.

Vilém shivered when he saw the picture at the top of the stack: a Nazi aiming a rifle at a woman who had collapsed while working. The Kommandant took the gruesome photo and opened one album, which was full of similar images. Dead Jews, injured Jews, smiling Nazis. Page after page of war crimes, so many pictures that he didn't have any room in the album for more.

He flipped through several more albums, searching for a space. When he found nothing, he opened a desk drawer and searched for another album, finding one at the bottom of his desk, an old brown book. The Nazi set the album on his desk and opened it.

His soul froze when he realized what he had uncovered. An old family album, filled with post-WWI pictures of little Hans Gerber and Isaac Goldstein.

Vilém could feel bile rise in Hans' throat, the ghost of his guilt threatening to haunt him. For a moment, he couldn't help but look down at the old memories. His eyes lingered on one picture of Isaac and himself as children sitting in front of a Christmas tree, leaning close, both hugging still-wrapped presents. Hans' gift was noticeably larger than Isaac's, yet it seemed that little Isaac hadn't yet realized how unfair everything was. He embraced his tiny box and grinned.

Hans stared at Isaac's bright, happy eyes for a moment. His own eyes began to sting, regret weighing down his heart.

A screech brought him back to his senses. He looked out the window and saw that a new train had arrived, filled with fresh undesirables to sort. He stood up, glanced back down at Isaac, and slammed the book shut. He grabbed his camera and rushed out of his office, fleeing from his not-brother's image.

Gerber ran out of Barrack One, which was being remodeled by several weary prisoners. He glanced at the Jews, smirking when they winced as he passed them by. He paused to snap a picture of the Jews painting over the old Barrack One sign and then strutted towards the Selection Platform. He arrived just in time to see the cattle-car doors slide open, and Vilém felt ill as eager interest took hold of the Nazi's mind, as though he had just walked into a new zoo exhibit.

"Good morning, Herr Kommandant," one Nazi soldier said. "Good batch today, fresh from the Sudetenland. Mostly Germans."

Hans turned to the young guard with a scolding scowl, and the Nazi hastily corrected himself.

"Jews who speak German," he stuttered, and the Kommandant nodded.

"No such thing as German Jews," he reminded his subordinate. "Get to it!"

"Yes, sir!" the Nazi cried, turning his furious attention onto the Jews.

"Men to the left, women to the right, children under fourteen form a separate group! Children under eleven must be surrendered to be cared for in the nursery!"

"Here we go!" whispered Hans, lifting his up his camera and

frantically snapping pictures as chaos erupted on the Platform. Jews tumbled out of the train cars and were yanked from their children before they even got a chance to say goodbye. Those who were too ill to move were shoved and beaten by the Nazis. Some people had died on the train, and their family members tried in vain to get them help while the Kapos carried their bodies to the Pit. The Selection was deafening. Wailing children, sobbing women, shouting Nazis, barking dogs.

Hans couldn't take photos fast enough. *Snap, snap, snap!* He tried to capture as many moments of terror as he could. One Nazi sicced a dog on a man who was refusing to leave his children. The Kommandant snickered, raising his camera and snapping away, as though he was on a safari and was watching a lion tear a gazelle to bits. The man's children bawled, but another Nazi grabbed them and dragged them away. They were far too young to be of any use to the Reich as slave labor. They would go to the Pit with the rest of the babies.

Vilém wanted to vomit again. He had seen the Selection too many times, but in every other memory he had experienced it through the eyes of the victims—save, of course, for Joseph Klammer, but the repentant Nazi had viewed the whole affair with disgust. Kommandant Gerber regarded it with delight.

Feeling the joy in the Kommandant's chest, the excitement, while dogs tore people to shreds and families were ripped apart...to hear these screams and feel nothing but satisfaction...it was sickening. It made Vilém's head hurt.

"He's eleven! He just looks little for his age!"

"He is not eleven, lying Jewish whore!"

The Kommandant turned just in time to see a Nazi slap a woman so hard she fell to the ground. Her son, whom she had been trying to protect, clung to her. He was obviously younger than eleven, five or six years old at most, and...

In unison, Vilém and the Kommandant were struck by a bolt of familiarity. The boy had curly ebony hair, soft blue eyes. Vilém released a shuddering breath, his heart pounding, but he kept his revelation to himself.

"Isaac...?" Kommandant Gerber whispered. Though the child didn't look exactly like Isaac Goldstein, the similarities were too numerous to be a coincidence.

One Nazi grabbed the little boy, pulling him away from his injured mother, carrying him towards the Pit with all the other useless young children.

"Wait!" Kommandant Gerber yelled, almost dropping his camera as he ran to the boy. The soldier stopped, holding the kicking, squealing child with both arms and regarding his boss with a raised eyebrow. The child's mother looked up at the Kommandant with a tiny dash of hope in her eyes.

"Herr, please!" she cried, grabbing Gerber's pant leg. "He's old, he can work, he can..."

"I don't care about that," grunted the Kommandant, pulling his leg out of her grasp and pushing her away with his jackboot. "Who is the boy's father?"

"His father was a German, sir..."

"His name, do you know his father's name?"

"It was Isaac Goldstein, sir, please, I...he wasn't even a Jew, his father..."

"That's a lie," snarled the Kommandant, turning away from the boy's mother and letting his eyes settle on Isaac's son. The boy had stopped struggling. He was watching the Kommandant with wide, inquisitive eyes, perhaps sensing that something strange was going on.

"I'm sorry, sir, please forgive me..." sobbed the mother.

"Were you married to Isaac Goldstein?" grunted Hans. "Tell me about him."

"He...he was a good man, but...he had problems with alcohol. We were never married...I loved him, but he left when our son was little and I don't know what became of him."

"The boy is definitely his, then?"

"Y-yes, sir...uhm...did you know Isaac?"

The Kommandant didn't answer. Too many feelings were clashing in his chest as he looked at Isaac's only son. Affection for his not-brother, an instinct to protect the last piece of him...but he had trained himself to be disgusted by Jews for so many years that hatred tried its best to batter love into submission.

He hesitated for a moment, letting the war rage in his soul until, at last, love won.

"The boy will not be harmed," he declared, striding towards his soldier and opening his arms. The Nazi handed the child to his boss, and the Kommandant started to carry the boy back to Barrack One.

"Wait, where are you taking him?!" the mother screamed, and Isaac's son started fighting again.

"Let me go! Mama! Mama!" the child screeched, and the Kommandant grunted in ire, glancing over his shoulder.

"Take care of her," he commanded his men, nudging his head to indicate the mother, and without another word he carried the howling, writhing boy back to his unfinished home.

I couldn't let him die...I thought that perhaps, even though Isaac's life was pointless, a waste...perhaps this child could be trained, raised as a German. Perhaps he could forget his origins and have a good life in the New World, with a new identity...

"You stole him from his people, from his mother!" hissed Vilém.

I saved him! He would have gone right to the Pit with all the other children!

"Because *you* would have sent him there!" Vilém argued.

"Heydrich said you were king of the Camp. You could have spared all the children if you wanted to!"

And waste valuable food and medicine on useless eaters? No. But for Isaac, and for my father, I took the boy in. I gave him a new life.

"Please hold still."

"I want to see my mother…"

"You may see her, but only if you hold still."

A new memory started, though they hadn't jumped too far forward in time. Isaac's son was cleaned, wearing a Hitler Youth uniform and resting in a bare room that Vilém realized was going to become his nursery. He was sitting on a stool while the Kommandant dyed his inky hair gold, making him look like a little Aryan.

"So curly, just like Isaac's…" muttered the Kommandant as he painted the black locks blonde.

"You knew my father?" the boy queried, and the Kommandant smiled.

"I did."

"He was drunk and horrible," the child sighed, crossing his arms and pouting. The Kommandant couldn't help but laugh.

"I can't argue with that, but you're going to be better than him," Hans said. "From now on, you'll be German. You will have a very nice life."

"But I don't wanna be German, I'm Jewish and Czech…" the boy argued, and the Kommandant's smile vanished.

"That's too bad," he said. "If you want to see your mother, you have to be a good German boy. You may not speak Czech or Hebrew or Yiddish, and you may not practice any Jewish ceremony."

"But God says…"

"God does not exist," the Kommandant declared, giving the

child's hair a slight tug to emphasize his point. "The notion is fanciful, and the Jewish religion is based on ancient nonsense. The Jewish people are a vile race…"

"I'm not vile!"

"No, and that's why I'd like to save you."

"And Mama too, right? Mama's not vile!"

"If you behave and do as you're told, your mother will not be harmed."

"Promise?"

"Yes. Now hold still, I'm almost done," the Kommandant said. With one final blot of dye, he transformed the little Jew into an Aryan cherub. He stepped back and observed his work with a grin.

"There! Now don't you feel better?" he asked. The boy's shoulders sagged and he kicked his legs anxiously.

"It feels wrong," he confessed. "Mama says God wants Jews to be proud."

"Jews have nothing to be proud of," the Kommandant sneered. He picked up his camera and grabbed the boy by the hand. As he pulled him off the stool, however, the child's sleeve slid upwards, revealing an enormous bruise covering his entire forearm. The child seemed unaffected by the sight of the huge black blotch, but the Kommandant immediately released the boy, worry filling his heart.

"What happened?" he asked. "Did you get that on the train?"

"Nah ah, when the Nazi grabbed me on the Platform," the boy said.

"That's impossible. He was only a little rough with you, he didn't beat you."

"I'm a hemo-fil-a-ac," the boy said, slowly pronouncing the word, which his mother must have trained him to say many a time. "My body's weird and if I get a little bump or a cut, it's like I'm about to die."

"You're not acting like you're about to die," observed the Kommandant, gently rolling up the boy's other sleeve and wincing when he saw another massive bruise.

"I get unlucky a lot, and I'm used to hurting," the boy said. The Kommandant nodded, dragging the boy's sleeves over the wounds.

"I see...well, I'll have to make sure you're not injured, then..." he muttered.

"Herr Kommandant," the boy said. "I thought it was against the law for a Jew to say he's a German. Isn't it illegal?"

"Hush!" hissed the Kommandant, lightly tapping the boy's cheek. "That is precisely why you must never say you're a Jew or behave like one. If you do, I will get in trouble and you and your mother will suffer. Come, we have to get your new identity card printed..."

He ushered the boy to a blank wall and had him stand against it.

"Your new name will be Martin Gerber the Second," the Kommandant said, and the boy scowled.

"But my name is..."

"Martin!" barked the Kommandant. "Your name is Martin! You are German! Be grateful for that. You will not be killed as a Jew, but your life as a Jew is over." He raised the camera.

"Smile!" he commanded. The boy refused, crossing his arms.

"I don't feel like smilin'..." he whispered. The Kommandant let out an irate growl.

"You *are* your father's son," he grumbled. "Be a good boy and do as you're told. Germans do as they are told; you are a German now."

"*You're* not doing what you're told," Little Martin argued. "You're not supposed to be doing this with me, I know that."

The Kommandant could not help but smile. "Fine, frown if you like. I guess it doesn't matter."

He pressed his eye against the viewfinder and snapped a photograph.

I will admit...I liked Martin. He was like a better version of Isaac. He reminded me of what Isaac was like when we were children. He was smart, studious, and polite. I was sure he would have a good future, and I did my best to give him everything a German boy could ever want.

"Martin! Come here! I have a surprise for you!"

A new memory started up. Vilém could feel the Kommandant clutching something small and stuffed in his hand as he entered his hearth. Little Martin came running, his eyes bright and eager.

"What is it?!" the child squealed, coming to a halt in front of the Kommandant, who examined the boy with a grimace of disapproval.

"Now, Martin, what have we talked about?" he chastised, and the boy's smile wilted. Martin submissively bowed his head and raised up a limp arm.

"Heil Hitler..." he grumbled through gritted teeth. The Kommandant regarded this proper German greeting with an approving smile, ruffling the boy's dyed hair.

"Much better, you'll get it," the Kommandant said. "I went to town and look what I got you!"

He held the gift out towards the boy, a small stuffed bear. The boy's optimism faded and he took the toy with a disappointed frown.

"Oh...another toy," Martin sighed. "Thank you, Kommandant."

"Look on the bottom!" the Kommandant said. "I had it monogrammed just for you. You should keep it on your bed instead of that old toy cat."

Vilém gripped the little cat tighter. Martin looked at the bear's rump and bit his lip when he saw the initials: "M.G."

"Thank you..." Martin mumbled. "I like my toy cat, though...Mama gave it to me."

The child put harsh emphasis on the word "Mama" and looked up at the Kommandant with a plea screaming in his baby blue eyes. Kommandant Gerber felt his chest tighten.

"I know you want to see your mother," he said, his tone icy. "But you must learn patience. You have been given a lot, and your mother is busy. You must be grateful for what you have."

"I am grateful, sir..."

"Good boy. Then let's not speak of this any longer. Have you finished your homework for the day?"

"I don't like my homework..." the child muttered, and though the Kommandant laughed, Vilém could feel aggravation boil in the Nazi's chest.

"Few children do! But your education is important. Come, let's see what you have so far."

The Kommandant started marching towards the nursery, Martin trodding behind him. The formerly bare room was now filled with toys of every sort. A train set, a stack of board games, and stuffed animals of every species.

See? So spoiled...and yet he insisted on keeping that little toy cat. Had me go all the way to the sorting barrack so he could get it back...

Martin set the new bear beside his favorite toy, the much cheaper and clearly beloved stuffed cat that Vilém was clutching.

"It meant something to him," Vilém said. "His mother gave it to him and you wouldn't let him see her...what happened to her?"

What happened? What do you think happened? I told my men to take care of her.

"Oh," Vilém seethed. "So you lied to him...and you murdered his mother."

His mother was a Jewess. She would have been a bad influence on him. I was trying to make him into a proper German. I worked very hard to make sure he was well educated.

The boy shuffled to a small desk that rested in the corner by the bed, grabbing a slip of paper off it and sheepishly handing his assignment to the Kommandant. Gerber read over the child's sloppy answers.

"Let's see how you've done in math. 'If a boy has one full German father, but his mother is half German and half Czech, what percent of the boy is racially pure?' Oh, Martin, you got it wrong. One hundred percent? It would only be seventy-five percent."

"General Heydrich says some Czechs can be Aryans," Martin argued, and the Kommandant chuckled.

"Clever boy, using my boss against me! Very well, I'll have to write out less controversial questions. Let's see...number two. 'To keep an invalid alive costs four Reichsmarks a day. At an asylum where one hundred inmates are held, how much does it cost a productive German citizen to keep them all alive for merely a single day?' Very good, Martin, four hundred a day! And that's only for one asylum!"

"Thank you, Kommandant..." muttered the boy, sitting on the bed and looking down at his feet. He reached out and hugged his favorite toy cat to his chest. When the Kommandant saw the child's obvious demonstration of nervousness, his pride petered into nothingness. He read the last question.

"'Two Germans enter a room, followed by two Jews. If one German leaves, how many people are left in the room?' Oh...silly boy. Three people are left in the room? No, only one person would be left in the room. One person and two subhumans. It's a bit of a trick question, I suppose…"

"These don't feel like math problems," whispered Martin, squeezing his toy cat. "And I'm a person."

"Naturally, you're a person, Martin," said the Kommandant, feigning a casual tone even as Vilém felt Hans' heart hammering with agitation. "You're a German."

"But I'm a J…"

"Hush!" snapped the Kommandant, and Vilém could tell that if the boy were not a hemophiliac and the Kommandant weren't afraid that a bit of corporal punishment could kill him, he would have smacked Martin across the face. Instead, he merely covered the boy's mouth with one gloved hand.

"We have talked about this, Martin," he hissed. "You want to see your mother again, don't you?"

"Y…yes…" hiccupped Martin, tears falling from his eyes, his cracking voice muffled by the Nazi's palm.

"Jews don't get to see their mothers. Good German boys get what they want. Good German boys who listen and obey and do their homework properly get everything they want. Now…"

He held up the homework sheet. "How many people are in the room?"

The child hesitated to dehumanize the people he belonged to, the people he loved, but his eyes flitted down to the little cat and the small hope that he could see his mother again made him whimper, "One."

Satisfaction and relief flowed through the Kommandant's bloodstream. He handed the boy his homework sheet and patted his head. "Good boy."

Normally, he was pliant as long as I dangled his mother in front of him. I hoped with time and isolation from the other members of his race, he would accept his new identity. But he always returned to Jewish nonsense, and it was easy for him to do so. His condition meant that he had to have a doctor nearby at all times, and naturally I couldn't have a German doctor stay in my house.

"Naturally," Vilém huffed. "He might have tattled to Heydrich."

Precisely. Too many private conversations were held in this building. I could only have undesirable doctors service him, and most doctors who arrived at the Camp were Jews. I warned them not to speak to Martin about Jewish matters, but so many didn't listen. We went through a lot of doctors...

"Martin, what is this?"

A new memory started, and Vilém could feel the Kommandant's heart pounding with fury and panic as he stormed into the nursery, two SS men flanking him. Martin had been sitting at his desk, doing another "math assignment", but when he saw the Kommandant, he dropped his pencil.

"What is...?" the boy stuttered, and the Kommandant unfolded a crumpled piece of paper.

"I found this in your trash," he snapped. He glanced at the scrap page and Vilém realized the paper was filled with Hebrew letters.

"K-Kommandant, please...I...I'll be a better Nazi if I know how to speak to Jews!" the boy cried, dropping to his knees in front of the Kommandant.

"By the time you're grown up, there won't be any Jews to communicate with," the Kommandant sneered, tearing the paper in two and dropping the halves in front of the boy. "Your doctor gave you Hebrew lessons."

"Please don't hurt him, he just did what I asked!" screamed the child, wrapping his arms around the Kommandant's leg, tears streaming down his rosy cheeks. "Please, please!"

"Consider this a lesson, boy," the Kommandant snapped,

gesturing for his men to enter the infirmary. The two SS men did as commanded and kicked down the door, dragging an old Jewish doctor out. Not Doctor Doubek. One of his unfortunate predecessors. The doctor screamed and begged for his life.

"I'm sorry, I'm sorry!" the doctor yelled, and Martin, bawling, tried to run towards the doctor, tried to defend him with his little body, but the Kommandant was quick. He scooped the boy into his arms.

"Stay calm, child," the Kommandant whispered in the boy's ear. "You've already misbehaved. Keep struggling and you won't be allowed to see your mother for another month."

But Little Martin, too concerned for the fate of his doctor, disobeyed, struggling and reaching for the prisoner as the two SS guards beat him. The doctor's blood splattered across the cushioned floor.

"Stop it, stop it, he didn't do anything wrong! Please! I wanna be punished instead!" screamed Martin, kicking the Kommandant in the gut. Gerber grunted, and Vilém felt his anger spike.

"Just take care of the fucking Jew!" he snapped at his men. "Take it out back and put it out of its misery!"

"Don't kill him, please, please!" screeched Martin. Vilém thought he might have to drop the cat again. The doctor, praying for mercy, was dragged out of the nursery. Martin was fighting, the Kommandant's soul was burning with hatred and ire, the child kept kicking and howling until...

BANG!

A gunshot echoed from outside, and the Kommandant dropped the child to the floor.

"Now," sighed the Kommandant, massaging his sore chest. "Next time, when I tell you not to seek out Jewish..."

But before he could say another word, Little Martin ran to his metal bedpost.

"I hate you, I hate you, I hate you!" the boy screamed, punctuating every pronouncement by slamming his head against the edge of the bedpost. The Kommandant watched the child self-harm, frozen with surprise, but after the boy struck himself so hard that Barrack One trembled, he came to his senses and intervened.

"Martin, stop! Martin, stop it!" he cried, grabbing the child and pulling him away from the bedpost. The boy had pierced his skin, and the minor gash he had created was gushing blood. The Kommandant grabbed a random stuffed animal, a smiling turtle, and shoved it against the boy's forehead in a desperate attempt to stem the flow.

"Stupid boy!" he snarled as the child's blood turned the emerald turtle scarlet. "Stupid little Jew!"

The memory shifted. Martin was lying down on the bed, his head wrapped in crimson-blotched bandages, hugging his little cat. The Kommandant stood above him, scowling.

"You shouldn't have done that, Martin..." he sighed. "You might have killed yourself."

"You killed my doctor," Martin countered, not daring to glower directly at the Kommandant, instead directing all of his anger at the roof.

"Martin..."

"Don't kill my doctors if you don't want me to die."

"I'll get you a new doctor, but you can't ask them to teach you about Judaism anymore. It's not my fault, I warned you what would happen. It's your fault."

The boy trembled, squeezing his eyes shut and turning his back to the Kommandant.

"I know..." he whimpered.

"Do not ask them again and no harm will befall them. And do not purposefully injure yourself."

"Why not?" the child hissed, his little voice cracking with guilt and hatred.

"You know you're very important to me, Martin," sighed the Kommandant, patting the child's back. The boy shrunk away from his touch.

"I want my mama..." the child sobbed.

"You didn't listen before, Martin. I warned you. You don't behave, you don't get to see your mother. One month. No mother. Be good and do your assignments and maybe I'll reconsider."

The boy hiccupped and nodded, still refusing to face the Nazi. Kommandant Gerber's heart reared up in fury.

"Martin, be a good boy and look at me," he commanded. "Good German boys are polite and grateful."

Vilém could see disgust hold the boy back, but love for his mother made him swallow his pride again. He turned to face the Kommandant, his cheeks red and stained with tears, his lips trembling.

"Yes, sir..." he said.

"Good boy. I'm going back to work now, say goodbye the right way."

The boy whimpered as though the Kommandant had told him to commit the unholiest sin.

"Martin..." the Kommandant warned, reaching out and putting a hand on the boy's cat. "Bad little Jews don't get to have toys."

Loathing glowed in the child's eyes, but he tightened his grip on the cat and obeyed, lifting up one little hand and squeaking, "Heil Hitler."

"Jesus Christ!" Vilém spat. "You *are* a monster!"

I was trying to keep the boy alive, to give him a better life...

"You *blamed him* for *you* murdering his friend!" snapped

Vilém. "You lied to him about his mother to try and morph him into a little Nazi! How can you *not* see what a shitbag you are?"

I genuinely don't understand. You're supposed to be seeing things from my point of view...

"Yes! And even from your point of view, you're a terrible human being!" cried Vilém. "It is *astonishing* how many hoops you're jumping through to continue to think you're a good person. Fuck! Even Heydrich let Iveta Sladký live, you didn't even spare the child's mother!"

I would argue that makes Heydrich a hypocrite. What is worse? Someone who follows his principles, or someone who bends them where it's convenient?

"You bent them too—you took in a Jew and gave him a fake ID! That was illegal! That was a violation of your so-called principles!"

Oh, I'm sure Heydrich would have said the same. Cold-hearted bastard didn't understand the difference between making my father's sacrifice worthwhile and letting his brat son keep a pet Jew. Nevertheless...I did owe him for the relative freedom he offered me. And besides, I hoped that an Aryan-looking Jew like little Fido...

"Iveta!" snarled Vilém. "At the very least say her real name."

You undesirables are so picky about your names. Fine, Iva or whatever her name was. She moved into the house, and I hoped that Little Martin would at least brighten up if he had a supposedly Aryan playmate. But while he played with her, he didn't like her very much. And whenever Heydrich would bring his little brat over to visit, Martin would be miserable.

"Gerber, I didn't think your boy would be so shy. Don't tell me he's afraid of being beaten by a little girl! Worse, a little Jewess."

Again, a new memory formed, and a familiar high-pitched voice made both Vilém and the Kommandant's chests tighten with aggravation. The Kommandant sat on the edge of his desk holding a half-empty bottle of beer. Heydrich was leaning by the open window, looking down into the garden. The Kommandant set his drink aside and slowly sauntered over, standing beside his mentor and peering outside.

Klaus Heydrich and Iveta Sladký were having a ball: both had taken up arms in the form of wooden swords and were engaged in a brutal duel. They laughed, a sweet sound that made Gerber feel like vomiting.

"See? He's by the doghouse. Why do you have that, by the way? You don't have a dog," Heydrich pointed out.

Gerber didn't answer. He glanced at Iveta's doghouse. Little Martin was sitting against the dilapidated structure, his back to the other children, anger etched onto his face as he stubbornly hugged his toy cat.

"Poor kid," Vilém muttered. Martin had no clue that Iveta was a Jew and Klaus was nothing like his father. If only he had known...perhaps they could have been friends, perhaps he could have had some moments of happiness at the Camp.

But Martin could only see Fido the Nazi Spy and Heydrich's little prince. He hid from them as though he was afraid they would start beating him with their wooden swords.

"I *told* him to play nice..." muttered the Kommandant, and Heydrich shrugged, taking a casual sip of his beer.

"Boys will rarely do as they are told. I love my sons, but my daughter is much easier to deal with. By the way, you should find a dog for that doghouse. Boys need pets, it teaches them to take responsibility. Klaus has our dog, some chickens that Himmler gave us, and I gave him his own horse just this year after our other dog died, poor Daxi..."

"And he has a pet Jew," the Kommandant snarked. Heydrich turned to his accomplice with a cold warning in his eyes.

"I'm joking," the Kommandant said hastily. "Klaus is too sweet for his own good."

"Yes..." muttered Heydrich. The Hangman realized his son had paused his duel with Iveta and was slowly approaching Martin. Klaus Heydrich gingerly tapped Martin's shoulder with the point of his sword. When Martin turned with a start, the younger Heydrich offered the sword to him.

Martin shook his head, clinging ever tighter to the cat. Klaus frowned with disappointment and his arm flopped to his side in defeat. Heydrich's son seemed to sense that he was being watched and looked up, his eyes locking with his father's. Gerber smirked as what little color remained in General Heydrich's cheeks drained away.

For a moment, they stood there in silence, Iveta watching the standoff with terror, Kommandant Gerber with amusement. If Heydrich didn't feel guilty about this entire affair, he at the very least felt embarrassed. Klaus broke first by raising up a hand and giving a tiny wave, a wave that his father slowly returned. Klaus offered his father a slight smile, then gestured with his sword towards Iveta.

"Go on..." Heydrich mouthed, motioning for his son to have fun. Klaus' eyes brightened with hope, and Vilém felt a stab of pity for the boy. He must have thought there was something good left in his father, some small sliver of kindness. He returned to Iveta with a bounce in his step.

Kommandant Gerber, whose chest was about to explode with anger, saw a teeny smile tease the corner of Heydrich's lips and he couldn't help but snap, "You're not being a good father, Reinhard."

Heydrich turned to face the Kommandant, raising an eyebrow and gesturing for him to elaborate. Gerber pointed at Iveta.

"You let your child associate with a Jew. Continue to do this and he will not be able to exist within the new world we're creating."

"Is that a threat?" Heydrich hissed.

"Not at all, but you're teaching him to have affection for a race we are going to exterminate. What will you do when he's older? What if he defects? Resists? Becomes an enemy of the state? It's not safe. It's *dangerous*. Were I you, I would have ignored his pleas, given him discipline..."

"I don't hit my children, Kommandant. I know you don't hit yours either."

"There are other ways to control a child besides physical force," the Kommandant argued, and Heydrich's face darkened.

"I know..." the Blonde Beast muttered.

"My point is, however you chose to deal with your son's misbehavior, you should have had the Jewess put down."

"I understand your argument, Hans," sighed Heydrich, glancing down at the glistening Nazi pin on his breast. "But you know as well as I do that when you love someone, you will bend politics for their safety and happiness."

"The Jewish Question goes far beyond politics, General Heydrich, as *you* taught me," the Kommandant snapped, an accusatory edge in his tone. "Besides, as far as I was *told*, the purpose of doing this work to solve the Jewish Question is to preserve our children's safety and happiness. Reichsprotektor, you might as well let your son keep a poisonous snake as a pet."

"You know, I don't take the Bible seriously," Heydrich sneered. "But I feel like you're 'casting the first stone', Hans. If I recall, you had your own *Edeljude* you wanted to protect."

"Well, maybe I was wrong!" the Kommandant hissed. "Why is it all right for you or I or Klaus to have an *Edeljude*? The average German does not get to keep their one good Jew, and I was under the impression that all Germans are equal under the Führer."

"If we let *every* German keep his good Jew, we would never solve the Jewish Problem..."

"But then *is there* a Jewish Problem?!" the Kommandant finally cried, and Vilém felt Hans' instincts scream for him to stop, beg him to take that back. He was questioning too much. It was dangerous.

But the dam was broken and he let his doubts out. "If *every* Jew has some upstanding German citizen willing to vouch for them—maybe not *every* Jew, but most German Jews—if that's the case, is there really a Jewish Question at all?"

Vilém expected Heydrich the so-called perfect Nazi to rebuke Hans like a priest might an altar boy who dared to question Church doctrine. He was surprised when the Blonde Beast's icy eyes warmed and he reached up, closing one gloved hand around his Nazi Party pin.

"You know..." Heydrich whispered. "Sometimes I wonder about that."

His grip tightened around the pin, as though there was a small part of him, the pinprick of goodness that Klaus could still see, that wanted to rip the pin off and stop the madness right then. The Kommandant watched his mentor, waiting...but Heydrich loosened his grip and brushed his thumb against the swastika.

"I guess it's too late to really ask those questions now...isn't it?" Heydrich said, and the Kommandant looked out at the Camp, at the ash-filled Pit, at the bodies of starved prisoners piled high in the distance.

"Yes..." Hans whispered, bowing his head.

"We've gone too far," Heydrich decreed, his high-pitched voice somehow rising an octave. "We *have* to finish it. We *have* to be right. We *are* right. People like you and I, through our sacrifices, we have earned our exceptions. It isn't unfair. It isn't."

"No..." muttered the Kommandant, barely keeping his tone

from wavering. Heydrich looked down at his own hand. There was a ring decorating one of his long, thin fingers, a ring shaped like a skull. He stared into the little skull's empty eyes for a moment before smiling bitterly.

"You know, Himmler was telling me the other day that he thinks when I'm gone, I should have all my medals and trinkets put in a museum. So my children and their children can see what I did and share it with the whole world."

He looked up, and if Vilém hadn't known the monster he was looking at, he might have felt pity for Heydrich right then. He had never seen a more uncertain face.

"What do you think, Gerber?" the Blonde Beast asked. "Do you want to be in a museum someday?"

"Ha!" laughed Vilém. "Well, Gerber, what do you think about your museum?"

I'm not fond of it, and I imagine if Heydrich could see his exhibit, he wouldn't like it either. But, well...he ended up becoming a martyr for the Cause.

"That 'martyr' sounded pretty sarcastic."

He didn't deserve one bit of the adoration he received. He was a pure hypocrite, and yet when he perished like a fool, the whole Reich was obligated to weep for him. Everyone...except one child...

"Kommandant Gerber!"

A new memory formed. Kommandant Gerber was standing before a large memorial that was drowning in wreaths and flowers. A bust of Heydrich sneered at him from the top of the memorial, and anger bubbled up in the Kommandant's belly.

"Kommandant Gerber!"

He turned and saw little Klaus, standing beside his younger brother and the head of the SS, Heinrich Himmler. Klaus broke away from his "Uncle" Himmler and darted towards the Kommandant. Gerber's anger elevated when he realized that the child was dry-eyed.

"Well, well, Klaus," he scoffed. "Aren't you putting on a brave face! You must be traumatized."

Klaus' eyes flitted towards his father's bust, and the Kommandant saw a strangely bitter smile flicker across the child's face.

"Boy, show your father some respect," the Kommandant hissed. "I assure you, if you were my son..."

"Thankfully, I'm not," Klaus declared, whipping an envelope out of his pocket and pushing it against the Kommandant's chest. "My father may be gone, but I can still make your life Hell if you hurt Iveta. Give this to her and keep her safe and happy."

"Ha! Well! Taking after your old man!" the Kommandant laughed, quickly pocketing the envelope. He shot a cautious look at Himmler, hoping he hadn't seen that exchange, but the Reichs-führer of the SS was too busy comforting Klaus' brother to spot anything suspicious.

"I take after Papa enough to be nosy," Klaus said, crossing his arms behind his back, his lively blue eyes suddenly becoming icy, a smirk that seemed too much like his father's blooming on his boyish face.

"So..." the child said, his voice dropping to a whisper. "How about you keep my Jew a secret and I won't tell my Godfather Himmler about yours?"

The Kommandant felt his heartbeat screech to a halt. He looked down at the insufferably snide child and barely suppressed the urge to deck the boy across the face.

"Martin told you?" he whispered. Klaus shook his head.

"I snooped. He writes things about you...he hates you, you know."

"You need to be quiet, boy..." snarled the Kommandant.

"So do you, *Kommandant*."

"I will not be ordered around by a dead General's brat...besides, you wouldn't say a word. You're softer than your father, Klaus, and you wouldn't want Martin's blood on your hands."

"Maybe..." Klaus said with a nod. "Are you gonna take that chance? You really shouldn't bet on a Heydrich being merciful."

"No...I suppose not."

"Good. I've gotta..." Klaus started to say, but the Kommandant suddenly reached out, grabbing the boy's wrist and pulling him back. The junior Heydrich turned with a look of disbelief, but his ire melted when he saw that the Kommandant's aggravation had morphed into dismay.

"What...did he write about me?" Hans asked. Klaus scowled, tugging his arm out of the Kommandant's grasp.

"What do you *think* he wrote?" Klaus snapped, retreating to Himmler's side without another word.

Heydrich's boy was right: I didn't want to test his mercy, so I kept Iveta around until he ended up getting splattered by a bus...but almost as soon as I got home from the funeral, I set out to find this secret journal Klaus had uncovered. You'll never guess where it was...

"He kept it in the cat," Vilém assumed, squeezing the old stuffed animal.

Correct! God knows how the little Heydrich brat figured it out so fast, I searched everywhere. But behind the button eye was a little hole, and in that little hole was a collection of papers. Letters.

"To who?"

His mother.

"'Mama, I hate every second of this, I hate to live a lie. Every time I say "Heil Hitler", it burns my tongue, but I will say it a million times to see you again. I pray to Adonai that I will see you soon and I pray that God sees all the evil in Gerber.'"

A new memory started, and the amount of fury that flowed

through the Kommandant as he read the little boy's letter aloud was almost painful. Vilém was surprised that the boy was still breathing, much less unharmed. But the Kommandant stopped himself from striking the boy, instead pacing in front of Little Martin.

Martin sat on the end of his bed, hugging his now one-eyed toy cat and staring down at the cushioned floor. The boy's face was unreadable. He refused to show any sign of how afraid he truly was, but Vilém could see tears clinging to the corners of his eyes.

The Kommandant finished the note, tore it into tiny pieces and hurled the shreds at the child, who winced as though acid rain was falling upon him.

"You really believe that about me?" Hans snapped. "After all I've done for you? After all I've given you...come here!"

He suddenly reached for the child, and Vilém was afraid he would grab Martin by the hair or wrist and seriously injure him. Fortunately, for as furious as the Kommandant was, he remembered Martin's condition and instead grabbed the little toy cat, knowing that the boy would refuse to let go of his most precious possession. Martin clung to the cat's tail and trotted behind the Kommandant, who gripped the toy's head and stomped all the way to the developing room.

"K-Kommandant!" Raya Pomnenka was busily hanging several pictures up on a wire. She paused her work and stood at attention, her head bowed, her burned hands at her sides. The Kommandant shoved her towards the door.

"Out, Pomnenka, go outside with Fido!" the Kommandant snarled. Raya didn't hesitate, scurrying past the Kommandant and the child, shooting the boy a sympathetic look as she fled. The Kommandant noticed this and slammed the door behind her, plunging the developing room into partial darkness.

"Does she know?" he barked, pointing towards the spot where

Raya had been standing. "Does she know you're a Jew? Have you talked to her too?"

"No, no! I haven't told her or Fido!" screamed the boy, falling to his knees. "Please don't hurt anyone! Please! I'm sorry!"

"Why should I believe a word you say after you wrote horrible lies about me?" growled the Kommandant, dropping the cat and crossing his arms. "I bet you told her...I bet you told her, and if you did...she has to go. Nobody who knows you're a Jew can be allowed to live! You know why?"

"Yes, sir..."

"Say it, you ungrateful brat!"

"Because you care about me and you're my protector," whimpered the child, pressing the cat to his cheek as though he desperately wanted someone to give him a comforting kiss.

"Correct! You see these!" The Kommandant snatched several pictures off the wire, blurry black-and-white images of Jews at work, Jews starving, Jews burning...he grabbed the boy by the hair and forced him to look up, shoving the photos in his face.

"This! This is what will happen to you if anyone finds out! If you tell a soul! Look, look!" Hans commanded.

"You're hurting me!" Martin squealed, dropping his toy and grabbing the Kommandant's hands, trying to pry the Nazi's fingers off his hair. The Kommandant released the boy, sneering when he saw that a few golden splotches of dye were staining his gloves.

"I've given you a new life," the Kommandant said. "I saved you from this!"

He tossed the pictures at the boy, who ducked and covered as though the horrifying photos were bombs.

"If you hate this life so much, perhaps I should let you go back to living like a Jew!" suggested the Kommandant. "You and your mother can be reunited, and you both can go to the Pit! If I'm so evil..."

"Please don't kill me!" whimpered Martin. "Please, I'm sorry, you're right, you're right, I'm ungrateful..."

"Damn right!" snapped the Kommandant, stomping his foot beside the boy's head, making the floorboards creak and bend.

"Please don't hurt me, please!" wailed the boy.

"You, I won't...for now. But if you think I'm so evil, perhaps I should take away your doctor. And your mother, perhaps she should be sent away...after all, I am *evil*."

"You're not evil!" the boy lied, clinging to the Kommandant's foot. "You're not evil, please, I was being silly! Please don't hurt anyone! Please, please!"

The Kommandant looked down at the sobbing child with disdain, remaining silent for a moment before sneering, "It seems your lessons have not taken hold. Really, maybe I should let you play with Heydrich's boy more often. He at least knows that German boys do not *beg*."

He pulled his foot away from the boy and declared, "A German boy *demands*. So, Martin, *demand* that I spare your mother and perhaps I will. Because I am not evil, I will be merciful, but I want you to show me that there's some German spirit in you."

He waved for the boy to get to his feet, to demand like a true German. The child remained on his knees, however, and the Kommandant began to feel nervous when he saw realization flaring in Martin's eyes.

"A German doesn't beg," the child whispered. "And a Jew doesn't deserve mercy...and Germans never give what is not deserved..."

"It seems you *have* been listening to my lessons," the Kommandant mumbled, arching an eyebrow. "Come now, let's see..."

"You wouldn't spare my mother," the child said, slowly rising to his feet, his face twisting with anger. "You said it yourself!

Anyone who knows I'm a Jew has to die, and my mother knows I'm a Jew!"

"Martin..." the Kommandant whispered, but the boy had figured it out. Martin lunged at the Kommandant, trying to shove him into the tub of chemicals behind him, screaming, kicking.

"You liar! You liar!" screeched the boy. "She's already dead! You liar! You never spared her! She's dead! She's dead! You killed her, you German bastard!"

"Martin, enough!" the Kommandant cried, grabbing the boy's wrists, having to keep a tight hold to prevent the boy from continuing his attack. The child bit the Kommandant's exposed wrist and Hans let him go.

"Ow! Little...!" the Kommandant cried, but Martin had already run to the tub.

"*My name is not Martin!*" the boy screamed, desperately trying to dump the chemicals onto the Nazi. The tub, however, was too heavy for Martin, and the Kommandant was easily able to capture him before he could tip anything over. He grabbed the child by his fake blonde hair and yanked him all the way out of Barrack One.

Vilém at first didn't understand what the Kommandant was doing, but then he realized the Nazi was dragging the howling, thrashing boy to a far-off corner of the Camp. The familiar, terrible stench of soft skin burning became more and more intense, but while Martin gagged and covered his nose, the Kommandant seemed unaffected by the smell.

They arrived at the edge of the Pit. A dancing flame licked the corners of the open-air crematorium. The Kommandant looked down into the Pit and smirked when he saw it was in use. Several new arrivals were being taken care of. The sick. The old. The young. They lay on grates at the bottom, their skin baking, their bodies burning into ash.

Vilém felt ill. He had seen a lot through the eyes of the other victims, but he had never seen what the Nazis did to their bodies. Worse, he felt a sense of satisfaction settle in the Kommandant's chest as he watched the bodies burn, like he was an artist admiring his own completed work.

"I can't breathe..." Martin whimpered, but the Kommandant forced him to look down into the Pit, forced him to stare at his fellow Jews' cremation. It was so hot that the boy's tears evaporated as soon as they left his eyes.

"Look, look boy!" the Kommandant commanded. "Is this where you want to be? You want to be reunited with your mother so badly? Huh? Is that what you want? Is this what you want or do you want to go back to being a good German boy?"

The boy stopped struggling as the Kommandant all but held him directly above the Pit. Martin looked down at the melting, empty eyes of his people. Ashes flew into the air, invading the child's lungs.

"Well? Well? Do you want to go in the Pit, boy? Do you want to be a Jew? Do you want to be a Jew?" the Kommandant snapped. "Am I evil, boy? Am I evil for *stealing* you from this? Go on! You want to go back to the house? Beg me to take you home if this isn't what you want!"

The boy kept his lips tightly pursed to keep the ashes, the taste of death, off his tongue, but he opened his mouth for a mere second to answer: "A German does not beg."

Pride filled the Kommandant's heart, banishing all anger, and he pulled the boy away from the Pit. He let go of the boy's hair and put his hands on his shoulders. Little Martin held his gaze. There wasn't any light in his eyes.

"Good boy," Hans said, patting the child's cheek. "Your mother would have wanted you to be safe. As a German, you will be safe. With me, you will be safe. Just be grateful."

"Okay..." Martin said, still refusing to let his gaze shift, and Vilém could tell that even the Kommandant feared the emptiness in the boy's eyes. Nevertheless, he ignored his own feelings of disquiet and offered the boy his hand.

"Let's go home..." he said. Martin didn't hesitate to cling to the murderer, and as a cloud of ash flew over the two, the memory faded into darkness.

And from there...from there, for some time, he was the perfect German. He didn't question, didn't argue, didn't make a fuss. He did all of his assignments perfectly. He never tried to speak with Pomnenka or any other Jew. When Klaus Heydrich died and I got rid of Fido, he didn't throw a tantrum...he was everything Isaac wasn't.

"He wasn't his own person, he was your puppet," Vilém snapped.

Oh, but not exactly. Under my nose, he associated with the traitor Klammer, he learned Jewish nonsense from the new doctor I got him...and he conspired, conspired to escape. Even when I gave him everything, he still wanted to live as a fugitive Jew.

"You killed his mother. You think for one second he actually wanted to be like you?"

Perhaps I was letting my wants get the best of me. The war was not going well. By the time Klammer pulled off his heist, I knew that everything we had been fighting for, killing for, the great future Heydrich had said I would build...it would never come. Martin was my last chance, my father's last chance, at having a purpose, leaving a mark. I prioritized him above everything those last few weeks before the train was set to leave for Auschwitz.

"Unwrap it, Martin, go on!"

A new memory formed. The Kommandant was sitting cross-legged in the nursery, surrounded by more toys and books than any child could have played with by themselves. A small pile of cards that wished Little Martin a happy birthday, decorated with swastikas and stuffed with Reichsmarks, sat at Martin's side. Martin had unwrapped all but one of his gifts.

"This one's from you?" the child queried, and the Kommandant nodded, grinning so widely that his cheeks hurt. If Vilém had been tossed into this memory with no context, feeling the Kommandant's giddiness and warmth, he would have assumed the child was Gerber's beloved son.

Martin tore the glistening wrapping paper to shreds and pulled out the gift. A smile lit up the boy's face as he hoisted the small machine out of the box. A camera, much smaller than the Kommandant's and clearly brand new.

"And before you ask, I didn't take that from the prisoners," the Kommandant said. "You kept borrowing mine, so I figured you would appreciate it. Do you?"

"Yes! Thank you!" the boy cried, hopping to his feet and wrapping one arm around the Kommandant's neck, giving him a half hug. The Kommandant's heart fluttered and he hesitated to return the embrace. Martin must have never shown him such affection.

"Do you want to take some pictures of your toys?" he asked, and the boy nodded. They spent a few moments posing Martin's stuffed animals and snapping pictures. The Kommandant allowed himself to be silly, letting the boy take pictures of him as he pretended the toys were attacking him.

"Here, sir," the boy said when they had gone through all the toys except one, the little toy cat, whose button eyes had been lovingly replaced. Martin picked it up and tossed it to the Kommandant.

"You can give that away," Martin said. "I'm done with it."

Surprise and joy filled the Kommandant as he looked from the ratty little toy to the boy who had once loved it so. "Are you sure, Martin?"

"Yes...I don't wanna look at it anymore. It's just a toy anyway," the boy said, lifting up the camera and snapping a picture of the grinning Kommandant. Gerber shoved the little cat into his pocket.

"Come here, you, I'm so proud!" he cried, lifting the boy into the air and spinning him around. Martin seemed surprised and frightened for a moment before he giggled. The Kommandant tossed the child onto the bed.

"Hey, be careful, you may bump me!" the boy cried. "The less I have to see that Jew doctor, the better."

"I'm careful, you know I'm careful!" the Kommandant retorted. "And you won't have to worry about the Jew doctor much longer. I'm looking for a replacement, a proper Aryan replacement. You've earned it, you've earned my trust."

Vilém could feel that announcing this made the Kommandant nervous. No doubt he remembered how Little Martin had reacted the last time he had disposed of a Jewish doctor. But Martin hid his true feelings well and smiled eagerly.

"Good! One less Jew in the house!" the boy declared. "Just don't get rid of my Jew until you find a *really* good Aryan doctor, I don't wanna die!"

Gerber's soul all but burst with happiness at seeing the boy's apparent anti-Semitism. He lovingly patted Martin's head. "I'll get you the best doctor in all the Reich, I promise! It'll be a belated extra birthday present."

"Oh! By the way," the boy cried, hopping to his feet and pointing to his skull. "I had a birthday request: I don't like that my hair's so curly, it makes me still feel like a Jew. Can we cut it really short so it doesn't curl? Can you use the razor on me?"

"The razor we use for the Jews?" the Kommandant said, grasping a curled strand of the boy's hair. "No, come, I'll trim it for you."

The Kommandant led the boy to his bathroom and pulled his personal razor out of a drawer. Vilém grinned: the Kommandant was unwittingly aiding in the boy's eventual escape.

"Smart kid..." Vilém whispered, but the Kommandant was none the wiser. He looked from the boy to the blade with innocent hesitation.

"Are...you sure?" Hans said, smiling gently. "Have I ever shown you a picture of your father?"

"Isaac Goldstein?" Martin mumbled. Still holding the razor, the Kommandant gestured for the boy to sit on his bed. Hans yanked his old album out of his dresser and opened to the image of him and Isaac as children.

"That's him?" Martin said, prodding the picture with his index finger and staring down at his father's grinning face.

"You look just like him, see? That's how I could tell you were his when I saw you on the Platform."

"I guess..." the boy mumbled, letting his fingers linger just above the faded image. The Kommandant started turning the pages, showing Martin picture after picture until they got to the very back. As he flipped through the album, as the years went on and Isaac grew older and older, Hans began to notice that his not-brother was smiling less and less.

By the time they reached the final image, Isaac was poker-faced. His eyes, once filled with mirth, had become empty.

He looked nothing like the boy in the Christmas picture. But the Kommandant glanced at stony-faced Martin and realized that the last picture of Isaac, the miserable picture...the resemblance was uncanny. If it weren't for the dye and the age difference, they would look identical.

Vilém felt something scratch against the Kommandant's soul. Not exactly realization, and not even close to guilt, but what little wisps of his conscience remained called to him, pointing out what he had done to Isaac, what he was doing to Martin.

Martin pressed his thumb against the solemn Isaac's face. "That's him," he muttered. "That looks like him."

The Kommandant nodded slowly, turning back to the first page, back to the happier Isaac. "You haven't...talked about what he was like to you before..."

"He left when I was little, I've told you that. He was drunk and horrible."

"All the time?" the Kommandant said. "Isaac, he...he had his sins but...he had his good moments."

"The good moments don't matter," Martin declared, shutting the album and shoving it back towards the Kommandant. "Not if everything else is terrible."

"I just...your hair reminds me of him...and..."

"He's the past," Martin proclaimed, grabbing a handful of his curly hair. "The past is gone. It's just sad now. All I wanna do is get to the future. Please, can we cut my hair...Papa?"

Vilém laughed at the boy's deception, and he felt the Kommandant's heart hop with happiness. The Nazi smiled at the new title and placed a hand on the child's shoulder.

"As short as you like!" Hans said. "It will make the dye easier to apply...let's do it!"

He threw the old album aside and took up the razor, cutting the child's hair extra short.

"Nobody will be able to recognize you, Martin," Gerber laughed, and the boy smiled widely.

"I'll thank all the guards for their gifts after the transport leaves tomorrow," Martin said, looking down at the mountain of curly hair that covered the floor and giving it a small nudge with his foot.

"Let's get a picture!" the Kommandant suggested with excitement. The boy posed in front of a swastika flag and shoved his arm into the air, grinning mischievously. The Kommandant, fully convinced that he had won, that the boy was his, snapped a picture.

And the next day...he was gone.

"Pulled one over on ya'!" Vilém laughed. "You didn't *really* think he loved you, did you?"

The spirit said nothing.

"Why would you even want it? A Jew's love?" Vilém inquired. "I thought they were all undesirable."

I thought Martin wasn't.

"Martin never existed, Kommandant!" Vilém snapped. "You tried to turn that little boy into Martin and you failed. And then what?"

And then? Well, of course I tried my best to get him back. I interrogated that traitor Klammer...

Fury and fear like nothing Vilém had ever experienced coursed through the Kommandant as a new memory started with a violent snarl and a kick to Joseph Klammer's face. Klammer was kneeling on the floor of his bare cell, his arms tied behind his back, his face bruised and bloody. Gerber grabbed him by the hair and lifted his head.

"*Where did they go?*" he demanded, and Klammer spat in his former boss' face.

"Fuck you," Joseph hissed, and the Kommandant, disgusted, threw the young hero to the floor again and kicked him in the stomach, kicked him over and over, his blood pounding in his ears, his heart racing...

And yet even as his bones cracked, even as he was beaten black and blue, Joseph laughed.

"What the *fuck* are you laughing at?" barked the Kommandant. Klammer looked up at Hans and grinned, showing off that the Nazis had knocked out several of his teeth.

"You!" he cried. "The Russians are right at our door about to butcher us and all you care about is killing more Jewish babies!"

"I *care*," the Kommandant insisted, striking Klammer in the gut once more, "that you let the Jews *steal my son*! Tell me where they are and maybe I'll consider letting you die quickly!"

"Your *son*, sure!" Klammer cackled. He sat up slightly, his bright, blazing blue eyes burrowing into the Kommandant's as the bitter mirth drained from his irises. "I talked to the kid. I talked to him. I know he's not your son. I know you stole him. I don't fucking know why, but you stole him...and he hates you. And he's gonna get away and live a nice long life raised by *Jews!*"

"Enough!" the Kommandant cried, kicking Joseph again, but the Sergeant refused to shut up.

"He's gonna get away, he's gonna be raised by Jews, and he's gonna curse your name forever! Worse! Maybe he'll just forget about you! The Russians will come, the Jews will be free, you'll be dangling from a noose, and all of this misery will be pointless! Your whole life is pointless!"

"ENOUGH! ENOUGH! ENOUGH!"

Hans felt like a bomb had gone off in his chest. He needed to let his anger out. He kicked the prisoner over and over and over...kick, kick, kick...

SMASH!

Until, in the blink of an eye, the memory shifted and in the place of Klammer, the Kommandant brought his boot down on his camera, crushing the machine. He heard a tiny gasp from the snooping Raya Pomnenka, but he ignored it, instead stumbling over to his desk. He grabbed a pack of matches and lit a fire in his trash bin.

Slowly, he started pulling out pictures. Pictures of Martin, smiling with empty eyes, waiting for his escape. Pictures of Martin pretending to be German, pretending to love the Kommandant. He tossed them all into the fire.

He pulled the boy's favorite toy, the little cat, out of his pocket and held it above the flames, but he couldn't bring himself to burn it. The boy had truly loved the cat. Unlike the pictures that were smoldering in his trash bin, the cat wasn't phony. He set it on his desk, and the little stuffed animal stared at him gloomily as he opened his old leather album.

The pictures of a broken Isaac went first. The Isaac he had poisoned, the Isaac who had lost the hope in his eyes, the Isaac that Martin had known best. They burned first. Slowly, he emptied the albums until only one picture remained: the photo of him and Isaac at Christmas, him and Isaac smiling, him and Isaac as brothers.

He held it above the flames, tears blurring his vision as he dropped it. He watched as the last image of Isaac burned like so many Jews. The ashes flew in his face and the world became gray.

And...well, you know what happened after that. The Russians came and I ended it all. Like Klammer said, it was all pointless.

"So..." Vilém sighed, gripping the family album that still sat on his lap. "You ended it...and then you stayed...because?"

Isn't it obvious? This is my legacy. This failed war, the Camp...this is it. This is all. And I want more. I want to know that my father and I left more than that.

"Through the boy."

He's never come to the Camp. I want to know what became of him. I want...I want for him to have done a great deed, to have become someone of note...I want him to give me meaning. If you can give me that, give me meaning through Martin, I will leave the Camp and move on to whatever's next.

"Right...well, I've got bad news for you. Good news and bad

news." Vilém set the cat on his knee and pressed his palm against the first page of his family album, tapping his finger against the picture of the Svobodas.

"Good news is I don't have to go on a quest. I know exactly what happened to 'Martin.' The boy you stole—his name was Fabian. He's my grandfather."

He peeked through his eyelashes at the picture in front of him, the picture of the grinning, happy Fabian Svoboda, formerly Martin Gerber II, and before that Fabian Goldstein. Vilém had finally recognized his young grandfather on the Platform, but he had bitten his tongue and now...now he could feel the Kommandant's spirit all but explode with surprise and anticipation.

Your grandfather...?

"Fabian befriended my great-uncle Danny. Joseph Klammer was hiding him in your house, right under your nose. Fabian pretended to be a good Nazi to keep you ignorant, to keep Danny safe. When he escaped with the rest of the Jews, my great-grandfather Sam took him in. He raised him as his own."

He...did you know him? Did you know Martin?

"*Fabian.* And I knew him very well. He was an amazing grandfather."

That doesn't matter to me! Did he ever talk about me? Or the war? What became of him? What did he do?

"Absolutely nothing," Vilém declared, his heart swelling with pride. "He kept cactuses. He painted birdhouses with his grandchildren. He was a house painter his whole life. Never stepped foot out of Czechoslovakia. He lived an ordinary life. No grand act of valor, no *point.* He lived, he forgot you, and he had a happy, normal life."

Vilém felt as though a thousand needles were pricking at his flesh as the Kommandant's anger consumed Barrack One.

Then my father died for nothing! I died for nothing!

"No!" snapped Vilém, tucking the toy cat under his arm and standing up. He held his family album like a shield and faced the Kommandant's burning rage. "Everyone in the Camp died for nothing! They died because of stupid, angry people that wouldn't move forward and only dragged their nation back! Fabian lived! Fabian lived a good, happy, gentle life! His life was worth living even if he didn't become a glorious hero or a soldier or whatever twisted creature you wanted to turn him into!"

He only lived because of me!

"You! You! You think everything is about you! But Klammer was right! Your life was pointless! Everything you ever did was pointless! *You* are pointless!"

He dropped the album and stepped forward, gripping the little cat by its neck, and he felt the Kommandant's fury fade into fear.

What are you doing?

"You are nothing! You're a name on a placard that people curse at! Legacy? Meaning? Point? This is your legacy, a legacy of pointless slaughter all done because you wanted everything to fit into a neat little Nazi storybook!"

Enough...

"Well, nothing panned out! You failed at everything! You failed to kill the Jews, you failed Isaac, you even failed to turn Fabian into Martin! And you know what? I'm getting married, and I'm gonna bring another Jew into the world. Fabian's name will carry on and on, but you? You? The only thing you'll do is *go to Hell!*"

In one swift motion, Vilém tore the toy cat in two. The artifact became nothing but stuffing, fabric, and bad memories, and the Kommandant's worthless soul vanished.

When Vilém opened his eyes, he found himself lying not in the barrack, but in a room drowning in white light. He sat up. He felt weightless; his skin tingled like a current was going through his blood. It was like he had just fallen out of his own body.

He looked to his side and his lips tightened when he saw that the album was gone.

"You can come out now, David!" Vilém cried. He heard the sound of a page flipping and turned around.

There was a boy sitting a few feet away, barely three years old. He was somberly thumbing through the Svoboda family album. He had curly black hair, curly and dark like Sam's, like Fabian's...

The little boy paused as he found one picture of Vilém's grandfather, scowling at Fabian's smiling face. Vilém cleared his throat. The child sighed and looked up, his soft blue eyes meeting the guard's. Despite his apparent age, the child had existed long enough to have gained maturity beyond his appearance. He greeted the Czech man with a crooked smile.

"Hi..." the child muttered. "You did it. Congrats...nephew? Should I call you my nephew?"

"You can call me whatever you want, David," Vilém said, crawling over to the boy and sitting across from him, offering David Svoboda a comforting smile.

"I get it now," Vilém sighed. "Joseph thought you survived...he thought you were my grandfather. But you...you died in the Ghetto the day before Klammer was reassigned to the Camp. Sam took Fabian in after they met, then they all found Rebecca and...I couldn't tell they weren't related. Fabian looked just like you..."

David nodded, touching the yellow '*Jude*' star that covered his heart. "He did...like an older me."

"How long have you been at the Camp, David?"

"I...move. I'm not like the others. I was never stuck in one place. I just...followed, watched...hoped someone would find out about me. I thought it would be your sister, Emma, the one studying history. But you...you got curious."

"Maybe a little too curious," muttered Vilém. "So...do you have a story to show me?"

"What's there to show?" David snapped, digging his ghostly fingernails into the soft leather of the album. "I got sick, I needed a doctor, I didn't get one...Joseph couldn't do enough. I died...and Mom and Dad replaced me."

The child chuckled ruefully. "Like a goldfish..."

"Or a cactus," Vilém said. "And Danny never even knew."

"He didn't remember me...and Mama and Papa forgot me..." Tears fell from the boy's eyes, dripping onto the album and hissing as they struck the paper, as though the images were an inferno.

"I'm sure they never forgot you, David," Vilém said, reaching out to the boy. "I saw what Sam was like after you died, he was destroyed. But he had to survive, live, keep Danny safe...and I think he just didn't want to feel sad anymore. He just wanted to keep moving forward..."

"Without me?" whispered David, curling into a little ball. "Because I made them sad."

"Please don't blame yourself, David. I think Fabian and Sam and Rebecca were all afraid of the past. They never talked about it, never got angry about it...but that's not much better than clinging to it like Gerber, hurting yourself and everyone around you to make all the pain worth it. I don't know how they *should* have moved on, but whatever they chose to do, they should have talked about you. You mattered."

"I'm pointless..." the boy said, resting his head on his knees. "I never did anything, never even lived...I just died and made people sad. As soon as they forgot me, they weren't sad anymore."

"David..." muttered Vilém, scooting close to his little great-uncle. He reached out and shut the album, shoving it aside so that nothing sat between him and the ghost.

"Look, I'm not God," he said. "I can't pretend to know how the world works, and I can't pretend to know what went through Sam's mind when he took Fabian in and pretended he was you...but I know that you're not pointless. You don't have to accomplish things or reach a certain age to be a good, worthy human."

"I'm just a number," sobbed David. "One in six million...people will remember Heydrich and the Kommandant...but not me."

"Raya thought the same thing. Was she just a number?"

"No, but *she* lived. Even if you wanna remember me, what's there to remember? I was born, I lived, I got sick, I died..."

"And your papa used to talk about you all the time. And you didn't say 'Papa' for the longest time and Sam was so happy when you finally said it. And when Joseph Klammer saw you...seeing you brought his heart a little closer to changing. You only lived for a few years, David Svoboda, but you changed so many lives, so many little worlds. You know, my grandpa said that Sam and Rebecca, they both passed really quick and really happy. I don't think they ever forgot you...I think they were looking forward to seeing you again. I think they miss you."

David sniffled, wiping his cheeks and gazing up at his great-nephew with wide, worried eyes.

"I'm still mad at them," he hiccupped. "For replacing me...I'm mad at them..."

"You have every right to be mad at them until the end of time, but don't let that anger keep you down here, miserable."

"I'm scared..." David confessed, reaching towards the guard, all semblance of maturity melting away. "What if they still don't wanna see me or think about me?"

"David, I barely know you, and I promise that I will not stop thinking about you. You deserve memory, and you deserve to move on and be happy, and you deserve a big fat apology from your parents...and a big hug too."

Vilém acted without hesitation, grabbing the little child's hand and gripping it tightly. The child exhaled as though amazed at the sensation of being held, seen, thought of. Slowly, David smiled, and it was a smile so lovely that even if Vilém had tried his hardest, he never would have forgotten it.

"Thanks...Nephew Vilém..." said David. "I'll say hi to Fabian...and Raya and Iveta and everyone else. I'll say hi to everyone."

"You'll be very popular, I'm sure," Vilém chuckled.

"Can you sit...here...with me...just until sunrise?" the boy begged, and Vilém squeezed the lost child's hand.

"Until you're ready," Vilém vowed, and he sat with the boy in the white room until slowly, the light consumed them both.

"Bye, Vilém!" David's little voice called to him, and he felt the child's hand slip away. "Thank you!"

"Vilém...Vilém!"

He felt as though he'd fallen from a two-story building and landed flat on his back. He awoke in Barrack One, covered in stuffing and sweat, blinded by sunlight, gasping for air.

"Jesus, Vilém, you weren't breathing! Are you okay? Don't fucking die in the Camp or I'll never hear the end of it from Ilona!" Alica Doubek's familiar scold alerted him to her presence above him. She helped him sit up, checking his pulse as she did so.

"I'm fine, I'm fine..." Vilém wheezed. "I did it...he's gone...they're all gone now."

"Good...that's good, but...you'll need to be gone...you..." Alica gestured to the remnants of the cat, grimacing as though the sight of artifact-destruction physically pained her.

"I'm sorry...it had to be done," Vilém said.

"I know, Rehor, I know..." Doubek sighed. "But I can't cover for you. You're fired...I'll write you a glowing recommendation and..."

She bit her knuckles and made a noise that sounded like she was choking on an almond. Vilém looked at his boss with concern, worried that she was being possessed, that perhaps the Kommandant hadn't been sent to Hell after all.

"Ms. Doubek..."

"And...you can have a bonus!" she finally gasped, pronouncing the promise in a tone that would have been more appropriate if she were confessing to murder. Vilém couldn't help it: he fell to the barrack floor, laughing.

"Oh, you!" cried Ms. Doubek, giggling and crying all at once. "When will I get a guard like you again?"

"Offer more bonuses!" Vilém joked, grabbing his album and pulling his boss into an embrace. "Bye, Ms. Doubek. You're still invited to the baby shower."

"Damn, thought I'd get out of it..." Doubek grumbled, returning the hug nonetheless. Vilém turned in his uniform, his badge, his flashlight, everything. He even left behind the album so she could use it for the new exhibit.

He left the Camp unemployed, empty-handed...and grinning so widely he drew disapproving glares from the visitors who saw him exit.

Many Years Later:

"Hey, Papa, David got beat up..."

Vilém Rehor stopped doing his homework right away. Normally, an interruption would have aggravated him when he was so wrapped up in finals, but of course his children and their well-being came first. He saved his history assignment and spun his chair around, facing his eldest child.

"How bad?" he asked, and Iveta Rehor, a pretty almost ten-year-old who had inherited her mother's looks, pursed her lips tightly together. It was, unfortunately, practically a rite-of-passage for the Rehor children to be beaten up by anti-Semites at some point in their young lives. Iveta had been beaten up, her younger sister Raya had been beaten up, and now it was the youngest Rehor child's turn to face the ancient hatred.

"Not too bad…" she intoned. "He's not happy, but Uncle Erik was nearby when it happened and beat up the bullies. It was some boys from school, but Erik beat 'em up and took him home."

"Good," Vilém said, rising from his chair. "Where's your mother?"

"Out with Raya. David's down in the shop with Uncle Erik. I put up the 'closed' sign."

"Good girl," Vilém said, patting his daughter's cheek. "I'll take it from here. We'll do our homework together later, okay?"

Iveta, who was the most studious of the Rehor children, smiled and nodded. She and her siblings loved that their father was in university. His status as a part-time student meant that they could all complain about homework together, albeit Vilém, who was pursuing an M.A. in History, certainly had a lot more to complain about regarding his assignments. Still, it was nice. It was something they could relate to.

Vilém sighed as he trudged down the stairs. Experiencing anti-Semitism wasn't something he could relate to. He could never understand what it was like to be his children, to be a minority, to live in the shadow of a genocide and still deal with the fear of it all happening again. He could never understand, but he could always support them, love them, and teach them.

"Hey, man!" Erik greeted him as he arrived down in the shop area. David was sitting at the booth, licking a lollipop and holding an ice pack over a bruised cheek. David looked like Vilém to an almost frightening extent, and even more than that, he looked like Fabian.

"Thanks so much for helping him, dude," Vilém whispered in Erik's ear. "He needs that, to know he has friends who'll defend him."

"I'll fucking deck a Nazi for that kid any day, and I know you would'a done the same for me when we were kids," Erik said with a smirk, patting his friend's shoulder. "Y'know...if all the little mini-Hitlers hadn't been too scared of my grandma to put a hand on me back then."

"Too bad Ilona's gone," muttered Vilém, glancing at a picture of the smiling matriarch that hung on a nearby wall. "If she was still here, she'd murder those little shitheads."

"I'll head up and keep Iveta distracted, you have a father-son whatever," Erik said.

"I'll try my best, but Jana's always better at this kinda thing," Vilém sighed. Erik ran up the stairs and Vilém slowly approached his son, ruffling the seven-year-old's curly hair. The boy looked up and offered Vilém a sparkling smile, a smile that bore a beautiful resemblance to that of his namesake.

"Hey, crazy," Vilém said, sitting beside his son and slowly unwrapping a blob of taffy, molding the candy into a little pyramid. "I heard Erik beat up some dummies."

"It was great!" David said, throwing his ice pack aside and joining his father in playing with taffy like play-dough. "He hit 'em with a plunger and called 'em the s-word."

"Oooh! Well, they earned it...open!" Vilém commanded, plopping his taffy pyramid onto his son's tongue. The boy giggled and the two of them delighted in being mutually gross for a moment.

"Sticky, beep!" David said, poking his father's cheek with a taffy-coated thumb. Vilém snickered and grabbed his son, lifting him onto his lap and squeezing him tenderly.

"You okay?" he asked. David leaned against his father, and Vilém could feel his son tense up.

"Yeah...yeah, Uncle Erik came in, so it's fine..."

"It's okay if it's not fine, son," Vilém said, hugging his child tighter, and he felt the boy settle.

"They said, 'Hitler shoulda' finished you off!' I dunno what they meant..." David confessed. "Who's Hitler?"

Vilém had been hoping that Jana would be the one to answer that question. She usually was. For Iveta, for Raya...but for David, it was Vilém's turn.

"That's an excellent question, David," he said, resting his chin on the boy's head and smiling as the boy's curly hair tickled his chin.

"This weekend, I'm gonna take you somewhere close by. It's a sad place, and it's a scary place, and it's okay if you cry when we go there. This weekend, you and me, we'll go together, and you can ask any question you want...and...I'll try my best to answer."

THE END